Archangel's
Light

NALINI SINGH

First published in Great Britain in 2021 by Gollancz
an imprint of the Orion Publishing Group Ltd
Carmelite House, 50 Victoria Embankment
London EC4Y 0DZ

An Hachette UK Company

1 3 5 7 9 10 8 6 4 2

A CIP catalogue record for this book
is available from the British Library.

ISBN (Mass Market Paperback) 978 1 473 23146 7
ISBN (eBook) 978 1 473 23147 4

Printed and bound in Great Britain by Clays Ltd, Elcograf S.p.A.

MIX
Paper from
responsible sources
FSC® C104740

www.nalinisingh.com
www.gollancz.co.uk

1

Yesterday

"Look, Illium." Sharine, the Hummingbird, squeezed her toddler son's hand.

He was so very small, his wings no more than suggestions of what they would one day become, but he insisted on walking. Aegaeon was proud of him for his stubborn determination, boasted that Illium had inherited his will.

What Sharine knew was that her son had more strength in his small body than she could've ever imagined when she cradled his infant form. He'd been such a fragile, tiny baby that the healer had worried, and Aegaeon had scowled. "How can I have fathered such a runt?" he'd said, offense in every line of his large and muscular body. "I am an archangel!"

Aegaeon had long forgotten his initial reaction, the memory overridden by the relentless drive of this small boy who was the center of Sharine's world.

"Look over there." She pointed out the similarly-sized child who played in a patch of wildflowers on the cold mountain plateau on which they walked.

Sharine's parents hadn't often allowed her such unstructured play, wanting her to be controlled and disciplined . . . and quiet, always quiet, but she allowed her son all the play he wanted, no matter how dirty it made him or how out of control it became. Yesterday, she'd discovered him climbing the kitchen pantry so he could get at the sweets she'd hidden at the very top. He'd been naked, a wild creature at home in his skin.

And such mischief he'd had in his eyes when she caught him with one pudgy hand clasped around a sweet far too big for his little body. He'd giggled when she took hold of him with a stern admonishment about the rules. Oh, but then she'd laughed, too, because his laughter was a thing infectious.

Sharine knew that was a bad way to teach a child not to be naughty. Aegaeon, for one, wasn't pleased by her gentleness with their son. Sharine, however, had no fears about who Illium would one day become. Her boy had a good heart. He'd never be cruel. If he ended up a little spoiled, well, that wasn't a bad thing, was it? Not if it was tempered by a kind heart and a generous spirit.

Now, he babbled up at her, the dark gold of his eyes shining.

Old eyes he had, her baby. Perhaps because she was such an old angel. She worried about that at times, that she was the wrong kind of mother for a bright, lively boy—too old and bruised and a little broken. But he laughed often, her Illium, so she must be doing something right.

"Shall we go say hello?" She didn't recognize the extremely fair-haired angel with wings of palest, *palest* gold who watched over the other little boy; she might be someone who worked often outside the Refuge. Or it might be that she and the boy lived on the far side of the Refuge and Sharine's path had just never crossed with theirs. Sharine knew she could be insular, content with a small circle of those she loved.

Illium tugged at her hand, trying to run on his wobbly little legs.

Laughing, she speeded up, and soon, wildflowers brushed

their legs. Sharine inhaled sharply at her first true look at the unknown child. He seemed a touch younger than Illium, and was a dazzlingly bright creature, as if every part of him had been designed to capture, then fracture light. His hair was delicate strands of diamonds, every filament of his nascent feathers akin to glass that had been formed into something soft and welcoming that drew light.

And his gaze, when he looked up from his seated position among the riot of indigo and pink, yellow and white blooms, was a fracture of blue and green that erupted outward from jet-black irises. But he wasn't looking at Sharine. He was staring at Illium, a tiny flower held in a soft baby hand.

A moment later, he smiled, this child of light, and held out the flower to Illium.

Sharine's boy smiled back, babbled happily, and took the flower before plopping down across from the other child. Sharine looked from the child of light to the green-eyed woman behind him, and said, "I think, our children will be friends."

2

A month before today

Elena slid her throwing blade into a forearm sheath as she strode onto the Tower roof on the hunt for her archangel. And there he was, silhouetted against the lush red-orange glow of the early evening sunlight, the golden filaments in the white of his feathers ablaze.

He turned toward her the instant she stepped out onto the rooftop, and though they had been lovers through a Cascade of change, their lives entwined since they met, the incandescent blue of his eyes stole her breath.

Dangerous and beautiful, the Archangel of New York owned her heart.

For an instant, she thought the Legion mark on his temple glittered, but then it was gone, nothing but an illusion caused by the setting sun. Her chest ached. She couldn't stop looking for that spark of life, couldn't stop hoping that the strange, ancient warriors who'd sacrificed their lives to protect the world from a reign of death would one day return.

Taking the hand that Raphael held out, she joined him on the edge of the highest rooftop in Manhattan, both of them looking out at their city. Almost a year after the war and it was still being rebuilt, construction equipment a familiar sight and cranes multiplying like overly fertile birds, while four city blocks near the East River remained black and barren despite their best efforts—but New York's heart had rebounded, unbroken. It beat with the dogged will of its people, mortal and immortal, human, vampire, and angel.

As in front of them thrived the verdant green of the Legion building. "I kept my promise," she said, a knot in her throat.

"You did, *hbeebti*." A kiss pressed to the top of her head. "You have kept their home alive."

Neither one of them spoke aloud the fear that haunted Elena: that the Legion's green home would remain forever empty, an echoing cavern devoid of the beautifully eerie presence of the seven hundred and seventy-seven beings who'd called it home.

The Legion, however, weren't the only ones Elena missed with feral desperation. "Tell me Aodhan will be coming home soon." He'd stood by Suyin's side as her second ever since her sudden ascension to an archangel on the far edge of the war.

Elena liked Suyin and didn't envy her the job she'd taken on as Archangel of China, but she wanted Aodhan home, surrounded by those who loved him. Aodhan trusted so few people, leaned on an even smaller number—and that trust had been years in the making.

She hated the idea of him being so far from all of that small group.

"Not just yet," Raphael said, his wing spreading in a caress behind her as the blazing rays of the sun set fire to the midnight strands of his hair. "That is why I'm out here. I've just had a meeting with Jason."

Elena hadn't realized the spymaster had returned from his latest trip. Hardly a surprise. The black-winged angel took pride slipping in and out of places. "He was in China?"

"He dropped by." A faint smile in Raphael's tone. "As Jason is wont to do now that one of our own calls it home."

"Did he speak to Aodhan?" Shifting so she could see Raphael's face, the sheer masculine beauty of him still a punch to the gut every single time, Elena resettled her own restless wings.

"Yes. He is strong, Aodhan, stronger than any of us realized. He does his duty."

"That tells me exactly nothing," Elena muttered with a scowl. "Is he okay? Homesick?"

"Jason found it difficult to judge—the two are blood-loyal to one another, but they don't have the kind of relationship where such intimacies are discussed."

Placing both hands on her hips, over the supple and well-fitted leather of her hunt-suitable pants, Elena snorted. "You mean they'd both rather slit their own throats than acknowledge they have the dreaded fee-fees?" Jason was the quietest and most reserved of the Seven, Aodhan not much better.

Raphael laughed, the sound a crash of joy in her veins. "Mahiya would disagree with that opinion."

"We all know she's the sole exception to the rule when it comes to Jason." Elena was glad for the spymaster that he'd found a lover he trusted with all of himself. Aodhan, however . . . "Sparkle is far from home, with none of *his* people around him."

"Yes, that concerns me, too." Raphael paused before adding, "I think it has been good for him to be independent from all of us this past year. I also believe it's time to remind him of home—I would not have him make the choice to come in a vacuum."

Elena didn't push for the why behind the first part of Raphael's statement; she knew Aodhan's past held a terrible darkness. Enough that he'd retreated from the world for a long, painful time.

He was so hurt, Ellie . . . the part that makes Aodhan who he is, it was so badly damaged that I thought I'd lost my friend forever.

Words Illium had spoken to her once, a wrenching agony to him.

The memory had helped her understand why Raphael had allowed it when Aodhan volunteered to stand as Suyin's second—so that Aodhan, in his full power now, no longer wounded or secluded, would have options, and wouldn't stay loyal to Raphael only because that was all he'd ever known.

Her archangel loved Aodhan enough to set him free.

"A choice?" Elena said, her stomach in knots. "So Suyin's done it? Asked him to stay on permanently as her second?" All of them had expected it—Aodhan was too strong, too intelligent, and too good at the tasks required of a senior member of an archangel's court for it to be otherwise.

To her surprise, Raphael shook his head. "She spoke to me of her desire to do so mere moments before Jason's arrival. She didn't wish to make Aodhan a formal offer behind my back."

"Yeah, she's not sneaky." It was part of why Elena liked her—and why Aodhan did, too. He'd said as much to Elena when they'd spoken prior to his move to China. "She has honor, Ellie, a bone-deep well of it. There are no masks with Suyin, no lies. If anything, she's too tied to behaving with integrity in all things. I can work with such an archangel."

Elena had no need to ask Raphael what answer he'd given Suyin—he'd never hold Aodhan back from taking the prestigious position, even if it broke his archangel's heart. "This is his time," she agreed, her voice rough. "And being second, new court or not . . . even I know it's a big fucking deal."

"Exactly so."

"But we're going to fight for him, right?" Elena said, while the last rays of the sun played on the side of her face, a touch of warmth on this cold day as the world slid from fall into winter.

"That would be a possessive action, and I have never been known to be such."

She grinned. "Of course not." Leaping into his arms, she pressed her lips to his as he wrapped her up in his wings. The passion between them was a thing of wildfire heat that made the world shimmer, a desert mirage of need and love and devotion.

"When are we going to fetch him home?" she demanded. "New York doesn't feel the same without him."

Raphael shook his head, no more humor to him, his face an unearthly creation of stark lines and cold power. "I don't think the time is right for him to make such a momentous move, nor that Suyin is the right archangel for him, but *he* must make the choice, Elena-mine. Freedom is the one thing I will never take from Aodhan."

Seeing the echoes of old rage in his eyes, hearing it in his tone—so frigid, the anger an old, *old* one—Elena stroked his nape, his hair heavy black silk against her fingertips. "Part of me wants to tell him to take the promotion and not look back." He was magnificent, their Aodhan, more than worthy of the position he'd been offered. "The rest of me wants to drag him home." A kiss pressed to Raphael's lips. "I'll keep it under control, though. I won't be anything but supportive."

"As will I," Raphael said. "But I also plan to fight dirty." A dangerous spark in the blue. "I have told Suyin I am sending her more help. I am a kind fellow archangel."

Elena whooped, her grin huge. "You're sending Illium."

"Of course I'm sending, Illium, *hbeebti*. Now, we watch, and we wait."

Life changes us. To wish otherwise is pointless.

—*Nimra, Angel of New Orleans*

3

Aodhan was tired.

Not the tired of the body. He was a powerful angel, and tonight, he flew patrol over Suyin's interim stronghold without any real drain on his resources. Young in the grand scheme of things at just over five centuries of age, but with veins bursting with an energy that made him suitable to be second to an archangel.

It was why Raphael had accepted his offer to assist Suyin as her temporary second.

It was why, three weeks earlier, Suyin had extended him a formal offer to make the position permanent.

Aodhan's first call had been to Raphael. His sire had told Aodhan that he wouldn't stand in his way should Aodhan wish to take up the position. "You are the only one who can make that call," Raphael had said. "Whatever you decide, know that you will forever be part of my Seven."

Aodhan's immediate instinct had been to turn down the position. "It is Raphael I call sire—and I do so of my own free will," he'd said to Suyin at the time. "It is a bond I will not break."

"You will never be second to Raphael," Suyin had said in her gentle way, her night-dark eyes vivid against the white foil of her skin and hair. "Dmitri has been too long in that position and is too good at what he does."

"I do not aspire to be his second." Aodhan already had another, equally critical position—to be one of Raphael's Seven was to be part of a group unlike any in all of angelkind.

Suyin had smiled, the sadness that lingered always in her easing for a fraction of a second. "You have honored me with your fidelity and courage, given me counsel wise and patient, and so I ask you to take more time, consider my offer in more than the moment."

And because Suyin was an archangel he respected, he *was* giving her offer the solemn thought that it deserved. To be the second of an archangel at just over half a millennium of age? It was unheard of; Aodhan would be the youngest second in the Cadre by far.

But, despite Raphael's promise, he would never again be one of the Seven. They would become the Six until and unless they accepted another into their ranks. Because no matter how friendly the relationship between two archangels, there existed a distance nothing could bridge. A thing of power and age, for two alpha predators could never successfully occupy the same space.

Even Caliane and Nadiel, beloved of one another, hadn't been able to always be in the same physical space. Aodhan hadn't been born when they were together, but their tragic love story was legend. Prior to Nadiel's madness and subsequent execution at Caliane's hand, however, they'd simply been two archangels in love. But never had they been able to spend all their time together.

Power was a gift that demanded sacrifice.

Should Aodhan accept Suyin's offer, Dmitri, Venom, Galen, Jason, Naasir . . . and Illium would be lost to him in a way that stabbed a stiletto blade straight into his heart, the cold steel severing their unseen bond even as it made him bleed. But was his vehement negative reaction not a bad sign? Could he say he was growing as a man, as an angel, if he clung to them with such fierceness? Or was he simply playing at freedom while keeping himself inside the cage that had altered the course of his life?

Then there was his tiredness. It was of the heart. He missed New York. He missed working by the side of his sire and the others of the Seven. He missed watching horror movies with Elena, both of them with their bare feet up on an ottoman and a bowl of popcorn in between.

He missed the new friends he'd begun to make in the Tower and in the Hunters Guild, those bonds one of the few good things to come out of Lijuan's obsession with New York. He even missed the noisy chaos of the city's streets, its drivers often yelling at each other as if for sport.

Wild blue flashed on the insides of his eyes.

Aodhan set his jaw and dived to do a wide sweep. He would *not* think about the person he missed most of all— because that person seemed to have forgotten him. Illium had sent him regular packages of items from New York alongside art supplies—only to come to a sudden screeching halt three months earlier.

The change had felt like a slap to the face.

Aodhan had called Elena to check that Illium was fine, that his silence had nothing to do with the sudden waking of his asshole of a father. He'd learned that his friend was hale and hearty and just ignoring Aodhan. So Aodhan had ignored him right back.

It was the longest they hadn't spoken to each other in his memory.

Even during his lost years, when he'd gone silent and withdrawn almost fully from the world, Illium had been there, a spark of light in the enveloping blackness of Aodhan's existence.

You are being childish, said a voice in his head that

sounded like his mentor, Lady Sharine. The woman Aodhan affectionately called Eh-ma, a term of respect and love used for the mother of a friend who had become cherished of the speaker. Lady Sharine was gentle and kind and, of late, with a new steel to her. Not that Aodhan had spoken to Eh-ma of this.

He would never put her in the middle of this fight.

"If I wish to be childish," he said to the cloud-heavy night, "I will be childish." Moonless nights such as this were his favorite time to fly, for he could be a shadow as he couldn't be in the sun. His body refracted far too much light.

Yet he missed Manhattan with its spiking towers of steel and light. So strange, that after a lifetime of solitude and distance, he should find such joy in a city that never slept. China, too, had once been that way in places. Shanghai had been a faceted jewel of technological marvels despite Lijuan's preference for the past, Shenzhen a glittering mecca where mortals and immortals alike came to source objects, clothing, and curios found nowhere else in the world. Just two of China's once-great cities.

Someone in Lijuan's court had obviously had some sway with her. Enough for her to permit such high-tech developments—though never in Beijing, which had been the heart of her empire until the loss of the Forbidden City. In Shanghai, her people had gone so far as to erect a hyper-modern glass and steel structure meant to function as her citadel there.

Aodhan had seen it. It was striking, with glass that shimmered a silvery blue, its lines clean and precise as it flowed into an elongated pyramid. Suyin, an architect born in a far different age, had spent their rest break in the city staring at it. "I can build akin to this," she'd murmured at last. "I understand it, see the beauty in its unadorned clarity."

Her smile—of delighted happiness—had been unlike any he'd seen on her face till that moment. "I was afraid, you see," she'd admitted to him. "That I'd been too long away from the world, that my art had moved on into places I couldn't follow. Today, I know different. Perhaps I will meld old and new when I build my own citadel in a future where it is possible."

She'd started the sketch for her future citadel that very day. As for Lijuan's Shanghai residence, Jason had told Aodhan that the Archangel of China had never once stayed there. Her dismissal had left Shanghai to languish as a third-rate city populated heavily by mortals and vampires. But that Shanghai was lost, its colors erased and its technology coming to a stuttering halt as its wide streets and tall apartment blocks stood hauntingly empty.

So many dead to feed the dreams of power of a megalomaniacal archangel, so many lives and futures destroyed. All for nothing. Lijuan was dead and so were the vast majority of her people. Those who remained were living ghosts with broken hearts and haunted eyes. Nearly all had migrated to the place that Suyin had chosen as her interim base—a small stronghold hidden within the verdant green forests and strange stone pillars of Zhangjiajie.

"I would build anew," she'd said at the time, "a place without any of my aunt's dark stain, but that would be a foolish waste of energy and power when we have so little." She'd looked at the neat stone edifice surrounded by lush green jungle, the air damp and humid then. "This will do. All signs are that she spent little time here—it wouldn't have been grand enough for her."

She'd made the decision before they'd discovered the secret beneath the stronghold, had decided to hold to it in the aftermath. Because by then, Suyin's people had already begun to cluster around her, and she welcomed them.

"I would not uproot them again," she'd said, strands of her hair flying across her face as they stood atop one of the pillars carved by time and nature, so high that it felt as if they could touch the clouds. "Not until it is time to move to my permanent citadel."

She was a good archangel, would become better with time. And Aodhan could be by her side as she grew into her power. He could be to her what Dmitri was to Raphael. Dmitri, too, had grown *with* Raphael, rather than coming into the position after Raphael was already an established archangel. It built a different—deeper—bond between archangel and second.

More than that, Suyin needed him as Raphael and the Seven didn't.

There was much Suyin didn't know about the ways of the Cadre. Aodhan didn't say that as an arrogant judgment—it was simple fact, the inevitable result of her eons-long captivity and abrupt rise to power. Young as he was, he'd stood beside Raphael for centuries, could assist her as she anchored herself in her new—

His nape prickled.

Halting in the air, his wings balanced in a silent hover, he looked around. His eyes had long acclimated to the dark, but the world was a stygian blackness tonight, the lights of the stronghold and settlement too small and few to make any difference to the sky. The suffocating weight of the night put him in mind of Lijuan's death fog, a thing of whispering evil that had murdered by its mere presence.

Its memory would haunt all who had witnessed it.

Despite his inability to see the intruder, he knew someone was heading his way. Since he hadn't been warned by the sentries posted farther out, either it was a cunning foe—or an expert at stealth like Jason. Aodhan respected the spymaster and fellow member of the Seven, but it turned out that the seconds of archangels did *not* appreciate stealth skills in the spymasters of *other* archangels.

"Oh, I love Jason and what he can do," Dmitri had said with a slow grin when Aodhan brought up the topic over a call. "But it drives me insane to know other spymasters are ghosting in and out of our territory."

At least Jason was no threat to Suyin. The same couldn't be said of all the spymasters—a year after the war and a number of others in the Cadre had rehabilitated their territories to the point that they had the time to turn a critical eye to China's untried new archangel.

Aodhan wasn't concerned about a martial assault—no one wanted China, not when Lijuan's malevolent shadow loomed large yet. The general consensus was that the territory wouldn't be fully "safe" for at least a millennium, perhaps more. However, the rest of the Cadre could make things difficult for Suyin if they judged her unworthy of her ascension.

It wasn't only the archangels, either.

Jason had passed on the tidbit that a few of the older angels had begun to mutter that her ascension had been a thing of war, an emergency measure that would've never kicked in were it a normal time.

That it *wasn't* a normal time even now seemed to escape them.

The world was still down one archangel, and while Elijah had healed enough to have made an appearance at the last Cadre meeting, Aodhan—attending out of sight at Suyin's invitation—had seen that he was far from his usual self. It was no wonder he'd turned down a physical meeting in favor of one held via technology.

Elijah wasn't the only one marked by battle scars. Neha had turned reclusive and—per Jason—her senior court had begun to whisper that she craved Sleep; it wasn't a future at which either her people or Aodhan looked on in pleasure. Whatever her faults, Neha had always been one of the most stable of the Cadre.

Added to that, Michaela hadn't returned and neither had Favashi or Astaad or any of the others who'd fallen. As for Qin, he had half a foot in Sleep, half in the waking world.

Where was the intruder?

Power wreathed his hand as he considered whether to light up the sky, but that would be a waste of energy and would frighten an already scared populace. It'd take a very long time for the people of this land to sleep easy. Most were probably still awake at this late hour, haunted by nightmares of grief and pain.

Then he saw it.

A glow.

Such as that emitted by the wings of archangels who were powering up to strike.

He should've alerted Suyin at once, but something made him hesitate, frown. He knew those wings. The shape of them, how the bearer held them in flight, it was all familiar on the deepest level.

But it wasn't Raphael, wasn't Aodhan's sire.

He sucked in a breath.

Because he knew one other person whose wings glowed at times. An angel who it was whispered would one day ascend.

His heart a huge ache, he altered speed to fly hard and fast toward that faint glow. With every beat, it grew brighter . . . before flickering out like a candle that had been snuffed out between uncaring fingers. But Aodhan was close enough to see.

He came to a hover across from the angel from whose blue wings the night had stolen all color, turning them obsidian. "Illium." The single word came out rough, gritty. "What are you doing here?"

4

"Nice to see you, too," Illium said with a smile that was false, didn't reach his eyes. Then he dipped into a flamboyant aerial bow. "At your service, Second to Archangel Suyin."

Aodhan barely heard words shaped to sound playful, but that held nothing of true emotion. He was fighting every muscle in his body not to slam into Illium and wrap him up in his arms and in his wings.

It had been so long since he'd had such intimate contact with another sentient being.

So long since he'd touched Illium.

His heart strained, threatening to burst. *"Illium."* It came out harsher than he'd intended.

Illium's smile didn't fade, still that undemanding and playful thing he pulled out for strangers and acquaintances. If you didn't know him, you'd think it real, think him amused and present.

To Aodhan, it was an insult.

"You going to keep me up here all night?" Eyes unreadable in the darkness, Illium reached up to massage one shoulder. "It's been a long flight and I could do with landing."

Aodhan narrowed his eyes; he wasn't sure what was going on with his friend, but he'd get to the bottom of it. Of the two of them, everyone always said Illium was the more stubborn—no, not everyone. Eh-ma had more than once pointed out that Aodhan could hold his own on that battleground.

"Follow me." It caused him physical pain to turn away from Illium and lead him to the far left corner of the stronghold.

He used his mental speech ability to warn the close sentries of their approach. He'd always been good at mental speech, but he'd grown stronger over the past year, after using it so much with people of far less power. In New York, he'd most often spoken this way with Raphael and others of the Seven. Bonded as they were by blood, it hadn't stretched him.

Now, he told Suyin of Illium's arrival.

Oh, Aodhan, I send you my apologies. Raphael did tell me he planned to send another one of his Seven to China to support you in your myriad tasks. It slipped my mind.

It is no matter, Aodhan said, well aware how much she was handling, and even though Illium's sudden appearance had thrown his world off its axis. Of all the people Raphael could've sent . . .

He inhaled, exhaled.

They landed at almost the same time, on a large flat balcony outside the wing of the stronghold that held Aodhan's small suite. He'd chosen it because it was private and offered him access to the sky at any time.

A rustle behind him as Illium folded in the distinctive silver-touched blue of his wings.

Aodhan turned, braced for the impact of the friend who was part of his very being, and yet who'd become a stranger to him in recent times. His eyes went first to those very wings. Elena'd had to amputate them during battle, to save

Illium's life, and though they'd all known they'd grow back, it had hurt to see Illium devoid of the dazzling feathers that were his trademark.

"Your wings?" he asked, though it was a foolish question; Illium had flown all the way to China on those wings.

"No problems," the other man confirmed. "Though I probably should've stopped more than I did—that's why I'm so stiff and tired." After flaring out his wings in a wide stretch, he closed them with the slow control of a honed warrior.

The night wind riffled the blue-tipped black of his hair at the same moment, the strands overlong and falling over his eyes. Those eyes were aged gold, his eyelashes the same blue tipped black. None of it was artifice. Illium had been born with those eyes, those eyelashes, that hair, his skin a sun-kissed golden hue from childhood.

His wings, however, had once been pure blue.

A severe punishment while he was a youth had altered their course. It happened that way at times. Aodhan had once had an art model with feathers of pristine white who'd endured a catastrophic fall that ripped off large parts of her wings. The damage had been so severe the healers had decided she'd be better off regrowing her entire wing structure.

Her wings had come back a pale lavender.

And none of that had anything to do with Illium. Aodhan was avoiding facing this head on—and he'd never avoided anything with Illium.

Child, be honest. You were the one who flew so far.

Again, the voice of Lady Sharine haunted him. She knew him too well, did Eh-ma. "Come," he said. "I'll show you to your quarters." There was an empty suite directly opposite his. Thanks to Aodhan's efforts, and self-driven interest from strong angels and vampires who wanted to take on the challenge of a new court, Suyin now had a stronger standing team. It was, however, still small enough that the stronghold was at nowhere near capacity.

Illium, this angel who was always talking, said nothing,

falling silently in step beside him. He was also careful to maintain space so their wings didn't so much as brush.

Aodhan's hand curled into a fist at his side.

Touch had been used to torture him once. Now, he craved it . . . but only from a scarce few. Illium was at the top of the list.

But that wasn't a topic he could bring up, not with this Illium. "Where are your things?" The other angel was carrying only a small pack designed to fit against his spine, between his wings.

"Should arrive by plane within the next couple of days. I have enough with me to get by until then. Just show me the laundry and give me a scrubbing brush." The amused comment was pure Illium, and yet it wasn't. That veil of distance, it lingered.

Striding inside the cool stone of the stronghold, Aodhan walked to the closest door to the left and pushed it open. "This is yours. I'm over there." He pointed across the wide hallway big enough for three angels to stand abreast without coming in contact with each other.

The amount of space and light within the stronghold was one of the undeclared reasons Suyin had chosen it for her interim base.

Because she, too, had once been a prisoner.

They'd never spoken of their confinements to each other, and he wasn't sure she even knew anything of what had happened to him, but they had the quiet understanding of people who'd survived similar pain.

The irony that this light-filled citadel had proved to be a place of the worst evil was nothing unexpected in a land stamped by Lijuan's mark, but it had caused Suyin to speed up her plans for the future. "For in this nexus of darkness, Aodhan," she'd said, "I cannot stay and my people cannot heal."

Another voice merged with the memory of hers.

"I see you decorated in my favorite color." Illium's lips twitched.

The room was pink and white.

Aodhan shrugged. "Mine's yellow and white. We think this wing was reserved for certain high-ranking courtiers." Lijuan'd had a large number of soldiers in her court, but like many angels, she'd also had a coterie of what Illium had been known to call "the pretties"—angels and vampires whose sole task was to be decorative.

All of them were dead.

Lijuan had spared no one in her quest for power.

Only their colorful, delicate rooms remained. Broken blooms, no life to them.

"Pink is supposed to be restful," Illium said, and stepped inside. "I need to get clean."

Then he shut the door in Aodhan's face.

Illium collapsed with his back against the closed door, his heart thumping like a metronome on speed and sweat breaking out along his spine. It felt as if his skin was about to burst, his muscles so tense they were going to pop.

To see Aodhan after so long and not touch him?

It was agony.

But something in Illium had snapped over the past few months. He'd taken heed of his mother's advice and supported Aodhan while his friend was in this place far from home. Hell, *not* taking care of Aodhan was harder for him than otherwise. He'd been watching over him for centuries.

But there had to be active participation for a friendship to continue.

And while Aodhan always responded with thanks to any care packages Illium sent, and replied to his messages, their conversations had been stilted, forced. Aodhan had only once reached out to Illium on his own. That had been when Illium's mother got together with Titus.

Aodhan had wanted to check in, see how he was doing with the news.

A whole year, and he'd been worth the effort of reaching

out to a single measly time? *Enough*. Illium was done with
this. He knew Aodhan as no one else did. His friend was a
warrior who'd stand his ground against any enemy, but he'd
never been a confrontational person when it came to his personal life.

Aodhan's response to emotional pain was to withdraw.

Illium had watched him do that two hundred years ago,
Aodhan's spirit more badly shattered than his brutalized
body, and Illium had never given up. He'd known Aodhan
needed him to persevere, needed his help to haul himself out
of his personal hell.

But now? When he knew Aodhan *did* call Ellie to talk,
that he stayed in regular touch with Illium's mother, and with
others in the Tower?

Illium had received the message.

Normally, he wasn't one to assume anything. Illium's way
was to ask the question to people's faces. He and Aodhan,
they'd never not spoken about things . . . except for the one
terrible act that had forever marked Aodhan. About that, he
spoke to no one. Not even Illium.

Perhaps that had been the first sign that Illium shouldn't
have ignored.

But even a man who always asked questions, always con-
fronted life head-on couldn't be expected to put himself out
there without any shields when he had been so quietly and
thoroughly rebuffed.

There was no need for questions or conversations.

The best course of action was collegial distance. The last
thing he ever wanted to do was make Aodhan feel obligated
to stay his friend—or worse, to make him feel coerced,
caged. The thought of it was a physical blow that made him
want to curl over his stomach.

Forcing himself to move away from the door, he took off
his pack and threw it on a flimsy-looking white chair with
curved legs and a velvet seat cushion, then headed straight
through a door he assumed led to the bathing chamber.

He was right.

Ignoring the empty and cold bath, he stripped, then stepped into the baroque shower with its ornate gold shower-heads. The tiles were pink marble, the abandoned shower brush fluffy white with a pink handle. A laugh bubbled out of him at the ridiculousness of it all, but it was a laugh without humor.

At least the shower area was open, clearly designed so it could be utilized by angels as well as vampires and mortals. Or perhaps it had been meant for orgies. There were multiple showerheads from every direction. He turned them all on, then stood there under the pounding spray.

He had to get a handle on his responses.

His and Aodhan's friendship might be dead and buried, but Aodhan was still one of the Seven, and Raphael had sent Illium to support him—including in his decision about becoming Suyin's second, no matter if that decision led to him leaving the Tower.

Illium would not fall down in that task, would back Aodhan every step of the way. When it came to their lost friendship . . . time would fix the bleeding wound inside him. It might take an eon, but it would.

His shoulders knotted, his jaw clenching hard enough to hurt as water pummeled his bare skin. He. Was. *Done*.

5

Yesterday

Sharine's heart bloomed at seeing Aegaeon bend down to grab their son, who was toddling toward him as fast as his little legs could carry. He was a big man, Aegaeon, with wide shoulders and muscled arms, his hair a vivid blue-green and his eyes the same vibrant shade.

His wings were a darker green interrupted by streaks of wild blue.

It was from his father that Illium had inherited the blue that tipped his hair. The same blue had begun to color the fluffy yellow-white of his baby feathers.

Now, Illium laughed in delight as his father picked him up and swung him around. Aegaeon laughed, too, open in his pride in his son, and in his happiness at being with him.

Sharine knew Aegaeon didn't love her, not in the way that Raan had loved her. Aegaeon kept a harem at his court. He had lovers aplenty. But Sharine was content. Because he'd given her Illium, the greatest joy of her life. And he loved Illium. That was what mattered.

They'd already spoken about when Illium grew older and

could be taken to Aegaeon's court for visits. Sharine would go with him, of course. That had never been in question. Aegaeon was a good father, but he didn't know how to look after a rambunctious little boy—he'd admitted that himself.

She hated the court, but Aegaeon had promised her that she and Illium would have an entire wing away from the venomous menagerie of his harem. "Even should your paths cross, they won't dare touch you, whether by voice or by act," Aegaeon had promised. "You are the mother of my *son*."

Regardless, Sharine wasn't looking forward to that part of things, but she was glad for Illium. Right now, at so young an age, he was happy to live with her, and to see his father only when Aegaeon came to visit the Refuge, but there would come a time when her boy needed his father's guidance.

She'd seen that with Nadiel and Caliane's boy.

Her heart ached at the thought of the new archangel who'd once been a youth devastated by the execution of his father. But Raphael had never blamed his mother for her actions, old enough to understand that his father was no longer who he'd once been, and needed to be stopped.

Still, she knew he missed Nadiel.

Boys and their fathers, it was a different bond than the one they had with their mothers.

Today, her boy sat proudly in his father's arms as Aegaeon closed the rest of the distance to Sharine's cottage. Aegaeon was shirtless, as was his predilection, and the swirl on his chest shone silver in the sunlight. He was a handsome man, and once, he'd taken her breath away.

That first flush of love had passed, but she still turned her face into his palm when he cupped her cheek, her heart sighing at his return. "Welcome home."

"It is good to be here," Aegaeon said, his voice a deep pulse she felt in her bones, and his smile blinding. "What a treat you are for my eyes, Sharine." A low rumble. "My court is a place of constant battle, but here, there is peace. I would live always in the Refuge were I able."

Sweet, sweet words that fell like nourishing rain on a

heart that had never again thought to fall in love. "We have missed you." Before him, she'd believed she was content in her aloneness, in her small circle of friendship and art.

Then he'd swept into her life, made his way into her heart, woken her up again. "I wish you could be here always, too," she said, pushing aside the knowledge of his harem, and of his life in a far-off land kissed by another ocean.

None of that mattered as long as he loved their son.

Freedom and love are entwined.

—*Lady Sharine*

6

Aodhan hadn't slept. He was old enough that he didn't need sleep as a mortal did, but he still usually got a few hours a night. That had been impossible last night, with Illium behind a closed door across from him.

At any other time in their history, he'd have thought nothing of just opening that door and walking in, sprawling himself down in a chair and talking to the other man while Illium wound down from the stress of the long flight.

Even during the years immediately after his rescue when he'd been lost in a nightmare so profound that he'd been all but dead, Illium had been a familiar and welcome presence in his life. Aodhan had stopped talking for a long time, but he'd always stayed in the room when Illium spoke to him— Illium had told Aodhan of his latest work for Raphael, spoken of his newest fleeting romance, or of things amusing and interesting that he'd thought Aodhan would enjoy.

Illium burned so bright with energy and life that it was impossible to be anything but compelled by him . . . overwhelmed by him.

Now, Aodhan stared at the single blue feather he'd painted in the hours since his shift ended. His preference was natural light, but he'd learned to work in artificial light. He'd only switched off those lights a half hour past, when early morning sunlight began to slant onto the balcony.

The dawnlight picked up the glittering silver he'd added to the filaments, the myriad tones of blue. Most people thought Illium's feathers were a single shade of blue, but they weren't. The shade people saw was made up of layers of others.

Aodhan knew every single one of them.

Dropping his paintbrush onto the small table he kept out here, he stared at the blue that stained his fingers. What the hell was he doing? Spine stiff, he walked into the suite's bathing chamber to wash off the betraying color. Nothing spotted the dark brown of his pants, or the simple white of his long-sleeved tunic.

He never wore sleeveless clothing in Suyin's court. These people didn't know him as those in the Tower did; the occasional accidental touch happened. Nothing overt and no one had pushed against his request that they keep their distance, but they forgot. No one back home ever did.

And back home, he had people whose touch he welcomed.

Aodhan. Suyin's mental voice was as elegant and gentle as her physical presence; it held none of the violent power of Raphael's. Yet it was unquestionable that they were both archangels. Aodhan had never experienced a clearer indication of different types of power.

Suyin. In an act of respect for her position—and though theirs was meant to be a temporary alliance, he'd called her sire at first.

It was Suyin who'd asked him to drop the distance. "You're the one person in my court who I can trust without worry at this point in time," she'd said. "Be my friend, Aodhan. You know far more than I about how an archangel–second bond should work. You've seen it firsthand in Raphael and Dmitri's long relationship. Teach me how that happens."

"I can't teach you that," Aodhan had said, because he wouldn't lie to her. "The sire and Dmitri were friends long before they were archangel and second." Neither one spoke often about their initial friendship, and Aodhan had picked up enough over the years to understand it was because in that deep past lay a haunting loss.

Dmitri'd had a wife he'd loved. Children.

Every now and then, however, a sliver of their history would slip through. Once, Dmitri had joked about Raphael's utter and total failure at plowing a field. "He wanted to help, so I let him—but I ended up laughing so hard I couldn't even supervise. You haven't lived until you've seen a mud-covered angel trying to command a pair of stubborn oxen."

So when Aodhan made his comment to Suyin, it had been a thing honest.

She'd accepted his words with grace. "I won't have that opportunity. I must choose a second who is already in their power." Eyes of impenetrable obsidian meeting his. "But at this moment, I need a friend even more than I need a second. Will you be that?"

Aodhan wasn't a man to make quick friendships, had a small number for an immortal of his years. But he saw in Suyin an echo of himself. She, too, had been held captive by a cruel jailor. She, too, had been thrust into a world for which she was unprepared. But where he'd been encircled by a wall of support, Suyin had only a limited number of people on whom she could lean.

Yes, Raphael was available to her at any time and would never lead her astray, but he was also a member of the Cadre. The same with Lady Caliane. It made their interactions complicated on a level no one who hadn't been around archangels could hope to understand.

So he'd said, "Yes, Suyin. I will be your friend."

Today, her voice held a thrumming tension that ignited his instincts. *I would talk to you. Will you join me in the wild garden?*

I'll come now.

Bring Illium if he is rested.

Aodhan's jaw set, but he made himself walk out and knock lightly on Illium's door. It opened moments later, a bright-eyed Illium looking at him. He'd changed out of his traveling outfit into faded old leathers of black with blue accents that left his muscled arms bare. Soft with wear and molded to his body, the outfit was genuinely ancient and one of Illium's favorites.

"I'm starving." A grin open and wide—and not fucking real. "Please tell me you're about to lead me to copious amounts of food."

"Archangel Suyin would like to speak to us," Aodhan said, his voice coming out stiff and formal. "We can eat afterward."

"We going off the balcony?"

"No, it's faster to go through the stronghold."

"Lead on."

They walked in silence. It should've been comfortable, just two warriors heading down to speak to their archangel, but it was like prickles on his skin. Illium was never like this with him. So charming and lighthearted without giving away the smallest piece of himself.

Pretty and amiable and so false that Aodhan wanted to yell at him, have it out in a knockdown, drag-out fight to end all fights. And Aodhan didn't yell or pick fights. Except it appeared, with everyone's favorite Bluebell.

"Nice décor." Illium pointed at a painting of a masked ball manic in its use of color, the brushstrokes going in countless serrated directions. "Good thing I didn't see that before turning in. Imagine my dreams."

"We haven't had the time to worry about aesthetics," Aodhan muttered, sounding like one of the stiff-assed old angels even to himself.

Illium didn't roll his eyes and tease him about his abrupt descent into crotchety old age. He didn't even scowl or make an annoyed face. He just carried on.

As if nothing Aodhan did or said mattered.

Aodhan's hand fisted at his side, his lips parting before he clamped them shut. This wasn't the time to confront Illium about his behavior.

Having reached the edge of the railingless mezzanine, he dropped down to the lower floor of the stronghold. As with most angelic residences, the central core of the place was open, giving him plenty of room to spread his wings to slow his descent.

He caught Illium coming down next to him—plenty far enough away that their wings didn't as much as brush at the tips. Polite, so damn polite when Illium was never *polite* to Aodhan. He was affectionate, irritating at times, wicked always. Polite between them was a calculated rudeness.

Teeth gritted, he led Illium through a side door and into the untamed garden that flourished despite the biting cold that foretold bitter snows. According to Suyin's scholars, this region wasn't one for severe winters, but no one knew what Lijuan's death fog had done to the land.

They wouldn't know the whole of it for years, decades even.

Aodhan had advised Suyin to prepare her people for a hard winter when she first chose the stronghold as her interim base, and she'd immediately put a survival plan into action. No one would freeze or starve even if the entire landscape became a sea of endless white.

Illium whistled, the sound low and musical. "Now this is more like it."

Having glanced at him in the split second before he breathed out that statement, Aodhan saw his first true glimpse of his friend. Illium's eyes sparked with unconcealed wonder as he reached out toward a lush white flower so big and heavy that it drooped from its own weight.

Aodhan instinctively shot out his arm, blocking Illium from making contact with the flower—without ever touching the other man. Illium had made it clear that such contact was unwanted. "It has a narcotic-like liquid on its petals," he explained. "Does actually affect angels if we forget we've touched it then rub our eyes or get it into our mouth. Visions, distortions of reality for an hour or so."

Illium sighed, his expression morose. "Why did I think Her Evilness would have a normal garden?"

Aodhan's lips wanted to twitch, the words were so Illium—though the moniker had come from Elena. "All of the plants in this garden are both lovely and peculiar."

When Illium said nothing further, Aodhan took him down a path bordered by trees that had been swamped by sweetly fragrant vines with shiny leaves of dark green and tiny white blooms. At the feet of the trees grew mushrooms in an array of colors unnatural and striking.

"We don't know the effects of all the plants, just the ones where an unfortunate member of the court has unintentionally made themselves a guinea pig." The subject held no emotional weight for Aodhan, was an easy one to use to fill the painful silence between them. "There's a pond deeper inside, the water a clear and cool green that's now filmed by ice in the mornings."

"Is it infested with flesh-eating fish?" Illium said sourly.

Aodhan did laugh then; it burst out of him without warning. He hadn't laughed since he'd come to this land, the sadness of it overwhelming. But Illium . . . Illium had always known how to make him laugh, make him remember what it was to be happy.

Illium fought not to stare at Aodhan. He was beautiful when he laughed—and it was a sight that had been missing too long in Illium's life for him to take it for granted. If Aodhan was a captured piece of light in normal circumstances, a dazzling star fallen to earth, he was beyond breathtaking when he laughed or smiled, the light of him a glow in his irises.

Jerking away his head when their eyes threatened to meet, Illium stared at a huge winter-blooming rose in a bluish-purple that would burn against the white of the snow to come. Inch-long thorns marched along its stem, ready to tear into the flesh of the unwary. He respected that plant. At least it declared itself exactly what it was—beautiful and deadly. No guessing games there.

"Not quite," Aodhan said, the laugh yet in his voice.

Having all but forgotten his sarcastic question, Illium forced himself to find that thread in his brain, somehow managed a light response. "Insects that will sting you to death?"

"The water is clear and uninfested, but there's a suction effect due to the natural mechanics of the pond. One angel who dived in ended up stuck at the bottom for six minutes before we worked out what was wrong and hauled him out."

"Just as well our kind doesn't always need to breathe." It was painful to suffocate, but no adult angel would expire of a lack of air. Of course, the younger the angel, the higher the chance of actual death as lack of oxygen killed the brain.

Put another way, suffocation for immortal children was akin to an unspeakable and slow decapitation. "Trust Lijuan to have an inviting pool that can keep you prisoner."

"A number of intrepid scholars have joined Suyin's court," Aodhan shared, and at that moment, he was Illium's Aodhan: curious about the world and giving of his knowledge, his presence warm and stable.

An enduring oak to Illium's changeable wind.

"One particular scholar has made it her mission to dig into the archives in the stronghold library, and she thinks the pond was used to torture immortals—and that this garden was originally set up as a maze, possibly one designed to drive those within it crazy as a result of the toxic botanicals."

"The underground complex? Any more news on that?" Illium had heard that Suyin called it the nexus of darkness.

Aodhan shook his head. "After our lead vampire squadron did a full sweep and found only skeletal remains in a few of the cells, Suyin made the decision to seal it back up." He rubbed his face. "It's an evil thing to find, and must one day be further explored, but right now, Suyin has to focus on the living not the dead."

Illium didn't disagree. The ancient underground prison would keep. Suyin's people wouldn't. "You didn't have to go underground?" The words spilled out without his conscious volition.

Aodhan's jaw was vicious stone between one breath and the next. "No." A single clipped word.

Aware he'd hit a nerve without meaning to, and furious with himself for it, Illium went to apologize, but then Aodhan spoke again. "Suyin decided it'd be more efficient to send in Xan's team. He and the others are highly trained, including in night maneuvers—and it's effectively night in the complex. They discovered no functioning light sources."

Since Aodhan seemed to have let his mistake go, Illium didn't bring it up again. He'd never knowingly dig up the past Aodhan wanted dead and buried. "I've picked up fragments of who's joined Suyin's court. Is she building a good overall team?" Jason had done his job, so Illium knew Suyin's court was growing—but it wasn't the same as being on the ground.

"You remember Xan?"

Illium's lips kicked up. "No one ever forgets Xan." The two-thousand-year-old vampire was a lethal fighting machine who could carouse even Titus under the table—and who led a team of the best mercenaries in the world. "It's been a long time since he's tied his flag to an archangel's."

"He epitomizes one group of those drawn to Suyin and to the task of rebuilding China," Aodhan said, his tone thoughtful. "The adventurers and explorers, you could say. Others are old immortals hungry for a challenge. Arzaleya, for one, requested leave from Lady Caliane to switch courts."

"Amanat's probably too staid for her." General Arzaleya had stayed awake while Caliane Slept, a loyal soldier who'd watched over her lady's interests. "That's a coup for Suyin. I think I remember hearing that Uram once courted her to be his second."

"Yes, the general stands as Suyin's third. She's blindingly clever and old enough to be a steadying presence. As for the rest of the main court, I'm ninety-nine percent certain I've succeeded in digging out any Lijuan sympathizers, and none of the rest of the Cadre appear to have tried to insert spies into the court."

"Not worth it," Illium said with a shrug. "They know Suyin is the least well positioned of them all to be a threat." Archangels could be brutal in their practicality.

"Yes—but I expected them to try to insert people just to know what was happening here."

"Not enough to risk a mutiny." When Aodhan shot him a questioning look, Illium filled him in. "Seems a lot of older angels still aren't sure China is safe—not after Lijuan's death fog." A veil of black that had swallowed up life after life, their screams locked inside her power. "They'd rebel if asked to come here."

An incline of Aodhan's head, his hair glittering bright despite the pale gray clouds that had moved in over the past few minutes. Illium's hand ached from the force he had to expend to keep from reaching out, pushing back a wayward strand of that hair so rare and precious that children in the Refuge hunted for fallen strands of it whenever Aodhan visited.

Then Aodhan's gaze shifted forward. "The archangel."

7

Suyin stood at the end of the pathway, under a tree that bloomed a riotous scarlet that colored the otherwise clear water of the stream below. Thankfully, it bore no similarity to the time the Hudson had turned blood red, the fallen blooms appearing nothing more than a natural garland on the water.

Suyin was a tall and slender woman dressed in leathers of dark brown that were surprisingly well-worn for a woman famed as an architect, and depicted in ancient paintings only in gowns flowing and delicate. The unbound white silk of her hair reached to the center of her back, a shimmering mirror.

Her wings, too, were snow-white but for the iridescent bronze of her primary feathers, and, when she turned to face them, her eyes gleamed a rich brown that was all but onyx. Those eyes tilted sharply upward at the corners, the cut-glass lines of her cheekbones striking accents that highlighted the near-painful beauty of her.

No flaws marked the cool ice of her skin—but for the beauty mark on the far edge of her left eye. And that was no flaw at all. She was a stunning woman by any measure, but all Illium saw when he looked at her was Lijuan.

It was an unfair, visceral reaction, one fueled by his jealousy at how close she'd become with Aodhan while the other man kept Illium at bay. But that was his problem, not hers. She could no more help her familial resemblance to her aunt than Illium could help having an asshole for a father.

As for the rest . . . No, not her fault.

Aodhan was the one who'd chosen to leave Illium in the past.

Suyin smiled, gentle and with too much weight in her eyes. "Ah, Illium. It has been too long."

"Archangel Suyin," he said, going down into a full bow on one knee, his wings flared and held in exactly the correct position for high angelic etiquette. She deserved his respect and he would not stint it.

Showoff.

His muscles spasmed at that crystalline sound in his head. Aodhan's mental voice was akin to the refractions of light that was his physical form. Illium hadn't heard that voice in his head since the war . . . and he hadn't been ready for how it would smash through the walls he'd tried to erect.

Just because you failed bow training, don't blame me. It was instinct to respond with the old insult that had never been an insult—they both knew Aodhan was graceful beyond compare and his lack of bowing skills had nothing to do with ability.

I didn't fail, was the response as familiar as the air in Illium's lungs. *I never tried to pass.*

Chest aching, Illium never wanted to stop this exchange. It was so effortless with Aodhan, so natural, a thing they'd been doing since they both developed the ability one after the other. Aodhan was technically younger than him, but the few years that separated them meant nothing in the context of an immortal lifetime. They'd developed near identically in strength and power.

"At times," the healer Keir had once mused, "I deliberate

on if you're so similar in power *because* you've been friends since childhood, and have somehow influenced each other's development. Or is it the other way around?"

A smile on that young-old face with its dusky skin and pretty features. "That you were drawn to one another as children because of your innate core of power. Like calling to like."

Illium didn't know and didn't care. Power had nothing to do with their friendship. It had been forged through a hundred thousand small acts of loyalty, of kindness, of adventure—and even of punishment taken for each other's crimes.

No one, not even Illium's mother, had believed that Aodhan ever came up with their antics. In fairness to Illium's mother, Aodhan *hadn't* come up with ninety percent of them. But the remaining ten percent had included several of their most glorious acts—for which Illium had been branded as the ringleader, despite Aodhan protesting that he was the one in charge.

No doubt because Aodhan had always been right beside Illium, confessing to all the things he hadn't masterminded. And vice versa. Never had they allowed each other to fall alone. And no matter what, Illium wouldn't do that now, either.

Even if it hurt to have Aodhan's voice in his head, Aodhan's presence beside him when he knew Aodhan was in the midst of walking away from all that lay between them, he'd give Aodhan what he needed.

That was what it meant to be a friend.

Illium would do this one last thing for his friend before he no longer had the right to use that word to describe their relationship.

"It is good to have you here, Illium," Archangel Suyin said as he rose to his feet and folded back his wings. "I have gathered a small court, but given the dearth of strong angels in the world, after the war . . . well, my territory is not a first choice for many."

"You're gaining a reputation as a strong and fair arch-angel." Illium dared the personal comment only because Suyin was a warrior beside whom he'd fought in battle. And though she'd ascended, she didn't yet have around her the cold burn of power held so long that it was in the blood. "Your court will grow."

"And, I suppose," Suyin replied, "I do not need a huge court when my territory is so very small."

He knew exactly what she meant—though China was a sprawling territory if measured by landmass, its population had been decimated by the choices of its former archangel. It would take Suyin centuries upon centuries to build it back up to anything near the powerhouse it had once been.

At some point in the far future, the other archangels would get over their Lijuan-induced skittishness and begin to look at this land with covetous eyes. Whether Suyin chose to fight to hold on to it, or accede to their demands in favor of ruling a more compact territory, it'd be a choice made on a strong foundation.

"Walk with me," the archangel said, and he and Aodhan fell into step on either side of her, all of them keeping a polite distance so their wings didn't brush.

Illium found himself surprised by Aodhan's formal deference. After so long working at Suyin's side, he'd expected more casual intimacy between the two. But that, of course, was none of his business.

Jaw set, he stared straight ahead at this strange garden that bloomed in the heart of winter. It made him remember what Ellie had told him about the red roses that had bloomed in the snow in Imani's garden. Those blooms had augured a time of death and blood and war. He hoped this garden was nothing but a small strangeness.

It was after they passed a tree blooming with trumpet-shaped yellow flowers that had dusted the path in sunny pollen that Suyin spoke again. "I've decided to begin the rebuild—physically speaking."

A glance at Aodhan. "I know we have spoken of priorities

many times, but I see now that I cannot move forward if I am always in Lijuan's shadow. I must make China Suyin's land rather than hers. And for that, I first need a citadel of my own choosing, with nothing of her in it."

Aodhan inclined his head in that way he had of doing, his face calm and his expression difficult to read. "I understand. Illium and I are at your service."

Illium, too, had no argument with Suyin's decision. Even setting aside her madness of the recent past, Lijuan had ruled this land for millennia, stamped every part of it with her mark. "Where are you thinking of building your citadel?"

"Ah, I made that decision some time ago." Suyin's face softened. "I will build on the coast, far from the places preferred by my aunt. A new start to a new reign. Also a place I can hold in battle when it comes in the future, for it will. No member of the Cadre can look at this empty land and not covet it."

Illium wasn't so sure about that; Raphael had never been land-hungry. It was part of the reason he and Elijah got along so well, their border having held since Raphael's ascension. Not many people remembered that Eli had actually governed Raphael's territory while the Cadre had been short an archangel.

When Raphael ascended, Elijah had given up that land without a fight, for he'd much rather rule well in a smaller sphere than spread himself thin. Raphael thought the same way.

Suyin stopped beneath a tree whose leaves were a deep ruby with fine veins of pink, the perfect foil for her coloring. *You should paint her this way*, he found himself saying to Aodhan.

I'm already making the mental brushstrokes.

"I will gather my people and head to the coast tomorrow."

Illium sucked in a breath at Suyin's pronouncement. "So soon?"

"Ah, Bluebell"—a soft smile as she used the nickname by which his friends so often called him—"none of us have settled here. Today, as I walked among my people, I saw most hadn't even unpacked their meager belongings."

The wind blew back her hair, revealing even more of the flawless lines of her face. "As soon as we unearthed the nexus, I knew I'd been wrong to believe this place had escaped my aunt's malevolent shadow—but though we kept the knowledge of the nexus from the mortals, they feel the lingering whisper of her evil."

A cloud of quiet sorrow over her bones. "They will die here," she murmured. "If I make them spend the winter in this place, I will wake in spring to a graveyard of lost souls."

She shook her head, steel cutting through the sorrow when she next spoke. "I refuse to permit Lijuan to reach out from beyond death to snatch victory. It may not be the best time to move, but move we will.

"We depart this place on the dawn to come, even if we have to leave behind a few objects and possessions. Who will steal them? We'll store them in the stronghold, lock it up against any curious animals, and I'll send a team back in the spring to do a retrieval."

"It should go smoothly," Aodhan said into the quiet after her words. "It's not only the mortals who haven't truly unpacked. We all knew this was only a temporary sojourn. No one has put down solid roots."

"Good." Suyin stopped, shifted so she faced the two of them, her face smooth and as hard to read as Aodhan's. Perhaps it was a mechanism of endurance, of protection—she had, after all, survived an eon in captivity.

As Aodhan had survived.

Illium's gut tensed, his rage as scalding and acidic today as it had been on that awful day when he'd learned what had happened to Aodhan, what had been *done* to him.

"We'll begin the journey to the coast without either of you." Suyin's words demanded all his attention. "I have another task for you." Hands on her hips and gaze attentive, she was the epitome of a warrior at that instant. "Vetra has come across something strange in her most recent survey of the territory."

Vetra, Illium knew, was Suyin's spymaster. She'd been junior to Titus's spymaster, and had moved courts with the blessing of her archangel. She'd never have progressed any further with Titus, since his spymaster was brilliant and long established in her position.

"Another surprise?" Aodhan's voice held a thread of the intimacy Illium had expected—the kind that formed between people who'd been fighting side by side for an extended period.

An ugly heat twisted his gut.

He clamped down on it. Hard.

His mother had given him good advice more than once in his life. But the piece that applied here was that he must not be jealous of Aodhan's growth—even if that growth took him away from Illium.

"What if he decides that the man he's becoming wants nothing to do with me?" he'd asked, his heart raw with the pain of it.

"Then you'll let him go." Love in every word, her fist held against her heart. "Freedom and love are entwined. And you, my blue-winged boy, you love more deeply than anyone I've ever known."

Suyin's voice broke into the echo of memory. "It may be nothing," she said in response to Aodhan, her eyes holding his in that secure, unforced intimacy that made Illium's gut churn. "But given how many secrets my aunt kept, I can't do anything but examine everything with a critical eye."

Illium had to admit he'd have done exactly the same in her position.

"On her way home, Vetra stopped at the hamlet beyond the stronghold."

Aodhan glanced at Illium. "A small group of citizens, about fifty or so, who survived the fog. They're based a ten-minute flight from here."

Illium had heard of these pockets of life—random and scattered across China. Never more than half a mile across, mostly much smaller than that. The working theory was that Lijuan's deadly fog had been thin in places, or had been affected by local geographical formations. No one knew for sure.

"The problem is that Vetra found no signs of life," Suyin said. "But she found no bodies or other signs of death, either. However, she had little time to investigate before she had to turn back—we got word of a group heading this way and she's gone to guide them safely to the stronghold."

Suyin pushed back her hair. "Given their slow speed, she won't make it here until late into the night—she's volunteered to go back to the hamlet, but I want her with us when we leave this place."

"She's been far from home for many weeks," Aodhan said in quiet agreement. "Even spymasters cannot always fly alone."

"Exactly so, my second." Pursing her lips, Suyin blew out a breath. "Vetra herself said that it's highly possible she missed things in the settlement. She *is* certain that all their belongings remain in the houses—boots, clothes, food supplies, tools—which works against the theory that they slipped off into the forests and away from me out of a lingering sense of loyalty to my aunt."

Illium thought of the events that had taken place in Titus's lands. It was instinct to reach out to Aodhan. *Could it be another infected angel?* Angels weren't meant to get sick, but the Cascade had brought with it the gift of disease. *The first known case was violent.*

Concern in the look Aodhan shot his way. *We've found no signs of anything like that, but it's an expansive territory.*

That an archangel as old and as formidable as Lijuan had left behind a plethora of deadly secrets was no surprise. Elena had muttered as much to him when she hugged him good-bye prior to his flight here. "Watch your back,

Bluebell—and remind Aodhan to watch his. I don't trust our psychotic neighborhood archangel not to have left behind a vicious surprise or three."

"Vetra," Suyin added, "would've taken the empty homes to be a result of human raiders who've escaped our net, or those few starving bloodborn vampires who remain in the wild, but she saw no obvious signs of violence or a hasty departure.

"The scholars keeping a record of the population have also triple checked with the mortals and vampires settled around the stronghold. The citizens of the hamlet are not within their number."

An eerie stillness in the air that made Illium's skin turn to ice as Suyin said, "Fifty people—men, women, children, mortal and vampire—appear to have vanished into thin air."

8

Suyin put her hands behind her back after that chilling statement, the hum of her power so subtle it was almost negligible. She had to be controlling it—archangelic power was never so muted.

Shaking off the shiver that wanted to crawl up his spine, Illium wondered if she was aware the problems her preference for such subtleties might cause her when the Cadre began to meet in person once more.

A sudden piercing look from Suyin. "What are you thinking, Illium? I can all but feel your concentration."

Caught by surprise, he nonetheless held his ground. "You're used to keeping your power contained." It had to be a remnant of her captivity—a subconscious survival mechanism to stop Lijuan from considering her a threat. "That won't do you any favors with the Cadre."

A long moment of unblinking eye contact, and for the first time, he felt it. The icily practical power of an archangel. It raised the tiny hairs on the back of his neck, but he didn't flinch. He'd been sired by an archangel, had grown up under the wing of another, had served Raphael for centuries. He understood that—no matter their outer skin—they were apex predators who didn't trust or value weakness.

Then she gave him a small smile and the threat passed like a summer rainstorm. "It seems the two of you are in agreement." A nod toward Aodhan. "But I will tell you this: thousands of years cannot simply be wiped away or forgotten. I have, however, never been called less than intelligent. I will take your advice onboard and attempt to appear more scary."

Illium blinked. "Have you been talking to Elena?" Because that had definitely not been Suyin's type of thing to say.

Laughter now, delicate and lovely. He could see why Aodhan liked being around her. She was like him. Gentle, artistic, kind.

"No," Suyin said at last. "Naasir."

That was when Illium remembered that it had been Naasir and Andromeda who'd rescued Suyin from Lijuan. "He told you to be more scary?"

Suyin pretended to form claws. "Show your claws, show your teeth," she said in an approximation of Naasir's blunt tone with people he knew and liked. "Or the bigger predators will eat you and spit out your bones."

Ducking his head, Aodhan coughed into his hand. "Good advice."

"Yes, yes." Suyin folded her arms. "You have all made your point." But then she smiled. "Do you think I have any chance of stealing Naasir and Andromeda for my court?"

"No," Illium and Aodhan answered at once.

What they didn't add was that so long as Dmitri stood as Raphael's second, Naasir would never go far. He was fiercely bonded to Dmitri—and now, to Dmitri's wife, Honor.

"That's what I thought. But to have two such trusted people . . ." Suyin exhaled. "I hope Raphael understands how lucky he is."

Andromeda didn't technically belong to Raphael's court, but that didn't matter here.

"It took him hundreds of years to put together his Seven," Aodhan pointed out, careful to do so in a way that wasn't about judgment but about offering his archangel clarity. "We were not Seven until roughly just over two centuries ago, when Venom joined our ranks. At the very start of his reign, the sire had only Dmitri by his side."

"You are wise yet again, my second," Suyin murmured. "I will think of this and I will practice patience." Wings held with warrior control she'd perfected since healing from her wounds, she said, "I want you and Illium to examine the hamlet.

"But first, we will wait for Vetra's return so she can more fully brief you—before she departed the area, she did a careful sweep over the forests to ensure the people of the hamlet were not hurt or lost in there. The trees stood silent, no voices to break its quiet."

Aodhan understood her meaning: Whatever had taken place, it was too late to save the residents. Waiting for Vetra wouldn't put them in harm's way—and, harsh as it was, right now they knew the people of the stronghold settlement were alive. And those people needed their help to prepare for the journey to come.

Suyin opened out her wings in a restless movement, closed them back in. "I don't foresee an easy answer—it is for this reason that I'd like you both to stay behind with the domestic team in charge of closing up the stronghold."

She held up a hand when Aodhan would've spoken. "You know we have the numbers to do this safely—and Caliane's elite squadron even now watches over the location where I intend to settle." A light in her eyes. "I think I will like my citadel by the sea, across from a friend."

Frown lines between her brows as she looked in the direction of the dark stone of the stronghold. "This is not a good place."

"Investigating the hamlet while keeping an eye on the stronghold shutdown team seems a small task. Illium and I would be more use to you en route."

Frown deeper, Suyin said, "I overflew the hamlet prior to our meeting to see if I could spot what Vetra might've missed. I had little time, but I felt an awareness of a cold evil. As if the silence of the hamlet made its whispers audible."

Aodhan raised an eyebrow. "Are you Cassandra now, Suyin? Making prophecies and talking in riddles."

Sudden laughter that brightened Suyin's eyes. "Truly, I did sound so, did I not?" She shook her head. "No, it's just an itch under my skin. You keep telling me to listen to my instincts and so I will. Stay until the shutdown team is ready to leave, see if you can unearth what it is that so disturbed me."

"If we find nothing?"

"Then join me by the sea." No laughter now, only a heaviness of emotion. "It may be that what I took for the kiss of evil may be a thing of quieter horror."

Not understanding, Illium glanced at Aodhan.

Many survivors can't deal with the grief and guilt, Aodhan told him. *They choose death—for themselves and their children*. Eyes of translucent blue and green shards held Illium's. *As I chose a living death for an eternity*.

Illium flinched. Aodhan never talked about those years. The odd allusion to it, yes, but never anything so full frontal. As he stood there, shaken by the unexpected blow, he realized something: *I don't know this Aodhan at all*.

9

Yesterday

Illium pointed. "Mama, look! Sparkles!"

His mother glanced over from where she was talking to the Teacher. Illium was too young to go to school yet, but he liked the Teacher. She was kind and had soft eyes, and when she smiled, he always wanted to smile right back.

"Oh," his mother said, her face lighting up in a way that made him bounce. "That's the little one you met once, when you were both babes. His parents took him with them to a remote posting soon afterward."

"But babies stay," Illium argued. "You said." That's what she'd told him when he'd asked to fly beyond the boundaries of the Refuge.

"Yes, mostly babies stay here." She ran her hand over his hair, and he saw that she had a streak of green paint in her own hair. "Unless their parents need to travel and the location to which they're traveling is a safe one for a child."

Illium's papa didn't live at the Refuge. He wondered if he could go with his papa. Only he never would. He loved his papa, but if he went away, then his mama would be all alone.

And Illium already knew that when his papa was at his court, he must be *very* busy. He was busy even when he came to visit Illium and his mama.

Seeing that the sparkling boy was standing alone while the woman who was probably his ma talked to another grown-up, Illium said, "I go play?"

"Be home before dark."

As Illium began to walk toward the boy, his wings dragging, he heard Teacher say, "Don't you worry about him wandering the Refuge on his own? He's so small."

"Oh, we all watch the little angels, Jessamy—you know you do it, too. And I know my tendencies." His mother's voice changed. "I would keep him tied to my apron strings, protect him from all harm, and in doing so, I would damage him beyond repair." A deep breath. "So I have learned to let him go, allow him to stretch his horizons."

Not really paying attention to the grown-up talk, Illium tried to pull up his wings as he walked over to the other boy, but it was hard. His wings were bigger than his body and they kept on scraping along the ground.

He wanted to fly, but he could only go two or three wing-beats before he got too tired and had to land. His papa had said he'd be able to fly farther and longer soon, but it was really, really, really, really, really hard to wait!

"Hello," he said to the boy angel, who was the shiniest person Illium had ever seen. Even his hair sparkled. "I'm Illium!" He knew the boy would understand him—*everyone* was taught this language even if they spoke lots of others.

The sparkly boy didn't smile, just looked at him with eyes that were all shattered but pretty. "I'm Aodhan."

"Wanna play?"

The boy looked up at the woman with a long fall of hair as pale as the dawn sunlight Illium's mama liked to paint, while Illium snuggled in a big and fuzzy blanket next to her, but she was still talking to that other grown-up. "I gotta wait."

Illium tried to be pa-pa-pa—tent. He truly did. But grown-ups talked a lot. Deciding that maybe Aodhan's ma just hadn't seen Illium, he tugged on the bottom of her gown. When she looked down with a little jerk that ran through her body—see, she *hadn't* seen Illium—he said, "Ah-dan go play?"

Green eyes bright like Aodhan's. "Yes." A smile that was quiet, but not mean. "It'll do him good to make little angel friends after his time away."

Not waiting for more, Illium held out his hand to his new friend. "We go play!"

The other boy took his hand, and they ran off, wings dragging on the grass. They only stopped after they were out of sight of the grown-ups, their chests huffing. Then they looked at interesting stones, and Aodhan found a spotted yellow bug that they watched for a while before they decided to go someplace else.

"Ah-dan," Illium said, trying out the name that made his tongue twist up.

"Ee-lee-um." Aodhan made a thinking face, then pointed at Illium's wings. "Blue?"

Laughing, Illium nodded, thought about it, then said, "Adi?"

Aodhan smiled.

At some point, they found themselves near the gorge, a massive split in the stone of the Refuge. Sneaking to the edge on their bellies, they peered down. Angelic aeries dotted the insides at the top, but there was nothing lower down. Only a darkness that made things secret.

"Papa says river there." Illium pointed.

Aodhan squinted. "I can't see."

"It's too far." Copying his friend's expression, Illium peered down, too . . . and noticed there were no grown-ups in the vicinity. "Wanna fly there?" he whispered.

Aodhan looked at him with those eyes that weren't like anyone else's. "Not allowed." Solemn words. "Mama said."

Illium looked down again, his heart beating too fast. "Yeah." But his wings twitched.

"Okay," Aodhan said suddenly.

Grinning, Illium rose and stepped a bit away from his new friend. Otherwise, their wings might tangle up. "Ready?"

Aodhan nodded, then the two of them stepped off the edge together before flaring out their wings. Illium wanted to yell in excitement but he tried to stay quiet so the grown-ups in the aeries wouldn't bust them.

When he looked over at Aodhan, he saw his new friend was smiling for the first time, his face bright not just because he was sparkly. It was bright from the inside. Illium grinned back and they both circled down . . . and down . . . and down . . . and down.

His wings were beginning to get heavy, and he thought he'd maybe begun to hear the first sign of a rushing river when a big hand grabbed him by the back of his pants and hauled him up.

"Hey!" He began to wriggle . . . and glimpsed wings of white and gold.

Poop.

Raphael grabbed Aodhan the next second, before flying up out of the gorge on powerful wings, taking the two of them into the sunshine once more. Illium looked across at Aodhan and shrugged. His friend grinned and shrugged back, and Illium had to fight off a giggle. They'd *really* be in trouble if they didn't take this see-ri-us.

He had to admit it was nice to get a ride up. His wings had been getting so tired. The gorge was big, far bigger than he could've imagined in his whole entire life. So he smiled when Raphael deposited them at the top.

Raphael didn't smile back. He folded his bare arms over his favorite old leather jerkin, one eyebrow raised. "Explain."

"It was me," Illium admitted. "I make Adi go."

"No." Aodhan scowled. "*I* go."

"But I said," Illium insisted, not wanting his new friend in trouble.

"No." Aodhan stood beside him, not moving, not trying to run away.

"I see," Raphael murmured. "So you are both culprits. Then you shall both be punished."

Illium groaned. "Rafa, we no do again."

"Do you think I was born yesterday?" Raphael's lips curved up. "Turn. March."

Sighing, Illium took Aodhan's hand as they began to head toward Raphael's stronghold.

"What the punish-ent?" Aodhan whispered.

"*School*. Write letters. Stay inside." Illium had once tried to point out that he was too young for school—and Raphael had pointed out that Illium was too young to be trying to fire a crossbow, and "yet didn't I just find you dragging a crossbow on the ground with felonious intent?"

Illium didn't know what that meant, but he'd understood the tone. So he'd kept on practicing his letters.

Aodhan didn't look worried. "I like inside." His voice was quiet. "People point and look outside." He made a staring face.

"Because you're so shiny." Illium had stared at first, too, but now Aodhan was his friend. He decided to tell him a very important thing. "My papa an archangel." It made Illium so proud.

Aodhan turned toward him, his eyes all big. Then he looked back at Raphael. "Papa?"

"No, Rafa friend." He felt proud to say that, too; not many baby angels were friends with an archangel. "My papa Aegaeon." It took him time to sound out his papa's name, but he got it right.

"Inside." Raphael ushered them into the cool stone of his stronghold, just as Dmitri was walking out.

Illium had used to think the vampire—who his papa called "Raphael's deadly right hand"—might not like small angels, but then one day, he'd fallen and hurt his knees bad, and Dmitri had brushed him off, then carried him all the way home. He'd stroked Illium's hair and told him he was brave, and Illium had felt good even though his knees hurt.

Today, Dmitri raised an eyebrow as dark as his hair. "In trouble again, Illium?"

"Yup."

Dmitri's smile was barely there, but Illium could tell it was real, not like the fake smiles some grown-ups used with kids. "And with a partner in crime now."

Illium smiled at Aodhan. "Adi. My friend."

Aodhan smiled back.

Illium and Aodhan, it is now nigh-impossible
to see one without the other. I find myself both
looking forward to and laughingly dreading
the day the two enter my schoolroom.
There will be chaos, this I predict with all certainty.

Aodhan is some few years younger, but I think I
must allow him to attend when Illium does,
else Illium won't concentrate for wanting to be
out playing with his friend, and Aodhan is already
such a quiet little one that I don't want
to separate him from his closest ally.
So together they shall enter their school years.

I can already feel the gray hairs
beginning to take root.

—*Jessamy, Teacher and Historian*

10

Today

Illium's luggage reached the stronghold just before sunset.

He'd been in the air at the time, had actually seen the transport vehicle arrive from the otherwise deserted local airport, flanked by angelic guards. Because nothing in Lijuan's land could be trusted. Not yet. Not before Suyin had dug out and eliminated every piece of darkness.

Supplies for Suyin's people filled the large transport vehicle to the brim. Illium's luggage had ridden in on the front passenger seat—it didn't amount to much, just a duffel of replacement clothing, a few extra weapons, and a stack of horror movies he was to pass on to Aodhan.

"He can download them," Illium had muttered to Elena when she put the package in his bag. "He knows how." Unlike with many other immortals, Illium hadn't had to badger knowledge into Aodhan; he'd learned as Illium learned, both of them in agreement that to be ignorant was to be left behind.

"Yes," Elena had agreed, "but I got copies of the original cases. See?" She'd held up a case with a garish-looking image of a woman in faux terror, her breasts all but popping out of her skintight nightgown.

"How is that meant to be comfortable for sleeping?"

Elena, who'd been dressed in full hunting gear at the time, every part of her bristling with knives, had dropped the object back in the bag. "It's not for sleeping. It's for running from an axe-wielding maniac. Just go with it."

Placing the stack of movies on the bedside table after Suyin gave everyone an hour off to rest and recharge, Illium scowled. A second later, he told himself to stop being an idiot and, grabbing the entire lot, headed across the hall. Aodhan's door was open. "Aodhan?"

"On the balcony."

"Elena sent you some horror flicks. I'll leave them on this table by the door."

"Oh, show me. I've got paint all over my hands."

Of course Aodhan's idea of taking a break was to pick up a brush. Illium's lips kicked up for a heartbeat, but the surge of affection was no match for his discomfort and hurt. He did *not* want to be in Aodhan's personal space.

But since he knew Elena would ask what Aodhan had thought of the original cases, he strode through the sunnily yellow room decorated with pictures of sunflowers and kittens wearing fancy hats. There was even a marble statue of what looked to have been someone's prized pug. A less Aodhan room he couldn't imagine—but for one thing: the wide balcony that spilled light into the space.

Light and more than one exit, those were the two nonnegotiables for Aodhan. He'd rather sleep under the stars than be stuck in a room that was dark. As for any room or apartment with difficult points of egress? Aodhan wouldn't even step inside.

Illium's chest ached under the weight of knowing why.

He also knew why Aodhan had gone straight to the balcony after Suyin mandated a rest break. The light at this time of day was coveted by artists everywhere. As a child, Illium had learned to amuse himself during those times—oh, his mother would've come to him at once if he called, but he'd seen such joy in her face when she painted in the evening light that he'd tried not to get into trouble then.

Later, he'd watched Aodhan fall under the same spell of light.

The sparkle of the other man's wings threw colors against the walls, making Illium's stomach clench. *Sparkle.* A name born in childhood friendship, but one Illium hadn't used for a long time after Aodhan was hurt. The sound of it had made guilt gnaw at him—because it reminded him of all Aodhan could've been if Illium had been a better friend, had found him sooner, had *not fought with him* in the first place.

Aodhan would've been with him that day if the two of them hadn't butted heads over Aodhan's infatuation with a flight instructor Illium couldn't stand. The asshole angel had been dangling Aodhan along on a string, while playing the same game with a female vampire *and* a mortal male.

Illium, furious on his friend's behalf, had muttered that the angel in question would "fuck a goat if he could get away with it."

Aodhan had taken that as a comment on his own intelligence and desirability when Illium had meant the opposite: that Aodhan was far too good for the likes of the instructor.

Such a fucking stupid thing.

He should've just shut his mouth, let the infatuation run its course.

But he hadn't. And his Sparkle had ended up in a nightmare that had stolen his light.

"Which movies did Ellie send me?" Aodhan asked the instant Illium appeared in the doorway to the balcony. "She promised to scare off my feathers."

Illium's breath caught, because this man ablaze in the warm light of day's end was *full* of light, of *life.* It glittered in his eyes, sparked in his hair, played over his skin. He sparkled once again and he was glorious.

"Here." Illium thrust out the stack of cases, his voice gritty.

His mother would be ashamed of him, but he hated that Aodhan had had to come to China, to Suyin, to find his light. His long years of friendship with Illium, even the relationships he'd made after he came to the Tower, none of it had brought him to this level of happiness.

It was walking at Suyin's side that had wrought this outcome—and fuck, that knowledge hurt.

Angling his body to look at the case on the very top, Aodhan held his hands to either side. Speckled with splashes of blue and green and white paint, they matched the scene taking shape on the canvas to his right. He'd always been a messy painter—and he'd never needed his subject in front of him to paint it—or them.

Aodhan's artistic eye caught moments, held them.

Today, he'd chosen to work on a scene from the Refuge that made Illium frown. Not realizing he was doing it, he leaned in toward the canvas as Aodhan leaned in to more clearly see the image on the case . . . and the edge of Aodhan's wing brushed his chest.

He jerked back. "Sorry."

Aodhan scowled. "Why?"

Illium had nothing to say to that, because one thing nothing and no one would ever steal away: though Illium's mother had held Aodhan often during his recovery, Illium was the first person whose touch Aodhan had actively sought when he emerged from his long sleep.

His fingers tingled at the memory of feeling Aodhan's skin against his after so very long, his chest compressing. Unable to stand the deluge of memory, of emotion, he stared at the half-finished scene on the canvas instead of replying.

It could've been many parts of the Refuge, but it wasn't.

That small stone house backed by jagged mountains, the flowers that bloomed outside, the path that led deeper into the Refuge. "That's our house." The place where Illium had grown up under the loving eye of his mother—and where

Aodhan had spent as much or even more time than he did at his actual home.

At least until they both grew older. Then, they'd been assigned their own small aeries in the gorge, alongside others near their age—though they'd both visited Illium's mother each and every day that they were in the Refuge, even staying with her during the worst times, when she forgot that they were no longer little angels.

Once they became permanent members of Raphael's team, they'd been offered rooms within his Refuge stronghold, but had declined. For one hundred years more, they'd kept the aeries—and taken youthful delight in racing and diving in the gorge.

"Batchelor pads," Elena had said with a laugh the last time she'd been in the Refuge. "I can definitely see the appeal."

Not quite the right term since the aeries weren't limited to a specific gender, but correct in tone, since no families called them home. For the most part, the aeries were favored by lone angels—with the age range skewing younger, though it did also house a complement of older angels who preferred their own company.

"You should paint the aeries," he said without thinking. "At night, when the lights are sparkling inside and angels are diving in and out."

He spotted something else in the painting before Aodhan could respond.

"What's that blotch of blue over—" Breaking off, he glared at his friend. "Is that supposed to be me?"

Aodhan's grin was a familiar thing that appeared too rarely. "Only the very beginning of you. I'm trying to capture that moment when you climbed onto the roof to try to fly off it, with me as the designated holder of the ladder."

Memory bloomed. Of how hard it had been to get himself up to the top with his wings heavy weights on his back, of how long it had taken them to move the big wooden ladder— he still wasn't sure quite how they'd managed that—and of how angry his mother had been when she'd caught them before he made it to the top.

"I had it planned," he said. "I was going to land in the soft jasmine bushes below if I didn't succeed in taking flight over the short distance."

Aodhan laughed, the sound rippling over Illium like a song too long unheard. "I don't recall you bringing up that piece of genius while Eh-ma was giving us both the dressing-down of our lives."

Illium snorted. "I knew I'd be in even worse trouble for the possible accidental destruction of her plants." Another burst of memory. "She didn't believe you when you confessed to coming up with the plan."

"That's because she knew I'd never come up with anything that put you in danger."

Their eyes met, the connection so profound, so full of shared memories that it stole Illium's breath . . . and then Aodhan's words penetrated, stab wounds to his heart. He knew his friend hadn't meant them that way, but while Aodhan had spent his childhood and young adulthood trying to keep Illium safe, Illium hadn't been able to do the same the one time it mattered.

He hadn't been beside his friend.

And they'd lost Aodhan, first to a monster and her monstrous lover, then to his nightmares.

Aodhan's smile faded, his eyes scanning Illium's face. "What's wrong?"

Shaking his head, Illium stepped back. "You should use the light before it fades," he said, his voice husky. "We'll have to head down to dinner soon." Suyin had asked all her senior people to gather after their break for a short meeting over a quick dinner.

"Vetra should arrive toward the end, be able to brief you regarding the hamlet," the archangel had said. "Prior to that, we need to go over the entire plan for the move one last time, ensure there are no holes in our strategy."

Illium had already learned that the travel plan had been worked out well in advance of Suyin's decision to move. It had been Xan who'd filled him in, while the two of them were strapping down a pallet full of tents.

"We always knew this wasn't our final stop," the vampire had said, his muscled upper body bare and several strands of black hair sticking to his cheeks after having escaped the tie he'd used to pull it back. "Even before finding that underground hellhole, we knew it was only a place to catch our breath."

"The underground complex? How bad was it?"

A flinty look in the rich brown of his eyes, Xan had said, "I found fangs on at least one set of bones. Locked inside a cell."

Vampires *could* starve to death, but it took a long, long time, most of it spent in agony as their body mummified around them. Such starvation could and had been used as a punishment for the most heinous of crimes, for many immortals believed death too easy a route. Illium agreed with them.

Yet to have been left behind to starve to the point of death?

Either the crime had been of the worst degree . . . or, given that the complex was under one of Lijuan's strongholds, it had been an act of cruelty. It was clear Xan believed it to be the latter, the people who'd died within guilty of no crimes.

The image of bones scattered in the dark was at the forefront of his mind as he stepped away from the balcony where Aodhan stood. The other man looked like he wanted to argue, but Illium didn't give him the opportunity—he turned and walked quickly out.

He knew he was avoiding the inevitable, knew they had to talk, put everything out in the open. But he wasn't ready, because there was only one way that discussion could end: with a final break.

The slow erosion of their friendship was over.
It was brittle now. Ready to shatter.

Aodhan felt the reverberation of the door Illium pulled closed behind him even though Illium hadn't banged it. It was as if the vibration had rocked directly into his body, fragmenting his thoughts and blurring his vision. He couldn't even remember the name of the movie at the top of the stack Illium had held out, a stack which he'd deposited on a decorative table on his way out.

Despite his state, he picked up his paintbrush. Art was how he'd always made sense of the world. His hand moved almost automatically, working to the blueprint in his mind.

As was his tendency, he left the depiction of himself to last. Because he'd never seen himself in these real-life scenes, he was the most difficult person to paint. Most of the time, his workaround was to ask someone else if they had a memory of that moment, and if they could describe him, his facial expression, his energy.

He should've asked Illium. For a few moments after Illium scowled at the blob-like depiction of himself, it was as it'd once been, with the two of them so comfortable with each other that they never had to verbally ask permission for anything. Not because of a lack of respect, but because they could read each other with a glance, give and ask with a grin or a touch.

Things had changed.

Aodhan accepted that he'd begun the change and, despite the pain of it, he would do so again; he had good reasons for his actions. This fractured friendship, this distance with Illium, however, had never been the intended outcome. "Be honest, Aodhan," he muttered to himself as he outlined half-formed wings of wild blue. "You never thought this far ahead. You were too angry."

I'm no longer a broken doll who needs to be protected from those who might play roughly with me.

It seemed so long ago, that fight inside Elena and Raphael's now-destroyed home in the Enclave, but that had been the beginning of everything. All the anger, all the frustration, it had been building and building inside Aodhan for years . . . only to explode outward in a merciless fury.

Of course it had landed on Illium. Because Illium had always been there, the strongest foundation of Aodhan's life.

That was the problem.

Aodhan had become so used to standing on that foundation that he'd forgotten to rebuild and strengthen his own—and he'd blamed Illium for it. He needed to apologize for that part of it. The blame was equally his. He'd allowed Illium to take the reins, allowed him to pave the way, allowed him to be Aodhan's shield against the world. That was on him.

But Illium had made his own mistakes. He hadn't listened when Aodhan tried to speak, hadn't accepted that his healing was done, that he no longer needed a keeper. Aodhan's jaw tightened even as he picked up his finest brush to add in the details of Illium's crouching form.

In this image, everything was as it should be, their friendship unbroken by time or atrocity or pain. But life moved on. To stagnate was to die.

Aodhan knew that better than anyone.

11

Sharine held one small hand in each of hers. She was holding on far too tight, but it was necessary for the two mischievous monkeys in her grasp. Honestly, she was giving serious thought to putting a leash on each of them—if Illium was naughty on his own, add in his quiet little accomplice and dear Sleeping Ancestors!

"He has never made mischief before," Aodhan's mother had murmured the last time around, after Sharine'd had to deliver Aodhan home with clumps of tar in his beautiful hair. She'd wanted to clip it, but hadn't felt she had the authority.

In truth, Sharine wouldn't have been surprised had Menerva decided against allowing Aodhan to play with Illium—though Sharine would've pled the boys' case. Yes, they got into mischief, but it was never anything mean or more than what could be expected of two smart little angels.

But Menerva had given her a small, shaky smile. "Rukiel and I used to worry that we'd stunted our son's development by taking him so far from all other angels his age. He's such a serious little man."

Affection in her gaze as she watched Aodhan sit glum-faced on a garden bench a little distance from them—but mingled with the affection was a sense of bewilderment. "I never expected to conceive a child so many hundreds of years after my first. I had settled into the next age of my life."

"I can but imagine your astonishment." The strange thing was that Sharine was far, *far* older than either of Aodhan's parents, but she'd been revived by Illium's birth. Menerva and Rukiel, in contrast, seemed perpetually perplexed by having a little angel in their vicinity—as Menerva had put it, they'd settled into an age of contemplation and scholarship, and for so long that they couldn't alter course after Aodhan's birth.

That day, Menerva had turned to Sharine, a touch of desperation in her tone. "But we love him. Never doubt that."

"I don't, Menerva. Of course I don't." Sharine had taken the other woman's hand, held it in both of hers. "And you don't have to worry about his development. He acts exactly as a boy his age should."

A look of gratitude from the fair-haired angel. "Do you mind his continuing friendship with your son? I know they are naughty together, but Aodhan makes friends so rarely that I would not get in the way of it."

"They *are* naughty," Sharine had agreed, "but they're also very good for one another. The way they encourage each other, it is a joy to watch." She'd squeezed Menerva's hand. "I think our boys will be just fine if we set them on the right path."

Which was why Sharine was today taking the two miscreants to school, to make sure they got started on that path. "Aodhan, you're technically too young, but Jessamy is happy for you to join in. The school has a morning session once a week for littles where the teacher tells stories, then the students play games."

"We play games," Illium said, a pugnacious look on his face.

Aodhan nodded firmly.

"These games involve more than just two players. They're about making more friends and having fun together." She didn't worry about Illium—her boy could talk to anyone. He already knew and played with most of the Refuge children. By the time Illium became a man, he'd no doubt have friends from one end of the globe to the other.

He'd gotten that from Aegaeon, she thought, a kind of wild charisma that swept everyone up in its wake. Illium's charm, however, was far kinder and without arrogance. But then, he was only a babe.

Aodhan, however, was like Sharine. Withdrawn around strangers, reticent with new people. Not that he was shy. He knew his mind, could speak it. Illium might've made the first move in their friendship, but Aodhan had chosen to accept the overture.

She'd heard them argue over decisions on what to play, which way to walk, and Aodhan never simply gave way. He won his fair share of battles. Theirs, she'd been pleased to see, was no uneven balance, but a true friendship of equals.

Now Aodhan looked at her with big eyes. "My friend, Blue."

"Yes. You'll always be friends with Illium. But that doesn't mean you can't have other friends."

"Adi, *my* friend," Illium said in his most stubborn tone of voice, his little forehead scrunched up darkly.

Oh dear. It looked like her son had inherited a possessive nature, too. From whom, she wasn't quite sure. Neither of his parents held on to one another. Perhaps she could find a grandsire to blame. Be that as it may, she'd have to watch him to make sure he didn't accidentally stifle Aodhan's attempts to make other friends.

Yes, Aodhan could stand his ground, but she wasn't sure he would when it came to making more friends. He had one true friend, and that was enough for him. Sharine understood. She had one true friend, too—that Caliane Slept at this time and place made no difference to their bond. But she was an adult, and she *did* have other friends who weren't as close to her as Caliane.

No, she'd make it a point to tell Jessamy to put the boys into different groups for games. Else, they'd pair up, demolish everyone else, and not widen their circle.

12

Today

Not counting the Tower, Illium had attended meals at the court of more than one archangel. The most recent had been at Titus's. His "stepfather" had threatened to deck him if Illium called him that one more time, while his mother smiled in a way that was dazzling sunshine full of humor.

For that alone, Illium would've loved Titus. But the archangel had many things to commend him—chief among which was how he treated his warriors. Never were they expendable to Titus. The Archangel of Africa valued each and every person in his forces and was known to take the time to train with even his most junior squadrons.

Of course, he did believe Illium too young to have so much power.

"You need seasoning, boy!" he'd boomed, slapping Illium on the back. "There's a reason ascension happens at a certain age."

The word "ascension" shot terror up Illium's spine any time someone spoke it in relation to him. He had no desire, *none*, to become an archangel. Maybe that would change in the future, and maybe it wouldn't, but one thing was true: he *was* too young for it to even be a whispered idea. The power would tear him apart. Even should he somehow survive—so remote a possibility as to be negligible—he'd be eaten alive by those of the Cadre who had no reason to care for him or call him a friend.

But the worst casualty of all would be having to leave the Tower, the Seven.

No, Illium was not on board with any talk of ascension. As a result, he'd been quite happy to watch Suyin ascend on the far end of the war. She might be untried, but she was thousands of years older than him, had a grace and a maturity that he was still in the process of developing.

He could be envious of her relationship with Aodhan and still accept her qualifications as a member of the Cadre—and more specifically, as archangel of this ravaged territory. This land needed an architect, a builder, far more than it needed an archangel of warrior blood.

As for Titus, despite his misgivings about the accelerated speed of Illium's power curve, the archangel had treated him with the respect due to a warrior of his skill and experience. There'd also been no formalities at his table, the three of them eating as family.

Even prior to Illium's mother's entanglement with Titus, the other archangel's table had been easy. Nothing could be like it was when Raphael got together with his Seven, but it had been close.

Neha's table, by contrast, was a thing of formal manners, every dish a work of art. Elijah's table fell somewhere in between—the familiarity of a warrior at ease in his home, but with a touch of elegance in the presentation. To be expected, since his consort was an artist.

Suyin's table reminded him of Dmitri's stories of how things had been when Raphael first became an archangel. Young and untried and with a furious intensity to him, as he learned to rule the land that was his territory.

The table at which they were to sit today was a huge slab

of wood on sturdy legs. It had been sandpapered to take off the roughness, but that was about the extent of the polishing. Illium didn't need to ask why Suyin wasn't using the formal table that must surely exist in this stronghold.

All the polish and shine would've brought Lijuan into the room with them.

This table represented Suyin alone.

Two long bench seats ran along either side, while at the head of the table was a single chair built for an angel. Four warriors were already at the table when he entered and they waved him over.

He knew Xan, of course, but hadn't yet managed to catch up with the other familiar face. His own cracked into a huge smile. "I heard you'd joined Suyin's court," he said after exchanging the embrace of warriors with a small bronze-skinned woman with wings of a blue so dark they were near-black.

Yindi would have the perfect wings for spying if she didn't have large splashes of white on the primaries. Also if she wasn't so loud and exuberant. He always had a good time with her when they met—the previous time around, they'd gone ice-flying below a massive glacier, nearly frozen off their butts, then drunk copious amounts of Illium's potent liquor.

"A better decision I've never made," she said, before introducing him to the vampire and the angel he didn't know.

Jae was the vampire, quiet but with a glint to her eye, Maximus the angel. And a bigger angel Illium had never met. The other man was more heavily muscled than Titus or Aegaeon, his body white marble sculpted to define every possible line. It was a wonder his wings could lift him aloft.

Beside him, long and lean Jae, her skin a rich brown, appeared as insubstantial as air—until you noticed the razor-sharp throwing knives in her arm sheaths. She'd braided her curly hair into two side braids that began close to her skull and carried all the way down to the middle of her back.

She looked nothing at all like Ellie and she reminded Illium of her all the same. When he said, "Are those garrotes woven through your braids?" she grinned, and Maximus leaned in close to examine the lethal tools that once more put Illium in mind of Ellie.

"Forget about Jae's obsession with hiding weapons," Yindi said with the rudeness of long friendship. "News, gossip, breaking stories, we want it all."

"We're insulated here." A freshly showered Xan, with a shirt on for once, threw back whatever deadly concoction was in his glass before continuing. "Not so much technologically—those links have been put back up, at least to a basic degree—but in terms of distance."

"The amount of work doesn't help," Maximus said in a voice deep and rumbling, but it wasn't a complaint. "We have little time to look to the outside when there's so much to do to rebuild China, build our archangel's land."

"And we're going to be building in truth soon," Xan said, the warrior's face bearing the refined beauty of an old vampire—the olive-gold of his skin so flawless as to be unreal, his cheekbones knife blades, and his lips delineated as if by a master artisan.

His eyes—thin, slightly hooded—gave him an enigmatic air, the entirety of Xan coming together to form a face so compelling that Xan only slept alone when he wished it.

"To tell my descendants that I helped build the court of an archangel?" Xan shoved a hand through the damp strands of his hair, broke out that berserker grin. "I will be even more of a legend than I am now."

They all laughed, and Jae threw a bread roll at him—which he plucked out of the air and began to eat. Feeling at home among the friendly group, Illium updated them on how the other territories were doing, what had been rebuilt, what hadn't. Additional senior members of Suyin's court joined them in the minutes that passed, the conversation flowing with ease.

Yet still—and though he had his back to the door—he felt it when Aodhan entered the room. The others had left a space to Suyin's right, and that was the spot into which Aodhan slid.

Because he was Suyin's second.

Illium forced himself to keep his wings motionless, didn't clench his fingers on the cutlery at hand, didn't even look away from his conversation with Yindi to meet Aodhan's gaze. The effort cost him, his abdominal muscles rigid and the tendons at his nape stiff.

"Mead?" It was a soft, feminine murmur at his shoulder.

He turned to smile at the mortal woman who'd appeared next to him, a jug in hand . . . and his heart, it stopped.

Kaia.

It was a roar of sound in his head, a thunder in his blood even though he knew Kaia was long dead and buried. But this woman, she had Kaia's face, had her high, flat cheek-bones, her soft lips, her wide and uptilted eyes, the long black silk of her hair. Only her skin tone was different. Kaia had been mountain born, her skin sun brown. This woman's skin was white with a pink tint to it.

"Angel?" A questioning lilt to her voice as she spoke in a dialect that was one of three he'd heard in common use here.

"My name is Illium." His voice came out rough, his breath stuck in his lungs. "Yes, thank you."

He watched her as she poured the old-fashioned drink into his tumbler, and he tried not to stare. He failed.

She had to be one of Kaia's descendants. The resemblance was too striking. But he couldn't ask her. She wouldn't know. Humans rarely had such long memories, or kept such records.

Smiling shyly at him, she moved away, to head to Aodhan.

Whose eyes were locked on Illium.

Do you see? Illium asked his friend, desperate to know if he was going mad.

Aodhan nodded. *She must have arrived with the newest group of survivors. I haven't seen her before.* He glanced up then, spoke to the woman.

Her reply was too soft to reach Illium, but it made Aodhan's face go eerily quiet. After she left to refill her jug, the shattered blue-green of Aodhan's gaze met Illium's. *Her name is Kai. A family name she tells me.*

Kaia. Kai.

Illium swallowed hard, then picked up his tumbler of mead and drank it down to the last drop. He was aware of conversation going on all around him, but it was all just a buzz of noise to him. It took everything he had not to get up and go after her. He just wanted to . . . what? Wanted to what?

That mortal woman wasn't Kaia, wasn't his long-dead lover.

And still his eyes watched for her, his skin tight with anticipation.

No matter Illium's reputation as open and friendly, Aodhan knew he was expert at hiding his thoughts when he felt like it. He'd learned to do it to protect Lady Sharine in her fractured years. Back then, no matter how bad his day had been, Illium could put on a perfect facsimile of joy to protect his mother's heart.

But Aodhan had been his friend too long not to see through any shield he might attempt. Right now, his friend's entire attention was on the pretty mortal woman who'd disappeared into the kitchen area.

Aodhan had witnessed Illium's shock, his own as powerful.

He'd never liked Kaia. She'd treated Illium as a trophy, her angelic lover to show off. He'd seen her as young and foolish and frivolous, a woman who'd never really mature. It had had nothing to do with her mortality—there were angels of three thousand who had as much air in their heads. It was a thing of personality.

He wished with all his being, however, that he hadn't been proven right.

Aodhan would've rather gritted his teeth through Kaia's entire mortal lifetime if it would've meant an end to Illium's hurt. Which made his next decision simple. *Illium.*

When his friend's head jerked his way, he said, *Suyin has been held back by fifteen minutes.*

Rising at once, Illium stepped away from the bench and toward the doors that led into the kitchens. Aodhan watched him go, unsure of his emotions. Illium had always been fascinated by mortals, compelled by them. It was by looking through Illium's eyes that Aodhan had first learned to value mortal hearts, mortal dreams.

But Kaia . . .

She'd been Illium's first love. Illium had given all of himself to her in that generous, uninhibited way he'd had as a young man. The same generosity existed in him to this day, but he'd directed it toward his friends, never again loving as he'd loved Kaia.

Aodhan's gaze went to the doors through which the blue-winged angel had vanished. *Face your ghosts, Bluebell,* he thought. *Conquer the phantom that haunts you.* Even as he thought that, he knew there was a very high chance that Illium would choose the very opposite path.

And if he does?

Aodhan swallowed at the question that bloomed bitter acid in his blood. Kai wasn't Kaia. Perhaps she would be the healing balm Illium needed, a mortal lover to vanquish the one who'd caused the open wound in his psyche. Perhaps Kai would finally effect what Aodhan had never been able to achieve.

His hand spasmed to lock around his tumbler.

Illium's Flaw caused Illium's Fall.

—*Angelic aphorism*

13

The kitchen appeared empty and for a second, sheared in two by a sense of keening loss, Illium thought he'd imagined her. But no, there she was in one corner, having just refilled her jug.

"Oh." She pressed a hand to her heart, her fingers long and slender.

"Sorry, didn't mean to scare you." He felt desperate, almost feral, but he forced himself to keep his distance, keep a smile on his face. "I finished my mead already." He held out the tumbler he'd somehow had the presence of mind to pick up. "I don't suppose you'd give me more?"

Her cheeks went pink. "Of course, Angel."

"Illium," he corrected again, keeping his voice gentle.

One sleek wing of hair sliding across the softness of her cheek as she poured his drink, she whispered, "Illium," and he fell back in time, to a laughing season of life when his heart had been unbruised and wide open and Kaia's wicked smile had owned him.

Her descendant's smile was softer and appeared more shy

at first glance, but the subtle sensuality to it tugged on his memories. "Thank you," he said after his tumbler was full, but didn't leave. "Did you travel far to come here?"

She nodded. "We heard the archangel had settled here, and so we came." Quiet, musical, her voice was pleasing to the ear.

Kaia had sung like a bird, her voice a clear mountain song.

This isn't her, he reminded himself, but couldn't help from asking, "Are you leaving with Archangel Suyin to-morrow?" If she was, he'd dream of her until he saw her again.

"No. I'm staying behind to help close up the stronghold, do the final cleanup."

His entire being exhaled. "Then I'll see you again soon," he murmured, forcing himself to step back.

She sucked in a breath, but her lips curved. And there it was—that hint of passionate confidence, the wildness of spirit that had so drawn him to Kaia.

He carried Kai's smile with him as he returned to the meeting table. Even as he replied to a comment from Yindi, he rubbed a thin metal disk between his thumb and fore-finger, having retrieved the keepsake from his pocket on his walk back to his seat. Old and smooth, it was no longer a memorial to all he'd lost, but a talisman to the future.

He'd be able to concentrate now that he knew Kai wouldn't disappear if he turned around. When Aodhan glanced at him, Illium found himself smiling, in charity with the world. Maybe his tour of duty here wouldn't be so bad after all.

A whisper of power as Suyin entered the room. It shouldn't have been a whisper, should've been a wall. But Illium had said his piece—there was a point beyond which you couldn't push any archangel.

Only consorts and seconds had that right.

When he turned his attention toward Aodhan, it was to see him looking at Suyin without any strong emotion on his face—but Illium knew he was speaking to his archangel mind-to-mind. Putting his neck on the line because it was a second's job to check their archangel if necessary.

Suyin gave a slight incline of her head before she took her seat.

Silence fell.

"You know that tomorrow," she began in her quiet, composed way, "we move from this stronghold, and toward the coast." She took a sip of the wine Aodhan had poured her. "During the break, I had a chance to assess our readiness, and I'm pleased to say the vast majority of the work has already been done."

"The mortals?" Jae asked, and as she leaned forward, Illium spotted the outline of a gun under her shoulder. "They've nested the deepest."

"I thought so, too," Suyin said, "but when I spoke to Rii—"

The one the mortals have chosen to represent them, Aodhan's voice filled in for Illium even as Suyin continued to speak.

"—he told me that most of them never unpacked. All were certain I wouldn't be content with a home borrowed from Lijuan." A faint, ironic smile. "It does terrible things to the archangelic ego when mortals see more clearly."

No laughter, because despite her light words, sorrow soaked her tone. "The mortals sensed what we all now know—that Lijuan stained this place with her evil." Sighing, she leaned back in her chair—one designed for wings, with a central spine and no sides. "I'm certain that some of the mortals continue to worship her as a goddess, but the rest see her for the monster she became."

"They are foolish," bit out Maximus, his fisted hand a mallet on the table. "Small minds, no sense of understanding."

Illium bristled. He'd always been far more connected to mortals than most immortals. Not only because of Kaia; he'd had mortal friends throughout his lifetime, and he remembered the name of each and every one.

Even as he went to open his mouth, Aodhan said, "Peace,

Maximus. You may as well say the same for those angels who remain loyal to her. You know they exist—any number of the survivors of the war are only in China and part of Archangel Suyin's forces because no one else will have them."

The rebuke was quietly delivered, its impact unmistakable.

Maximus sagged, then raised those big, square-fingered hands to rub at his face. "You're right," he said afterward. "At least the mortals have the excuse of a short lifetime—for anyone who wasn't born outside the territory, all of it will have been spent under Lijuan's reign. Our kind have no such excuse. They know everything of what she did, were right in the thick of her madness and evil."

He slapped one hand palm-down on the table. "Why do they continue to revere her?" His voice held confusion, his eyes oddly lost for a man so solid and certain of himself.

Suyin shook her head.

"Mortals have a theory," Illium said, and all at once, was the center of attention.

"What can mortals know about Lijuan?" Maximus demanded, his eyebrows lowered over eyes of faded blue.

Illium wasn't in the least cowed; he'd dealt with rough and rowdy warriors far more belligerent than Maximus. "It's not about Lijuan. About why people remain in bad situations. The theory is one based on the fallacy of time sunk and resources invested.

"At a certain point, say mortal healers of the mind, walking away no longer seems an option—even when a person knows that it's the only right choice. It's not logical, but is rather an emotional reaction. It's why cattle remain with vampires who bleed them dry, and vampires serve cruel masters even after their Contract comes to an end."

A pause around the table, as the others chewed over his words.

"I think the mortals are right," Suyin murmured. "All these warriors made a choice, and they know the choice will sully their honor for an eon. So they cling to the falsehoods she peddled in order to justify their choice, and to continue to believe themselves righteous."

A sudden shake of her head. "Enough. Let us have no more talk about my aunt. Her time is done. Let's cleanse our palate by talking of my new citadel." She turned to Aodhan. "I've asked my second for his thoughts on the design."

Pride speared Illium's veins. Suyin was an architect of great renown, had designed buildings that were revered to this day, yet she respected Aodhan enough to ask his opinion. She valued him. Truly valued him. As much as Raphael valued him. Aodhan would lose nothing by staying with her, while gaining incredible prestige.

The realization was a boulder in Illium's gut.

"What you propose is lovely and graceful and true to you," Aodhan said, the light playing over the faultless line of his profile and picking out the sparkle in his hair, in his skin, in the feathers visible where his wings arched above his shoulders.

Suyin raised an eyebrow. "But?"

"You should remember Naasir's advice."

A buzz of conversation around the room, as one and all wondered what Naasir might've said. Illium's fellow member of the Seven was well-known in angelkind—though not many *truly* knew him. Strangers and acquaintances might be excused for believing him contained and tight-lipped, a deadly predator who could be an assassin or a courtier.

His friends knew a far different Naasir: a man who was wild at heart, capable of endless affection and gifts that made sense only to him. Women tumbled headlong into love with him, but he loved only one woman. His treasured Andromeda. His Andi.

Soft laughter from Suyin as she raised her glass to Aodhan. "I take your point." Then she turned to the table to put them out of their misery. "Naasir has advised me to be more scary."

A pause before every single person at the table nodded in firm agreement.

Even as Suyin groaned, Yindi was saying, "We love you, sire, and we think you the greatest of archangels with your compassion and your courage—but that isn't the fuel on which the Cadre runs."

"Yindi is, alas, correct," Maximus intoned with unexpected glumness.

"Enough, enough." Suyin laughed, and in that moment, Illium saw the archangel she was under the weight of sorrow and the pain of the past. A woman of great power and great beauty and even greater heart. "I will be certain to add several spiky turrets and perhaps a gun wall or three. Aodhan can surely fashion skulls out of bone-appearing material for me to mount on the walls."

Raucous laughter vibrated through the room at the idea of Suyin sullying her elegant design with such abominations. Xan snorted, he was laughing so hard, which had Yindi spraying mead out of her nose and Maximus guffawing. Even Aodhan's lips flirted with a smile, the light of his amusement reaching his eyes.

Illium sat back, his breath lost under the inadvertent body blow.

He'd convinced himself that Aodhan wasn't happy here in China, that he couldn't be happy anywhere outside the Seven and Raphael and Elena. But Aodhan *was* happy. He'd found a place for himself in this court, and by this archangel's side.

She held him in high esteem, and the others in the court— from wild Xan to cool-eyed Jae—looked to him with respect. Aodhan had become a true second to Suyin.

Perhaps, Illium forced himself to admit, this was where he was meant to be.

14

Yesterday

Aodhan sat next to Illium on the roof of Aodhan's home. It was nearer the side of the Refuge from which Illium's father would come, so they'd decided it would make a good lookout. "How do you know he's coming?"

"My papa's friend Meri said," Illium answered with an excited smile. "He saw Papa at Neha's court, where they were having a meeting. Papa told him to tell me that he was coming this way today or maybe tomorrow."

He took a breath, finished. "Meri said dates, but I can't tell dates, but Mama told me not to worry, that she'd tell me the day when it came—and she told me today!"

"Will we stay here all night?" He would if Illium wanted; he knew his friend missed his father.

Aodhan's father lived in the Refuge, so he was always close by except for the times he had to go be a scholar in a court. He and Aodhan didn't do things together a lot, not like Illium did with his father when Aegaeon came, but Aodhan knew Father was there if he needed him for anything important. Mostly, he didn't. Mostly he tried to find the answer by himself, or with Illium's help.

"No." Illium's lower lip jutted out. "Mama said I have to come in before dark. Papa will come to me if he flies in late."

"You should listen to Eh-ma." She was Aodhan's favorite grown-up, even more favorite than his own mother. He never said that anywhere except inside his head, though. He knew it would hurt his mother's feelings. He didn't know how he knew that, but he did.

Illium kicked his feet, but not enough to unbalance himself from his perch. "I will." But he still looked grumpy. "I told her I'm big now, and she said I'm her baby boy. Ugh."

"But we are babies," Aodhan pointed out. "We don't even go to proper school yet!" Only the special one for little angels.

Illium scowled at him. "Papa says I'm a little man. He says I'm going to be in his army when I'm bigger."

Aodhan wished Aegaeon wouldn't come at all, even though he knew that was a mean thing to wish. Aegaeon played with Illium lots, and even sometimes invited Aodhan, but Aodhan didn't like how Eh-ma was when Aegaeon was in the Refuge. It knotted him up on the inside.

It was like she . . . faded.

He fisted his hands, frustrated because he didn't have the words to explain even to himself what he meant. All he knew was that Eh-ma was different when Aegaeon was here. Like he was a big insect that sucked up all her brightness, that was it.

But even though Aodhan shared everything with Illium, he didn't share this. Illium would be mad if Aodhan said that about his papa.

Illium loved Aegaeon.

So when Aodhan spotted a glimmer of color on the horizon while Illium was searching another part of the sky, he said, "Look. I think it's your papa."

Illium's entire face lit up. Jumping up onto his feet, he began to flare out his wings. But Aodhan pulled at one wing. "You can't fly so far. You'll fall."

Illium tugged away his wing. "I can fly there." His forehead creased.

Aodhan also didn't like how Illium was when Aegaeon was in the Refuge. His friend was still his friend, but he was also . . . hungry to be with his father. Aodhan didn't mind about that. He still saw Illium all the time. He was mad for Illium, that his father made him so scared about missing time with him that Illium got all tight inside, as if he'd burst if he didn't grab on to every minute.

"If you fall and break your wing," he said, repeating something Eh-ma had said to both of them more than once, "you won't be able to do anything with him."

Illium's scowl got darker, but he didn't fly away. And, after a while, his scowl faded into a smile. He laughed and bounced on his feet. "Aodhan, my papa is coming home!"

Aodhan smiled because his friend was happy, but he didn't fly out with Illium when Aegaeon got close enough that it was safe. Moments later, someone scrambled up to crouch on the roof next to him.

Naasir's silver eyes were fixed on the spot where Illium flew toward his father. Illium's flight path was wobbly, but he was going faster than Aodhan could fly, faster even than some of the older young angels. "It's Illium's papa," he said, even though Naasir probably knew that.

Naasir wasn't like the other grown-ups in the Refuge. He wasn't an angel and he wasn't a vampire. He was just Naasir. He knew grown-up things, and Aodhan had seen him be very serious-faced and "normal" around some people, but he was himself with Aodhan and Illium.

One time, Eh-ma had said Naasir was barely over a hundred. Aodhan had been so surprised, because Naasir didn't act like the young angels. But he didn't act like an old angel, either. When he'd asked Naasir, Naasir had told him it was because he was a "one being." "There's no one like me in the whole world."

He was right.

The last time he'd been in the Refuge, he'd played hide-

and-seek with them and he hadn't just pretended like other grown-ups did. He'd *played* for real, and it had been the best game ever because Naasir was a good hider—and he was *really* hard to hide from.

Naasir said he could sniff them out, so Aodhan had been tricky and dunked himself in water before hiding, and it had taken Naasir a long time to find him. His silver eyes had been bright when he succeeded, his grin wild. "Good game," he'd said afterward, then left to take a training session for a group of halflings.

Naasir was fast and a good fighter.

Today, he said, "I don't like Aegaeon."

Aodhan's eyes rounded. He turned to look at Naasir, able to see his profile because Naasir had pulled the shaggy silver of his hair into a short tail, except for a few strands that lay against the dark brown of his skin. Naasir had skin that looked warm, like it had sunshine in it, and people wanted to touch him sometimes, like they did Aodhan—except they were too scared of Naasir to try.

Aodhan wanted to be scary like him. But today he was only thinking about what Naasir had said. "That's not . . . paw—paw—"

"Polite," Naasir completed, then shrugged. "Polite is for pretending. You don't like him, either."

Aodhan bit his lower lip, worried Illium would see his secret, too.

It was as if Naasir could read his mind. "Don't worry, small sparkles." He patted Aodhan on the shoulder. "Small blue wings sees only his father."

Exhaling, Aodhan looked to where Aegaeon was now hugging Illium, holding him close. "He makes Illium too hungry." He knew the words weren't the right ones for what he meant, but Naasir nodded.

"Yes. He creates a desperation in the child." Right then, Naasir sounded like a proper grown-up. "I wanted to bite him when he came to visit Raphael, but Raphael said that might cause a political incident."

Aodhan only understood part of that, and it made him grin. "I would bite him if I had sharp teeth."

Colors rippled over Naasir's skin for a moment, like the fur of a tiger. His teeth glinted, his eyes reminding Aodhan of a snow-cat's. "Too bad we have to be polite."

"Too bad," Aodhan parroted.

They sat there, watching the reunion in the sky until Aegaeon flew off with Illium, toward Eh-ma's house.

Aodhan stayed where he was, not wanting to go there while Aegaeon was around. He'd rather stay with Naasir. "Are you a proper grown-up in Raphael's court?"

"Sometimes." Naasir yawned. "It's annoying, but I only do it when I want. Dmitri told me to be myself, but I know Raphael is a new archangel. I know others watch him."

Aodhan didn't understand much of that at all. "Are you here to do work for Raphael?"

Naasir nodded. "But I have time to see small sparkles and small blue wings." A wild grin. "Come. I brought you presents. One from me and one from Raphael."

"What about Illium?"

"We'll give him his presents later." Naasir scrambled off the roof with a grace that Aodhan had seen in no one else.

Stomach still in knots, but knowing Illium was happy for now, he flew down to join Naasir. He was still wobbly in flight, so often it was much easier to walk. And he liked to walk with Naasir. He always saw interesting things and pointed them out so Aodhan could see, too.

Once it had been a giant spider as white as the snow.

Lifting his hand, he slid it into Naasir's warm one. "His papa's not mean," he said, feeling a little bad for not liking Aegaeon.

Naasir didn't say anything for a long time.

"Nasi?"

Silver eyes locking with Aodhan's own as Naasir crouched down in front of him. "Sometimes, small sparkles, meanness is hidden inside." He tapped the place over Aodhan's heart. "You see it with your heart. Listen. Remember."

He got up, squeezed Aodhan's hand. "But right now, you are a cub. Cubs don't have to worry about things like that. You just have to be Illium's friend."

"I'll always be his friend." He looked up. "And yours, too."

Naasir's smile was a dazzling white. "One day, small sparkles, we will be allies in battle, and we will bite all our enemies."

Laughing together, they walked through the Refuge hand in hand, while in a cottage not far from them, a little boy grinned in his father's arms.

15

Today

Aodhan hadn't been able to talk to Illium at dinner, they'd been seated too far apart. He could've initiated mental contact, but this wasn't a conversation he wanted to have while surrounded by others—especially when Illium's eyes kept flicking to the doors that led into the kitchen.

His muscles threatened to knot once more, but if there was one thing he knew, it was that Illium could be brutally stubborn. There was no point in attempting to lead him away from Kai even when Aodhan knew there could be nothing healthy there for his friend. Kaia was dead and gone. No matter what, Illium couldn't re-create the past. Aodhan hoped he didn't; hoped he didn't talk himself into another obsession.

For now, he pitched in with the final necessities of the move. Vetra had been delayed due to injuries sustained by the people she was escorting in, would be hours yet. She, too, Aodhan thought, would appreciate the move to the coast for she loved to surf the waves. But no one wanted it more than Suyin.

"I hunger for the freedom of the endless horizon, Aodhan," the archangel had said to him an hour earlier, as the stars glittered overhead. "Zhangjiajie has made me see that no longer am I a child of the mountains as I once was. They loom over me now, throwing shadows I cannot escape. The sea and its vast openness is what I need for this eon of existence."

Aodhan knew her meaning well. Part of the reason he'd been able to move to New York was its proximity to the ocean. But unlike Suyin, he also loved the mountains, the reason why he'd stayed so long in the Refuge. The sunlight there was brilliant, dazzling, even painful at times. And light of any kind was freedom to him. He'd been trapped in the dark, light the taste of hope.

"Aodhan, could you carry this out?" Jae's request had him glancing back to see her indicating a box that he knew held heavy weapons.

No one expected war, not now, but it would be foolish to go out unprepared when so many of Lijuan's sympathizers still called China home.

"Of course," he said, and picked up the box.

Jae herself was laden with two bags, one on either shoulder.

"Food," she said to him. "Emergency supplies in case the hunting fails or we hit one of the toxic areas."

Those areas were dead patches in the landscape where it was as if Lijuan's death fog had permanently settled, turning the soil black and the area shadowy even on the brightest summer's day. Suyin had banned angels from landing in those areas, while mortals and vampires hadn't needed her order—they refused to go near the tainted sections.

Rii, the forty-something man who spoke for the mortals, had shivered when he told Aodhan of one such patch he'd passed on his journey to Suyin. "It smells of the dead." Then he'd muttered prayers to a god older than Lijuan had ever been.

Despite Suyin's order banning angels from making contact with the blackened and dead surface, Suyin had planned to land herself, to bring back samples for the scientists.

It was Raphael who'd talked her out of that. "We know I'm immune to Lijuan's poison," he'd pointed out at the time. "Why should you take the risk when I can do the same task without risk? Remember, Suyin, the Cadre is already down multiple members, with more than one either not at full strength or with no willingness to be in the world."

Aodhan had been able to tell that, newborn archangel or not, it went against Suyin's territorial instincts to acquiesce to Raphael's suggestion, but she had finally agreed. She'd accompanied Raphael to the chosen location, however, as had Aodhan—both of them staying in the air while Raphael landed.

Aodhan had hated seeing his sire disappearing into that murky place devoid of light, had been unable to stop himself from saying, *Be careful, sire. How will I face Ellie if any-thing happens to you on my watch?*

Do not worry, Aodhan. Elena has already threatened to kill me dead if I dare get hurt. I will take every care.

Raphael had confirmed that the toxic pocket held nothing of life. No animals, no insects, no plants, not even any moss. Everything was shriveled and dead. The tests on the soil had come back inconclusive but the general consensus was to treat it as poisonous. And even though animals seemed to avoid the areas, Suyin had declared that there was to be no hunting within a mile radius of each such spot.

No one dared defy her for the simple reason that they didn't wish to be poisoned by the darkness. Not even Lijuan's most ardent supporters.

"Will it be enough?" Aodhan took a critical look at the amount of food in the supply truck to which Jae had directed him.

Each supply truck held a portion of everything—food, weapons, other necessities—so that the loss of one vehicle wouldn't threaten to wipe out an entire chunk of a certain item. Aodhan hadn't been in charge of that aspect of things, now wondered if someone had made an error—the food stores were lower than he'd have thought prudent. "How fast is Suyin planning to travel?" He slotted the box of weapons securely in between two other boxes.

Jae dropped her bags on the ground, then jumped up into the truck. As Aodhan passed her the bags to stack into place, she said, "It's all sorted. Vetra did a flyby during this most recent run of hers to confirm any toxic spots in our travel zones, so even with any new eruptions of the fog we should be fine to hunt to bolster our supplies. There's no lack of game—and we've got the gear for winter hunting."

True enough. Nature had responded to the mass disappearance of so many mortals and immortals by filling the gap with life. Rabbits, deer, and waterfowl were just a few of the species that teemed across the landscape. The rabbit population, in particular, had exploded with a vengeance.

As if she'd read his mind, Jae said, "That ecology scholar—Mila—she says we need to control the rabbits anyway, before they push out other species. We might get sick of eating rabbit, but it'll keep us alive."

Satisfied, Aodhan helped the vampire finish loading the truck, then the two of them moved to stack supplies into a carrier designed so six angels—three on each side—could carry it with ease. No reason for angels not to help out with carriage of goods, especially since it meant some of their supplies would be safe in the air and not subject to any sudden eruptions of the black fog.

Those eruptions weren't exactly rare, the reason why Aodhan, Arzaleya, Xan, and Vetra had planned out multiple travel routes for when Suyin decided to move her people to the sea. The eruptions didn't cover as large an area as the toxic patches, and it was possible to predict them through ground-sensing equipment—but the scholars manning the sensors had to be within meters of the oncoming eruption.

Aodhan's respect for them was enormous.

Some of the eruptions turned into "stable" toxic patches, while others faded away after a few days. But regardless, the travelers would have to find an alternate route to avoid any such.

In terms of general safety, the angels would go first, with the mortals below the second half of the winged cohort. The vampires would bring up the rear, with an elite squadron above them. The strong bracketing and protecting the weak.

Aodhan had become used to seeing New York's Guild Hunters as part of the strong—highly trained and lethal, they'd fought with Tower troops during the war. It was during the war that Aodhan had truly come to know and call a number of them friends. The cheerful and witty Demarco, for one, was one of his favorite hunters. Elena had grinned when she'd found the two of them talking, but she'd never tell Aodhan why she found their friendship so interesting.

Lijuan had, however, decimated China's Guild.

Many had left prior to the final annihilation, pulled out by the worldwide leadership of their organization when it became clear that Lijuan was no longer paying any mind to the risks to hunters in the tasks being handed to them. Many, however, had stayed.

"To leave would've been to abandon the entire population to vampires gone bloodborn," Elena had said when they'd spoken on the subject. "Hunters can be mercenary, no doubt about it, but most of us are driven to do what we do— especially the hunter-born. We want to protect mortals and weaker vampires. We want to hold the line."

The end result of it all was that there were no living hunters of the Guild currently in China. Though the Guild had reviewed its stance against China after Lijuan's death, there'd been no need for hunters in the immediate aftermath of the war—China'd had no real vampire problem, while other territories had been overrun by bloodborn. As if with the end of war had come a blood madness.

Add in the fact that Lijuan had siphoned all other trained humans into her army, and the vast majority of China's surviving mortals were considered vulnerable. Prey to the toxic patches in the landscape as well as to animals emboldened by the dearth of a sprawling civilization. Tigers prowled abandoned cities and wolves howled in the night.

"Illium! Over here!"

He looked up to see wings of wild blue against the night sky, Illium diving in to assist a squadron as they finalized the balancing of another sling—which was currently swinging wildly. Moving quicker than any other angel Aodhan had ever met, Illium switched sides, spiraled up, and fixed the strap that was causing the problem.

Aodhan's best friend had always been that: quick, dazzling, overwhelming in his drive and goals.

Aodhan hadn't cared about that for a long time, content to be in his shadow. But things had changed.

16

Sharine was painting a meadow scene while the two boys played through the flowers, their laughter keeping her company, when she became aware of a sudden quiet. Mother's instincts on alert at once, she looked around her canvas.

Illium was seated in among the bluebells, his wings a carpet of an even more vibrant blue. He was watching what was probably a bug. He was of an age to be fascinated by them—but he never hurt them, not ever.

Aodhan, however . . . was right beside her.

Hand pressed to her heart, she glanced down at the little boy who'd become as dear to her as her own son in a very short time. "What is it, little one?"

Aodhan pointed with a soft child's finger at her canvas.

Sharine smiled. "Yes, I'm painting." Then, because she'd seen his interest other times, she picked up one of the sheets of rough handmade paper that she'd brought with her for this very reason and attached it to a thin wooden board using the device Naasir had made for her. A clip of sorts that worked with a string tie.

Her Illium would be surprised to learn that Naasir had climbed onto her roof long before Illium attempted it. He'd been so nimble as a babe that she'd known she'd never catch him, so she'd coaxed him down with his favorite treat of dried meat strips.

He still came to visit her at times. And he brought her gifts like this clip. Naasir had a very clever mind.

"Sit here," she told Aodhan, and the gentle-natured boy sat down in the flowers next to her. "This is your canvas." She put the flat "easel" in front of him. "And this is your brush."

The smallest brush she'd brought along proved too large for his tiny hand, but that wouldn't matter. Illium got tired of the "painting game" after a few minutes and ran off to do wild little boy things. No doubt Aodhan would as well once he'd satisfied his curiosity about this new thing.

Next, she put a small dab of different paints on a spare old palette.

"Yours," she said, putting the palette on the ground next to Aodhan, since he didn't yet have the manual dexterity to hold it in one hand, the paintbrush in the other.

Then, those extraordinary eyes focused on her, she showed him how to dip his brush in the paint, how to put that paint onto canvas—or in his case, paper. He watched with care, then copied her with equal care.

He was far gentler with the brush and paints than Illium. As she watched, he put a dab of blue on his paper, then looked out at Illium and frowned before speaking. "Not blue."

"Yes, that's blue." Sharine frowned inwardly, surprised he was uncertain of his colors at this age. "Beside it is red, and—"

"*Not blue*," Aodhan insisted, and when she looked at him in confusion, he pointed his paintbrush.

Right at Illium.

Oh.

"I see," she murmured softly. "You want to make the blue of Illium's wings?"

At Aodhan's strong nod, Sharine showed him how to mix the colors to get different tones and shades. After she was done, she dabbed a new blue on the paper. "How's this?" It was the exact shade she used when she painted the base color of her son's wings; Aodhan was too young yet to learn about layering.

A huge smile. "Blue," he said happily, and began to paint.

His creation ended up a huge blobby mess, but she could see what he'd been trying to do. He'd gotten the proportions of Illium's body correct as compared to his wings, and he'd even managed to make a passing facsimile of flowers. Not only that, he'd made a different color *on his own*, melding blue and yellow to create green.

She hadn't shown him that . . . but she had mixed up a shade of green while he sat next to her. "Well now," Sharine murmured after Aodhan finally got up, put down his brush, and ran off to join Illium—who'd fallen asleep in the blue-bells. "I think you, little Aodhan, have a gift."

Putting down his first painting on a thoughtful nod, she turned to add to her own painting. She'd painted Illium asleep in the flowers, now added in a sparkle-eyed child seated next to him, tapping at his cheek with a bluebell.

Two wild little children as bright as stars.

17

Today

Illium was about to land when a flickering light to the far left of the stronghold caught his attention. Since the packing was done but for the final things that'd be put in right before the beginning of the journey, he decided to investigate the light in case one of the mortals had gotten caught out and was heading home in the dark.

Maximus had told him they'd seen no signs of surviving reborn, but no one was breathing easy, not after Neha's discovery of hidden nests along her border with China. The creatures were intelligent to some level—and the general consensus was that Lijuan must've left nests in reserve, to act as her seed group should she lose all her reborn in the war.

That no one had found any such seed groups in China didn't mean the theory was worthless. Especially not after the discovery of the nexus.

"Who knows how many underground lairs that monstress had built?" Maximus had growled as he threw large pieces of furniture into the back of a truck. "And what interest does any sane archangel have in an underground lair, you tell me that, Bluebell of the bluebells!"

The big angel had picked up on Illium's nickname from Yindi, found it hilarious to make that ridiculous play on it. When Illium retaliated by threatening to call him Bighead, he'd laughed even louder before pounding his massive fists on his chest and saying, "Me giant! Me crush you!"

So of course now Illium liked the big idiot.

But jokes aside, Maximus's statement had been apt. Illium could stand being underground, but he didn't like it. And that was before he got to what had been done to Aodhan, how he'd been caged away from the sun.

The light flickered out just before he reached it. Concerned, he threw a little of his power into the air. It wasn't something he did often—a showy thing, it served no purpose but to use up energy for a short burst of light. But it was worth it this time, because it illuminated the huddled body of a young girl crouched against a tree, her lantern dark at her feet and her face twisted into a rictus of terror.

Illium's light faded even as he landed, but he could tell the girl hadn't moved. The world was too still. And when his eyes acclimated again to the night, he easily picked out her frightened form. She'd ducked her head onto her arms, her lank hair a curtain around a body that shook.

Shifting closer, he crouched down, his wings spread behind him. "Hello," he said gently in the dominant tongue of this region. Immortals often knew many languages but a younger Illium had made it a specific point to learn at least one language in each of the territories of the Cadre—he'd seen it as another element of being a successful warrior.

Over time, his knowledge had grown, with each new language or dialect coming easier, as if his mind had built pathways along which the new words could travel. He wasn't anywhere near as good as Dmitri and nothing close to Jason's fluency in too many languages to count, but he was good enough for this.

"My name is Illium. I'm from New York's Tower, sent here to help the new archangel." It was a deliberate thing to make sure she knew he wasn't of this land, and that he'd played no part in what Lijuan had done.

Her quivering seemed to stop, a wary creature who was listening.

Encouraged, he said, "Did you get separated from your family? I can escort you back to the settlement."

Her head lifted, her eyes inky pools swimming in a pale oval face of astonishing beauty. When she spoke, it was in a whisper so low that he had to ask her to repeat herself.

"Dead," she rasped. "My family is all dead."

Grim as it was, at this point in history, that wasn't an unusual thing in this territory. "I'm sorry." That the dreadful loss of life was a national tragedy didn't make it any less painful. "But I don't think they'd want you out here alone. Let's walk to the stronghold."

A jagged shake of the head, her body hunching in on itself. "The archangel is there."

"Archangel Suyin means her people no harm."

"No, *her*." The girl's voice was an urgent whisper. "*She's here*. She walks in death."

A shiver rippled up Illium's spine. Fighting past it, he made his tone blunt. "I saw Lijuan die. I saw her be erased from existence by the combined might of many archangels. She's not coming back from that."

"Goddess," the girl whispered. "Goddess can't die. I wanted to go home. But the goddess can't die. She can't die."

Rising to his feet, Illium decided it was time for harsh reality. "She's not here, and the settlement moves tomorrow. If you don't join them now, you'll be left behind."

A moment of motionless silence before his words seemed to penetrate. Unraveling from her tight curl in jagged movements, she stood—and he realized she wasn't a girl after all, but a young woman. Nineteen or twenty mortal years perhaps. Her hair proved to be waist-length and was matted with leaves and other debris, and what he could see of her clothing was torn and dirty.

The smell that came off her was of old sweat and dirt.

Nothing nasty. No indication of festering blood or putrefying wounds. Simply as if she hadn't bathed for a few days.

"Did you go looking for greens and get lost?" He'd noticed any number of mortals scavenging in the forest for greens and mushrooms to supplement their diet of hunted meat. Yindi had told him that the mortals had also begun to preserve greens and fruits from the start.

"With farms lying fallow until we settle," she'd said, "it's a necessity. And the mortals want to contribute—they know they can't fight off any predators, or scout for danger, and most have never hunted, so this—and donations of blood—are their contributions to our food supplies."

But the young woman next to Illium seemed to not even hear his comment about the gathering of greens. Head down as she trudged beside him, she said, "Run. Run. Run. She walks."

Her voice was an eerie monotone that raised all the hairs on the back of his neck. This was why he didn't watch horror movies with Aodhan and Ellie. There were enough scary things in real life. *Especially* when it came to the megalomaniacal archangel who'd made the dead walk.

Deciding to leave the traumatized woman be for the time being, he led her to the stronghold, then around it to the large human encampment. It spread out for some distance, the area a bustle of activity in the daylight hours, but quiet now, as most people tried to catch a few hours of sleep before beginning the long migration home.

Most of the hearths had already been extinguished, with only a few left banked in order to provide hot drinks in the morning. Those last hearths would be safely extinguished after breakfast, the few permanent buildings locked against scavengers. The latter structures had been put up to house the very young and the very old. The rest was all temporary habitation that could be broken down within an hour, ready for transport.

The young woman looked around, her eyes wide, dazed.

Glimpsing the mortal named Rii, Illium caught his attention. "I found her coming out of the forest. She seems disoriented. Can you find her people?" Yindi had told him that the mortals were tight-knit, creating new families out of the wounded pieces of all who remained.

The man's eyes were close-set with thick lashes, his salt-and-pepper hair buzzed close to his skull. "I don't recognize her," he said, his heavy accent telling Illium this dialect wasn't his native one. "But no fear, my wife will know. My Lili knows everyone." A hint of a chuckle in his tone. "I will take care of it, Angel." He bowed.

Illium found the deference awkward. In New York, he'd land on a city street and people would grin and wave and the cheekiest would ask him to pose for a photograph with them. Venom was of the opinion that Illium was on more people's social media accounts than the rest of them combined.

"That's because I like people," Illium had said with a grin. "I'm not a tall, dark, and brooding type like you. You know you have a hashtag."

Viper green eyes glinting, Venom had slid on his sunglasses. "I'm not going to ask."

"SuitPornV," Illium had said, staying out of Venom's viciously fast reach. "Full of sneakily taken 'thirst' pics of you."

Venom had looked so utterly appalled that it had sent Illium into fits of laughter. Meanwhile, Venom's love, Holly, had already been on her phone scrolling through the hashtag. "Your stalkers have good taste," she'd said, then tugged a scowling Venom down for a kiss. "Don't worry, cutie, I'll chop off the hands of anyone who dares touch you."

Illium hadn't pointed out that tiny, fierce Holly had her own following. But that was the thing—in New York, immortals were part of the rhythm of life. Not the same as mortals, but still woven into the city. He knew the current levels of interaction had a lot to do with Ellie, but New York's immortals had never been *this* remote from the rest of its people.

Here, a film of fear colored every contact between mortal and immortal. Even Rii, who appeared at ease with angels and vampires, had given the slightest flinch when Illium re-settled his wings.

As if bracing for a blow.

Illium didn't know how Aodhan had lived with it for so long; his friend's personality was such that he tended to keep his distance from most strangers, mortal or immortal, but neither one of them was comfortable with obsequiousness. That wasn't how you built a strong people, a strong city.

None of this, however, was Suyin's fault. She couldn't just erase the memory of her aunt's heavy-handed rule. It would take time for the new culture to form and then permeate the population.

Leaving the young woman in Rii's safe hands, Illium rose into the sky. When a flash of color caught his eye, he looked down to see Kai carrying out a tray of food to an angelic security team on break. It was the yellow scarf she'd used to tie back her hair that had caught his attention.

When she looked up, he dipped his wings.

Her smile held a playful impudence to it this time, and it caught at his heart, made him remember another woman, another smile. Kaia had beamed at him with bold flirtatiousness from the first. He'd blushed from the pleasure of it.

"Will you walk with me?" he'd finally screwed up the courage to ask.

Basket of flowers held to her side, she'd given him a saucy look. "If I have the time." Then she'd giggled and walked off, a lovely young woman unafraid and intrepid.

If he had been Cassandra, able to see the future—if he'd known the heartrending loss to come, would he have chased after her as he'd done that day? He'd flown over her, doing aerial tricks until she dropped her basket of flowers and clapped, and he'd known he'd won her.

Then he'd lost her. In the most absolute way possible.

As he was now about to lose Aodhan. "But I can't force him to be my friend," he rasped to the night sky. "I can't hold on to him if he wants to go."

We're all a little broken.
No one goes through life with a whole heart.

—*Keir, Healer*

18

Yesterday

Aodhan flew toward Eh-ma's house. Illium had stayed with him at his house the previous night, and Aodhan's mother had baked them sweetcakes and his father had taken them for a walk along the top of the gorge.

Aodhan had been so happy. So had Illium. Especially when Aodhan's mother let them eat *three* sweetcakes each! She'd seemed to like being with them, and his father hadn't been distracted by his books. Those were Aodhan's favorite times and he'd felt proud to have Illium see how his parents could sometimes be.

"Your ma is nice," Illium had whispered before they went to sleep. "And your pa, too. He has a lot of books."

"Yes. Like Eh-ma has paints and brushes everywhere— even in her hair!"

They'd giggled at that and slept.

Aodhan had thought Illium would stay in the morning, too—Aodhan's papa had promised to make honey oats for breakfast and Illium loved those—but then Raphael had come and taken him away and Aodhan had a knowing in his heart that something was very, very wrong. But when he'd asked his parents, they'd just said, "Oh, Aodhan. This is a thing for adults."

That was wrong. It wasn't a thing for grown-ups if Illium had been taken away. Aodhan's best friend wasn't a grown-up.

So he'd waited and waited and waited until his parents were busy with their books, and now he flew toward Eh-ma's house in the evening light. Yesterday, on their walk, he'd found a pretty stone that he'd thought she'd like. He'd give it to her, and he'd ask her what was happening. Eh-ma would explain. She always explained things.

But it wasn't Eh-ma who came to the door. It was a far taller and thinner angel, her hair the color of chestnuts after his father roasted them, and her eyes soft. Aodhan had known she was kind the first time he'd seen her, even before she'd ever said a word.

"Aodhan." Smile as soft as the feathers of a color like pink—but deeper—that he could see over her shoulder, Teacher Jessamy knelt in front of him. "I'm afraid you can't visit Lady Sharine today."

Aodhan's heart beat too fast. "Is Eh-ma all right?"

A sadness to Jessamy's smile. "She's had a big shock, and she needs time to rest." Leaning in, she kissed Aodhan on the forehead. "I'll tell her you came by, I promise."

Teacher Jessamy never lied to them, so Aodhan knew she'd keep her promise. Digging inside his pocket, he pulled out the stone. "This is for her."

Light filled the warm brown of his teacher's eyes. "Oh, how lovely. I'm sure this will brighten her day."

"Can I see Illium?"

"Oh, of course—I think that would be very good for him." Jessamy touched his cheek. She'd asked on the first day of school if he minded if she hugged him or touched him in such small ways, and he'd told her he didn't. He liked her. She was warm inside like Eh-ma. "He's with Raphael. You know where Raphael's Refuge stronghold is?"

When Aodhan nodded hard, Jessamy said, "I'm sure he'll

be very glad to see you. But Aodhan, if he's mad at you, or doesn't act like himself, please know it has nothing to do with you. He's had a bad shock, too."

Aodhan's best friend was never mean to him, but he nodded again. "Is he hurt inside?" It was something Eh-ma had taught him, that sometimes, the hurts weren't ones you could see.

Jessamy gave him a solemn look. "Yes, sweet boy. He's hurt inside."

"I'll go see him now." He couldn't leave his friend alone when he was hurting.

Jessamy stood and watched as he walked to the edge of the drop-off beside Eh-ma's home, and flew off it. He couldn't do vertical takeoffs like the big boys yet, but he could fly good enough to get to Raphael's stronghold.

Still, he was puffed by the time he reached it, his wings drooping as he came in to land on the big flat balcony that Raphael had said he and Illium were allowed to use.

Raphael was already on that balcony. "There you are, Aodhan," he murmured.

"Did Jason see me?" Aodhan huffed, gulping in the cold air.

"No, Jason is in my territory. Another sentry spotted you." Raphael held out a small glass of water. "Drink this first, then we'll talk."

Thirsty after his long flight and wanting to see Illium, Aodhan gulped down the drink, gave Raphael the glass, then took the hand Raphael held out. They walked together into a big room that had lots of sitting places. Putting the glass on a nearby table, Raphael lifted Aodhan up onto a bench seat by a window.

The archangel then sat down next to him, his huge wings taking up all the space behind Aodhan. His face was more serious than Aodhan had ever seen it.

Scared, he said, "It's something really bad, isn't it, Rafa?"

"Yes, Aodhan, it is." Raphael met his eyes. "I've spoken with your parents, and they've agreed with me that you need to be told. You're too important to Illium for it to be other-wise."

Aodhan bit his lower lip. "Did you make my parents?" Because they'd been patting him on the head and telling him he didn't need to know.

"Perhaps I applied a little pressure." Raphael's tone was . . . different. Hard. "But there are times to protect a child, and there are times to trust a child's heart and strength. I think you have plenty of both."

Aodhan swallowed, squeezing the edges of the bench on which they sat. "What happened? Did Aegaeon do a mean thing?"

Going as still as one of the snow leopards that Naasir had shown Aodhan, Raphael murmured, "Now, why would you say that?"

Aodhan shrugged. "I don't like him." He flicked up his eyes to see if he was in trouble for saying that.

"Neither do I." Raphael's voice was even harder. "And the answer is yes, he did." Swiveling so he was straddling the bench, Raphael helped Aodhan get into the same position, so they were face-to-face. "Aegaeon went into Sleep. He didn't warn Lady Sharine or Illium. He just went into Sleep without warning."

Aodhan knew about Sleep. His grandmother who was his father's mother had gone into Sleep before he was born. It meant she was resting because she didn't want to live in the world anymore. One day, she'd wake up, but it might be a long time from now. Maybe even after Aodhan was a grown-up.

"But Aegaeon's a papa." He scrunched up his face. "Mamas and papas don't go to Sleep." Not until their children weren't little angels anymore.

"Even a small child knows our unwritten laws," Raphael said, his eyes like the blue stones in Aodhan's mama's favorite bracelet, "and yet that ass thinks he is above them all."

"Ass" was a bad word when used that way. Aodhan knew that, but he didn't say anything. Raphael was an archangel.

And it sounded like he was using the bad word about Aegaeon. If Aegaeon had done such a horrible thing, then he needed to be called bad words.

"Is Aegaeon going to wake up soon?" he asked in hope, because even though he didn't like Aegaeon, he knew Illium loved his papa.

A shake of Raphael's head. "All signs are that he intends this to be a long Sleep. He's set up a transition team in his court."

When Aodhan just looked at him, Raphael shook his head. "Of course you don't understand. None of that matters, Aodhan. What matters is that Illium is—"

"—hurt inside," Aodhan interrupted. "I know. Can I go see him?"

A faint curve to Raphael's lips. "Naasir says you have a heart like a tiger, fierce in your love."

Antsy to see Illium, Aodhan said, "Did Illium cry?"

When Raphael nodded, Aodhan banged his fists against the dark blue cushion of the bench seat. "Illium *never* cries! He's happy all the time!" Now Aegaeon had made him cry. "I hate Aegaeon!"

Raphael didn't tell him not to say those things. He just said, "You can be angry, Aodhan. But today, you need to listen to Illium. His heart is broken. He's very sad. We can hate Aegaeon, but he's Illium's father."

Aodhan's eyes were hot, but he nodded. Raphael was talking to him like a grown-up, talking to him like Aodhan could understand. So he would. He wouldn't talk about how horrible Aegaeon was; he'd let Illium say whatever he wanted. "I promise," he said, his voice wobbly.

"Aodhan." It was a murmur as Raphael took him into his arms and held him close to his chest, the huge breadth of his wings wrapping around Aodhan in a wave of warmth and protection that made it okay for Aodhan to cry.

After he finished, he wiped his eyes and sat up. "I can see Illium now. I won't say mean things about his papa."

Stroking back strands of hair from Aodhan's face, Raphael

met his eyes. "You have a tiger's heart indeed, small sparkles." A gentle smile as he used Naasir's name for him. "I think Illium will be quite all right with you by his side."

After they got up, Raphael used a wet cloth to wipe Aodhan's face so he didn't look like he'd been crying, and then they walked down the hallway of the stronghold, all the way to a room that was big and full of light. In the center of it stood a bed, on which lay a blue-winged boy curled up into a small ball, his body jerking as he slept.

The angel who'd been seated by the bed rose. "Sire. He hasn't woken since you left him."

"Thank you, Adaeze. You can return to your duties, now."

She inclined her head before walking out the door, her wings held neatly to her back. Aodhan didn't see what color they were; he was already climbing onto the bed to pat Illium's shoulder so his friend would sleep without bad dreams. It took a few pats, but Illium stopped jerking and soon, his face wasn't scrunched up anymore.

Raphael, who'd sat on the other side of the bed, reached out to brush Illium's hair off his forehead. "I will leave you be," he said. "Illium and I have spoken, and he knows I'm but a single call away. Now, I think he needs his closest friend."

Aodhan nodded. "I can come get you if he wants." He knew all he'd have to do was step into the hall and stop the first grown-up he saw; they'd find Raphael for him.

Raphael's smile was of a kind that made Aodhan feel good inside. It was how Eh-ma looked at him when he finished a piece of art. "I'll have Adaeze bring up a tray of food for you two. She has a little one of her own and tells me that everything is better with small sweets and savories."

Aodhan wasn't too sure about that, but when the angel with curly black hair and skin almost as brown as Naasir's walked in with a tray of things that smelled nice, his stomach rumbled.

Adaeze smiled. "There you go, sweet little child." She placed the tray on a table right beside the bed, so Aodhan could reach it from where he sat. "It's usually no eating in bed for little angels under my care," she murmured, her voice holding a rhythm that was like music, "but today's a special case. Don't you worry about crumbs now, and if you spill anything, you just let Adaeze know."

Aodhan nodded. "Thank you."

"You are most welcome." Soft eyes on Illium. "Poor baby. But he is loved, so loved. I see that, I do."

She left the door half-open when she went out, but Aodhan got out of bed after and quietly nudged it all the way shut. Illium wouldn't want anyone to see him crying if he wanted to cry some more. Raphael was different. Raphael was part of their family. Then, his tired wings dragging on the floor, he walked across the carpet and climbed back onto the bed.

Illium stirred.

Seated beside him, Aodhan patted his shoulder so he'd know he wasn't alone. Rubbing his eyes, Illium sat up. He had marks on one side of his face, and his hair was all mussed up and his eyes were big.

"Want a snack?" Aodhan picked a small pie thing he thought his friend would like.

Nodding, Illium took it, and they sat side by side, eating snacks from the tray until Illium spoke. "My papa went to Sleep."

"You're sad."

Illium nodded. "How come he went to Sleep? Papas don't go to Sleep."

Aodhan remembered what Raphael had said and he didn't say anything about Aegaeon being a bad papa. He just said, "I'm sorry. But Eh-ma is here, and Raphael is here. And I'm here."

Illium put his head on Aodhan's shoulder. "Do you think he didn't like me? Was I bad?"

"No," Aodhan said at once. "Even Brutus said he'd be proud to have you for his son, and he doesn't like any kids." Aodhan was careful to shape the words as the old warrior had said them, with a kind of half smile in his voice. "He yells at any other little angels who land in his garden, but he doesn't yell at you."

"My papa didn't stay. He didn't want me."

Aodhan couldn't stand that tone in his friend's voice. Illium was always laughing, always playing jokes—never nasty ones, just funny ones. He wasn't sad like this. "Your papa is old," he said. "Maybe he was just so tired he couldn't stay awake anymore."

Illium chewed on a piece of dried fruit. "Do you really think so?"

"Yes," Aodhan said, and it was a lie he didn't mind telling—not when it made some of the sadness fade from Illium. "He played with you all the time when he came to the Refuge. My mama says that sometimes, angels just get old and tired. That's what happened to my grandma. Remember? I told you."

"My papa is old," Illium murmured, but he was frowning. "Mama is old, too, and she's not Sleeping."

Aodhan shrugged. "Eh-ma is different. Special."

No hesitation from Illium. "Yes, she's special." He sighed. "Do you think my papa will wake up soon and not be tired anymore?"

"I don't know," Aodhan replied. "But I know he'll come to see you when he wakes up."

The faintest hint of a smile on Illium's face. "He will, won't he? Because I'm his boy."

19

Today

Illium. An archangel's voice in his head. *Vetra is here. She will meet you and Aodhan in the stronghold.*

Yes, Archangel Suyin.

Switching direction, he landed on the cobblestones of the main courtyard, then made his way inside to the large gathering room with huge windows where they'd had dinner. Aodhan was already there, pouring Vetra a drink as she ate.

She was as he remembered from Titus's court: a tall, leggy woman with a tumbled cap of mahogany-dark hair streaked with bronze, her skin the kind of white that tanned to a pale gold, and her wings as rich a brown as her eyes. She had the type of mobile face that seemed to mark spymasters—distinctive and vivid when she was with friends, she could turn it bland and forgettable while she was working.

It was a trick he'd seen Jason pull to great effect, and he had no idea how either did it. Jason had a tattoo that covered half his face and people *still* didn't see or remember him when he didn't want to be seen or remembered.

When Vetra lifted a hand in a silent apology aimed at Illium, he said, "Eat. You must be exhausted." He grabbed a seat on the other side and took the tumbler of mead Aodhan passed across.

Their fingers brushed for a second.

He jerked back without meaning to, the mead sloshed—and Aodhan went motionless. *Shit*. It was just that he hadn't expected it . . . and that Aodhan meant too much to him.

Vetra spoke before he could attempt to say something. What, he didn't know.

"I didn't find much else on my second glance," she said. "Just the abandoned hamlet, everything neat, no rotting food in the fridges, no signs of people having packed up and left, no blood, no bodies."

It was a haunting image she'd placed in their minds, of a place just waiting for its people to come home. "Fifty residents, right?" he said.

It was Aodhan who answered. "I checked with the scholar who did the headcount for our records—he puts the exact number at fifty-one. The woman you found? She told Rii her name is Fei. If she's from the hamlet, that means we're missing fifty. Thirty-nine mortals, eleven vampires."

"High percentage of vamps. Unless they were getting blood shipped in before everything went to hell, each of the adult mortals would have to be a regular donor."

"Yes." Vetra took another bite, swallowed it down after a cursory chew. "I planned to look into that on my return but . . ."

She put down her sandwich, deep grooves in her forehead and lines flaring out from her eyes. "I looked for tracks, for burial places, didn't find any. But there's a lot of forest and I couldn't do an in-depth search. If they've been dumped at the bottom of even a shallow ravine and covered with foliage, they'd be invisible from the air."

She looked at the curved wall of windows at the front of the generous space in which they sat, beyond which lay the main courtyard. "Soon, the snow will come."

Burying the dead in their forgotten grave.

A bleak and sad image that would haunt Illium until he found these lost people.

But though he and Aodhan spoke to Vetra for another quarter of an hour, she had precious little to add to what she'd already told them.

"It infuriates me that I'm so in the dark." Her hand tightened on the tumbler. "I left the task unfinished, secrets hidden. More than that, I didn't assign anyone to keep an eye on the place from the start, check regularly on the residents."

"You have but a small team, Vetra," Aodhan murmured, his deep voice soothing. "And the hamlet appeared well-established, its residents happy to stay outside the borders of the stronghold—you had no reason to expect a mass vanishing."

"I should have," Vetra muttered, her eyes like flint. "This is still Lijuan's land."

"No." Aodhan's tone was unbending. "She may have left behind some echoes, but it's Suyin's land now."

A pink flush under the tanned gold of her skin, Vetra dropped her head. "You're right. I'm just frustrated. How can fifty people vanish without a trace? Even when the black fog erupts out of the earth like pus ejected from a rank wound, it leaves behind shriveled bodies, bones."

That was another horror of which Illium had become aware—that every so often, remnants of the black fog seeped out of the earth. As if it had been trapped in some pocket.

"None of it makes sense." Vetra shoved both hands through her hair, then looked from Aodhan to Illium and back again. "I need you two to solve this. I must go with my archangel, but I won't sleep easy until I know what could've possibly happened to so totally erase fifty living, breathing people."

The vast majority of both immortals and mortals were in a deep sleep, and pack-up was complete but for odds and ends.

It was one of the latter that currently held Aodhan's interest: he was helping a human resident tie their belongings to the roof of their vehicle. The man had already done it, then woken up unable to sleep, decided it was badly arranged and restarted.

Aodhan understood needing to do something, anything to keep the nightmares at bay, so he'd said nothing about the unnecessary work, just stepped in to assist. He didn't need to sleep tonight, and—with Illium—was part of the crew on night watch. He and the young mortal were almost done when Suyin's voice entered his mind.

Aodhan, please find Illium, then meet me at the edge of the settlement—near the sleeping hazel tree.

I just saw him. We'll be there soon.

The mortal's belongings secured, he rose up into the sky in the direction he'd spotted Illium.

Illium turned at almost the same instant, as if he'd sensed Aodhan.

Their awareness of one another was part of what made them such great partners in battle. It was nothing mystical, rather the result of centuries of friendship and knowledge of each other.

Not mystical but . . . special.

Waving for the other man to wait, he headed over and told Illium of Suyin's request.

Illium frowned even as they turned to fly toward the tree devoid of blooms or leaves, a bleak sight that would've blended in with the night sky if not for the portable "street light" that stood close to it. Those lights would usually be dotted heavily throughout the settlement, for Zhangjiajie was otherwise a cool darkness after nightfall.

Most, however, had already been packed in readiness for transport, only a final few left to act as beacons for anyone who woke before dawn. In a land known for a death fog that devoured in chilling silence, no one found comfort in the pitch dark of a moonless night.

"I wonder if it's about Fei," Illium said, the words traveling easily to Aodhan on the motionless air.

Aodhan didn't have a chance to respond. They'd arrived at the meeting location. Rii, who'd been speaking to Suyin before they arrived, slipped away even as Aodhan and Illium folded back their wings. The mortal headman passed under the street light for a second, and Aodhan saw that his features were pinched, his lips pale.

Suyin allowed Rii to get out of hearing range before she said, "We have a problem."

No warrior working at his archangel's side ever wanted to hear such a statement. That went double-fold—triple-fold— in what had once been Lijuan's land.

Illium groaned and slapped a hand over his face. "Go to China, they said. It'll be a cakewalk, they said. Nothing much to do, they said."

Suyin stared at Illium, while Aodhan shifted a minute fraction toward his friend, fighting the urge to wrap Illium protectively in his wings. Suyin didn't know Illium's humor, didn't understand how he used it to try to lighten the dark, and despite her lack of "scariness," she *was* an archangel, an archangel who was highly stressed . . . but then she burst into such laughter as Aodhan had never before heard from her.

It filled her eyes, broke the tension that locked her shoulders, lit her skin from within. At that instant, she was glorious, and he knew he'd paint her exactly so, with her body clad in warrior leathers, her wings held with strict control, her hands on her hips, and delight on her face.

"Would it not be splendid were it so?" she said to Illium, her lips curved and eyes dancing. "I dream of ruling a boring land in a boring time where the most exciting event will be the escape of someone's prize bull, or perhaps a shocking fashion faux pas where two angels turn up to a court dinner in the same clothing. Would that not be a wonderful life?"

Illium's grin was so real it stole Aodhan's breath. "At least for a century or two."

"Yes, but it appears we are not to have even a few days of peace." Smile fading, she ran her hand through her hair. It rippled through her fingers like silken water. "The woman you found—Fei—no one in the entire settlement knows her or of her.

"General Arzaleya, who is in close contact with the scholars charged with keeping track of our population, confirmed the same just prior to your arrival. Fei did not exist before this night."

"'She's here. She walks in death.'" Illium shifted to look over his shoulder on that eerie recitation, in the direction from which the stranger had come. "Guess there's no question now. She must've come from Vetra's troubling hamlet."

"Just so," Suyin said. "I would tell you to speak to her, but our senior healer, Fana, visited her earlier this day after Rii became concerned about her increasing lack of responsiveness. Fana was unable to get through to her. She has turned mute but not in the way of stubbornness, in the way of a being with a wounded mind." Compassion in Suyin's tone. "I'll get word to you if she comes out of it once we are away from here."

As an archangel, Suyin could've literally broken into the woman's mind—but given Suyin's own past, such an action was not one of which she was capable. It would damage her as badly as it would damage the mortal.

So it was that Aodhan made no effort to remind her of her ability. "It can't be the reborn." Their intelligence didn't rise to the level where they could cover their tracks. "An infected angel as was discovered in Africa?" Only the very senior immortals knew of that abomination.

"Let us hope not." Suyin rubbed at her eyes for a moment before she dropped her hand. "The one grace is that after tomorrow, there will be no prey here on which this threat—whatever form it now takes—can feed.

"Arzaleya has informed the staff who are to remain behind to stay inside unless you or Illium are nearby—the vast majority of their tasks lie within the stronghold so my order will not hamper them." A faint glow against the darkness of the tree trunk, Suyin's wings afire in a silent indication of her rage at all her aunt had done.

That it was viciously contained made it no less deadly. In truth, Aodhan worried at how Suyin stifled her anger. He knew it was hypocritical of him when he'd shut out the world for so long. But by that same token, he understood how much damage such a choice could do.

"Do you think you need more backup?" she asked Aodhan, none of that cold rage evident in her tone. "I may be able to spare you—"

Aodhan was already shaking his head. "No, Suyin, you can't." They were working with razor-thin margins. "Illium and I can take care of ourselves. You need every warrior you have to make sure all the survivors make it to their new home."

Illium gave a silent nod.

Not arguing, Suyin flared out her wings. But before she took off, her voice silvered into Aodhan's mind. *An angel who can bring laughter to the darkest time? Such a being is a gift, Aodhan. I see more and more why you have called him friend for these many centuries.*

20

Sharine knew something was wrong with her. Her mind hadn't been the same since . . . since . . . She let the memory float away, focused on trying to paste together the broken fragments of her thoughts.

"He doesn't ask as much anymore," she said, her eyes on the small blue-winged boy who was doing drills in the air with his class of fellow young angels. Learning to use their wings more precisely, learning to land with more control.

"His youth is a mercy," said the archangel who stood by her side, his hair a familiar midnight hue and his eyes as blue as the heart of a sapphire she'd seen once.

Child of her closest friend in this entire world.

Her friend who had gone quite, quite mad.

A moment of clarity that whispered of her own madness, and then it was gone, slipping away like a wisp of mist from her grasp. "He learns new things, makes new friendships, doesn't stand any longer at the edge of the Refuge waiting for . . ."

"That's good." Caliane's son nodded at the children. "I see Aodhan beside him."

"Always." She smiled. "They are so different, but they are the best of friends." Her smile faded as she experienced another moment of clarity. "My boy has always wanted to be a warrior. But I know nothing of this. Who will give him his first sword? Who will teach him those things that—"

A big hand closing over her one, the touch gentle despite the power that burned off him. "You need not have any concern on that score, Lady Sharine. I will ensure Illium has all that he needs."

A stirring in the back of her head, an echo of a time she couldn't quite see now. "Did I hold you once?" she asked, staring down at their linked hands. "Did I stroke your broken wings and tell you it would be all right?" It seemed impossible that she could've done so for this archangel strong and so much taller than her.

Raphael's voice was solemn. "Yes. More than that, you loved me at a time when I was a beast with a razored spine, unwilling to allow anyone close. You will always have my loyalty."

She looked up at him, smiled. "Raphael. My oldest boy." Raising her hand, she waited for him to lower his head, then stroked his cheek. "Caliane will be so proud to see who you've become. As Aegaeon will be of his boy."

An alteration in Raphael's expression that she couldn't read, but all he said was, "Your pride is the most important to him. He looks to you even now to see if you witnessed his latest achievement."

Sharine laughed and waved at her son.

Illium's responding smile lit up her world, until the fragmented edges of her mind almost came together, almost became as they'd once been, almost . . . "My pride in Illium will never be in question. My son is a light in this world."

21

Illium landed sometime around five a.m., after ensuring the other nightwatch sentries were all happy for him to take a break. He needed to eat; his body required extra fuel as a result of his long flight to China. It wouldn't harm him to go without, but it would slow him down a fraction and he wanted to be at full speed in this land.

When he saw that Kai was one of the two staff members in charge of the late-night meal station for those still awake and/or working, he smiled at her. The person with her, a vampire of a certain age, sniffed. "Don't trust this pretty one, Kai. He breaks hearts all over the world, I hear."

Kai's eyes went huge at the plain speaking, but Illium grinned. "Such lies you tell about me, Li Wei."

The small and pretty woman who looked around twenty-seven, but was actually nine hundred years old with the tendencies of a strict school matron, huffed. But he caught the smile in her dark eyes. He and Li Wei had met for the first time some three hundred and fifty years past, when she'd held a position in Neha's high-court kitchen.

On an errand for Raphael, he'd landed late into the night and had snuck into the closed kitchen desperate for a snack. Two minutes after he entered, Li Wei had busted him poking through her cupboards, delivered a sharp reprimand, then made him the best sandwich of his life—with a side of a cold potato-spice soup for which she'd refused to share the recipe no matter how much he begged.

The woman was so good a cook that she could pick and choose her employment.

It surprised him that she'd chosen to come to this place so unstable when he'd always seen her as efficient and warm-hearted, but also stodgy in terms of her preferences.

"Hungry, are you?" she said now, and passed across a roll she'd filled with layers of delicately flavored meat, caramelized onions, and more deliciousness. "Eat, skinny boy."

Illium liked her a whole lot. She'd lived long enough that she had no time for anyone's bullshit. Next to her, Kai—despite her innate confidence—was a fragile bloom barely budded, to be treated with care. He spoke to her as he ate, learned that her entire family had survived the fog.

"Our village was in a valley where the fog didn't seem to be able to reach," she said. "It hovered above us like a horrible cloud, but it never dropped."

"Hell, that must've been terrifying." Illium couldn't imagine the kind of fear her family and the others with them must've experienced.

But Kai shook her head. "We didn't know, you see. What the fog was doing. We thought it was a bad storm—so bad that it had cut off all communication with the outside world. It was only after that we . . ."

She took a shuddering breath. "Later, when the archangel flew away with her army, she didn't call us up. We think perhaps she didn't know us because the fog didn't touch us."

It was an excellent theory, the fog an extension of Lijuan's power.

"More?" Li Wei asked after he was done, and had chased it all down with a tall glass of water.

"No." He grinned and bowed over her hand. "I thank you for the sustenance, my beauteous Li Wei."

"Ha! Off you go, you scamp."

He left with a light salute for her, and a soft smile aimed Kai's way. While he was assisting with the sentries so they could take more breaks, he had no official assigned area. He decided to use that freedom to check on Aodhan, having not seen his friend for the past hour.

This place . . .

He shivered, just not liking the feel of it. Especially now that they had a survivor who'd come out of nowhere and who spoke about Lijuan walking the earth.

Aodhan stood underneath a sky smudged a charcoal gray that said night hadn't yet released its grasp on the world. Having flown to the highest point in the area—the forested tip of one of Zhangjiajie's unearthly pillars—Aodhan waited for the light, his intent to search for any signs of unusual movement or activity.

Lijuan's monstrous creatures weren't the smartest when they were hungry or injured.

"Why are you lurking in the dark like a bloodborn vampire out of one of your horror movies?"

Aodhan didn't startle; he'd heard the snap of Illium's wings as he landed behind him, felt the wind it generated. "Since when do you know anything about horror movies?" he said, light bursting inside him in tiny bubbles at the fact Illium had hunted him down.

"I know many things, young grasshopper." The other man came to stand beside him. "Oh, I see. This is the best vantage point in the area. You're waiting for the dawn?"

Aodhan nodded, his throat dry without warning and his face hot. It happened like this sometimes, a sudden flashback to the endless darkness that had been his world once upon a time.

He'd learned to live in the night again, learned to

accept that the sun and the moon couldn't always be his companions—but right then, he came to understand that part of why he so loved New York was that Raphael's city was never truly dark.

A brush of a wing across his own.

His heart twisted, clenched, clung. He said nothing. Nothing needed to be said. Illium knew his nightmares, had seen him at his most broken, when his wings had been nothing but tendons held together by rotted webbing, and his spirit a thing splintered. Illium understood the horrors the dark held for Aodhan, understood that as long as the night existed, Aodhan could never truly forget.

He didn't know how long they stood there in a silence that wasn't comfortable or uncomfortable. It was . . . It had no words. No description. It was a thing formed out of time and friendship and loyalty.

Only when a sliver of light lit the horizon on fire did Aodhan take his first real breath in what felt like hours. Air stabbed into his lungs, filled his nostrils, made his skin ignite with life.

When he felt Illium begin to slide away his wing, he reached out and grabbed the other man's wrist. Solid bone and warmth, the contact made his world shift the right way up for the first time in more than a year.

Then Illium's muscles went rigid under his touch, his arm unmoving.

"Let go." Illium's voice was a harsh thing full of ground-up rocks as he gave an order he'd never before used on Aodhan. Not for this.

Aodhan never disregarded such requests. *Never.* But he had to force himself to lift his fingers from around Illium's wrist one by one. And the words that should've come, they stuck in his chest, the silence between them a spiked mine that stabbed and cut.

The image was enough to smash an anvil into his chest, release his words. "What is wrong between us?" It came out almost angry.

Illium's eyes were aglow when he looked at Aodhan, a sign of the violent power that shadowed him, and haunted all those who loved him. He was far too young for it, needed time yet to be part of Raphael's Seven, to be a senior squadron commander, to be everyone's playful Bluebell.

"There's nothing wrong," Illium said, his shoulders set as hard as his jaw, and his voice that of the senior squadron commander. Mature. Remote. Professional. It was a face that he'd never before turned toward Aodhan.

"Blue." The old nickname was torn out of him.

Illium didn't budge. "We're just different people now," he said.

It was a truth, but only *a* truth. They'd grown as people throughout their lives, yet always remained bonded in blood, their friendship so deep that nothing and no one could shake it. "You're avoiding the question."

"You told me you needed freedom." Illium's words were rough shards that sliced into them both, the distance exploding in a million deadly pieces. "That night during and after the dinner at Elena and Raphael's Enclave home, you told me you wanted freedom. As if *I* was a cage." He thumped a fisted hand against his chest. "So go, be free, Aodhan. This cage will never again hold you."

Spreading wings of wild blue and silver in a violent snap, he rose up into the air before Aodhan could respond. He could've flown up after him, but no one could catch Illium when he didn't want to be caught. Aodhan would wait, be patient. They'd be alone soon enough, and then they'd have this out.

Because he hadn't *ever* implied that Illium was a cage, much less used the words Illium was trying to put into his mouth.

He remembered exactly what he'd said: *I'm no longer a broken doll who needs to be protected from those who might play roughly with me.*

Then later, when he'd tracked Illium down as he sat alone on one of the powerful columns that arched over Brooklyn

Bridge: *I don't need to be tied to your apron strings any longer. I don't need to be babied and kept safe from myself.*

He'd been frustrated but no longer furious as he'd been at dinner. He'd needed his best friend to understand what he was trying to tell him, to *see* Aodhan as he was then and not as he'd once been.

But Illium, hurt by his earlier words, had been in no mood to listen.

If he could go back in time to that night, would he say the same? No. The apron strings comment had been out of line and Aodhan owned that. As for the rest . . . He wouldn't use the term "broken doll" for that brought up a memory so ugly it should be forever forgotten. But the rest? The meaning behind it? Yes, he'd speak of that again. It had needed to be said.

22

Yesterday

Illium had just finished his sword training with Raphael—
the archangel made him use a stubby wooden sword even
though Illium had *told* him that he wouldn't accidentally stab
him or himself, but it was still the best fun. He hardly ever got
to train with Raphael; he was an archangel, had lots of important business, and was often in his territory far, far away.

Mostly, Illium trained under people Raphael had chosen
for the task.

But Raphael was the one who'd taught him his first
skills—he'd spent an entire month with Illium for that, had
even asked permission from Teacher Jessamy to take him out
of school for it!

It had been amazing.

And even though he couldn't spend so many days with Illium often, he always made time for a session or sometimes
even two whenever he was in the Refuge. Today, he'd been
waiting at the house when Illium flew home from school; he'd
been seated at Illium's mother's table while she sketched him.
In front of him had been a plate of cookies, and a glass of milk.

Illium's eyes had gotten round. He knew that was little angel food. He still liked it, but Raphael was an *archangel*. But Raphael was never mean to Illium's mother. Not ever. Not even when she did things that weren't quite right. Today, he'd drunk the milk, and eaten the cookies before he took Illium out for the training session.

Once, when Illium had said thank you to Raphael for being so nice to Illium's mother, Raphael had stopped walking and crouched down so they were eye to eye. It stopped Illium's breath to be that close to Raphael—his eyes were like blue fire and Illium could feel a pressure against his skin, like he could in the air right before a storm.

That day, Raphael had said, "You need never say such to me, Illium." He'd cupped one side of Illium's head, his fingers brushing Illium's hair. "Lady Sharine has every claim on my loyalty, love, and care. She was a mother to me when I needed one most. Whenever she calls, I will come."

Illium hadn't understood all of the emotion in Raphael's voice or face, but he'd understood that his mother had a history with the archangel. Maybe one day, he'd be old enough that they'd tell him about it. It was annoying being a little angel—but at least he wasn't any longer considered a baby.

"Ugh," he said as he struggled up the steep climb. He could've flown home, but Raphael always said that he couldn't only be strong in the air—to be a truly well-rounded warrior, he had to be strong on the ground, too. Because otherwise, what would he do if his wings got wounded in battle and he fell to the earth?

Illium had no plans of being useless if he ended up groundbound. So he made it a point to walk as much as he flew. Sometimes, when the ground wasn't this uneven, with craggy edges and sharp rocks, he even ran. But today, Raphael had made him do a hard training, and the ground was all broken up, so he was huffed by the time he made it to the top of the incline.

When a burst of light landed beside him, he bent down with his hands on his knees, his sword strapped safely to his back, and gasped. "Sorry. Training."

Aodhan didn't say anything, standing in quiet next to Illium until Illium could breathe properly again. He could see
half of Aodhan's legs and part of Aodhan's wings from his
bent-over position. His friend was wearing brown sandals,
and his favorite old pants that had started out white but were
now kind of a dull light brown, with small rips in them. His
wings glittered like the stones in Lady Ariha's necklace.

Light shattered off Aodhan, was drawn to him.

Though Illium was used to it, it was still kind of difficult
to look at him in the bright sunshine. Playfully pushing his
friend into the shade of a nearby tree when he could stand
straight again, he said, "I think I see stars."

It was an old joke between them, from a time when Illium
had fallen and hit his head and thought he was seeing stars
when really, it was just Aodhan leaning over him with the
sun sparking off his hair.

The two of them found it hilarious.

But today, Aodhan didn't laugh. His face was still and
tight. Illium immediately stopped joking around. "What
happened?"

Aodhan kicked at a piece of rock. "Can we go flying?"

Illium had intended to walk all the way home, but he said,
"Where do you want to go?"

When Aodhan just shrugged, Illium said, "I know where
we can fly." There was a place his mother had shown him—
a mountain field with lots of flowers and butterflies. Aodhan
loved butterflies, even though he liked to pretend he didn't.
Illium didn't tease him about it; teasing was for stuff that
wasn't important. Butterflies were important to Aodhan in
some way.

They took off soon after. Illium couldn't do vertical takeoffs yet, but they were at a high point near the gorge. So he
walked to the edge of the massive split in the earth, and took
off from there, sweeping down on the air currents, then rising up into the clear blue of the sky. The two of them still
didn't have permission to gorge dive, but this—using the lift
created by the air cradled in the gorge—was allowed.

Illium didn't complain when Aodhan flew much higher. Aodhan liked doing that because he attracted too much attention when he flew closer to the ground. Littles their age weren't usually allowed at such high elevations, but Aodhan had been given special permission after Illium's mother went and talked to the other adults.

Now, Aodhan was a spark in the sky.

"He is a little sun," Mama had said one day, her voice dreamy as she looked up at the sky where Aodhan flew. "So bright and open and full of an inner light that I worry will be bruised by the world."

Her fingers in Illium's hair. "I worry about both of you, my two bright sparks."

Today, Aodhan followed Illium until they reached the field of flowers and butterflies. Then he came straight down to land on his feet. He wasn't anywhere near as fast as Illium, but he was much faster than other children around their age.

A huge butterfly of jewel green settled immediately on his shoulder. It fluttered up when Aodhan slumped into a seated position on the field, then settled again. Other, smaller butterflies found spots on Aodhan's wings, his hair, even his legs. Each time he moved, the air shimmered with color.

Illium's mother had painted Aodhan covered with butterflies and even though Aodhan had gone a funny color at seeing it, he kept the painting in his bedroom. He wouldn't even give it to his own mama, even though she'd pressed both hands to her cheeks and asked with shining eyes.

Sitting down beside his best friend, Illium pulled off his practice sword. It might be stubby and made of wood, but he loved it because Raphael had given it to him once he decided Illium was old enough for sword training. When it broke—because all practice swords broke after a while—Illium was going to save a piece and see if his mother's friend who carved things could carve him a tiny sword out of it, for Illium to put in his box of keep-things.

He put down the sword with care, then fell back in the grass so he was looking up at the sky, with the flowers waving alongside him, and Aodhan's bright presence to the left. Then he waited. Trying to make Aodhan talk when he didn't want to talk was stupid. All it got anyone was a tired voice.

Aodhan's mama and papa didn't seem to understand that. They were nice, but they thought Aodhan was like his sister Imalia, who was already a grown-up. If they'd been his parents, Illium would've been mad at them for not knowing him, but Aodhan never got mad. He just said, "Eh-ma knows me. You know me. Teacher knows me. I don't need a lot of people to know me."

So because Illium knew him, he closed his eyes against the sunlight and began to talk about his training, including the new moves Raphael had taught him. "I'll teach you," he promised his friend. Aodhan was good at physical things, but he only did them because Illium did, so they could play battle games together.

Mostly, he liked making art.

"Thanks," Aodhan said, speaking at last. "You were tired."

"Raphael is a tough teacher." Illium loved that the archangel didn't baby him—he wasn't dumb, he knew that Raphael didn't treat him like a warrior. Because he *wasn't* a warrior. You didn't just decide you were one. You had to become one. Other warriors had to evaluate your skills and decide you were worth the title. "One day, I'm going to be in his seniorest squadron."

"That's not a word," Aodhan said, but Illium could tell he was smiling. "Seniorest."

"Who says?"

When Aodhan laughed, Illium opened his eyes—to see the butterflies take flight in tiny bursts of colors. Slumping back into the flowers and grasses with Illium, their fingers just touching, Aodhan sighed. "I was trying to show my art to this artist Eh-ma said I might like to talk to—she even gave me an introduction letter."

"Was he horrible about your art?" He didn't think his mother would've suggested a person like that, but her art friends could be strange. In their own worlds, but not like his mother. Different. And a few of them were plain odd or rude. They said things that weren't polite and thought it was all right because they were great artists.

Illium spoke his final thought out loud to Aodhan. "You know that's not right," he added. "My mother is the greatest artist of all and she's kind." That wasn't only Illium's opinion, either—people across the Refuge, even archangels like Uram and Lijuan, they called her art a "gift to angelkind." "Don't pay attention to the ones who think they're so important they can be mean."

"It's not that," Aodhan answered. "I don't mind being told I'm not that good or could improve—I want to learn, want to get better."

Illium broke off a grass stalk, chewed on it. "Yeah, that's how I feel when I mess up in training and get shown what I did wrong."

Aodhan stirred up into a seated position, pulling his knees to his chest. His skin glimmered in the sun. Not with sweat. With the sparkle that was buried in his skin. That was why Illium, inspired by Naasir, had begun to call him Sparkle a long time ago. He only did it in fun, and he knew when Aodhan would laugh—and when it wouldn't be right to use it. Like today.

"Adi?" he said, using the old baby name he'd used back when they didn't even go to school.

Aodhan shifted again, flopping down onto his stomach this time. It disturbed the butterflies once more. The big green one fluttered over him in irritation before landing on his hair. "He barely paid attention to my art," Aodhan said, his voice gritty. "He kept staring at me."

"A lot of people stare at you." It was a fact of life.

"Not this way. He kept saying how he'd heard I was beautiful, but that I was 'simply astonishing' in the flesh, and he couldn't wait to capture 'my essence' on canvas. On and on." Aodhan was ripping out hunks of grass as he spoke. "It was like he didn't even see me as a person. Just the outside! Just the shine! He ignored my art, Blue. Ignored it like it was nothing."

Illium frowned. "I don't know how anyone can ignore your art."

Aodhan's work was really good and even if Illium was a young angel, art was a topic he knew better than many adults. Growing up with his mother allowed for nothing else. Their home was filled with art, artists came and went on a near-daily basis, and his mother talked about art like warriors talked about battle tactics.

As if it was her air.

Illium wasn't that interested in art for himself, but he loved how happy it made her, so he listened. And now, he listened because it made Aodhan happy, too. Just like they listened to him talk about swords and hand-to-hand combat, and flight squadron war tactics.

You listened to the people you loved. That was how it was.

"Well, he did," Aodhan muttered, pulling apart the strands of grass. "He didn't see anything but the sparkle and the shine." Reaching up, he pulled at his own hair. "Sometimes, I wish I could rip off my hair, peel off my skin, tear out my feathers, and just be a normal angel!"

"Don't say things like that! You're you. I like you."

"I want to be normal!" Aodhan's fingers worked on the strands of grass. "So people won't be distracted by me. So people will see the art I create, the things I make!"

"They will," Illium said, then used his strongest weapon. "Mother sees you, and she's the best artist of all."

Aodhan was quiet for a little while. "She's different. She's better than everyone else."

"I know. But Raphael sees you, too—and not because you're pretty."

Aodhan glared at him for using that word.

Illium grinned. "I'm prettier."

A tiny twitch of his friend's lips. "Ha-ha." But he wasn't scowling so hard now. "Raphael did say I have good grace in the air."

"Yeah, and the trainer said we could always stain your wings and hair another color so you wouldn't stand out in battle." It had been during a strategy discussion after their flight tactics session—they were only short lessons, since they were so young, but Illium took it seriously and the trainer rewarded him by teaching him extra things.

He knew Aodhan had only joined the class to keep him company, but his friend wasn't bad at warrior skills. Illium was only ahead of him because he spent so much more of his time on it.

"He said the same about your wings," Aodhan murmured.

"Uh-huh, and even about Rufi." Their fellow trainee had wings of orangey yellow that made her look like a tropical bird—like the one Illium had seen in a drawing in a book in the Library.

Aodhan nodded again. "They treat me normal." His voice wasn't so angry anymore. "Not like I'm a thing they want to put on a shelf or make art about."

Illium hated that anyone had made his friend feel that way, but he also knew Aodhan would have to deal with this for the rest of his life. He hadn't been meant to be listening, but he'd heard their teacher talking to his mother about Aodhan, her kind voice full of worry.

"If he was another kind of child," Jessamy had said, "I'd worry he'd become spoiled. But Aodhan is so private that I'm increasingly concerned the attention will drive him more and more inward."

Illium's mother had been like before-times that day, her eyes clear and her mind in the here. "Aodhan doesn't need many anchors to steady him in life," she'd said. "As long as he has two or three strong lines, he will be content."

"That's good to hear, Lady Sharine. You probably know him best, even more than his parents."

"The trouble," Illium's mother had added, "will come with those who can't see beneath the unique beauty of his outer skin. They will hurt him—and so we must focus on teaching him that their blindness takes nothing away from his light and his gifts."

Illium had thought a lot about that. Often, he had too

many thoughts in his head and couldn't sit still, but that day, he'd gone off to a favorite spot and really thought about just that one thing—and he'd come to a conclusion.

Today, he spoke that conclusion aloud: "There are stupid people in the world—but them being dumbos doesn't change that you're my friend, or that you're an artist, or anything else about you." He was pretty sure that was what his mother had meant. "You have to learn to ignore the stupids."

Then he added a thing he'd thought up on his own. "Those people are still going to be stupid tomorrow, but you're going to be getting better and better in your art and in your warrior training—until one day, you'll be in an archangel's court"— with Illium, because the two of them were always going to be friends—"and they'll still be here, being stupid in stupid world."

Aodhan snorted out a small laugh . . . that grew and grew and grew. Illium grinned. Nobody else could make Aodhan laugh that way, and it was one of his favorite things in the whole world when it happened.

When he stopped laughing at last, Aodhan held out the strands of grass with which he'd been fussing. He'd woven the strands into a perfect star. Illium stared at it, turning it this way and that, fascinated by the intricate work. "Can you do other shapes?"

"What do you want?" Aodhan pulled out more grass. "Stupids in stupid world." He laughed again. "Yes, they are. They're not my people. I don't care about them." Then he began to weave again without waiting for Illium to choose a shape.

Illium didn't mind. He was just happy that Aodhan was smiling again, his shoulders no longer weighed down and his wings no longer limp. They arched against the sky as he lay on his stomach, shards of light falling off them to hit Illium's face in a shower of stars.

23

Today

Illium rubbed at his wrist, but he couldn't rub away the feel of Aodhan's hand. The memory of the contact burned, ice against the fire of his skin. He knew his response had been graceless; he just hadn't been ready and the anger that had been simmering inside him ever since that night in the Enclave—the night it all began to go wrong—had burst out.

So go, be free, Aodhan.

Shit, shit, *shit*! Why had he said that? He hadn't meant it. Not in the way he'd made it sound. He didn't want to cut bonds with his best friend, had never wanted that. *And* it wasn't why Raphael had sent him here. He'd been sent to support Aodhan, not to make life difficult for him.

Shooting high into the sky, he allowed himself a scream, then dove back down toward Aodhan.

His friend scowled when he made a high-speed landing. "Trying to turn yourself into paste?"

"If I was, I'd be paste," Illium said lightly, his heart thudding. "I'm no turtle. Want me to showcase my precision turns?"

Returning to his survey of the area, Aodhan said nothing.

"Sorry about earlier," Illium said, because he'd never had a problem apologizing when he'd got it wrong. "You startled me." That was as far as he could go.

Aodhan shot him an unreadable glance before returning to his task.

Before, when they'd argued and Aodhan got like this, Illium knew to leave him alone for a few hours. Aodhan wasn't built for quick changes of mood like Illium; he needed that quiet time to work out things in his own head. Then he'd either accept Illium's apology—if Illium was the one who'd screwed up—or he'd apologize himself. And they'd be over it.

It had never taken longer than half a day at most.

But things weren't like how they'd always been. Their relationship had altered—no, Aodhan had altered—to the point that Illium couldn't predict his reaction to any given situation. And right now, it wasn't only about their relationship. "What are you searching for?"

"Anything," Aodhan said. "If we put aside the nexus—"

"Because of its age?"

"Exactly. It wasn't constructed during Lijuan's age of madness, and Xan's team found no evidence it had been in recent use."

Illium nodded as a crisp morning wind brushed over their bodies like an affectionate pet, the world in front of them shaded in that cool color between gray and yellow that only exists in the moments when the sun has just begun to emerge.

"Once we take the nexus out of the equation," Aodhan said, "so far all we've found are the odd starving reborn, bursts of trapped fog, and the toxic patches, but we know that Lijuan must've left more behind. She was arrogant but she was also intelligent. She didn't hold on to her territory for millennia through blind luck."

Folding his arms, the pale dawn sunlight welcome on his bare skin, Illium scowled. "I don't know. She was a raving lunatic by the end even if she fooled most people into believing otherwise. She was greedy for power and certain that she could hold on to it. My opinion? Her Evilness didn't have a backup plan."

Lijuan had once been a respected archangel—Illium could accept that. He'd seen her from a distance more than once as a youth, witnessed how Raphael, Elijah, even Michaela interacted with her. As they would with a senior whose life and experience they held in value. But that Lijuan had begun to vanish long before her public descent into power hunger and madness.

It was Jason who'd said the latter to Illium, after the spymaster returned home following a postwar survey of China. Illium had ended up beside Jason while Dmitri, Venom, and Raphael looked over a map on which Jason had marked points of interest in Lijuan's former territory.

New York's damaged buildings spread out below them in a broken carpet of light, Illium had said, "How long do you think she was on this track? Lijuan, I mean. Her madness. Her fever for power."

"Centuries." No hesitation in Jason's response, the pure black of his wings motionless and the curves of his facial tattoo standing out against skin that had lost some of its warm brown tones over the cooler months.

"The Cascade might have accelerated her descent," Jason had explained, "but the more I look, the more I uncover of her belief in herself as a goddess. Prior to Caliane's waking, she'd already begun to believe herself not just the most senior member of the Cadre, but the most powerful archangel of all time."

Jason had paused, taking time to put his thoughts in exactly the right order. The spymaster didn't waste words, but that wasn't to say he didn't have important things to say. Quite the opposite. When Jason spoke, Illium listened.

"If you look at the pattern of her senior recruits over the past half millennia," Jason had told him, "they were all . . . damaged in ways that made them easy to manipulate. They wanted a path, a being in whom to believe—she used that need to feed her ego while turning them into zealous acolytes no longer capable of independent thought.

"The temples built to her, they didn't emerge in the century past, or even in the past half millennia. Lijuan allowed her people to worship her long before that—such a desire strikes often in mortals, but most archangels don't nurture it. Even Michaela nixed mortal plans for a temple to her—not ones to her beauty as exist now, but to her as a goddess."

"You've surprised me with that one, Jason." Michaela's vanity was legend. "But then, she turned out a surprise all the way around, didn't she?" The former Queen of Constantinople had fought with selfless courage in the war, even though she'd recently borne a child, could've been excused for taking a back seat.

"Archangels," Jason had murmured that night, "have as many facets as a gemstone cut by a master artisan."

"One of Lijuan's was her comfort at being worshipped."

"More than comfort, Illium. She wanted her people to view her as an omnipotent force. You could term that mere arrogance, but there were signs of a disturbed mind even then—such as the fact she collected unique pairs of angelic wings."

"Yes, Ellie told me." Illium's skin had chilled at the memory. "She pinned dead angels up like butterflies." Elena had warned him to never put himself in a vulnerable position with Lijuan. *She'll take you, Bluebell, pin you up on her creepy board.*

Tonight, Illium reminded Aodhan of that—and of her other madnesses. "She thought the reborn were life."

Aodhan stood unmoving, but the wind couldn't stop itself from riffling his hair, the elements entranced by his beauty. A single butterfly as pale as snow landed softly on his shoulder. "Just because she was mad doesn't mean she wasn't also cunning and smart. She might be dead, but there's a prickling in the air, a sinister energy that whispers at the back of my neck."

Illium wanted to scoff, but fact was that Aodhan had always had an eerie instinct about such things. As if he was attuned to strands of time and life the rest of them couldn't access.

No, that wasn't right. Aodhan *had* always had an affinity for the natural elements of life, but it was only after his captivity that he'd become sensitized to the darker rivers of existence. Prior to that, he'd attracted butterflies until he turned into living art, laughed at the diminutive birds who perched on his shoulders, and been embarrassed by how much he loved his tiny familiars.

Though the butterflies and birds had never left him, he'd left them for a long time.

Pain slicing at him at the thought of those silent years, Illium turned to look in the other direction. "I'll keep watch this way so you can focus on that side."

"I can do it alone." It was a comment as sharp as the edge of Illium's sword.

"I know, but I'm here to be your backup." Words he'd never before had to say aloud; it had always been understood between them that one would watch the back of the other, that they'd pick each other up if they fell, that they'd stand as a united wall against all threats.

Only once had Illium failed . . . but it had been a spectacular failure that led to Aodhan's devastation. Illium's gut still churned when he thought about that day, about their stupid fight, about what had happened in the aftermath. And about the silence that had followed. Aodhan's silence.

24

Yesterday

Aodhan was so proud of Illium. His best friend had just been given the highest honor available to trainees their age—it put him at the top of their class. Had he been an adult, he would've held the rank of squadron leader. As it was, he was now First Wing of their training squadron.

It was a big thing, and the trainers had held a small ceremony for it. Their teacher, Jessamy, had come, as had Aodhan's parents, even Archangel Raphael. But the most critical person in Illium's life was missing; Aodhan had expected to see sadness in Illium because of that, but instead, when he finally got his friend alone, Illium's face held only worry.

"My mother's not having a good day," he said, turning his head in the direction of his home. "She's somewhere else today. Healer Keir is with her. I didn't want her alone."

"I'm sorry, Blue. I know you wanted her here."

"She was so excited about me becoming First Wing." Illium's hand clenched around the small pin he'd been given as part of the honor. "When she realizes that she missed it . . .

it'll make her so sad, Adi." His eyes shining wet, he swallowed hard. "I don't know how to fix that."

Aodhan's chest got all tight. He couldn't bear it when Illium was sad. "I have an idea," he said. "Wait here." He left his friend in the company of two other trainees who'd run over to congratulate him—no one was jealous of Illium gaining the honor. No one was ever angry at Illium. He was everyone's friend, often helped others better their skills—and they all knew how hard he worked.

Aodhan's Blue put in twice the hours as most trainees.

It took Aodhan a bit of time to twist and duck and make his way close to Raphael, and then he had to stand off to the side until the archangel noticed him. Youngsters didn't go up and interrupt archangels while they were in conversation. But Raphael turned to him far quicker than he'd anticipated.

"Aodhan," he murmured, after excusing himself from his discussion with a senior trainer. "Where is Lady Sharine?"

Raphael was one of the few people who used Eh-ma's name. Most people called her the Hummingbird. "She's away," Aodhan said, knowing Raphael would understand. "Illium is sad because her heart will break when she realizes she missed this."

Raphael's eyes darkened, and he brushed his fingers over Aodhan's hair. "He's too young to have such worries on his shoulders."

"I was thinking," Aodhan blurted out because he could see someone else heading this way, no doubt wanting Raphael's attention, "that when she's better, you could come and present him with his pin again, and we could pretend it was the ceremony?"

The intense, dangerous blue of Raphael's eyes pierced Aodhan, the power that burned off him an incandescent heat. "I do not believe in lies, Aodhan," Raphael said at last, "but there are some lies that are told to save a heart. So we will do this so Lady Sharine's heart doesn't break."

A firm, reassuring touch on Aodhan's shoulder. "Tell Illium

not to worry and to enjoy his day. He's earned it. I'll speak to the head trainer and make sure he's also present at our private ceremony—he's a good man, and he loves Lady Sharine as well as you or I."

Eyes hot, Aodhan wanted to wrap his arms around Raphael, but he was nearly a halfling now, and such impositions into an archangel's personal space wouldn't be forgiven as they would in a child. But then Raphael enclosed him in his arms and in his wings, and murmured, "You are a good friend, Aodhan."

Power isn't everything—
the bonds that tie us to one another,
forged by emotion and battle and friendship,
that's what makes us strong.

—*Illium*

25

Dawn had come.

Suyin's people had woken and broken bread.

It was almost time for Aodhan to say good-bye to his archangel as she led the survivors toward the open, windswept piece of the coast where she would build her new stronghold—a place of grace and beauty that was true to her. The defenses would be external, the home within a balm to her wounded soul.

Even now, she chafed against the need for what she termed a "defensive display." "It doesn't suit who I am, Aodhan."

About to remind her that necessity had to trump her dedication to architectural form, he stopped and thought about it. "Raphael's Tower is in the center of a thriving city, and has no battlements," he said. "But everyone knows that sentries monitor all approaches to it. It's also no secret that the top of the Tower can be turned into a battle command station."

Aodhan had never thought about the subtleties of Raphael's

show of power until that moment. "The display doesn't have to be overt," he verbalized to Suyin. "It just has to be known."

Suyin gave him a long look. "You've taught me much, Aodhan." A fleeting touch of his hand, a gentle softness to her expression. "Would that we could be more as desired by so many, but we are too akin, you and I."

It was the first time she'd made any reference to what others in angelkind had whispered of for the past year. Aodhan knew of those whispers because his sister had passed them on—they'd become closer after the birth of his nephew, Imalia having pronounced him the best of uncles, and now she spoke and wrote to him on a regular basis. She also loved to gossip.

"Most of the Refuge is convinced you'd make the perfect couple," she'd said early on in his sojourn in China. "Both of you beautiful and artistic and quiet. They're saying your home would be a place of perfect grace and harmony."

Aodhan didn't know his sibling that well, not when they'd so recently reconnected, but he knew her enough to pick up a particular tone in her voice. "You don't agree."

"It's not my place."

"Imalia."

A long, dramatic sigh, eyes of clear green rolling upward in an elfin face. "No, I don't agree. Your home with Suyin would be quiet and peaceful and it would *bore you out of your gourd*."

A tilt of the head as she pressed her lips together and shot him what he'd decided was a patented older sister look. "There's a reason you've been best friends for hundreds of years with an angel made of quicksilver and mischief and wit."

So unexpected that she saw so clearly, his sister who'd been all but a stranger to him these many years.

"Yes," he said to Suyin under the pale gold of the morning sky. "We would amplify each other's sadnesses." As it was the first time she'd broached the rumors, it was the first time he'd put their past scars out into the open. "I feel it every moment we're together."

Suyin inclined her head, the silk of her hair sliding against her skin. "You speak a painful truth, Aodhan. But we shall be friends, yes?"

"Yes." He genuinely liked Suyin, and when together, the two of them could talk forever about art and architecture. But there were also places he could never go with her. "We must talk about your second."

Dark eyes searching his. "Ah, I see the answer before you speak it. You won't reconsider?"

"This isn't the right place or time for me to be second." He knew that in his gut, tried not to look too deep, see the image of the archangel for whom he was waiting.

Suyin's sigh was heartfelt. "I shall miss you by my side, but a large part of me was expecting your final response. I'll use the journey to our new home to consider my options."

Aodhan knew exactly who he'd place in the position of her second, but he couldn't influence Suyin, not in this. Being second wasn't only about power and skill but about the ability to bond to your archangel. "I will remain as long as you need."

"I know." A smile that spoke of her faith in his honor, this extraordinary new archangel who'd helped him find his wings by accepting him at her side. "Take care as you investigate the oddities here. I would not have harm come to you or Illium."

"I'll keep you updated." He'd attempted to teach her how to use a phone and—to her credit—though she'd failed to retain the knowledge, she'd tried her best despite her age and distance from the current world. That was the difference between her and a pompous ass like Aegaeon, who refused to "lower himself" to modern technology.

How Illium could've come from such "a stinking blot of donkey excrement" Aodhan would never know. He'd also be forever grateful to Titus for that description of Aegaeon, which Aodhan hadn't been meant to overhear—but he had, and it gave him great pleasure to use it even if only inside his mind.

An hour after his meeting with Suyin, Aodhan stood with Illium on the same stone pillar from which they'd watched dawn caress the landscape, a lover too long gone.

Now, they watched Suyin lead her people home. She flew at the front, on alert for any danger, a combat squadron behind her.

Far below the sea of wings moved a line of vehicles. Mortals in the core, ringed by civilian vampires, with trained vampire warriors on the outside. Because even a vampire untrained in combat could survive a lot more than a mortal, up to and including being disemboweled.

"Still can't believe there are no combat-capable mortals," Illium said as he waved to a mortal boy who'd leaned out a window to look back and up at the two of them. With the sky a cloudless chrome blue, Aodhan glittered with light—there was no way for even those far below to miss the two of them.

Illium's new friend waved back with enthusiasm.

"Do you think the mortal-immortal cooperation in New York was an artefact of war?" Aodhan asked. "Will the Tower's link to the hunters and other mortals hold in the aftermath?"

"Yes." No hesitation in Illium's response. "It's Ellie. She'll never lose her humanity—I guarantee you that. And it's that humanity which brings mortal trust to the door. Without her, they would've still assisted us, but it wouldn't be like it is now."

Aodhan believed his friend's assessment. Of all the Seven, even the vampires who'd once been mortal themselves, it was Illium who best spoke the language of that firefly race whose lives blinked out between one beat and the next.

"Remember how Raphael was becoming before her?" Illium added as wing after wing passed overhead. "Remember how Dmitri used to be? You were in the Refuge during that period, only saw them the odd time, but trust me, Aodhan. I witnessed the change day by day, saw they were getting harder and more cruel. Even their friendship, it changed."

This wasn't the first time Aodhan had realized he'd missed far more than he knew when he'd sequestered himself. Oh, other than the immediate period around his healing, he'd done his duty, upheld his vows to his archangel. But it had all been at a distance, physical and emotional.

"They've been friends for a millennium," he said, struggling to understand. "What could've possibly happened to alter that?"

"Immortality." A short but full answer.

Aodhan had seen the effect of an endless life on many of their kind. Some grew while remaining true to themselves at the core. Others altered beyond compare. The ones with the greatest power seemed the most vulnerable to the slow corrosion of their hearts. Such as archangels . . . and those powerful enough to be their seconds.

"The vampire in Times Square," he murmured. "The one whose bones Raphael crushed to pebbles." Aodhan hadn't been in the city then, but everyone in the world had heard of that very public chastisement against a being who'd thought to betray his archangel. "I can't imagine a younger Raphael ever doling out such a harsh punishment."

Illium shrugged, his shoulders rippling under the faded black of his tee. "Maybe. Maybe not. Remember—we keep telling Suyin to be scary for a reason. A lot of our kind are so jaded that nothing but the most extreme punishment makes a mark." He shoved a hand through his hair, the blue-tipped black strands so long they were getting into his eyes.

"The thing that changed wasn't his ability to do what was necessary, it was his empathy," Illium said. "Raphael could've snuffed out a thousand mortal lives without thought—as can most of the archangels. Now . . . now Raphael loves Ellie, and he's remembered what he almost forgot: that while mortal lives are short, they're no less valuable than ours."

About to reply, Aodhan's eye caught on the profile of a woman who sat in the back of a truck that currently had its covers rolled back. As with most angels, his vision was acute, so he had no trouble distinguishing her features. "There's Fei. Do you know if she's said anything else since our last update from Rii?" Aodhan had meant to follow up on that, forgotten in the rush to ensure a smooth departure.

Illium shook his head, his skin strained over his jawline. "I caught Rii right before he got into his truck. He says if you press her she just keeps repeating 'Goddess Lijuan'—other than that, she's turned mute."

"You'll have to get used to Lijuan's shadow." Aodhan had had to do the same after he first relocated to China. "No way to avoid it here."

Illium said nothing, and they watched the departure in silence. Even with the limited number of survivors, it took a long time for the last of the convoy to pass below—then overhead.

General Arzaleya and her squadron dipped their wings in a coordinated good-bye, while the vampires driving below flashed their lights. No honking horns. No making extraneous noise that might draw out the dangers hidden within China's beauty.

Then they were moving on, slowly fading into the distance.

Inside Aodhan's mind came a familiar voice, elegant and feminine: *Take care, Aodhan. Never forget that my aunt ruled this land for an eon. Her mark endures.*

I won't forget, Aodhan promised. *I would urge you to do the same. Simply because you're far from her strongholds at any one point doesn't mean it's safe to drop your guard.*

Soft laughter. *Oh, Aodhan. Do you think either of us will be capable of true trust ever again?*

Aodhan glanced at the blue-winged angel who stood next to him, straight backed and alert—and, despite his apology for how he'd blown up at Aodhan—still so angry under the skin. And yet who would, without hesitation, step into the path of a killing blow aimed at Aodhan. *Yes. I'm capable of great trust, as are you. You trust me.*

So I do, my friend. I will see you soon.

Her presence faded from his mind.

And though the convoy would take a long time to vanish totally into the distance, they were now far enough away that it was difficult to make out individuals. Aodhan stirred his wings. "Shall we eat, then do a survey of the hamlet?" Neither one of them had eaten this morning, while burning considerable energy.

Illium even more so than Aodhan, because Arzaleya had roped him into doing a rapid scouting run a significant distance out along today's proposed route. Aodhan had watched Illium take off, a streak of blue against the cool light of dawn, and his stomach had wrenched at seeing him out alone in the sky of this dangerous land.

Now, his friend gave a curt nod before lifting off.

Eyes narrowed, Aodhan spread his own wings before rising more slowly into the air. No more, he thought. No more unsaid things, no more distance, no more simmering anger. Now that they were alone, it was time the two of them had this out.

Only . . . they weren't alone, were they?

Kai, lovely and sensual and a mirror of Illium's youthful obsession, was still here.

26

Yesterday

Illium landed in front of the small studio Aodhan had claimed as his own on the outskirts of the Refuge. No one had been using it, and no one seemed to know to whom it had ever belonged, so Aodhan had asked permission from the second of the archangel in charge of that part of the Refuge—Uram—and been granted it.

He and Illium had basically rebuilt the dilapidated structure, until it was now a place full of light where Aodhan could paint. Illium didn't usually interrupt his friend while he was creating—he knew the kind of concentration Aodhan demanded of himself. But he was too excited to stop himself today.

"Adi!"

Aodhan looked up from the huge canvas he'd laid out on the floor, his face dotted with bits of paint and his hands a mirage of color. His eyes were unfocused, and for a moment, Illium felt a sudden strange panic. But Aodhan hadn't gone away as Illium's mother had done; he snapped out of his art and into the present in a matter of heartbeats. "Did you pass the squadron entry tests?" A quick, eager question.

When Illium screamed out a yes, Aodhan threw down his brush and rose in a glitter of light to grab Illium in a bear hug. Despite being younger, he'd grown to be a little taller, a little wider of shoulder, and being hugged by him felt like being enclosed by light, powerful and loving.

They laughed as they drew apart, Aodhan slapping him on the shoulder. And even though he wasn't an angel who liked big parties, he said, "I'm throwing you a celebration! Does Eh-ma know?"

"No! I'm flying to her next! I'm so proud, Adi." He'd wanted to be in Raphael's forces as long as he could remember, but he'd known he'd have to earn it.

He'd *wanted* to earn it.

That he'd just done so at the earliest possible age he was eligible to take the test—a hundred—was a thing of incandescent joy. His day of birth would forever also be the date he became the most junior member of Raphael's most junior squadron.

"She'll be so happy." Aodhan was smiling as hard as Illium. "Let's go."

As they went to move out of the studio, their wings companionably crushed against each other, Illium said, "Are you going to take the test when you're eligible?"

Aodhan was powerful, and had trained alongside Illium after the archangels made it clear Aodhan needed that training so he could better handle his growing strength. Illium hadn't known until then that the Cadre had a team that kept an eye on the little angels in the Refuge, to ensure no unruly powers went off into the world.

"It wasn't in my plans," Aodhan said with a grin rare and beautiful. "I want to be an artist, not a warrior."

"Too bad you're so powerful." It had been made clear to Aodhan that he was too strong at too young an age to be left to his own devices. Either he aligned himself to a particular archangel's court after his majority, or he ran the risk of being considered a threat by all.

"I talked to Raphael." Aodhan ruffled Illium's hair, his happiness for Illium a dazzling brightness. "He told me I can work as a courier for his court after I come of age—it'll give me more time to decide, and I can keep up my sparring with you."

Joy burst to life inside Illium. Even though it was his dream to be in Raphael's forces, he'd hated the idea of being separated from Aodhan for significant stretches of time. "Good plan. I know you want to focus on art, but you know you get frustrated without a physical outlet."

Aodhan wasn't like Illium's mother, content with weeks, even months, of solitude; he and Illium would've never become friends if he hadn't also had a wildness inside him. Only three days earlier, it had been Aodhan who'd talked Illium into a late-night session of gorge diving.

"I'd like to be in a squadron with you," he admitted, knowing it was a selfish need—but it wasn't one he could fight, not when Aodhan was one of the solid foundations of his life. "If you don't want to, though, it's all right. You just have to be aligned to a court—you don't have to actually be part of a squadron."

"No, that won't do." Aodhan threw an arm around his shoulders. "I have to pass the damn test now—just to keep you out of trouble."

"Ha!" Illium elbowed his best friend. "You wish. I'm going to be the one riding to the rescue, Mr. Turtle."

"We'll see." Another grin. "So what's the first thing you're going to do now that you're an official adult?"

Illium's cheeks grew hot. "The girl I saw in the meadow when we did that overnight flight? I found out her name. Kaia." As an underaged angel—even if only by a few months—Illium hadn't been allowed to land or speak to her. Angels were only permitted to interact with mortals after they gained their majority.

"Yeah?" Aodhan's eyes twinkled. "Are you planning on courting her?"

"I'm going to try. I look at her and I can't breathe, Adi." He rubbed a fist over his heart, massaging away the ache.

"Just flutter your pretty eyelashes at her, and she'll fall." After ducking to avoid Illium's mock punch, he came up smiling. "Seriously, though—congratulations, Blue. One of these days, you're going to end up second to an archangel."

"No. That's Dmitri's spot—and I'm not leaving Raphael for any other archangel." Illium's loyalty was a thing of blood and stone. Once given, it would take an earthquake of monumental proportions for him to shift allegiance.

Eyes yet bright, Aodhan gave a slow nod. "No, you're right. I can't see either of us being happy in any other court. Is it arrogant to say that Raphael and Dmitri and Naasir and Jason are like family now?"

"Not when it's the truth." It was Raphael who'd taught Illium how to raise a sword, Dmitri who'd tutored him in strategy, Naasir who'd shown him the wild places in the Refuge and taught him the value of stealth.

Jason was different; quieter, more distant, but he was also the one who'd passed on advice about the motives of certain people in the Refuge. He'd also made sure Illium knew to protect his mother from the attentions of those who'd take advantage of her generous soul and fragmented mind.

The four had mentored Aodhan nearly as much. And not only because he and Illium were always together. No, it was because Aodhan had scholars for parents. Menerva and Rukiel'd had no idea what to do with a son so powerful.

"Family isn't only blood," Illium added. "Dmitri and Raphael are each other's family, too."

Aodhan gave him a thoughtful look. "Are we family?"

The answer should've been easy, but Illium hesitated. "No," he said at last. "We're beyond that."

Aodhan nodded, his expression suddenly solemn. "Yes."

27

Today

Illium was already putting together a sandwich in the stronghold kitchen by the time Aodhan made it there. No sign of Kai. When Aodhan touched his mind to Li Wei's, she told him that the staff was in another wing, closing it up room by room. But they'd be in the kitchen in five to ten minutes, for their lunch.

Damn.

Shelving his discussion with Illium for now, Aodhan made his own sandwich, then the two of them ate standing up. Neither one of them had to be reminded to use high-energy items, but Aodhan ignored the Medjool dates that Illium snacked on, instead choosing a handful of dried fruit.

"Still hate dates?" Illium asked, no anger in him at that instant.

"Hate is a strong word. Despise beyond bearing would be better."

A grin that hit Aodhan right in the gut, it was so familiar. "There's chocolate in my backpack. I can get you some."

Aodhan smiled, went to answer . . . and it hit him then.

His willingness to fall right back into the uneven relationship that had been so easy—and a cowardice. It had nothing to do with the offer of chocolate and everything to do with how quickly he was willing to turn his face from all that he wanted to change between them, how ready he was to forget the difficult conversations they needed to have, just to keep that smile on Illium's face.

Stepping back without thought, he said, "No, the fruit is fine."

Grin erased, Illium finished a glass of water and said, "If you're ready."

Aodhan wanted to kick himself for his panicked reaction—because it *had* been panic. This past year, he'd convinced himself he was growing, becoming stronger, more who he would've been had an act of suffocating evil not derailed his life. But that was before his greatest temptation landed in the territory.

Illium, so bright and charismatic and generous.

Illium, so sure of what he wanted in life.

Illium, so easy to follow.

And follow him Aodhan had. Nearly all his life.

"Illium." He lifted a hand, dropped it when Illium went motionless. "That wasn't—"

"No explanations necessary." A small meaningless smile. "My fault. We agreed to treat each other like squadron mates on a task. I'm the one who keeps overstepping."

No, Aodhan wanted to yell, *I didn't agree to any such thing! We've never been anything so mundane, have always been* more. Yet how could he say that, how could he demand more than this strained silence between them without falling into the gravitational force that was Illium?

If he fell, he'd remain stuck in amber. That was his greatest fear: that his dependence on Illium would leave him frozen in time, while his extraordinary friend grew and changed until he was a star Aodhan couldn't touch.

He said none of that. He wasn't quicksilver like his best friend. He needed time to think, to get his thoughts in order.

And he could hear the faint murmur of voices in the distance as Li Wei and her team headed to the kitchen.

The idea of coming face-to-face with Kai when he felt rubbed raw turned his tone flat and curt as he said, "Let's go."

Illium was glad of their short time in the air after that ugly moment in the kitchen when Aodhan had taken a physical step back from him. Illium had seen Suyin touch Aodhan this morning, so it wasn't as if Aodhan's trauma had reared its horrific head, his friend fighting the dark.

No, it was Illium specifically that Aodhan didn't want close.

Illium's breath came out ragged, his chest crushing in on itself. The quick flight was just long enough for him to raise a shield that had been faltering, put it back in place. Patched and repaired it might be, but the fucking thing would hold. All he needed to do anytime it weakened was to remember that instant in the kitchen.

When Aodhan had broken his fucking heart.

Keep it together, he ordered himself as they reached the hamlet. "Looks normal at first glance."

Hovering overhead, they took in the small grouping of homes. Each had its own vegetable garden and enough space for a domestic animal or two, but it wasn't a large settlement by any measure.

The forests and pillars of Zhangjiajie surrounded it on every side. Even the gravel road that led eventually to the main road, on which today traveled Suyin's people, was heavily shadowed, the greenery encroaching on it from above and on either side.

"It could be a painting of a sleeping woodland village." Aodhan's voice was a little rough. "Like from a children's book."

"As if it wasn't abandoned, but closed up for a long absence." From what he could see, the doors were shut, the windows latched. No cars sat on the single main street that ran through the small settlement, and there were no abandoned items or pieces of lost clothing on the street or elsewhere, as might happen if people left in a rush.

The vehicles he could see were parked in what looked to be their usual spots beside houses, or at the side of the road. He spotted a few garages, guessed other cars lay within. "It's like Vetra said, it looks like an average settlement in the middle of nowhere."

Similar settlements existed in Raphael's territory, usually made up of people who were self-sufficient and preferred to live off the grid. "I believed her when she said it, but I have to admit I still wasn't expecting anything *this* normal." He could see why she'd been so disconcerted.

"I, too, thought she must have missed some small sign of trouble since she was tired and on her way home from a long survey mission," Aodhan admitted.

"I guess we both need to mentally apologize for our doubts. I'm going to land."

"I'll keep watch, see if your presence stirs up anything."

With that, Illium arrowed himself to drop down in the center of the street. The susurration of his wings folding back was the loudest sound in the area. Even the trees had stopped rustling. *It's eerie,* he thought to Aodhan. *Like the world has stopped here.*

I see movement to your left, near the yellow house.

Illium shifted his attention, didn't see what had caught Aodhan's eye. Walking closer while Aodhan shadowed him from above, he went to slide out his sword, when he heard a small sound.

He halted.

It came again.

A smile curving over his lips, he crouched down and looked under the raised porch to meet the scared eyes of a kitten so small she'd fit in the palm of his hand. "Hello there," he murmured, and held out his hand for her to sniff.

She scrabbled back instead.

"Don't blame you," he murmured, "It's creepy out here." *Aodhan, it's safe. Our intruder is maybe eight inches long and probably weighs as much as a puff of air.*

Aodhan joined him moments later. "Here," he said, after digging into a wide side pocket of his rough canvas pants. "I grabbed a couple of packs of jerky on my way out of the kitchen, in case you got hungry later."

When Illium scowled up at him, Aodhan a glittering silhouette against the sky, his face shadowed, Aodhan said, "You didn't eat anywhere near enough to refill your energy reserves."

Still annoyed, Illium grabbed the packet, and opened it to pull out a piece of dried meat. He put it where the kitten could get at it. Then he rose—while eating another slice. He slid the extra into a pocket. He wasn't going to cut off his nose to spite his face—even if he really felt like it.

"Let's leave her to decide whether to trust us or not. We can always bring some food out here for her if she stays skittish." It was obvious from her skinny frame that she hadn't been able to forage enough to thrive. Probably because she was too young to have those skills and had been someone's pet.

Which made him frown. "Where are the chickens, the dogs, the goats?" The silence was absolute and he'd seen no other signs of life from above. "They took their animals with them, but the kitten escaped or got scared and bolted and so got left behind?"

"None of it makes sense." Aodhan slid out one of his twin swords. "Let's check the houses."

They looked through eight different ones together, found clothes still hanging in the wardrobes, shoes sat by the front door, furniture standing unmolested, curtains neatly pulled or tied back. Other than large bags of rice and flour, there was no food except for the odd forgotten can in the back of a cupboard—but that could be explained by the residents taking all the easily transportable items with them.

To go where?

With no clothes or shoes or suitcases.

Standing in the center of the street again, surrounded by an echoing, inexplicable emptiness as clouds began to dim the sunlight, he said, "What are the chances Vetra looked in the same houses we did?"

Aodhan glanced at the homes they'd entered. "High," he said after a while. "This is the logical place to land if you want to assess the situation. She also had no backup so wouldn't have risked entering the houses that make a quick exit difficult."

He touched the pocket of his cream-colored shirt with its raised collar and long sleeves. "I can call her."

"The place isn't that big. We could take a good look inside all the houses within the hour if we split up, take half each."

"No splitting up," Aodhan said at once. "Not here, Illium. China is . . . There are too many echoes."

Illium had parted his lips to argue that he was fully capable of handling any random reborn that showed up, but shut his mouth on the second part of Aodhan's statement. His friend had far more experience in this territory—and it *was* seriously creepy here.

Raphael would not be impressed if Illium got wounded because he'd gone off in a huff due to what was happening with Aodhan.

Instead, he just gave a nod, and the two of them began to go methodically through the houses. At some point, he heard a small meow and looked back to find the tiny gray-furred kitten following them—at a safe distance. Deciding to leave the scared creature to make up its mind about them without pressure, Illium kept watch while Aodhan searched, then they swapped.

It wasn't something the two of them had to discuss. After so many centuries working side by side, they had a rhythm familiar and effective. So this entire operation was effortless . . . except for the tension that hummed beneath the surface. When their wings brushed as they passed in a hallway, Illium bit back his jerk and just continued on, not looking at Aodhan to see how he'd reacted.

He couldn't bear to witness him pulling away again.

His mind went to earlier that day, to the moment he'd witnessed Suyin make contact with Aodhan's skin. He hadn't meant to see it, hadn't been spying; he'd been on his way to talk to General Arzaleya when he'd overflown the spot where Suyin and Aodhan stood talking.

The touch had been nothing much. A mere brush of her fingers across his forearm, but Illium knew Aodhan. He could read his physical comfort. Aodhan had been fine with that touch. It hadn't been unwanted.

Illium was glad his friend was increasing the circle of people with whom he was comfortable when it came to touch, but he was also jealous. It made his cheeks heat to even think that.

What the hell kind of friend was he to be resentful of Aodhan healing?

He shook his head in furious denial. No, that wasn't it. He loved that Aodhan was healing. He wouldn't mind if Aodhan touched Jae or Xan or General Arzaleya or literally any other person in this entire territory.

It was *Suyin.*

Kind, artistic, powerful Suyin who was the perfect match for Aodhan's own strong, kind, artist's soul. The last time Illium had spoken to his mother, she'd told him that Aodhan and Suyin sketched together at times.

"I think she feels guilty for taking even an hour for herself," his mother had said. "But I've told Aodhan he must make sure she does take it. It's critical—she's had little time to adjust to her new circumstances, needs to stabilize and nourish herself in the way that means the most to her— through creating."

Illium understood all of that, but the idea of Aodhan and Suyin sitting companionably together while they created, it made him grit his teeth. Aodhan hated people in his space when he worked. Usually, he only allowed Illium or Illium's mother into his studio. Illium had spent many an hour quietly cleaning both their weapons while Aodhan painted.

It was *their* thing.

"Now I sound like a jealous fuck even to myself," he muttered under his breath.

And that was when he saw it. "Aodhan."

A rustle of wings, and then Aodhan joined him in the kitchen of the small home. It was impossible for their wings not to touch in the compact area, and Illium bore the contact with a clenched abdomen and tight tendons. "Look." He pointed to the small pool of rust-brown below one of the three chairs that bracketed the round table. "That seem like blood to you?"

Aodhan crouched down, his wings folded in and confined by the wall at their back. "Yes. But it's too old for any kind of scent. We'd need to get a scientific analysis."

"Yeah, I know. It could as easily be spaghetti sauce." He shoved a hand through his hair. "I'm jumpy. Sorry."

Aodhan rose, his wing brushing over Illium's arm and chest. Unable to stand it, his eyes hot in a way that made him feel stupid, Illium stepped out of the room and continued to explore the home. Neat, lived-in, normal. No signs of struggle or violence.

Next house over and it was his turn to keep watch. He did so in silence.

The kitten stood three feet away, staring at him out of bright blue eyes. He raised his eyebrows. "Meow?"

She skittered back.

Great, now even tiny helpless creatures were pulling away from him. Scowling and feeling sorry for himself, he folded his arms and turned to the right. Washing hung lank and brown on the line of the house next door. He frowned, took a step toward it. There was something . . .

"Aodhan, I'm just moving a few feet away to look next door."

"I'm done here anyway," Aodhan said, exiting the house. "What did you see?"

"I'm not sure . . ." Walking over, with Aodhan by his side, and the kitten padding along a little farther back, he saw that the piece of washing was stiff and marked by bird droppings. "Oh, it's leather," he said. "That explains—Fuck!"

28

Illium wrenched back his hand before his fingers could brush over the skin.

Because that's what it was. And not an animal skin.

Not an angel, either, because there were no marks or holes where wings grew out of an angel's back. Mortal or vampire, then. A fly buzzed over to sit on the skin. That there were no other insects on or around it told him the skin had been hanging there long enough to dry out, lose its smell. Would that happen naturally? Or had someone prepared it?

He swallowed repeatedly.

"Now we know." Aodhan's voice, his tone even but his face expressionless. "Something bad did happen to this settlement, and to its people."

Having managed to get his nausea under control, Illium moved around the line to look at it from the other side. It was no less horrific from that side. "I can see why Vetra didn't notice." From above, she'd have seen what he originally had—an old brown shirt on the line.

Aodhan, who'd stepped toward the house, said, "There's

more here." He shook his head when Illium went to join him. "No, Blue, you don't want to see this."

Blue.

A nickname so old that only Aodhan used it, and that rarely. Almost everyone else used Bluebell, a moniker he'd picked up later in life.

Illium froze, caught by the solemnity of his friend's voice. "What is it?"

"Stacks of skins," Aodhan told him. "Cured and neatly folded up into piles."

Illium had seen horror, survived it. But today, his gorge rose for a second time. Swiveling away from the doorway, he breathed deeply to try to keep it contained. When Aodhan walked over to put his hand on Illium's shoulder, he didn't shrug it away.

"How?" he said at last. "How could someone capable of *that* be so calm and controlled that they left behind no chaos?"

It made no sense to him.

"How, too, did the murderer manage to do this to so many people without causing them to flee?" Aodhan said. "Why is Fei the only survivor?" Aodhan ran his hand down Illium's spine, his fingers brushing the inner curve of his wings.

It was an intimate touch, but again, Illium didn't shrug him away. He needed his friend at this moment, needed the connection. "We have to tell Suyin." Illium might be jealous of Suyin, but she was the archangel of this territory, needed to know its horrors and dangers. "She has to know to keep an eye on Fei—I think the girl's mute out of terror, but we can't discount the possibility that she might've been involved."

Aodhan pulled out a phone. "I'll call the general—she kept up with technology while Caliane Slept, seeing it as part of her duty to be ready for the day her archangel returned to the world."

"What about Suyin?"

"She's working on it, but current technology is difficult for her."

"You should push her," Illium muttered. "If Titus can learn, so can she."

"She's far older than Titus, Illium."

"She's not older than my mother." Illium knew he was being obdurate, but he also knew he was right. "Staying stuck in the past won't exactly help her."

Aodhan stilled. Yes, Illium could be militant about technology, but the particular words he'd just spoken held far more meaning than was apparent on the surface. Because Illium was the child of the Hummingbird, whose mind had been stuck in a whirlpool of the past for most of Illium's life. He'd never blamed his mother for her fractured mind and he probably wasn't even conscious of why, his obsession with Kaia aside, he refused to cling to the past—but Aodhan had always seen it, known it.

Reaching out, he brushed the back of his fingers over Illium's cheek. He didn't take it badly when Illium flinched. There were scars in both of them that hurt, and this was one of Illium's. Which was why he didn't put it into words, either. Illium didn't need the connection made apparent, didn't need the torment of history to color his present.

As he placed the call, Illium walked away to examine the closest edge of the forest, his wings spread as if to block Aodhan from following. Illium was the one who'd first taught him to use this device and the ones that came before it. No matter the origins of his fascination, Illium had always been far more in tune with the technology of any given era than Aodhan, whether it was a teletype machine, steam engines, or computers.

Once, during Aodhan's dark years, Illium had brought him a mechanical paint-mixing apparatus. It hadn't been anywhere near as technologically advanced as what existed in the current time, but it had been a thing strange and fascinating, and it had pulled Aodhan a little further into the light.

"Aodhan?" Arzaleya's voice held an echo that said she was in the air.

"Hello, Arza," he said, for though the general could be formal with juniors, she was no stickler when it came to interactions with senior staff; she also had a dry sense of humor that amused him—and that he thought would be the perfect foil for Suyin's quiet sorrow. "I need to talk to Suyin."

"She's flown down to talk to the mortals and vampires. Is it urgent?"

"No, it can wait a few minutes. But call me back the instant she's free."

"No, wait, she's flying up now." A short pause.

"Aodhan, you've found something." Suyin's voice was alert, ready for another nightmare.

Aodhan told her what they'd discovered. "Right now, we have no answer for any of it."

"I think we all knew something was coming." There was nothing of defeat in her tone. It held only the bite of a simmering anger.

That anger had been a part of Suyin since before her ascension. According to Naasir and Andromeda, both of whom had stayed in contact with Suyin since the day they helped her escape Lijuan, her anger had woken as her body knitted itself back together.

"At first, she was a wounded bird," Naasir had said. "Stuck on the earth, unable to fly." His silver eyes had been bright. "But strong, not willing to bow down to pain." A glance at the angel he loved with all his wild heart. "Wasn't she, Andi?"

Andromeda had nodded, her thick hair a beautiful chaos of golden-brown curls, aglow in the evening sunlight. "There was always grit to her. It just took her a while to find her way back to herself.

"But I don't think she came back the same Suyin she was when Lijuan put her into captivity." Thoughtful words from the woman who was Jessamy's right hand. "Before then, all the records talk of her as a great architect, a woman of grace and art. No mention of the rage that lives in her today."

Aodhan hadn't needed Andromeda to spell out the latter;

he knew better than most that some moments altered you forever. Suyin's anger was now an indelible part of her, as his shadows were a part of Aodhan. She'd asked him once, if he thought her rage made her weak.

"As long as you don't let it control you," Aodhan had answered. "I allowed evil to steal away a part of my life that I will never get back, and I regret that."

Suyin had returned the unadorned honesty of his words with her own raw truth. "I won't allow my aunt to be a malignant ghost riding my shoulder, I promise you this, Aodhan. My anger . . . it fuels me."

"Then use it."

Today, she said, "Do you need more people? I can—"

"No. We can handle the situation." Suyin's circle of trust was incredibly tight. Aodhan wouldn't deplete it without desperate need.

Her next question had nothing to do with their horrific find. It seemed, in fact, to come out of left field. "How is Illium? Have his power levels stopped fluctuating so dangerously?"

Aodhan went motionless.

Correctly interpreting his silence, Suyin said, "Vetra is a good spymaster."

His hand clenched on the phone at the realization that Suyin was spying on Raphael, even though he knew his response to be irrational. Raphael was also spying on Suyin. It was a game with the Cadre, though right now, it was also about unearthing any threats that might emerge in the postwar period.

He went to ask what any of that had to do with Illium—because he would never betray his closest friend, not even for his archangel—when he got the import of her question. "If you're worried I don't have stable backup, don't. To save my life, Illium would get in the way of an archangel's strike."

Suyin's response held a tone he couldn't identify. "I ask only as a friend. He saved my life, too, in battle, though he likely has no memory of it, we were in such fierce combat at the time. He warded off a blow from a morning star aimed at my face—the spikes would've surely shattered my skull into a hundred pieces."

"It's who he is," Aodhan said, his gaze going to the wings of defiant blue on the edge of the forest. "I'll let you know the instant we learn any kind of an answer."

"Stay safe, Aodhan."

"And you, Suyin."

They hung up on that sentiment, Aodhan happy to have gotten through it without having to chase after Illium. His best friend could be impulsive when angry or emotional. Aodhan had been half prepared for him to stride off into the trees.

As Aodhan slid away his phone, Illium crouched down, stayed that way for several seconds. When he rose again, turned, a tiny, furry face looked out at Aodhan from Illium's muscled embrace.

Of course he'd charmed the wary kitten.

Aodhan couldn't help his lips from curving. "Another conquest."

Scratching the top of the kitten's head, Illium looked around. "Aside from the odd fly and a couple of birds, she's the only sign of life in this place." No longer was there anger in his body or in his voice, his attention on the eerie quiet of their surroundings.

That was the thing with Illium—he was rare to anger and quick to forgive. Aodhan was far more likely to hold on to a grudge. "Let's finish the search. Once we know all there is to know, we can make a plan for our next step." He nodded at the kitten. "We'll take her back to the stronghold with us."

"Yes." Illium scratched the kitten again, this time under the chin.

She purred, her eyes closing. "That's my girl," Illium said, his tone warm with affection. "I think I'll call you Smoke, for this pretty fur."

Smile deepening, Aodhan shifted to face the house again. And no longer wanted to smile. His skin chilled.

"Aodhan."

"We have to look inside, find the extent of . . . whatever this is."

"Here, you hold Smoke and I'll—"

Aodhan rounded on his friend. *"Stop it."* It came out far harsher than he'd intended, and he was sorry for it at once when Illium's beautifully mobile face went blank. "Fuck." He wasn't one to use profanities, but it was the only word that seemed appropriate.

Shoving a hand through his hair, he said, "I'm not incapable. I've been surviving this territory for a year. You don't need to babysit me."

Illium's eyes glowed gold. "Why are you so fucking stuck on that?" It came out hard as stone. "We've always had each other's backs."

"No, Illium. *You've* been watching *my* back for over two hundred years, and I'm over it." Aodhan's skin burned now, his muscles tense wires. "I'm not a child, and I'm not—"

"Don't you say it," Illium gritted out. "Don't you fucking say it."

Hand fisting at his side, Aodhan said, "I'm going to check the house. Keep watch outside."

Illium stepped closer instead of backing away, the heat of his body buffeting Aodhan and his power a storm in the air. "No." An unbending response. "That house is going to smell like a fucking coffin and you don't need that."

Aodhan's stomach twisted on itself, his throat threatening to choke up. "It's time," he said, his voice rough. "I decided not to hide anymore when I first came to New York. I won't go back on my promise to myself. I won't, Blue."

Illium's gaze turned stark, all anger melting away. *"Aodhan."* It was a plea.

"No. Stay here."

Illium's jaw worked. "I should knock you out, you stubborn asshole."

"Try it and see who comes out the winner." Illium might be the better trained, but Aodhan was a fraction taller and had a little more heft to him. Enough to balance them out in a hand-to-hand combat situation. Because the two of them were never going to fight with angelic powers—it would always be hard and dirty, a thing of muscle and skin and bone.

"Don't," Illium said, the single word a request that stood on foundations laid centuries ago. "Don't do this to yourself. Or to me."

Aodhan gripped the side of Illium's neck, pressed his forehead to Illium's for a single potent second. "If I keep on hiding," he whispered in a rough rasp, "I might as well still be in that box, Blue."

Illium's wings glowed, streaks of red on his cheekbones, but he didn't try to get in Aodhan's way this time.

Holding the warmth of Illium's skin in the fingers he'd curled into his palm, Aodhan stepped into the center of the horror.

I am a goddess.
I will rise and rise and rise
into my reign of death.

—*Archangel Lijuan*

29

Death had a smell pungent and old and putrid.

The skins might've been cured enough not to rot, but not enough to eradicate the smell associated with dead things. Or live things that had partially rotted.

Aodhan's stomach wanted to eject all the food he'd eaten that day, eject itself, but he held his breath and forced himself to go on. An angel his age could survive a long time without breathing, though it was uncomfortable. Far better that, however, than to have the fetid scent in his nostrils.

Memories threatened to rise, threatened to hijack his thoughts.

I'm going to tell Mother you did this.

He clung to Illium's voice, that thread of wild blue normality. *I'll tell Eh-ma you've been snapping at me since you arrived in China.*

I have not.

It was a silly, juvenile conversation, and it was exactly what Aodhan needed to find his feet. Which Illium would well know.

Sometimes, of late, Aodhan wanted to strangle his best friend—but then Illium would do something like this, and all Aodhan wanted was to hold him close and fix what had broken between them.

Even as they continued their ridiculous back and forth that fixed nothing, and yet bolstered Aodhan's ability to do this, Aodhan made himself count the skins. *Only ten.*

Even though he hadn't specified to what the number referred, Illium said, *Add in the one on the line and it's still nowhere enough to account for the people who lived in this village.*

No, Aodhan agreed. *I'll keep looking.* His fingers feeling soiled from having had to touch the skins to count them, Aodhan kept them by his sides, not wanting them to come into contact with any other part of his body.

The room just beyond the back entryway was a kitchen that appeared to have been in use in the recent past. An onion sat badly chopped on a wooden board, tomatoes that looked foraged from the garden outside sat beside it, and there was a large pot on the unlit stove. Green mold furred the vegetables.

Aodhan didn't want to look in the pot, but he knew he had to do this, had to finish it.

Blue? Talk to me about something, anything.

Demarco and his girlfriend held a party at their new place, and I went. Drunk guild hunters have nothing on drunk tattoo artists. I almost ended up with a rose tattoo on my butt.

Aodhan clung to the steady rhythm of his friend's voice as he forced himself to approach the large pot. *There's a pot,* he told Illium when he reached it. *The state of the onions and tomatoes on the board says someone was here a number of days past. It could be nothing, just an abandoned meal.* Except it was the first such scene they'd discovered. The rest of the village was almost pathologically neat and tidy.

Illium said, *Venom swapped out Dmitri's Ferrari for an old Mini as a joke.*

Aodhan's hand trembled as he lifted the lid off the pot. *Dmitri called me after. He was pissed.*

But laughing, too, right?

Yes. He had plans for Venom's Bugatti. The word pink came up a lot.

Illium's laughter in his mind, the strain in it unhidden— but it was enough to hold Aodhan steady as he looked in the pot.

Slamming the lid shut, he stumbled away from the stove. "Aodhan!"

"Stay outside!" Aodhan yelled. "I'm fine!" *I was just startled,* he added, because he knew Illium, understood that for him to remain outside would push him to the edge of endurance.

"I hate this!" Illium's voice was taut. "Hurry up and get the fuck out of there!"

His protectiveness raised Aodhan's hackles, made him want to snap back—and the surge of frustration was exactly what he needed to deal with the ugliness of what he'd found. *There are rotten human remains in the pot.* He didn't enumerate on what he'd seen—the hand floating in a watery soup, the chunks of meat that had probably come from a fleshier part of the body.

All of it putrefied to noxious green and crawling black.

Whoever this was didn't know how to cook. It looks like they just put the remains in the water. Though his gorge roiled, he made himself finish the report. *There was no sign of any kind of seasoning, no herbs. If not for the onion and tomatoes, I'd have said they were just boiling the flesh off the bones.*

A pause, then Illium said, *You're okay.*

His relief was sandpaper over Aodhan's senses. *I'm not going to retreat back to my lair in the Refuge,* he bit back, even though he knew, he *knew* he was being irrational. Illium had every reason to doubt Aodhan's stability.

Fine. Stop arguing with me and get the fuck out of there. I need to check the rest of the house. Now that he'd seen what he thought would be the worst of it, he took a deep breath—and only then realized he'd begun breathing again at some point. Autonomic reflex. Hard for even an angel to resist.

The scent of rot coated his nostrils now, familiar and ugly.

At least he could wash his hands. There was soap by the sink, and the water still ran. It wasn't like he had to preserve the scene for a forensic team. He and Illium were it as far as any kind of investigation. But he did check the sink and the cupboard underneath for any clues before he ran the water.

One newly clean hand fisted so tight that his tendons ached, and his neck stiff from the tension in his spine, he then made himself look in the old fridge in the corner. Meat sat stacked up in neat piles in the fridge section, cut up and put into plastic containers, or wrapped up in paper.

The freezer compartment was also packed to the gills, as was the dented chest freezer that sat next to the fridge—and some of the pieces in the latter hadn't been sliced into chunks. He recognized a human thigh, an arm, thought there might be a head at the very bottom.

Sweat broke out over his body, his pulse in his mouth. *We need to check the fridges of all the nearby properties, see if there are any chest freezers in the garages.* He couldn't remember if they'd done that, being more interested in outward signs of violence and death. *I think I know what happened to at least some of the bodies.* The existence of the chest freezer inside the house was likely the reason the killer had chosen this otherwise ordinary house as their home base. *The rest have to be buried in the forest.* Where it would've been impossible for Vetra to spot the graves from the air.

Can you imagine what Ellie would say about now?

The distraction worked. Aodhan stepped away from the horror in the corner of the kitchen. *Of course there are body parts in the freezer. Of course. Why should the land of Her Batshitness return to normal now that the wicked witch is dead? Because that would be far too easy.*

Startled laughter from Illium that Aodhan heard both in

his mind and in the real world. *That's good. You make me miss her even more.*

Aodhan almost smiled, and that, he could've never predicted only a minute earlier. Fortified by the interaction, he carried on down the small hallway lined with what looked to be family photographs. An old woman, perhaps the grandmother, with a younger couple. No children.

"Thank you," Aodhan whispered, though he didn't know to whom he was speaking. Maybe the Ancestors. He was just glad he hadn't had to face the remains of an innocent, though he knew some must've lost their lives during this neat and tidy massacre.

Then he saw it: image after image of a child from birth to about ten years of age, that last one with one foot on a soccer ball, the child dressed in a blue sports uniform.

Fuck.

Swallowing his rage, he carried on.

Another frame held a black-and-white photo of a middle-aged man. Probably the grandfather, passing away before he got to old age. He'd been lucky.

A few other photographs, then an amateur watercolor that had been lovingly placed inside a golden frame. Beside it was an equally nicely framed cross-stitch of a rabbit in a field.

People's lives. People's dreams.

It hurt him to know that something monstrous had ended those dreams. Another angel might not have reacted that way to the death of mortals, especially mortals he didn't know, but another angel hadn't grown up with Illium for a best friend.

Illium and his wonder about mortals, his respect for their short, bright lives.

It wasn't linked to Kaia but rather the opposite way around. Illium had been fascinated by mortals since he and Aodhan were halflings.

"So many things they've invented, Sparkle," he'd said more than once during their friendship. "Our kind gets lazy.

We live such long lives that we think we have forever to solve problems and make discoveries—and so we rarely do anything. But mortals, their lives run so fast that they're always racing to solve the next mystery, unearth the next secret."

Illium's wonder in the mortal drive to grow and change the world had opened Aodhan's eyes to the same. Along with that had come a far deeper understanding of what it meant to have a human friend. It was why, for so long, he'd kept his distance from those brilliant firefly lives.

Because he'd known that one day those people would all be gone, nothing but memories that made his heart hurt. Then he'd come to New York and it had become impossible to ignore how much he liked certain mortals. So now he had friends who would one day break his heart by dying.

"Perhaps it's a kind of insanity," Illium had said a couple of years ago, after returning from the funeral of another mortal friend. "To keep on trying even though each loss puts another scar on my soul."

Aodhan's mind hitched on something important in that memory, but right then, his attention caught on an empty spot on the wall. It held the ghostly echo that forms when a picture has been hanging in the same place for a long time, a perfect rectangle of jarring brightness.

He looked back down the hallway again. All those photographs, only this one missing. Could be a coincidence, the image removed for some reason before the inhabitants were butchered.

Aodhan's instincts said otherwise.

Which was why he wasn't the least surprised when he reached the doorway to the left, and looked inside to find a small but tidy living space. In the center of it was a small table of carved wood. On top of that table sat a framed image of the right size to fit into that missing space in the wall.

Around the image were arranged candles, fresh flowers that had long wilted and turned black, and what looked to be keepsakes from the family—a makeup compact, a journal or notebook, a bracelet of delicate metal flowers of a size unlikely to fit a man's wrist, a lightweight top of pale citrine that had been neatly folded, and a bottle of half-finished nail polish of a shade the woman in the photograph might wear.

No, not items that had belonged to the family. Items that had belonged to her.

Aodhan recognized her as the same woman who'd been in the family photograph—but she was a touch older here. And in her arms, she held a baby, her face beaming as she looked down at the infant's scrunched-up little face.

The child wore a hospital bracelet on his little ankle, the mother one around her wrist. Her hospital gown was pale blue, the baby wrapped up in what looked to be a hand-knitted or woven blanket of what might've been yellow, though the color of the photograph had faded over the years so it now looked cream.

Aodhan, what's happening in there?

I don't know. He described what he was seeing. *It's almost like a shrine. The candles appear to have been lit at some stage.* Droplets of wax pooled against the wood of the tabletop.

If, Illium said, *the rest of the hamlet wasn't empty, too, I'd say that someone became obsessed with the mother of the child and decided that if he couldn't have her, no one could.*

Yes. Aodhan looked around the room. *But this . . . it's different. There's an absence of the kind of sexual perversity that accompanies such obsession. A pretty top chosen rather than intimate garments, a total lack of violence. The way the photograph has been cleaned of dust, the arrangement of the candles and the flowers, it almost looks like love.*

Is the boy of an age where he could've done this to his family? Illium asked.

The last photo I saw of him was of a child—nine or ten—and that photo was bright, not faded by the years. That leaves the husband . . . but none of that explains the silence of the village.

Are you coming out soon?

Aodhan's neck muscles tensed. *No. There are more rooms*

to check. He tried to keep his voice even. There was no use snapping at Illium, no use stirring up a fight they'd been having for over a year. Not right now.

Because sooner or later, they had to finish that fight.

Just be careful.

Aodhan bit back the words that wanted to escape. Failed. *I was planning to take every dangerous risk possible, but you've made me think better of it.* He wanted to kick a wall the instant the words were out. Why had he just said that? He wasn't like this with anyone else.

A pause, before Illium said, *You know what? Why don't you come stand out here, while I go into the house with THE SKINNED PELTS OF MORTALS and then we'll talk about why you're snapping at me for behaving normally.*

Aodhan closed his eyes, took a second, opened them again. *You're right. You be careful, too. I think this house is empty—which means the danger is outside.* And now that he'd put it into words, his skin prickled with the urge to get out there, shield Illium from harm.

I have a fierce kitten protector, was the outwardly insouciant response. *She'll keep me safe with the power of her ferocious meow.*

Blue.

I've got my sword out. Happy now?

Yes.

Exactly. Don't get all sarcastic with me for worrying about you.

Having reached the next room down the hall—on the opposite side and just offset from the living area—Aodhan didn't reply in favor of keeping all his attention on what he was seeing.

It wasn't much. The room held a single bed, the mattress covered by a handmade quilt soft with age. The scents of talcum powder and a faint sweet perfume permeated the space. His mind flickered with the memory of Demarco's grandmother. The trim older woman had dropped by Guild

HQ while Aodhan was there one day, having brought her grandson a "birthday treat."

Demarco had grinned, lifted her up off her feet, and swung her around. "Thanks, Gams," he'd said after she slapped at his shoulder and told him to put her down. Then she'd smiled and kissed his cheeks.

A look at the brush on the small table placed in front of an old mirror confirmed his guess that this was the grandmother's bedroom—caught in the bristles were a number of gray hairs. The black-and-white photograph of the man he'd assumed to be her deceased husband sealed the deal—it sat on the bedside table, where she'd have seen it each night as she went to sleep.

Next to it was a lopsided clay mug as might be made by a child. A gift from grandson to grandmother. A cherished one, for in that mug were handcrafted cloth flowers with green wire stems.

"I'm sorry," he found himself murmuring, though none of these people would ever again hear him.

This family was forever broken.

30

Yesterday

"Mother?"

"Oh, my baby boy, do be polite." Illium's mother's face was serene, her eyes a joyful sparkle. "Can't you see we have a guest?"

Illium glanced at the empty armchair of champagne-colored velvet that faced his mother's seat. His heart hurt. "Oh, I'm sorry."

"It's no matter." She held out a hand, and when he placed his in it, she tugged him to stand beside her. "See how strong and tall he's become?" she said to her invisible guest. "Aegaeon will be so proud when he wakes and sees the man his son's grown into."

Rage threatened to burn Illium's irises, but he kept his expression even. This wasn't his mother's fault. All she'd ever done was love him. Even now, when her mind was shattered glass that reflected everything and nothing, when she forgot herself much of the time, she didn't forget him or how much she loved him.

Always when he came home, she'd say, "My son," or "Baby boy" and hold him.

No, this was no fault of hers. It was Aegaeon who'd broken their family.

"Illium," his mother said now, "have you met Raan?"

"Isn't that . . ." He stopped himself just in time. Raan was the man his mother had loved a long, long, *long* time ago.

Raan was also dead.

He only knew the latter because his mother had been talking to herself one day, and he'd put together what she'd said with her visit to a memorial long forgotten by most of angelkind.

Recovering quickly, he bowed. "I'm honored to meet such a great artist."

Sharine patted his hand when he rose back up, her eyes aglow with pride. "Raan taught me to paint, taught me to fly." She cocked her head, listened. "Oh yes, so much has changed."

A softness to her as she turned her face to the empty armchair. "We were beautiful once, my Raan. But our time has passed. Now it is the time of my son." She smiled up at Illium. "He has fallen in love, you know." Mischief in her eyes. "He thinks his mother doesn't know."

Illium felt his cheeks color. He *hadn't* thought she knew about his tumbling heart, his desperate devotion. "Mother, you're embarrassing me."

Laughing, she rose from her seat, tucked her arm through his, and said, "Come, I have made you a cake. Where's Aodhan? I made it for him, too." The way she didn't even glance at the chair told him that she'd forgotten her ghostly visitor.

"He's in the Library, looking at copies of Gadriel's early work." The originals were held in Lumia, which Aodhan hoped to eventually get permission to visit.

"Oh yes, I did tell him to study the angelic masters. He will learn much by not forgetting the past. Every artist thinks he invents this brush stroke or that—but the good ones know that we build on the strokes of all those who came before us."

At times like this, when she sounded so pragmatic and like herself, Illium allowed himself to believe that she'd never fractured, that she was still the mother to whom he could go with any problem and know it would be fixed. In these moments, he could be her son, carefree and reliant.

Today, he smiled and sat down at the kitchen table while she cut the cake, and made him a drink. They sat, talked, and he confessed to her about Kaia. "I know everyone thinks I'm too young to understand love, but they're wrong. I love her until it's hard to breathe without her."

"I was young, too, with my first love," she said with a tender smile. "My Raan. Such a kind man he was, Illium. I wish you could've known him."

It was clear Raan was on her mind today, and he was grateful for it, for it was obvious the memories brought her joy. "Will you tell me about him?"

"Another day." She leaned forward, her hands around her mug of tea. "Today, tell me about your pretty Kaia."

So he did, pouring out his heart. Unlike so many others, she didn't patronize him or dismiss his love as a fleeting infatuation. She listened, and she accepted that he knew his own heart.

Another kind of desperation choked at his throat: the need to have this woman as his mother always, rather than her fractured counterpart. He loved her in any guise, but to see who she could be . . .

His hate for his father burned even hotter.

After he'd finished his cake and talked his fill about Kaia, he told her about his continuing studies. "I keep thinking I'm done, but then I get hit with more. Today, Dmitri told me to follow around one of his junior assistants. At first, I thought it would be boring—Mirza isn't a warrior, but a scribe."

Shame heated his cheeks. "But, Ma, you should see all the things she handles. None of the warriors would even *have* their weapons if Mirza didn't put in the orders for various materials. I think that's what Dmitri wanted me to learn—that there's a lot more to being part of an archangel's court than just being able to command a squadron or strategize in battle."

His mother's eyes, such a light, bright color, were fuzzier than when they'd started, but she was still present. "He's begun to teach you how to be an invaluable member of the senior court, rather than simply a sword hand. There are many of the latter, only a rare few of the former."

Illium hadn't thought of it that way, quickly saw her meaning. "When I'm older and more senior, I have to be able to step into any position, don't I? I mean, even though Dmitri is Raphael's second and I don't want to be second, I have to be *able to* if they need me to.

"I suppose Dmitri must sometimes want to go do other things," he said dubiously, unable to imagine the tough-eyed vampire away from his position at Raphael's side.

"Yes, you are clever," his mother said, and he could see her fighting to get the words out past the veil dropping across her mind. "They know you are clever. So they try to show you that life is far bigger and more complex than you understand at this time—and that to stand at Raphael's side, you must be a man of many skills."

Illium took his mother's delicately-boned hand in his. "It's all right, Ma," he whispered gently. "You can let go. It's all right."

Tears shone in her eyes, the color an effervescence of palest gold. "My baby boy. No, this isn't right." But she was fading even as the last word left her lips, disappearing into the kaleidoscope.

Yet her hand, it remained tight on his, and the love that burned in her vague gaze, it wasn't vague at all. It was for him. Her son. Her baby boy.

31

Aodhan finished checking the grandmother's room. There wasn't much else in there. A small potted plant that had wilted and browned from lack of water, a cardigan left on the bed, and a pile of clothing squares in a basket by the window. Grandmother was the quilt-maker, likely the person who cross-stitched.

Who'd been the water colorist?

He took care as he opened the small closet, but it held no horrors, only the older woman's clothing, and a few personal items.

Leaving the room with a sense of melancholy heavy in his blood, Aodhan went to the next door down.

It had once been part of a bigger room, but someone had put up a rough wooden partition at some point.

The first room was of the couple, the one next door the child's.

There were no surprises in either, but Aodhan felt a heavy weight crush his chest as he stood in the doorway to the latter, and saw the small table beside the window. On it sat three toys, two pretty-colored stones, and a handheld device that he recognized as a cheap game player once advertised on huge billboards in Times Square.

Cheap, but expensive when it came to a family who lived as did the one in this house. Everything neat and tidy, but nothing new, nothing extravagant. All the clothes worn and repaired, many of the dishes chipped. That game would've equaled weeks or months of saving up, and it was obvious the child had treated it with care. It was placed carefully in its open box, as if the boy put it back there after every use.

Aodhan rubbed his chest, began to step out.

The light changed outside, perhaps a cloud moving, and the shift caught his eye, brought it to the wooden flooring.

There was something not quite right about it.

Striding over, he flipped the bed so it leaned against the makeshift wall that had given the boy his own private space. He'd been loved, this child. And under his bed was a stain of blood so large that no child could've survived it.

Forcing himself to keep going, Aodhan glanced at the slats of the bed. The bottom of the mattress was clearly visible . . . and it was soaked in rust red. Bringing the bed back down, he flipped away the hand-stitched quilt.

The child's bed is soaked in blood, he told Illium, his throat hurting from all that he didn't say. *Enough of it that the smell hasn't fully dissipated.* He'd caught the faint whiff of cold iron the same instant he flipped back the quilt.

Rage against the child? Or was the mother there, trying to protect the boy?

No way to tell. Aodhan left the room, and checked the only other doors. One led to a small but crisply clean toilet, the other to a shower that made him suck in his breath. *Someone bloody showered in here and didn't clean up.*

Dried blood flecked the plastic of the shower walls, while streaks of watery brown clung to the faded shine of the sink taps. A full handprint marked the wall next to the sink. The size said woman or a small man to him. Perhaps even a teenager. Definitely not a child as young as the one in the photo.

He turned his attention to the characters written in blood on the mirror. His local language ability was good as far as speech went, but he wasn't confident when it came to his writing skills. Taking an image using his phone, he sent it to Illium. *Can you read what I just messaged you?*

No. I think it's an older version of the language most often used in this region—see how complicated it is, how many lines? I don't think most people these days use it.

Aodhan nodded, though Illium couldn't see him. It was obvious now that his friend had pointed it out. *Suyin will likely recognize it. I'll send it to the general to show her.*

A reply buzzed his phone just as he left the house.

First, he took great gulping breaths of the clean air, while Illium stood on alert watch, the kitten sitting at his feet with its ears pricked and claws unsheathed. "It feels as if the scent of death is in my mouth, coated on my tongue."

"Here," Illium said. "Had it in my pocket."

It was a small piece of hard candy, one of Illium's little vices. Aodhan far preferred chocolate, but he took the candy with a grateful hand and, peeling off the wrapper, put it into his mouth. The flavor—a fresh mint—was a gift that cleared his nostrils and overwhelmed his senses.

Shoving the crinkled paper of the wrapper in his pocket, he gave himself another moment—then looked at the message from Arzaleya. Unable to make it make sense in his mind, he just held out his phone to Illium.

"'Why doesn't it work, Mother?'" Illium read out. "The same question repeated three times."

"Perhaps we're wrong," he said, "and it *was* the husband, and this is all about his mother."

"Humans are fully capable of committing a massacre," Illium murmured. "And how hard would it be to wipe out a settlement if everyone knew and trusted you?"

The other man rubbed his jaw. "Fifty or so people . . . it's not that many, Aodhan. Especially given that a number were elderly, and a few children. A single man could have done it.

Invite a whole bunch for dinner, poison or drug them, and take care of the others in the night."

"He'd have had to behead or remove the heart from the vampires." Aodhan considered that. "Doable. Vampires sleep, especially the less powerful type of vampires who'd have made their home in a small town like this."

"Fei must've gotten lucky, seen something, run." Illium's voice was grim. "No wonder she's all but mute: imagine seeing your neighbor skinning people you knew, perhaps loved."

"Could be she tried to find help, only to realize she was the sole survivor."

"Maybe," Illium postulated, "she wasn't in the village when this took place. She talked about wanting to go home. What if she was out foraging for mushrooms or checking rabbit traps in the forest, and ran late?"

"And everyone was dead by then."

They both stood, thought that over.

Awful as it was to imagine, a single mortal madman *could* have done this. It also made sense that, in his home, he'd cleaned up only enough so that the carnage wouldn't be obvious to a visitor.

All the better to lure people inside.

Which made Aodhan think of another possibility. "He could've invited people over one by one. Time it well enough and the living residents would just assume they were out foraging, working inside their homes, or sleeping."

"Can you imagine the terror of the ones left at the end? They'd have known something was wrong but not what."

"Let's go through the other places again now that we know he focused on hiding the evidence of what he was doing," he said to Illium. "I think he got careless here because it was his home—a place where he had full control."

This time around, they found more evidence of a stealthy slaughter. A cushion placed over a small stain on a sofa, a kitchen rug thrown over evidence of blood, a door pushed back to the wall to hide the fact that the back of it was finely splattered in gore. You could easily dismiss it as nothing but dirt at first glance.

Still, it wasn't much, not given the scale of the slaughter.

The two of them ended up back in the center of the street after completing their second inspection.

"It took time and effort to clean up, skin, and butcher people." Aodhan couldn't believe he was saying those words, but they couldn't hide from the ugliness of what had gone on here. "A lot of work for a single mortal."

"We don't know the timeframe over which it took place," Illium pointed out. "He could've also kept Fei captive—or she could've been wandering lost and disoriented in the forest. She was very thin."

Aodhan looked around again. "Do you believe it?"

The gold of Illium's eyes was bright even in the dull light of the day now that the sun had been totally eclipsed by clouds. "It all makes sense, but there's an itch at the back of my neck, a feeling that it's all too perfect."

"Yes." Aodhan scanned the line of trees beyond the houses to his left. "Whoever it was, we need to track them down."

Illium bent to pick up Smoke, petted her as he followed Aodhan's gaze. "He's going to have the advantage if he's hiding in the trees. We could do with ground support—Jae would be perfect."

Aodhan knew Illium was right about their wings making a search more difficult, but—"Suyin will send her back if we ask," he said to his friend, "but we'd have to go out and escort her here." He reached out to scratch the top of Smoke's head—the kitten had followed him around earlier, now purred. "I don't want anyone making that journey alone, even in a vehicle."

Illium's expression went suddenly flat. "Aodhan, what are the chances the person or people behind this are trailing the resettlement caravan? What if that's the reason for Fei's continued fear?"

The world turned silent, Aodhan's mind a place of icy

peace. "There's no way he—or they—can get through the rear guard," he said at last, then looked toward the skins again. "That's a hoard. No one who went to all that trouble would just abandon it."

After putting Smoke on the ground so she could explore, Illium stared in the same direction. "Yeah, I have to agree with you there."

"I'll warn Suyin regardless." Aodhan proceeded to do just that. Afterward, he turned to Illium. "To be absolutely certain, one of us needs to fly toward the caravan, see if we can spot any signs of pursuit, while the other one stays on watch here."

Illium looked up at the sky now licked with a darkness heavier than the clouds—night was coming. "I don't like the idea of splitting up. What if we're totally off base and this was an angel? Either one of us could be ambushed."

"No feathers, no sign of damage caused by angelic wings crashing into things," Aodhan said, but he didn't like the idea of Illium flying off alone—because they both knew it made sense for the faster, more agile flyer to go.

"On the flip side," he said, "Suyin is with the caravan and will be able to take on any threat." No angel, regardless of their strength or age, could stand up to the might of an archangel. "The vulnerable are well protected in the center of the caravan—and the fact this assailant avoided the stronghold tells me they aren't confident enough to take on people more powerful."

Hands on his hips, Illium glanced over to where Smoke was pouncing on invisible prey. "Aerial sweep? Then we decide on our next step."

After Aodhan nodded his assent, Illium said, "I'll go to the right." Striding over, he picked up the kitten and put her inside his tee—after tucking the hem into his jeans.

"She'll claw you bloody."

Illium stroked the small creature who'd poked her head out of the neckline, a furry little growth with twitching whiskers. "Nah. She likes me." Another stroke. "Stay in contact."

"Don't take chances."

Illium gave a small salute and they took off in a rush of air, their wings powerful in flight. Neither one of them blended into the dark gray of the sky, but that was a risk they'd have to take. Aodhan's section included the strong-hold, and he took care to check every corner of it. If the killer or killers had been watching events unfold, they could now believe the stronghold empty, open for squatting.

He saw no signs of an attempted incursion. No shards of glass glittering in the dying light of day, no damage to the areas with shutters. Regardless, he landed and spoke to Li Wei. "Stay inside until we return," he told her.

"If a vampire or mortal comes to the door asking for sanc-tuary, don't allow them inside. Throw out food or bedding from a higher floor if you judge it safe. If not, or if it's an angel, hide in the most secure place in the stronghold—underground." No one who didn't know of the nexus would ever find it.

Li Wei nodded, her cream-hued skin holding the smooth beauty of an old vampire and her eyes sharp. "Our work is inside regardless. I'll make sure my staff understands."

Aodhan spotted Kai in the background as he left, found himself irritated by the way she smiled at him. What was wrong with him? His and Illium's problems had nothing to do with the mortal woman who wore Kaia's face . . . but he still wished she weren't here, in this time and place.

Her mere existence threatened to derail any healing Il-lium had done, to throw him right back into an agonizing moment that had almost broken Aodhan's bright, blue-winged best friend.

Love has a way of crushing a man
until nothing remains.

—*Dmitri, Second to Archangel Raphael*

32

Yesterday

Aodhan went looking for Illium as soon as he found out what had happened. Even though he knew all the places his best friend went to when he wanted to be alone, it still took him hours to track him down.

Eschewing all his favored locations, Illium had gone to a cold and craggy outcropping on the far edge of the Refuge, a place overhung by spears of ice above a carpet of shattered boulders. Nothing thrived here, not even the tiny frost-resistant succulents that grew in other icy places. It was often called The Cold because no matter the season it was a place of no warmth, all hardness and jagged shards.

Illium hated it.

Now he sat hunched over on one of the rocks, the stunning blue of his wings violent slashes of color against all that grim gray and ice. He wore only his faded boots and an old pair of pants that he used for training, his upper body bare.

Landing, Aodhan sat down next to him and immediately wrapped a wing around his exposed upper half. Angels didn't feel the cold as mortals did, but Illium was barely beyond his majority. The cold might not kill him, but it could cause vicious hurt.

"Your skin is like ice." Aodhan curled his wing tighter even as he curved his other wing around in front of them, to better conserve the heat in the space in between—where Illium sat cold and silent. "We have to get you off this mountain."

Illium said nothing—and he didn't move. And while Aodhan was strong, he wasn't strong enough to carry an unwilling Illium down into the warmer zones. Instead he tried to use his nascent power to warm up his friend. That power was less than nothing in immortal terms, but as young as he was, Aodhan wasn't complaining.

The only angel similar to his age he knew of who had even a hint of power sat mute beside him. And mere droplet or not, it was enough to add a whisper of heat to the air, enough to bring a little color to Illium's skin. But still he didn't move or show any other sign of life.

"I know you're proud of your coloring," Aodhan said, as his heart squeezed, "but trying to turn yourself blue is taking it too far."

Illium didn't react to Aodhan's attempt to lighten the moment—of the two of them, it was Illium who was the one forever trying to make people smile. Aodhan didn't do jokes except for rare low-voiced pieces of aggravated sarcasm that sent Illium into choked laughter.

"Warn me next time, why don't you?" he'd said the last time around, after he'd nearly lost it in public.

"Sorry," Aodhan had muttered. "I can't predict when someone will be idiotic enough to set off that part of me." Because it took a *lot*.

Illium had grinned and thrown an arm around his shoulders. "If only your legions of admirers knew the things you think in that pretty, sparkling head."

Today, there was no laughter, no gentle ribbing, no sound at all from the friend who usually spoke a hundred words to every one of Aodhan's.

Aodhan had never seen Illium so broken—and it broke

him. His heart hurt. He'd do anything to fix this, make Illium smile again, but he couldn't bring back Illium and Kaia's love.

"She's fine," he said, hoping it wasn't the worst possible thing to say. "I flew over the village to check on her." Aodhan had spotted her in the act of taking the washing out to the cold, clear waters of a nearby stream, laughter in her pretty and lively face as she spoke to another young woman.

Illium stirred at last, eyes dark with anguish looking at Aodhan. "She is?"

Aodhan's lungs expanded on a rush of air. "You know she feels no pain." That was the sting in the tail of Illium's punishment—his lover would feel no torment, suffer no loss. Because her mind had been erased of all memories of Illium, as had the minds of everyone else in the village.

To them, he wasn't even a ghost; he'd simply never existed.

Illium's voice shook as he said, "I'm glad." Brokenhearted love in his words. "It was my fault. I told her something I shouldn't have."

The secrets of angels were not for mortal ears. A truth—a *law*—drummed into them from childhood. To tell a mortal such secrets was a crime that could lead to execution for all involved—but Kaia's life had never been in danger. "You know Raphael—"

"I know." Shuddering, Illium leaned forward with his elbows on his thighs. "He never threatened her life. Not once. 'All I'll take are her memories of you,' that's what he said." Illium's body hunched in on itself. "The look on his face, Aodhan. I hurt him by making him do that, making him punish me."

Aodhan stroked his hand down Illium's back and wings. It was a good sign that his friend was already thinking about Raphael's reaction to his transgression rather than the fact he'd lost the lover with whom he'd been obsessed. Illium had courted Kaia with gifts and acts of romance, run to her every day that he could, dreamed of her when he slept.

Aodhan had never said anything against her, but he hadn't

liked how she made Illium act, how she'd pushed him and pushed him and pushed him for more and still more. Never had she been satisfied with the gift of *him*. Illium, who was so beloved of so many, hadn't been good enough for her without all the gifts and the romantic gestures, and the public devotion.

She'd treated Aodhan's friend like a trophy—the angel who was in thrall to her.

Aodhan's reticence had been for more than one reason. The first was that while he'd had small romances, he hadn't yet fallen in love himself. As such, he was aware he had no real experience to inform his opinions. He'd also received advice from an unexpected source: Dmitri.

Raphael's second was so much older than Illium and Aodhan that, most of the time, he treated them like awkward, fumbling pups. But, on that one occasion, Dmitri had seen something in Aodhan and pulled him aside. "He won't listen to you right now," the vampire had murmured.

"That first love is a small madness." Haunted echoes in his voice. "For some, it leads to a bond indestructible. For others, it ignites fast and fades as quickly. This shows all the hallmarks of the latter. Leave him be to make that discovery himself rather than turning yourself into an enemy of his love. Be there for him when his heart breaks."

Aodhan had followed Dmitri's advice, gritting his teeth and staying quiet whenever Illium mooned over Kaia. What he'd never expected was that he'd have to be there for Illium because he'd breached such a fundamental law that it gave Raphael no choice but to punish him with utmost harshness.

"Are you grounded, too?" To not be permitted to fly, to miss his squadron training, it would hit Illium where it hurt him the most.

A sharp bark of laughter. "He's taking my feathers. It's what I deserve."

Aodhan swallowed hard. The taking of an angel's feathers by an archangel was just one step below total excision of healthy wings. The impact of the process would leave Illium with translucent wings that, unlike an infant's, could be spread and stretched—and that were hauntingly beautiful when opened in the light, a shimmering mirage of flight.

Only a member of the Cadre was capable of doling out the punishment—which, despite the visual impact and painful surface burns, caused no serious damage to the underlying wing structure. So it was another mercy that Raphael was doing Illium. But an angel wasn't designed for featherless flight; to lose your feathers was to lose your wings.

Aodhan didn't know how long it'd take for Illium's extraordinary feathers to return, how long his friend would be tied to the earth. Despite his question, however, part of him had known this was coming; he'd just hoped for leniency. But Raphael had already shown the greatest possible leniency by allowing Illium's lover to live.

Not many of the Cadre would have been that kind.

Aodhan was happy for that mercy for Illium's sake, but he worried at the repercussions. He knew Illium. As soon as he healed, he'd be unable to stop himself from going back to the village to watch over his lover from a distance.

That was how Illium was about his loves—he held on to them with teeth and claws. It made him capable of a depth of loyalty rare and precious, but it also left him wide open to devastation.

Today, that devastation was a gray rain that washed all the color from Aodhan's best friend. Heart aching for him, Aodhan sat in the cold and held him, and let him talk. Then he flew beside Illium as he made his way back to Raphael for the final part of his punishment. Aodhan was the only witness, for Raphael would never make Illium's chastisement a public spectacle.

As long as he lived, Aodhan would never forget the searing flash of archangelic power, the voiceless agony on Illium's face, the dragonfly shimmer of wings gone translucent before they blazed red from the burn . . . or the carpet of wild blue left behind in the aftermath. Neither would he forget how hard Raphael embraced Illium once it was done, the archangel's eyes glittering with rage and sorrow.

33

After leaving Li Wei and her team safe within the stronghold, Aodhan flew a grid over the thick forest between it and the hamlet, his eyes trained on the landscape below—though he never lost track of his aerial surroundings. Lijuan still had many angelic admirers in this land.

The wind was cool over his wings, the sky darker with every moment that passed—but when he looked in the direction Illium had gone, he was still able to pinpoint the dot of blue that traced a grid in the sky. Illium was a dancer in the air even in so repetitive and routine a task; it was a pleasure to watch him fly.

As a child, he'd always tried to teach Aodhan the tricks he could do in the air. Aodhan, in turn, had tried to teach him how to draw the lines and shapes that came naturally to his hand. Illium had produced enthusiastic blotches on canvas—and Aodhan had tangled his wings more than once while attempting fancy flying tricks.

They'd laughed hysterically at each other's failures, but it had been a laughter without malice, the kind of laughter shared between fast friends. Soon enough, they'd understood that their abilities were divergent and couldn't be shared—and so had switched to supporting each other's efforts.

Aodhan had turned up to all of Illium's flying contests and races, and Illium had attended every showing of Aodhan's art—where he'd once talked up a painting with such enthusiasm that it had ended up being bought by an angel of old who'd once shared a bottle of honey wine with Gadriel himself.

In the distance, the dot of blue halted, hovered.

What do you see? Aodhan asked.

Something we need to explore—but I don't think we should do it in darkness.

Aodhan frowned. *Phone flashlights?*

You really were paying attention when I gave you phone lectures. Yes, that should work for a while.

I'll finish the sweep on this side, then join you. There was no point in leaving things half-done when that might mean their mouse fled through the hole.

But he found nothing, and twenty minutes later, was hovering beside Illium, night on the horizon. There was just enough light to reveal the face of a short, squat pillar that looked a bit "off." It took him a minute to work out why. "There's no moss or other greenery growing in a pattern that looks like the outline of a door."

"Good to know I'm not seeing things," Illium murmured. "I think our hopes of a human psycho were premature and are about to be dashed." He withdrew his sword from the sheath on his back, the sound a quiet slide.

Aodhan left his dual blades on his back, and they landed together in silence as night fell in a pitch-black curtain. Though he'd mentioned the phones, he wreathed his hand in light instead. That part of his ability had always been brighter than Illium's for one simple reason—any light near Aodhan was multiplied many times over by his skin, his hair, even his eyes.

It was why he so often wore long sleeves even when around people who never made a mistake and forgot his aversion to touch. The coverage made him a little less like a streak of white fire in the sky. But today, he'd pushed up his sleeves as he landed, and so the light bounced off the skin of his arms to throw a glow around them.

"Way better than a phone flashlight." Illium grinned before crouching down; the kitten, who'd climbed up to sit on his shoulder, stayed quiet. "Signs of recent movement."

The dirt was rucked up, the small plants crushed.

"Could be an animal," Illium added as he rose to his feet, "but I don't think so, not with the door to nightmares right there."

"I've always liked how you think positive."

A snort of laughter that actually sounded real, sounded like Aodhan's Illium. "Sparkle, there's thinking positive, and then there's suicidal mania. I have the sword, I go first."

Aodhan rolled his eyes. "I have the light, you idiot."

"Which is quite wide enough for me to stand in. You also can't focus on that and still focus on attack or defense."

Aodhan shrugged. "I can see over your head anyway. I'll just shoot bolts of power at anything that comes."

He could all but hear Illium's narrowed eyes in his response. "You're exactly one and a half inches taller than me. Don't try to convince anyone otherwise."

Oddly happy with their bickering—normal, so fucking normal—Aodhan didn't argue any further as Illium stepped in front of him and they began to move toward the door that shouldn't exist. His heart was quiet, his breathing calm. He'd moved into full combat mode, with no room for extraneous emotion.

It wasn't how all soldiers worked, but it was how Aodhan worked.

Having reached the strange pattern in the rock, Illium pulled, pushed, and had no success whatsoever in opening it. "Well, phew, false alert."

Aodhan blinked out his light . . . and there it was, the faintest glow emanating from the rock . . . in the shape of a rounded door.

"*Fuck.*" Illium followed up the harsh expletive with

words far quieter—and far more potent. "Adi, you can't go in there."

Aodhan bristled against what sounded like an order. "I got over my fear of confined spaces a long time ago."

Raphael had never pushed him, never made overcoming his phobia a condition of his position in the Seven. It was Aodhan who'd been desperate to shake off the chains left behind by his captors. He'd gone to Keir, and the healer had worked with him over a period of a decade to patch over that broken piece inside him.

"Don't snarl at me," Illium muttered, his face invisible in the pitch-black of the night. "I know you can do it. I also know you hate it beyond anything else in the entire world."

"No," Aodhan said. "I don't hate it beyond anything else. It would have to be underwater for that."

The words fell between them like bullets fired point-blank.

A slight movement, as if Illium had staggered back.

"Blue?" Aodhan went to reach out, but a noise from the forest had them both going motionless.

When the noise came again, Aodhan recognized it as the rustling made by a small nocturnal predator. Two glinting eyes low to the ground confirmed his supposition. The kitten hissed. "There," he said to Illium, "your new love will protect us."

"I swear to—" Biting off whatever he'd been about to say, Illium moved again, and Aodhan brought back his light.

It took them over ten minutes to trigger the door open, both of them just pressing and pushing at various points on and around the door until the mechanism finally clicked. Aodhan half-expected a groan as he pulled back the door while Illium stood guard, but it moved smoothly . . . and he caught a hint of cooking oil.

He moved his light toward the hinges to check. They gleamed; there were also stains on the floor that could've come from oil. He swiped a finger over a hinge to confirm. "Recently oiled."

"Those hinges would need it—they're ancient."

Aodhan saw his friend was right. The hinges weren't simply old, they were from a different time. "What was Li-juan keeping inside?" Because he had no doubts, none, that this was the doing of the Goddess of China, the archangel who'd believed herself above life, above death.

Illium stepped forward, stopped. "Aodhan, are you sure?"

Aodhan fought back his aggressive response. "I won't break," he said, the words stiff. "I can watch your back."

"That's not what I'm worried about and you know that." It was a dangerously quiet statement.

The kitten hissed again.

"She's going to give us away," Illium muttered, "but I can't exactly leave her outside. What if whatever this thing is eats her? She'll be scared in the dark, too."

That was Illium, forever a collector of the lost and the weak, forever the angel who protected those who couldn't protect themselves. Aodhan was his most long-lasting project.

"I can put her into a doze," he said past the knot that final thought put in his chest.

"New power?"

"No, just an extension of the butterfly entrancement." He didn't often bring up his ability to call butterflies to him, since it wasn't exactly the most practical power, but it turned out it had hidden depths. "I worked out that butterflies are kind of hypnotized around me, and before I left New York I accidentally called five kittens, who all laid around languidly and watched me, so . . ."

Illium took Smoke from his shoulder, held her out. Scared by the situation, she bared her teeth at Aodhan, but was soon heavy-lidded, her mouth opening in a yawn before she curled up on Illium's hand. As he placed her back into her safe spot against his chest, Illium said, "Can you affect larger animals?"

"Not as far as I know. Just butterflies, tiny birds, cats, and"—he sighed—"bats."

He saw Illium's shoulders shake, his eyes brighten, but he

didn't tease Aodhan about his strange little side ability. Instead, he focused on the barely lit passage they'd exposed. "You're really sure?"

"Go before I fry your hair for asking again."

"How would you explain my bald head to my mother?" Illium muttered on a snarl before they stepped into the passage.

Aodhan couldn't see any lights, but the tunnel wasn't dark. *Bioluminescence?*

Could be. We survive this, the scientists can run tests. Or, you know, Lijuan figured out how to lock her energy into external things. Maybe she did a Uram and left behind a batshit piece of herself.

Aodhan was not even going to entertain that idea. *All her lingering energy died with her.* The biggest evidence of that was the mass "death" of her black-eyed automaton soldiers. They'd fallen from the sky, rotting from the inside out.

I don't trust even my own eyes when it comes to Lijuan, Illium muttered. *But yeah, it's probably bioluminescence. I can see what looks like moss on the walls—glow seems to be coming off that.*

A part of Aodhan was fascinated by this living thing that thrived without sunlight—an act impossible for Aodhan—but the rest of him was hyperfocused on watching Illium's back. Despite his earlier teasing, their height difference was minimal, and he couldn't see over Illium's head, so he had to watch and listen with all of his sensory energy to ensure he didn't miss a threat.

But there was nothing to miss, not for a long time as they went steadily downhill. He had to fight every step of the way not to turn back and run screaming into the night. That was what his work with Keir had done—taught him to feel the fear and go forward anyway.

"Your wound is great," the healer had said, his eyes too old for his age, and his face a delicate beauty of fine bones and soft lips. "But our lives are measured in millennia. This step is just the first one on your journey."

That step was enough for now. It allowed him to do all his tasks as a member of the Seven—and it had kept him from faltering in his position as Suyin's interim second. His muscles might be locked in painful tension, his head pounding from his awareness of being in a place that might turn into a tomb, but he could function.

Aodhan? A single word that held an entire question, as if Illium could feel his increasing inner panic even though Aodhan's breathing hadn't altered, his step steady.

I'm maintaining, he said, because Illium was his partner in this walk into the unknown, and needed to be aware of Aodhan's status. But then he said other words, venturing into a past long shrouded in curtains he didn't part for anyone. *It helps that we're moving. I couldn't move then.*

Then.

A single word to encapsulate the months of horror that had changed him in a way that could never be reversed. *The Aodhan I am today,* he found himself saying, *isn't the Aodhan I would've been without what happened.*

Illium inhaled sharply. *You're still you,* he insisted. *Still the Aodhan who makes art that stuns people to silence, still the Aodhan who's gentle with the vulnerable, still the Aodhan loyal to those you call friends and family.*

Aodhan shook his head under the weight of the mountain pressing down on him. *I used to be made of light, Blue. Now . . . now there are patches of indelible obsidian within.* So strange, that he'd railed against his blazing presence as a youth, a presence that meant he could never walk in the shadows, and now the shadows lived and breathed inside him.

34

Illium fought to keep himself from stopping and turning to Aodhan. He'd never pushed Aodhan to talk about the twenty-three months when they'd lost him, or what had followed in the aftermath. Had he imagined Aodhan bringing it up one day of his own volition, he'd have guessed it would be in the brightest light, in a wide-open space.

Not in near-darkness in a tunnel dank and echoing.

Yet this was the location Aodhan had chosen, and Illium wasn't about to push against the opening of a door that his friend had bolted shut for hundreds of years. *Aodhan,* he said. *Trust me when I say you didn't lose anything of yourself. You're still—*

You're not listening. Hard, angry words. *You've never listened, never accepted that I'm* not *who I was before I was taken. I can't be* your *Aodhan. That Aodhan died over two hundred years ago and you can't pretend he didn't!*

Illium's heart shuddered at the blows Aodhan was landing, his first instinct anger that his friend would talk about himself this way. But then he remembered what his mother

had said to him one of the times he'd talked to her about his
and Aodhan's disintegrating relationship.

"It's like he's put up a wall I can't cross," he'd said, angry
and confused and hurt. So badly hurt.

"Has he, my heart?" Gentle eyes. "Or are you just seeing
a newly awake part of him?"

At the time, emotional and wounded, Illium hadn't really
paid attention to the meaning behind her words. But now,
under the silent whip of Aodhan's anger, he forced himself
to consider every aspect. Was it possible Aodhan's current
behavior was just a sign of growth . . . and that his friend had
grown away from him?

Everything in him rebelled against that conclusion. Because even though the two of them had been fighting for
more than a year now, even though he'd believed Aodhan
wanted distance from him, there was no sense of distance in
either one of them now. Naked emotion pulsed against the
walls of the tunnel, angry and intense, with not even a hint
of fucking remoteness.

You're not listening to me, he argued back. *I know what
happened changed you. I fucking know!* He'd witnessed it
firsthand. *But those monsters didn't succeed in erasing you.
They didn't kill Aodhan.*

If they had, he added before Aodhan could interrupt, *you
wouldn't be capable of making whimsical art like those
fairies everyone stole off the tree on the High Line, and
you wouldn't have played baseball with me in the sky, and you
wouldn't have allowed my mother to hold you when you rejected everyone else! That all means something.*

A long pause as they trudged on into the darkness.

Sometimes, Aodhan said at last, *I feel like I'm pretending
to be the person that you want me to be.*

Illium flinched. He hated that they were doing this in the
dark, where he couldn't see Aodhan's face, where he couldn't
look into his eyes. But it was happening and he had to deal
with it—only, the narrow passageway suddenly widened, the
light in the walls brighter. *Aodhan.*

I see it. No anger or old pain in his voice now, just the acute alertness of a warrior.

Illium kept moving forward, reminded of how Elena had described finding the place of captivity of her grandparents. He didn't allow himself to think of another cold, dark place that had been made a cell. That memory was too vivid, too painful, too much a thing that tormented him.

But why did immortals do this? Make hidden prisons underground where they did things terrible and evil? Or perhaps the tendency to go underground wasn't so unexpected in a race known to Sleep for eons in secret places around the world, the pull toward the dark a primal impulse.

In some, however, that impulse had been badly twisted.

He looked from right to left as they emerged into a large cavern lit by the same sickly green bioluminescence. His attention was on scanning for threats, so it wasn't until after he'd crossed the cavern to take a position by the passageway that seemed to lead deeper within that the horror of what he was seeing truly sank into him.

Aodhan had stayed at the opposite end, and now, the two of them looked at each other over the splintered remains of a table and four chairs. Playing cards lay scattered on the floor, their white backgrounds snapshots of light in this subterranean place.

At first glance, that was all there was to see: the remains of a single small table and four chairs.

No bodies. No blood. No other signs of violence.

But, when Aodhan stepped away from the tunnel through which they'd entered, and began to move around the room, he saw other things. A steel bowl lying upside down in a corner not far from a badly dented metal mug.

An instant later, his light glinted off another piece of metal: the remnants of a plate that had been twisted and torn apart from one corner to the other. He crouched over it, angling his hand so that the metal was bathed in light.

This is tough material, he said to Illium after examining it. *It would've taken a good deal of strength to twist it into this state. Only the rare human could've done it. Most likely, it'd require vampiric or angelic power.*

Rising, he continued to move around the room and soon discovered a bread roll encrusted in green mold. He tapped it. *Hard as stone.*

In the end, he found enough other mugs, bowls, and plates to line up with the four broken chairs that lay sprawled on their backs on the pounded dirt of the cavern. Also among his discoveries were what looked to be the remains of more than one set of ceramic chopsticks.

The most interesting item however, was a functioning battery-powered lamp. *Should we use it?* he asked after switching it on. *My light doesn't take much energy, but we may as well conserve it.*

Can it be dimmed?

Aodhan worked the device again and the light turned from harsh to soft.

Illium nodded. *It's not much brighter than using your power.*

After doing another sweep around the room, Aodhan joined Illium. *Lijuan kept Suyin captive for thousands of years, but she did so in one of her strongholds. Why would she keep anyone in a place like this? Unless the inhabitant was meant to be kept in the cells beneath the stronghold, but it didn't work for some reason.*

No question in Aodhan's voice that this was a place of captivity, this outer cavern a guardhouse of sorts. Illium didn't argue with the assumption—he'd seen what Aodhan hadn't, knew the other man was right. *Lijuan was quite mad in her final years,* he pointed out. *Who knows why she did anything?*

Then he shifted so Aodhan could take in the broken chains that lay by his feet. Each link in each chain was of such heavy metal that the entire thing would've been more than the weight of either one of them.

A gate, he said, pointing out the places where the anchors for the chains had been embedded into the stone on either side of the passage entrance. *You and I could break that, but there aren't many angels as strong as us, even fewer vampires.*

There's no blood, Aodhan pointed out. *No skeletal or other remains.*

Illium had been thinking about that. *Could be the guards abandoned their post after Lijuan's defeat. Either out of fear or out of self-interest. No one would look kindly on them for taking part in the captivity of another immortal.*

Whether others in the Cadre had been guilty of similar outrages wasn't the point—it was an undeniable fact that immortals could be cruel. Lijuan, however, had pushed it too far, and now all she'd touched was tainted with the odor of death, and of madness. And the latter was a quiet fear that lurked in the minds of most immortals.

I can see that, Aodhan murmured. *Especially if the captive was only kept under control by others more powerful—who Lijuan likely sucked into her army. Bad planning on her part.*

Illium thought of the wall of flyers that had come at New York. *She had only one priority at that point. She must've thought this barrier would hold until her victorious return.*

If she thought about it at all, Aodhan said. *I think she was so obsessed by then that she wasn't thinking of anything beyond her desire to be a goddess.* He nodded toward the unknown passageway.

Illium stepped into it without further question, not wanting to drag out the experience. He hated that his friend was being subjected to this. At the same time, he was furiously proud of Aodhan's refusal to bow down under the weight of what had been done to him. Which was why it so frustrated him that Aodhan thought the events of the past had destroyed all he'd been.

You've never listened!

The memory of Aodhan's earlier response stung enough that he found himself picking at the wound. *If I never listen,* he said, *it's because you never talk.* He wanted to kick himself even as he spoke the words. The two of them had danced around this topic for centuries; Illium had kept his silence because it was Aodhan's pain. Aodhan was the one who needed to bring it up.

Now he had, and Illium was sniping at him. *Sorry,* he said on the heels of his words. *I'm being an ass.*

Stop it. Hard, angry words. *I'm not a whimpering wounded animal to be scared off by plain speaking.*

Illium wanted to pull out his hair, but they'd reached the prison cell. A much larger cavern than the one outside, it was set up like a full living space. An area with seating—not just one, *two* seats made for angels, with the spinal column designed so wings would fall on either side of it.

Seeing the space held no dangers to Smoke, he took the kitten out and put her on the bed to nap. That bed, too, was large enough to fit two angels, but when Illium checked the closet, he found clothing of a single size—no dresses, just tunics and pants. Going on rough average sizes, the clothing could've fit either an adult woman, a teenage boy, or a smaller man. Definitely a person shorter and slighter than Illium.

He looked down, frowned. *There are no shoes.*

Harder to escape barefoot, Aodhan said, a frigid cold in his tone.

Unable to stand it, Illium moved to brush his wing over his friend's. Pulling him back from the ice of the past with the warmth of today. Aodhan didn't say anything, but neither did he put distance between them. Rather, he brushed his own wing over Illium's before they parted to check other areas of this subterranean apartment.

Illium's soul hungered for more, but he also felt a wave of relief at this silent indication that, no matter what, Aodhan still trusted him. With that as a foundation, they could damn well sort out all the rest.

Putting that aside for now, he focused on the situation.

Angels fly, younglings. Never forget that danger can lurk above.

Words spoken by the first weapons-master who'd had a

hand in Illium's training. Naasir, with his habit of prowling
the rafters, had taught him that lesson long ago—but it had
been good to have it spelled out. Driven by the memories, he
looked up. But there was nothing and no one up there.
However . . .

Flaring his wings, he rose up and up. *There are small
holes in the rock. Sunlight probably lights this space up during the daytime.* Press an eye to a hole and you could look
outside, but there was no hope of escape. The holes weren't
close enough together to in any way weaken the fortress of
stone.

Enough to read with? Aodhan asked.

I think so. Why?

Come, have a look.

Illium landed, walked over to Aodhan. Once again, he
stood close enough that his wing touched Aodhan's, and
once again, Aodhan didn't move away. Instead, he handed
Illium a text, then held up the lamp so Illium could read it.

"This is a teaching text." He frowned. "I'm sure I saw
something like this on Jessamy's desk the last time I was in
the Refuge." The angel who'd taught Illium and Aodhan as
children was now the love of another member of the Seven—
but to them, she'd always be the teacher who'd been exasper-
ated by them more than once, but who'd also taught them
with love and grace.

They both adored her and, back when she and Galen first
got together, they'd told Galen they'd shun him forever
should he hurt her. The weapons-master had threatened
to beat them both bloody for daring to think he'd ever hurt
his Jess.

The two of them had kept an eye on him nonetheless—
because while he'd become Raphael's weapons-master and
they'd given all respect to his position, *and* they'd liked him,
he'd still been an unknown. Now, some four centuries later,
they'd long known his promise for truth, were bonded to him
in friendship.

"I think it's for an angelic teenager or teenagers," Aodhan

said. "The level of the calculations, that's what I remember learning around sixty, seventy years of age."

That was what mortals and vampires often didn't realize about angelkind. They grew very slowly as children, including in their mental development. Even at a hundred, they were considered callow youths at best.

The last mortal to whom Illium had explained that—a baker named Catalina—had gasped and pressed a hand to her heart. "Dios mío, your poor mamá. I had sprouted endless gray hairs by the time my first child reached sixteen, and to think she had to keep you out of trouble for many times those years."

Illium had laughed. They were friends, he and Catalina, even though he knew she'd one day leave him, as all his mortal friends left him. As Catalina's Lorenzo had already left them both. "No," he'd said that day, "my mother would have been horrified at the idea of losing me after a mere eighteen years. Time moves differently for us."

It was hard to explain the passage of years to a mortal from an immortal perspective. But today, as he looked down at the study items, his gut churned. "If a child or children were kept in this darkness . . ." Time would've moved at the speed of sludge, a slow creep of nothingness, the only view of the outside world a pinprick that looked out into stone and green.

Aodhan said nothing, and when Illium glanced at him, he saw that his friend had gone motionless, the pale hue of his skin making him appear a sculpture carved by an artist who had fallen in love with his subject.

Beautiful but cold. Distant. Unreal.

As Aodhan had become after healing from the physical wounds of his captivity. As if once he was no longer distracted by the injuries to his body, he needed to turn inward to escape the horrors that haunted him.

Horrors far too near to what had taken place in this cavern.

Illium didn't even think about his next action. He slipped

his hand into Aodhan's and squeezed hard. "Whoever it was, they escaped," he said, because that was the critical factor, the one that would smash through the remote ice of Aodhan.

It took a long time for Aodhan's fingers to curl slowly around his, his skin chilled from how far he'd gone, and his breathing so slow it was nearly imperceptible. "If it was a child, they will be insane, that much is certain." His voice held the eerie echo of distance.

"Then who better than us to find them?" Illium squeezed his friend's hand again.

At last, Aodhan turned his head to meet Illium's eyes. His own were icy mirrors that reflected Illium's face back at him. "Do you think this maddened, abused child is responsible for what we discovered in the hamlet?"

"I don't know." Illium's gut churned at the idea of it. "Either way, we have to find them." If they had become monstrous after being kept enclosed in the dark the entirety of their life . . . that was a problem to consider later.

Aodhan's entire body shuddered as he exhaled, his hand clenching on Illium's before he broke the contact. "Did you notice the neatness, the cleanliness?"

Illium hadn't, but now that Aodhan had pointed it out, you couldn't miss it. No dust on any surface—which should've been impossible in a cavern—all the spines in the bookshelf aligned to a precise degree, the texts and scrolls on the desk positioned at exact right angles. The bed, too, had been made so that it bore no wrinkles, the sides the same length.

It sent a chill up his spine—because the massacre had been as neat and tidy. "A form of control."

"Yes, I think so." Aodhan picked up a scroll.

Leaving him to examine that by the light of the lamp, Illium returned to check the door to a second closet. It proved to lead to a large area set up with bathing and sanitation facilities. Plumbed the modern way. So the residence had been upgraded at some point—while continuing to leave the occupant without light.

Mouth tight, he exited, then returned to the clothes closet

for a second look, his aim to find something that would give this child solid form in his mind.

At first, he saw nothing. Just bland tunics and pants that gave no clue as to gender or personality, the colors brown and black. He was about to move on when the beam of his phone flashlight picked up glints of silvery white on the shoulders of a black tunic.

Heart thudding, he reached out and picked up the fine, fine threads. Only, they weren't threads at all. "Shit. *Shit.*"

35

Aodhan was by Illium's side in a split second. "What?"

Illium just held up the long hairs, the icy white hue a recognizable symbol to anyone in the angelic world. For white hair in immortals was a genetic marker. A thing of family, not of age.

"Lijuan's kin." Aodhan took the hairs from Illium. "But Suyin knows of no other members of the extended family who have vanished or died in mysterious circumstances."

"How sure is she of that?"

"Very. Tracing the members of her family was a task she took on while she healed after her rescue. Andromeda used her research skills to assist, while Lady Caliane put her in touch with genealogical scholars among our kind; the end result is that she managed to trace each and every individual.

"Even the ones said to have gone into Sleep did so in a way that makes it impossible for Lijuan to have disappeared them. Not that she used such subterfuges. When she took Suyin captive, Suyin just vanished without a trace. And," he added, "theirs is an old line. No new births for over a millennium. There is no one young enough for those texts."

It was a good reminder. Living as Illium did in the Tower of a young archangel, and surrounded as he was by relatively young immortals, he occasionally forgot that immortality was an endless thread.

"Then maybe it's not a relative." He held his sword ready by his side even as he thought. "Hairs could belong to Lijuan herself."

"That would mean she came here." Aodhan turned, examined the semidark space. "If you strip away the absence of sunlight and the lack of freedom, it's a comfortable setup." His voice was tight, and Illium knew he'd had to force himself to say the words.

Because no prison was ever comfortable.

But Illium saw his point.

The bed was large and plush, the blanket and comforter folded at the end of fine fabrics. The rest of the furniture was equally well made, if in an antique style. There wasn't any food, but when Illium walked over to examine the round table in one corner that held an empty metal pitcher, he found a couple of tins of high-quality tea.

"This tea"—he held it up—"Lijuan drank that."

"How do you know?" Aodhan's forehead crinkled.

"She came to New York once, back before she lost her freaking mind," Illium muttered. "She was a guest, and Raphael asked me to source some of this." He'd forgotten that random piece of information until he laid eyes on the tin.

"So," Aodhan said, "the child in this place might have nothing to do with her bloodline."

"Makes sense if Suyin isn't aware of anyone who's missing." Crouching down, Illium opened a small cupboard. "Empty. No food." He stood. "Lijuan could've arranged for fresh meals to be sent through from the stronghold."

"Signs are that she closed it up a while ago." Aodhan's voice held a creeping darkness. "The hamlet, Blue. In the middle of nowhere. It could've been started specifically as a kitchen for this child—and as the home of the guards. It'd also explain the rage behind the massacre. To the child, every resident of the hamlet was their jailor."

The ugliness of an entire community conspiring to hide this unpardonable secret . . . Illium clenched his gut, fisted his hand. Raging would do no good, wouldn't erase all that had been done. "If the guards deserted their post after Lijuan's death, the child would've been left to starve."

"That bread roll," Aodhan murmured, "it's old, but surely, it would've disintegrated or been in a far worse condition if it was lying there for a year?"

"Yeah, you're right." Illium chewed on that. "Could've been Suyin's arrival in the region that spooked them." Picking up another book, he flipped the pages to check the language. English. Another proved to be in French. "An angelic halfling could survive such a short starvation."

"The guards who did this," Aodhan murmured, "they would've had to be some of her most loyal people, must've considered her their goddess. They'd have clung to the hope of her return long after any hope was lost."

"Yet to assist in the torture of a child?" Putting down the book, Illium shook his head, his jaw working. "That isn't serving your goddess; it's an embrace of evil."

"Yes." Nothing could ever justify this place, this act. "What have you found?" he asked Illium, well able to see the tic in Illium's jaw, the whiteness around his mouth.

No quicksilver heat this, but a bone-deep rage that echoed Aodhan's.

"The child had an extensive study schedule and, from the handwritten notes, kid's smart."

"So there's reason to hope they aren't responsible for the carnage."

"Yes." Despite his answer, Illium's gaze was bleak. "I can't imagine what this life would do to a child's psyche. We have to be prepared for the worst."

Neither one of them spoke again until they'd looked over every inch of the space, then—retrieving Smoke, who was now awake enough to hold on to Illium's shoulder when he tucked her up there—made their way back outside. Illium was on alert for any sign of distress from Aodhan, but his friend's simmering anger seemed to have pushed out every other emotion.

Illium was glad for it. Aodhan was slower to anger than Illium, but when he did reach that point, his anger burned for far longer than Illium's own fury. The only living person against whom Illium had held a long grudge was Aegaeon. Even then, he was fairly certain Aodhan's grudge on his behalf was a harder, darker thing.

Once outside, they flew up into the sky to speak, on the off chance the child was hiding out nearby, watching them. Hovering opposite Aodhan, the kitten held to his chest with one hand, Illium said, "I've been thinking about the lack of dust. Tidiness is one thing, but a place like that wouldn't remain dust-free without maintenance. I think the kid's been coming back on a regular basis."

"It's the only stable place in their universe," Aodhan said, his voice gritty. "The only place that they know in great detail."

Illium chewed the inside of his cheek. "Aodhan, any angelic child that grew up in there wouldn't be able to fly." Flight required muscle strength, and that strength developed over a childhood of *trying* to fly. Sunlight was also a requirement for much the same reason mortal children needed sunlight—it helped with bone growth and the health of the mind.

Aodhan's shoulders were tight as he said, "It's possible Lijuan did allow the child small trips outside. If so, that would make them even more inclined to madness. Because a child who grew up in there would know nothing else, but one who knew an outside world existed and had seen it? Then to become aware they were trapped?"

Nausea threatened to strangle Illium. He stroked Smoke's warm, fragile body—all fur and bone, she was—in an effort to comfort both her and himself. "We need to come back here in the daylight." With all that had occurred, it wasn't far off now. "We'll see more. And we need to bring food."

Aodhan looked at him. "You want to lure the child here?"

"Think about it—if they're used to being fed by others, it won't seem unusual to them. They might even be comforted by the idea of being given food."

Illium made himself take the next step. "I think they ate their way through the easy consumables that they could find in the hamlet, but don't have the cooking skills to use the staples like rice. And if it was the child . . . it makes sense that they didn't know how to make such a simple thing as soup."

Aodhan looked in the direction of the hamlet. "Why would a child do such horrors, Blue? I can't believe it."

It wasn't the first time this day that Aodhan had slipped into using Illium's childhood nickname, and, to Illium, it was a measure of his friend's mental struggle with all they'd seen and experienced today. He wanted desperately to wrap Aodhan up in his wings, protect him from the nightmares of the past, but he'd gotten the message there: Aodhan was in no mood to be protected.

It grated on Illium to not be able to do anything, but he kept a grip on himself. "We know Lijuan was a monster," he said. "We have no way of knowing what she did to this child, what she raised them to be."

Eyes of crystalline blue and green, shattered outward from a black pupil, as familiar as his own, looking into his. "Do you think she purposefully raised a child capable of such evil?" He shook his head on the heels of his question. "Why am I asking you questions you can't answer?"

Shoving a hand through the glittering beauty of his hair, he said, "You go and get the food, take care of Smoke. I'll keep watch here in case the child returns."

Illium hesitated. "We don't know the danger—"

"Go, before I lose my temper again," Aodhan muttered. "How do you think I've survived without you this past year? *Go*."

Narrowing his eyes, Illium decided not to argue. Not when lines of tension marked Aodhan's face and his skin was an unhealthily pale shade. Tucking Smoke close so she wouldn't be buffeted by wind, he arrowed his body toward the stronghold—but couldn't help throwing back a final caution. *Don't land. You're harder to jump in the air.*

One more word and I'll pluck out your feathers one by one.

Even as Illium scowled, relief bled through his veins. Aodhan was sounding more and more like himself—though he was more irritable than Illium had ever before known him to be.

"He is the deep, boundless ocean to your tempestuous storm," his mother had said to Illium once, her smile wide. "He anchors you and you take him flying."

"Right now," Illium complained to an alert Smoke—who didn't seem to mind flying at all, "he's a grump." But he was Illium's grump and this was far from over.

Alone in the stygian cold of the night, Aodhan began to do slow, steady sweeps over the area around the cavern while never losing sight of it. Given the darkness, it was likely he'd miss any signs of movement were his prey stealthy, but none of Raphael's Seven ever just gave up. That wasn't who they were—alone or as a group.

The forest and the pillars of Zhangjiajie remained motionless. Even the wind had fallen to silence.

Then it came, the first breath of air that held not only cold but an icy chill.

He glanced at the horizon, but of course there was nothing to see. When he looked straight up however, he could make out a sudden heaviness of clouds in the night sky. Snow? Possible in this time and place.

Zhangjiajie tended to have light snowfall in general, but angelic and mortal meteorologists had both warned of a high chance of a nasty winter across China due to the way Lijuan's fog had altered the atmosphere. Not a permanent change, it was thought, more a lingering aftereffect that would fade after one bitter season.

If only Lijuan's evil would fade as fast.

On the heels of that thought came another: would a child who'd grown up in that dank prison know how to survive in the snow? Even an angelic child was still a child, without the recuperative capacities of an adult angel. It was part of the reason angels were so careful to keep their children out of sight of mortal eyes until they were of an age where injury wouldn't lead to death.

They were called immortals, but angels *could* die. It just took so much to achieve such a result that the point was moot—except when it came to children. Children could be killed far easier than adults. And this child's growth was apt to already be stunted as a result of their captivity.

Fine white flecks began to hit his face—a pretty spray of sugar if not for what the cold of it could mean for the vulnerable. Like a child with no armor.

No, this wasn't good.

He said as much when Illium appeared out of the softly falling snow, his wings dusted with white in the moments before each wingbeat. "We have to make it so the child feels safe to return to his cavern," Aodhan said. "Else he'll be out in the snow—and I can't see him having the skills to survive that."

"It's cold in that place," Illium said. "Did you notice? I don't think an angelic child could've survived there while a babe. I'm guessing there must've been some system to provide heat—might be it broke down after Lijuan's fall."

Aodhan's skin prickled under a memory he'd done his best to bury for two hundred years: of cold, cold water dripping onto his face, seeping into his skin, rising up past his nostrils until he drowned and drowned.

It had taken him until the war to realize he couldn't outrun that piece of his past; he had to face it or he would always be the prey and the memory the hunter. He'd spoken to Keir privately in the immediate aftermath of Lijuan's defeat, and the healer had made time for him many times this past year, regardless of all the other demands on his attention.

"Why now?" Aodhan had asked while New York lay devastated around them. "Is it because of the horror of what Lijuan did? It's awakened my own horror?"

"I can't answer that," Keir had murmured, his wings a stir of golden-brown next to Aodhan and his power a quiet thing of profound depth, "but I think I have earned the right to say I know you, Aodhan. So I say with certainty that the memory rises now because you are ready now."

Keir had been right. Aodhan had been ready to face the nightmare head-on. And so today, while it whispered to him, it didn't derail his thoughts or suck him back into the darkness. "Do we still lure the child with food?" He knew he wasn't rational on this topic, needed to rely on Illium's clearer vision.

"It's our best bet of catching them," Illium confirmed. "Which is why I spent a few minutes heating up the food. The scent might help. We're here to scare off any predators who might be drawn to it."

Aodhan stayed on watch above while Illium landed. *Where's your new pet?*

I left her with Kai, who will undoubtedly spoil her.

They both went silent as Illium stepped inside the passageway to place the food. *I'll leave it close to the door. More chance of the scent reaching them—and less of us having to chase them deep inside the cavern. Last thing I want to do is freak out a kid.*

An out-of-control and scared child would be no match for two angels of their strength—but they'd be trying not to hurt the child, while that child would have no such compunction.

Blue?

I'm done, but I was thinking I should go farther inside, hide in the shadows. If the child does come in, you can land behind them, while I'll be in front. We should be able to make a quick capture.

Aodhan's neck muscles knotted, his biceps rigid. *It's not safe down there.*

Illium didn't give him a smart-ass reply about how the mountain wasn't about to fall down on him. He said, *I'll stay in touch throughout. In fact, I'll tell you bedtime stories while you freeze your ass off in the snow.*

The snow *was* increasing in force, but Aodhan had flown for hours through worse. *I hope the caravan is out of range of this snow front.*

Even if not, Illium said, *they're prepared to hunker down. Still . . . I didn't want to bring it up with Suyin, but were things really that bad with the survivors that the move had to be now? Everyone looked like they were soldiering on to me, but I know I only glimpsed the surface.*

Yes, Aodhan confirmed, remembering the hollow-eyed man who'd woken to repack his belongings. *China's people are broken. Not only the mortals. Any surviving vampires and angels, too, even those that followed Lijuan into war. Being close to a physical reminder of Lijuan, it was leeching away their ability to be happy in any real sense.*

We saw it, but thought they would make it through winter. I, myself, hadn't understood the depth of their growing depression until Suyin made her pronouncement and I saw hope return to their faces—she proved herself a true archangel that day, Illium, by seeing what even those living the pain couldn't.

In angelkind, such depression was simply called "mind darkness." Aodhan's mind had gone dark for a long, long time after his captivity, the shadows so infinite that he'd barely been able to glimpse the light. He would've castigated himself for not picking up the populace's increasing despair if Suyin alone hadn't been the one to spot it.

Sometimes, it took an archangel. Because an archangel wasn't formed by power alone.

One angel said to me that they'd rather fall under the weight of snow on their wings, than shrivel up inside the tainted walls of the stronghold.

Illium's response was swift. *I get it.*

Of course he did. Because he'd witnessed Aodhan's spiral into despair firsthand. It hadn't been right after his rescue. He'd been badly physically injured then, but he'd been present—and focused on his recovery. The mind darkness had come after his body was whole once more, his wings capable of flight. But he hadn't flown.

He'd fallen.

36

Yesterday

It was Naasir who finally found Aodhan.

Twenty-three months of relentless searching and it was Naasir's primal ability to follow scent trails that led them to Aodhan. Raphael had made the strategic decision to pretend to stop looking and allow everyone to believe they'd given up on the lost young angel—but he'd made the decision on Naasir's advice.

"Sometimes, predators hide their prey," Naasir had said, his eyes not in any way human. "Hide it so well that no one else can find it. They only come out when they think the coast is clear—that's when they can get careless, and that's when we'll strike."

Because they all, each and every one, knew this had nothing to do with an accident on a courier run, Aodhan's body lost to the ocean. Aodhan had always been coveted—unhealthily so by many.

Now, one of those ugly obsessives had taken him.

Raphael respected Naasir's advice and wild instincts, but he hadn't been certain the gambit would work—and he'd hated the anguish of Aodhan's parents and Lady Sharine. They all believed he'd given up in truth—because he couldn't let them in on the plan; they all loved Aodhan too deeply not to give away the game.

Illium, of course, had had to know. The three-hundred-year-old angel who'd been on the road to make squadron commander of an elite squadron prior to Aodhan's disappearance, had lost considerable weight, his cheeks hollow and his shoulder blades sharp—but he'd lost none of his strength. Rather, he'd made a concerted effort to force nutrition into his mouth.

"I can't help find Aodhan if I'm in the infirmary," he'd said, his face grimmer than Raphael had ever seen it. "Whatever it takes, I'll do."

But even Illium, with his fierce faith in Naasir's strategic thinking abilities, had hesitated when Naasir first suggested his idea. It was Dmitri who'd put it all into stark perspective. "We have no other option," he'd said. "We have to try this—if it fails, we restart the open search. Nothing is lost in attempting to mislead our quarry."

What was left unsaid was that they'd failed in their open search. Not only Raphael and his people, but the people of friendly archangels and senior angels. Even Neha, busy with problems in her own territory, had assigned squadrons to search India. Uram, too, had come through, as had Elijah and Titus, and they weren't the only ones.

The cooperation wasn't only because of their friendship or respect for Raphael, but because of the gift of Aodhan. It had become clear in the last century that Aodhan was the Hummingbird's artistic heir. Their styles and pieces were unique to each, but the glory of their work . . . One day, Aodhan would be as revered as Lady Sharine, but for now, he was a bright, bright light no one wanted to see extinguished.

All of angelkind knew that to hide a single angel wasn't a difficult task, especially had the hiding place been prepared in advance. What Raphael refused to believe was that Aodhan was gone forever. He'd shut his ears to those who whispered that talented, loyal, quietly powerful Aodhan had been stripped of his wings by an angel who coveted his beauty, then murdered.

He wouldn't believe Aodhan lost forever until he saw concrete evidence. Given how obsessed certain angels and vampires were with Aodhan's unique appearance, captivity also made far more sense. There were many stunning immortals and near-immortals in the world, but there was no one like Aodhan.

"I don't want the attention," he'd said to Raphael as a youth on the verge of manhood, a flush on his cheekbones and confusion in his unusual eyes. "Why do they keep insisting?"

"Is it any particular person?" Raphael had asked.

"A few." Aodhan had given him the names, and those names had spanned the gender and age spectrum, Aodhan's astonishing beauty a drug to many. "I don't want to get them in trouble . . . but they make me uncomfortable."

"I'll deal with it." He'd gripped Aodhan's shoulder when the youth went to open his mouth. "What they are doing is unacceptable, Aodhan. You've made it clear that you aren't interested. They have no right to keep pushing—so now they will get a personal visit from your archangel."

Raphael would've done the same for any young person in his court. He did not intend to keep a court like Charisemnon's, where sexuality was encouraged to the point that it enveloped every part of court life—and ensnared those far too young.

"What about the others?" Aodhan had asked, his voice hesitant. "The ones who don't push into my space, but who stare? How do I handle that? When I was a kid, Illium told me to ignore the stupids and it worked . . . but now . . . The attention makes me feel soiled." He'd swallowed. "I know they're not touching me, but it feels like it."

Raphael had considered his response with care. "It's not of your doing. Know this first of all. Those are the actions others choose to take." He'd wanted to make it clear that no blame lay on Aodhan for any of this.

"You can call it out when you're comfortable—some will then back off. Others won't and justify it to themselves and to you by terming it admiration." It was an unfortunate truth that such was the way of those who thought only of their own needs, immortal or mortal.

"But," he'd continued, "there are many who will be embarrassed and aghast to realize they are causing you discomfort." A lot of people were so struck by Aodhan that they forgot themselves; this didn't excuse their actions but at least they could be taught to be better. "And, Aodhan—there will come a time when you are so strong that no one will dare look at you with such open greed."

A quick, shy smile from the youth that had Raphael ruffling his hair as he so often did with Illium. "Whatever happens," he'd added, "always remember what I said first—these are the actions of others. They do not in any way define you."

Aodhan had taken a deep breath, exhaled. "At times, I wonder what it would be like to be normal."

"Naasir says normal is overrated," Raphael had answered. "He says it's far better to be a one-being and keep everyone guessing."

Aodhan's smile had turned dazzling, his entire being alight. "I will aim to be more like Naasir, sire."

That delighted smile was what burned in Raphael's mind as he flew high above the clouds, while Naasir ran far below, a hunter invisible. Illium flew slightly behind Raphael, Jason with him, while Dmitri held the fort for Raphael, and Galen kept an eye on the Refuge base of their enemy.

Because that angel *was* now Raphael's enemy. Sachieri had dared take Aodhan, dared take one of Raphael's people. She would pay the price. At present, she and her equally guilty lover, Bathar, were in her Refuge home, but even had she been at the stronghold where she'd most likely imprisoned Aodhan, it wouldn't have mattered.

Sachieri was a dealer of rare antiquities for immortals. No warrior, no power, certainly no match for an archangel. What mattered was to find Aodhan before any of her people got to him and attempted to use him as a hostage.

Which was why all the angels were above the cloud layer, while Naasir crept up to the stronghold. He wasn't quite human today, hadn't been quite human since he'd passed Sachieri in the Refuge a week earlier and caught a hint of Aodhan's scent on her clothing.

Not an old, faded scent like Naasir told him existed yet in parts of Aodhan's studio, but a fresh, bright scent that spoke of recent contact. That Aodhan was an angel uncomfortable with touch except for his closest family, lovers, and friends, just made the implication of the scent all the more enraging.

"I would rip out her throat," Naasir had said to Raphael, his silver eyes as bright as a tiger's and a growl in his throat. "*After* we find Aodhan."

"If she has a throat left after I am done with her." Raphael's rage was a cold, cold beast, one who understood that vengeance could last an eternity.

Naasir had tilted his head to the side. "He is one of your cubs. You can go first."

Despite having seen Aodhan grow up, Raphael didn't think of him as a child. He saw in him a young warrior any angel would be proud to have among his people. But Aodhan *was* his, and no one was permitted to hurt Raphael's people. *Jason, how is Illium?*

In control, was the cool response from the spymaster who'd searched with a relentless will that had left him as thin as Illium, yet who blamed himself for not having found Aodhan. *He won't act precipitously and put the operation in jeopardy.*

And you, Jason? Can I trust you to maintain?

Yes, sire.

His word was enough for Raphael. Jason wouldn't be his spymaster if Raphael didn't have implicit trust in him. What Sachieri had done, however, had damaged the black-winged angel, as it had damaged all of them—including the already

fractured Lady Sharine. At least her broken mind had protected her somewhat; at times, she forgot Aodhan was gone
and talked as if they'd painted together the previous day.

Strange mercies.

But when this is done, Jason added, *I intend to erase Sachieri and Bathar from angelic history. I plan to steal every
document in which either of their names is mentioned, and
to strongly encourage anyone who has had dealings with
them to forget they ever existed.*

Jason wasn't a violent angel—but he burned with a smol-
dering power. For most, his encouragement would be difficult to resist; Raphael would take care of any who remained.
*I think, Jason, you will have the cooperation of more people
than you know.*

Angelkind's fascination with Aodhan could be used to
gain him justice of a kind that would be a horror to an immortal: to be so forgotten that thousands of years of life
added up to nothing. *Neither has a child. Their bloodlines
end with them.*

For Aodhan's captors would both die. But it wouldn't be
quick. Not for this crime.

They flew on.

Until at last, Naasir's mind touched Raphael's. Technically, the other man shouldn't have been able to speak to him
this way, not given who and what he was—but Naasir had
never been one to follow the rules. *Sire, I am going inside.*

*We'll hover above the cloud layer until you give us the
go-ahead. Take care, Naasir. You are smarter and stronger,
but vicious cowards are not to be underestimated.*

I will be the stealthy hunter, Naasir promised. *Our prey
will never see me.*

Raphael kept an eye on Illium as they waited, all but able
to see the rage that boiled in his blood. Illium hadn't laughed
or smiled for anyone but Lady Sharine since the day Aodhan
failed to arrive at a courier waypoint; and even for his cherished mother, he could only manage bright falsehoods that

didn't fool her except for when she was far into the kaleido-scope.

The rest of the time, he was grim rage.

Raphael could've never imagined such an incarnation of their laughing, playful Bluebell.

I have Aodhan's scent. Sharp. Strong. He can't be far. Fierce exultation in Naasir's voice. *The servants are weak and lazy. No threat. But I will find our sparkles, make sure he is alone.*

Blood fury hazed Raphael's mind the next instant, Naasir still connected to him as he went into a sudden killing frenzy. *Go!* he ordered Jason and Illium, even as he dived through the clouds toward the stronghold situated in the midst of what would be rolling green hills in the summertime.

Cloaked in snow and ice this winter's day, it appeared a beacon of glimmering gray stone—look only at the elegant outside and you'd never deduce the filth and malice that coated its walls.

The counterfeit sense of peace broke right then, trans-formed into screaming anarchy.

Angels flew up from every corner, their wings beating in terrified desperation, while below, vampires ran out into the snow. A number stumbled and fell, crawling insects who de-served no mercy.

Raphael struck them all down with a single modulated blow of archangelic power. Enough to slam them into unconsciousness—and cause a few broken wings and bones for the angels in flight.

No death. Not yet.

Anyone who'd worked in this stronghold was liable to be guilty of abetting in Aodhan's torture, but he would make certain of that. No one who'd helped harm Aodhan, if only by their silence, would ever again know anything but terror.

Jason.

I'll take care of the stragglers. Sire—Illium won't stay with me. He's heading after you.

Let him come. Aodhan would need his best friend.

Raphael landed on a wide balcony. Aware of the streak of blue landing hard behind him, he blew open the closed doors, stepped inside.

Silence. No more screams. No more panic.

Naasir.

Sire, they hurt *him.* Naasir's voice shook with rage. *They took him out of the light and they buried him in water and they* hurt *him.*

"Basement," Raphael said to Illium, and they both stepped off the railingless edge of the upper level, their destination the ground floor.

While small angelic homes had no basements, they were often added into large strongholds as extra storage. It made sense, since such strongholds almost always had non-angelic staff—the vast majority of whom felt no sense of confinement at going into the basement.

Quite the opposite of winged beings.

Raphael's feet hit the floor at the same time as Illium's.

"Sire!" Illium sprinted to the left, having spotted what Raphael just had—fallen and broken vases, tumbled furniture. Casualties of the staff's rush to escape Naasir's rampage.

Raphael pounded after the young angel, his boots crushing the flowers scattered on the floor as his wings took out other items. A painting fell with a splinter of glass. A mirror followed right before a small marble statue thudded into the spilled water, broken porcelain, and bruised petals that were all that remained of a floral arrangement.

Ahead of him, Illium disappeared through a wide door that proved to lead to a set of stairs that headed down deeper into the earth. Blood splattered the walls around the stairs, and a vampire who'd been disemboweled by claws as lethal as razors lay gurgling blood on the floor, his hands lost in the rippling folds of his intestines.

What had Naasir seen or smelled on this man that had set him off?

Ignoring the vampire—weak, not one who'd quickly re-

pair the grievous wound especially with no blood to fuel it—
Raphael followed Illium down the stairwell. He noticed a
lever as he did so, noticed, too, that it had bloody prints on it.
Naasir had turned that lever.

Water. Buried.

His gut churned as the scent of damp, cool and unmistakable, hit his nostrils. The stairwell, however, showed no signs
of water. It was softly lighted, the walls lined with art . . .
Aodhan's art.

A glow hit the air.

His wings were afire.

Raphael called on all his strength to keep his rage from
blinding him. Aodhan needed him to be his archangel right
now, not the man who'd seen him grow up, not the one who'd
taught him how to use a crossbow, and not, too, the laughing
new archangel who'd caught him when he tangled his wings
as a babe and fell.

"Adi, Adi, I'm here."

He'd half expected a scream from Illium, but his voice
was quiet, gentle.

Raphael turned the corner and saw.

37

Pieces of iron had been peeled up from a narrow and long box that sat on a stone floor still pooled with glimmering wet. The box had been manacled with chains now broken. Naasir's bloody hands were jagged with embedded shards as he sat crouched on one side of the open part of the box, struggling to tear back more of the iron, while Illium knelt on the other side, his hand trembling as he reached within and brushed back Aodhan's hair.

Sachieri had kept this angel full of light in a box in the dark.

Going frigid within as that was the only way he could deal with this, Raphael said, "Naasir," and the other man moved with primal speed.

A single flick of archangelic power and the iron box was nothing but dust. But he'd been careful, so careful, that nothing he did hurt Aodhan. Striding forward, he saw eyes of translucent blue and crystalline green shards turn toward Illium.

No other part of Aodhan moved.

Couldn't move.

His wings . . . his beautiful wings . . . battered and damaged to the point that they were nothing but strings of tendon over rotted bone. His body was emaciated, his skin broken and bloody and scarred.

It took a long, long time to do that to an angel, but Aodhan was young yet. Young enough to hurt. Young enough to hurt to the point that he hadn't been able to break out of the box. Sachieri had to have struck him a near-fatal blow at the first, then kept him too weak to heal. Else, he'd have used his power to smash out of the cage.

Raphael would find out. He'd find out all of it. He'd strip her mind bare until she was nothing but a sniveling shell. But not today. Today, he would take Aodhan home.

Raphael contacted Dmitri and Galen the instant they were close enough to the Refuge to speak through their minds. *Cage Sachieri, Bathar, and their entire household. I will deal with Elijah.* It was in the other archangel's Refuge territory that Sachieri made her home, and she was bound peripherally to his court.

Dmitri was the one who replied. Unsurprising. Galen, on watch with a full squadron, would've sprung into action. The weapons-master was also apt to be in a rage; Raphael would get no words out of him until his task was done.

I'll speak to Elijah's second—he won't stand in our way. Sire, Aodhan?

He's badly wounded. Warn the Medica that I'm bringing in a critical case.

How do I stop myself from killing them?

No fast death for either of them, Dmitri. No mercy. That goes for you, too, Galen. Keep them alive.

A grunt of acknowledgment from Galen.

Nothing from Dmitri, but Raphael didn't need it. His closest friend had too close an understanding of the need for vengeance—and for justice. He would do nothing to diminish the harshness of the punishment Raphael intended to mete out.

What Dmitri did say was, *I'm near the Medica. I'll see Aodhan first before I join Galen. He doesn't need me for anything but dealing with Elijah's people. Our Barbarian is not the best at politics.*

Raphael didn't deny him. Like him, Dmitri had watched Aodhan grow from when he was a babe. He'd once walked hand in hand with Aodhan when Aodhan got it into his head to visit an angelic monument on the far edge of the Refuge. Naasir's "small sparkles" was beloved of them all.

Raphael looked down to make sure that the cushion of power he'd wrapped around Aodhan's blanket-enveloped body was still holding. He lay in Raphael's arms, unconscious and without any real weight to him. He'd reacted only once—when he'd tried to speak to Illium. Then his eyes had closed, and he'd slumped into this state.

Raphael had known he'd likely gone to a place beyond pain; he'd wrapped the cushion of power around him nonetheless. Never would he risk being the cause of even a minute trace of pain for this angel who was the gentlest member of his court, the one who saved small insects caught in pools of water and made sure the wild birds were fed.

Illium had tried to pace Raphael, inevitably fallen behind. He was fast but didn't have the endurance to keep up with Raphael over a long flight. *Go, sire!* Illium's mental voice had been fierce. *I'll follow!* He was doing so alone, Jason and Naasir having stayed behind at Sachieri's stronghold to secure the prisoners.

So when Raphael landed on the wide landing area outside the Medica, he was alone but for the wounded angel in his arms. Keir and several other healers were waiting for him, and he saw the horror on all their faces as they laid eyes on Aodhan. But it lasted the barest moment before they snapped into action.

Dmitri stood off to the edge, out of their way—but plenty close enough to see Aodhan. *Hurt them,* he said to Raphael in a short, clipped voice, the skin of his face bloodless, it was pulled so tight over his bones. *Break them.*

Oh, I intend to. He strode inside on Keir's orders as Dmitri shifted on his heel to go join Galen. Once inside, he forced himself to relinquish Aodhan by laying him down on a large bed designed for angelic beings. But Aodhan had no wings to speak of, looked lost in the whiteness of the mattress.

When Keir and another healer unwrapped him from the blanket with careful hands, Raphael was hit once more with how little of Aodhan remained. "You must heal him," he ordered Keir, his voice a thing of grit and stone.

Keir had known Raphael all of Raphael's life, and had little fear of archangels in general. "This is our place now, Raphael. Go. We'll work better without your wings blazing fear into my staff."

It was only then that Raphael realized his wings were glowing.

Hands fisted, he glanced around and saw faces bleached of color. Keir might not be afeared of him, but the same couldn't be said of the others. He had to go, but he wouldn't leave Aodhan alone without one of his people. "I'll wait outside this room until Illium arrives. He is not to be separated from Aodhan, understood?"

Keir nodded. "I was planning to ask you to send Illium here, regardless. The child will need his heart's mirror to pull him back to us." He brushed tender fingers over the broken straw of Aodhan's hair. It still glittered bright under the light, but it was faded, brittle.

Retreating to the doorway, Raphael stayed out of sight while positioning himself so he could see inside the room. When a sweaty and breathless Illium ran into the Medica some time later, he grabbed the young angel and crushed him close until Illium's wings stopped fluttering and his breathing evened out, his heartbeat no longer a drum against Raphael.

"Aodhan doesn't need your anger or your panic," he murmured in Illium's ear. "He needs your friendship." That term wasn't enough to describe the tie between the two, Keir's use of heart's mirror far more fitting. "Be as you've always been with him. *Do not* treat him as broken. Be his friend, the one he's always known."

Illium's arms clenched around him as he nodded with jagged movements. "I understand."

Pulling back, Raphael met eyes of aged gold, saw more calm in them than he'd expected. But then, Illium was Lady Sharine's son. He held far more maturity and kindness within than was apparent to those who saw only the surface flash. "Good. Don't get in the way of the healers or I'll pull you out."

"I won't do anything to harm Aodhan." Illium looked over Raphael's shoulder into the room where Aodhan lay, then back at Raphael. "I want to torture and kill her."

"No, Illium." Raphael gripped the side of the young angel's face. "Your job is here. It is the duty and the pleasure of your archangel to take vengeance." He pushed Illium toward the room. "Go. And know this—she will suffer."

Another angel might've argued with Raphael, but Illium and Raphael had a bond different from the one Raphael had with any other of his people. Where Raphael saw Aodhan as a warrior first and foremost, it wasn't the same with Illium. For him, Illium would forever be the little boy he'd cradled in his arms after Aegaeon's cruel departure, the child to whom he'd given his first sword, the youth who'd run to him in breathless excitement after he gained a place in a junior squadron.

Today, Illium's eyes glittered, but he nodded, trusting Raphael to do what he would've done had he had the chance. He need not have worried. Raphael's anger was of an archangel's—nothing could match it.

Keir, he said, touching the mind of the senior healer. *I interrupt only to say that every resource I have is at your disposal. If you need something me or mine can't provide, tell me and I will obtain it.*

I know, Raphael. But while we'll do all we can, this battle will, in the end, be fought by Aodhan. A pause before he said, *We must amputate what remains of his wings. They are rotting into his back and will only harm him at this point. Do you give permission as his sire?*

Raphael didn't point out that Aodhan's parents were alive and awake. Aodhan had handed Raphael the power to make such decisions when he signed onto his team. *Yes, you have my consent.*

Better to do it now, while Aodhan was so weak he was unlikely to notice. By the time he recovered enough to do so, his wings would be in the process of growing back. *Can you tell me anything of what was done to him?*

I need more time to examine him, but I can tell you that his wings were clipped. An icy calm to Keir's mental voice. *The damage to the section that should hold his primary feathers isn't a result of rot. I can see the wounds where his tendons and bones were severed—there are scars that say it was done over and over again.*

Raphael could feel the glow coming off his wings begin to intensify, forced himself to get it under control. *The instant you know more, tell me. I don't care if you discover it while it is the darkest hour of night.*

I will do so. Now go, leave me to my work.

Before he exited the Medica, Raphael made sure to tell Illium what was about to happen to Aodhan's brutalized wings. *Don't try to stop the healers. This is necessary for Aodhan's healing—and you know Keir will do Aodhan no harm.*

The young angel's response was calm. *If he wakes and panics, I'll remind him that I all but lost mine when I was far younger than he is today, and my wings are now so glorious others are jealous.* His attempt at humor was shaky at best, but that he was trying was a good sign.

Illium would hold for Aodhan. As long as Aodhan needed, Illium would hold.

Raphael left not for his stronghold, but for the home of the enemy. Dmitri was waiting for him outside, on the wide stone path that led to the main doors. Others who belonged to Raphael guarded the entrances to the property.

"It's done. Elijah's people have disowned both of them," his second said. "*She*"—Dmitri turned and spat hard onto the path—"is in an upstairs room with Galen standing guard. He didn't want to risk that she'd take the coward's path out. He threw that pathetic piece of shit Bathar in with her."

Suicide was difficult for angels who weren't incredibly young, but it *could* be done. "Good." He put a hand on his best friend's shoulder, squeezed. "Will you take the task of informing Aodhan's parents?"

Raphael would normally pay them that respect, but Menerva and Rukiel were frightened of him. Not so odd if you considered that many people were frightened of archangels, but he found it strange when their son had never been scared in his company.

"Yes." Dmitri's hand fisted at his side, his jaw working.

"He is strong, Dmitri. He will return and he will be as powerful as always. Remember that."

Neither one of them brought up the little boy who hadn't survived abduction and torture, the little boy whose sobs and cries for his papa haunted Dmitri, but the ghost of little Misha stood between them—as he lived in the nightmares that haunted Dmitri hundreds of years after Misha had turned to dust.

Misha. Caterina. Ingrede.

Aodhan would not be another name to add to that litany of loss and grief.

Dmitri's hand flexed, then curled inward again. "What will you do to her?" His eyes glowed with a red tinge—it was the first time in centuries that Raphael had seen his friend and second so close to bloodlust. Dmitri's control over his vampiric urges was legendary.

"What she deserves."

Dmitri didn't question him further; he understood Raphael better than any other person walking this earth, and so he knew that the vengeance Raphael took would be appropriate to the crime.

Waiting only until his second had left to inform Aodhan's parents, Raphael considered Lady Sharine. *Jessamy,* he said, reaching out to the kind angel of whom Illium's mother was fond. *Have you seen Lady Sharine today?*

I'm with her now. Dmitri told me something was happening, that I should shield her from any news until you came to her.

Of course Dmitri had done that; that was why he was Raphael's second. Because a second had to think for himself, do things without being ordered to do so. And because a second had to understand his archangel's heart.

She's quiet today, Jessamy continued. *She's painting while I sit with her and read.*

Raphael considered which action to take first, decided on vengeance. Only once that was in play would he be calm enough to talk to Lady Sharine. To her, he would give a full accounting, nothing left undone. *Can you stay with her awhile longer?*

I'll stay as long as needed, Jessamy said, her mental voice as gentle as her physical one. *Rafa, is Aodhan home?* It was a measure of her emotional state that she'd called him Rafa. These days, though she was the beloved of one of his Seven, she tried her best to remember his status as an archangel—rather than as her former troublemaker of a student.

Raphael felt no anger at the familiarity; he never would, not toward Jessamy. *Yes, he's home. But he's hurt. I will have to break the news with care.*

I will be a wall against all others, Jessamy promised.

Leaving her that trust, he strode toward the small stronghold. Trace, a vampire known for his suave ways and mild manner, stepped aside from the door he'd been guarding. He said nothing as he pulled that door open, but his eyes held the same red tinge as Dmitri's.

All of Raphael's people were angry.

Raphael had no need to ask for directions to Sachieri and

Bathar. He could feel Galen's rage like a beat in his veins. To his right hung the terrorized silence of a huddle of staff. Members of Galen's squadron watched them with merciless eyes. Those eyes didn't move off their quarry even when Raphael entered the space.

Leaving the warriors to their duty, he flew up to the mezzanine, then walked to the room that held the two people who had dared take one of Raphael's own.

38

Galen's pale green eyes flashed when he saw Raphael, his anger a flame as fiery as his hair.

Go, Galen. Watch over Lady Sharine with your Jess. Ensure no one gets to her.

I would see him.

Don't get in Keir's way—and, Galen? Be ready. They hurt him.

A curt nod and Galen was gone . . . but Raphael saw the shine of tears in the weapons-master's eyes as he left. Raphael knew the angel's huge heart was full of rage, Galen the most volatile of the six men he trusted most. Jessamy would help him find ease. Protecting Lady Sharine would further that aim.

He shut the doors behind Galen, then turned, looked.

Sachieri, she of the golden curls and sky blue eyes, sat on a heavy wooden chair, her arms twisted behind her back and tied tight. Her legs were tied as fast to the legs of the chair, each ankle secured with a separate rope. She was dressed in a gown of silken white that flowed like ice water, except where it'd been caught by the ties around her ankles. The cream hue of her skin bulged red-black around the ties.

No doubt, her wrists were as bruised.

The gag around her mouth dug into her skin and her eyes beseeched Raphael to set her free. She couldn't touch his mind however, was too weak—and even had she not been, no one could touch an archangel's mind that he did not permit.

Ignoring her for the time being, he glanced at the second prisoner.

Bathar had been hog-tied and left on the floor, discarded angelic trash. He was a follower, always had been. That Sachieri was behind Aodhan's imprisonment wasn't in question, but that didn't make Bathar any less guilty.

Pulling over another chair, Raphael sat down in a spot from where he could see them both—and where they could see him. "You took one of mine," he said with utmost calm. "What I will do to you in turn will make you forget that you were ever sentient beings, your minds and bodies a ruin."

He used the barest flick of power to burn the gag from Sachieri's mouth.

She began to babble at once in that pretty, high voice she used to make herself appear small and weak. Girlish. "I'm so sorry, Archangel Raphael! I didn't want to do it, but he made me!"

Bathar bucked in violent protest, making stifled sounds behind his gag.

"I didn't know he needed light to survive!" Sachieri continued. "If I had, I'd have made sure he had more! I tried to help him!"

Raphael smiled, and both angels went silent, the blood draining from their faces. "You do not need your mouths for me to learn what occurred. I'm considering obliterating your lower jaws to stop the whimpering and the lying and the begging."

Silence now, huge eyes.

He went into their minds without warning. Small, weak,

covetous minds. He saw that Aodhan had been Sachieri's obsession, an obsession that caused an ugly jealousy in Bathar. Sachieri had driven the crime, yes, but Bathar had participated to the fullest extent.

He saw, too, how the two weak angels had captured Aodhan in the first place. Brave of heart and kind of character, he'd gone to help her as Sachieri feigned distress—a desperate broken-winged angel stranded on an isolated stretch of land between two courier waystations. They'd stalked him long enough to know his favored flight path on this route, had been willing to try again and again until they succeeded.

Bathar, concealed in a hide that made it impossible to spot him from the air, had shot a heavy-duty crossbow bolt into Aodhan's throat the instant he landed. In the interim, Sachieri had retrieved the crossbow on which she'd been lying, and followed that first devastating blow with one to his heart, while Bathar shot another two bolts into his wings.

The wounds—especially the heart-wound—had been enough to weaken him for the next assault: the total removal of his heart. An angel could survive that, especially an angel of Aodhan's age, but he couldn't regrow his heart and fight for his freedom at the same time.

It was while he was unconscious that they'd clipped his wings and put him in a box of cold iron that they'd then had a squadron of their staff fly home. Raphael made note of each and every one of those faces, for they, too, would pay. The squadron had landed twice during the journey, so Sachieri could brutalize Aodhan's healing heart.

Once at the stronghold, they'd taken the iron box inside via a wall from which the bricks had been removed. They'd then rebricked it, and flooded the room . . . and the box.

A badly wounded angel couldn't heal while his body fought the urge to drown. As an archangel, Raphael would feel no ill effects from being immersed in water—his cells had developed past that point. But Aodhan was only a few centuries old. He'd have been terrorized, his lungs searching for air and finding only water.

Too old to die and too young to survive without unrelenting agony.

Raphael's eyes went to Sachieri's chest, to the oval-shaped locket of bright yellow gold that sat against the lush cream of her skin.

Rising, he ripped it from her throat, leaving behind a line of wet red.

When he opened the locket, it was to reveal a single tiny feather of glittering diamond light. He slapped her with the back of his hand, so hard that blood flew out of her mouth, and bone cracked. Then he went to her coconspirator and broke one wing in a single movement.

A muffled, high-pitched scream, Bathar's eyes rolling back in his head.

Returning to his seat, with Aodhan's feather held carefully in hand, Raphael continued to trawl through their memories. *Keir,* he said when he realized the pattern of injuries, *Aodhan's heart has been removed at regular intervals. They allowed him to heal just enough that he'd remain conscious, but never enough to become strong enough to fight them.*

It would've also left him too weak to slip into Sleep—not that Aodhan would've made that choice. In his situation, with Sachieri and Bathar slavering for his responses, it would've equaled suicide. And Aodhan would've never given his captors the satisfaction of thinking they'd broken him to the point of fatal surrender.

That explains the scarring I'm seeing, Keir replied, his voice curt in the way of a man who was busy doing another task. *Angels don't scar this way. Find out what they did to his skin and wings to make them rot. Immersion in fluid alone—even long-term immersion—doesn't do this to our bodies.*

Recalling Sachieri's babbling at the start, Raphael dug through her mind for proof. *He needs sunlight, Keir. Needs it in a way the rest of us don't.* He fought the urge to fly to the Medica, cradle Aodhan in his arms and fly him high up into the atmosphere, until not even a cloud stood between him and the sun.

As for Sachieri and Bathar, they'd figured out Aodhan's need by a process of trial and error when his wings began to deteriorate. So, every six months, they'd torn down the brick wall to drag him out into the sunlight. Not enough to make him strong. Barely enough so he wouldn't die.

Of course we wouldn't know that, Keir muttered. *Why would we? Our Sparkle has always had the sun on his skin. I'll make sure his room is full of direct sunlight.*

Raphael didn't pass on the rest of what he'd learned: that the two evil cowards in front of him had used Aodhan's weakened state to touch him in ways abhorrent and unwanted.

That healing would have to come after the physical. And it would take a lot longer. Because while Aodhan was affectionate with those he loved, he was exquisitely private with everyone else. He took care with even the most inconsequential touch. Perhaps because all his life, people had wanted to touch him, tried to touch him.

Aodhan valued his ability to decide who he wanted that close.

Sachieri and Bathar had stolen that choice from him, stolen it in a way that made Raphael's hand glow, his need to annihilate them almost overwhelming. *Almost.* "Oh, I'm not going to kill you," he said when a wet patch spread on the front of Bathar's pants, and Sachieri began to snivel and plead all over again.

He smiled again. "First, I will ask master artisans to build an iron box for each of you, lined with spikes and infested with spiders and biting insects, so that you can never rest, never not be touched." As they hadn't permitted Aodhan to escape their touch. "They will crawl into your mouths, set up home in your orifices, dig their teeth into your eyeballs."

Sachieri threw up.

Ignoring the stink of it, Raphael continued. "Then I will

bury those boxes so far beneath a weight of soil and stone that only an archangel will be able to retrieve you. And I *will* retrieve you. I don't intend for you to fall into a stupor and miss out on the experience of being buried alive."

"Please!" Sachieri screamed, her beauty lost in a tracery of burst veins and smeared cosmetics. "We're sorry! He's so beautiful! We just—"

Raphael flicked out a hand and her lower mouth and jaw broke apart in a splatter of blood, bone, and flesh. Her head dropped. He raised an eyebrow at Bathar, then burned off his gag with a carefully modulated use of archangelic power . . . just enough to sear off the first layer of his skin. "Would you like to speak?"

A convulsive shake of his head, his eyes all but bulging out of his head as he fought not to scream at the agony around the red flesh of his mouth.

"A good choice. Now, to wake your lover." Raphael dug his fingers into her mind, wrenched her out of the peace of unconsciousness.

After he had the full attention of her bloodshot, terror-filled eyes, he tapped a finger on the arm of his chair, Aodhan's feather still curled safe in his other hand. "You took Aodhan from us for six hundred and ninety-nine days.

"Now, I'm not so severe that I'll make you serve a year for each day." A small smile of apparent boredom. "That would be tedious after a while, as you'd be so insane you wouldn't understand what was happening."

He spread out his wings, folded them back in. "And it would be a merciless thing to offer you no hope of survival. So I will say . . . one year for each month. Twenty-three years is not so long in the scheme of an immortal life."

Gratitude in two pairs of watery eyes.

Raphael leaned forward. "After those years, if you are yet sane," he said softly, "I'll put you both in the same box—wooden this time—so that you'll have company as I take you to an island far from all else, and set you aflame."

It took a long time for an angel to burn to death, especially if the fire was set to be a slow, slow torment of embers. "I will only scorch you for the first week, sear you for the second, then burn you down to ash over the next seven days. A mere three weeks, then death. Is that not merciful?"

Bathar screamed, while tears rolled out of Sachieri's staring eyes.

In truth, Raphael didn't expect either one of their minds to survive even the year. They were worthless worms, with no bravery in them. But they would now spend what little time they had thinking of the other horror to come. And it *would* come. Because Raphael would watch their minds— and he would dig them up the instant before the final insanity.

Each would go into death knowing for what crime they burned.

You must understand—for Aodhan,
the Seven and Raphael are family,
the bonds between them far beyond blood and bone.
It is a thing elemental.

—*Lady Sharine*

39

Today

It was only ten minutes after Illium went into the tunnel with the food that Aodhan saw a stirring in the trees. *Movement*, he warned.

The snow had fallen steadily in the interim, and had long erased any evidence of Illium's passage. So it was on pristine white ground that the newcomer stepped, their head swiveling this way and that on a thin and small body as they ran toward the cavern.

Their hair was a river down their back that shone as white as the snow.

And their wings . . . they dragged on the cold earth, weak and twisted.

Then Aodhan saw that the angel below had no primary feathers.

Rage a hum in his cells, he said, *Get ready, Illium*. He began to drop down at the same instant, careful to do so in silence.

The runner had entered the tunnel by the time he landed. A scream sounded even as his boots touched the snow, followed by the sound of movement . . . then a relatively light body slammed against his chest.

Aodhan had the runner's hands manacled behind their back before they could claw at him. "We mean you no harm," he said in the tongue Lijuan had used most often. It was an older dialect, but all of Raphael's people were fluent in it, for to know your enemy was the greatest advantage in battle.

The person in his hold continued to twist, the long strands of their fine white hair obscuring their features. It was only when Illium emerged and took charge of restraining their captive that Aodhan was able to see enough to—

He sucked in a breath.

This person wore Lijuan's face . . . on a male body. Slightly harder angles, but the same pearl-gray eyes, the same white skin, the same proportion to the features. "Was Archangel Lijuan your mother?" he asked the boy—because it *was* a boy. Young. Maybe fourteen in human years, which would put him at about seventy or so in angelic terms.

The boy spat at him.

Avoiding the spittle with a small movement because he'd been expecting an assault of some kind—the boy was a creature trapped and scared—Aodhan spoke to Illium. "Let's take him to the stronghold, get him out of the cold." Everything else could wait.

Illium shook his head. "We can't fly him if he doesn't cooperate. He'll cause a crash."

A sudden quivering motionlessness to the boy. Aodhan realized Illium had continued to speak in Lijuan's favored tongue—and the child had understood. His eyes went to those stunted wings, the rage within him a cold, coiled thing born of a dark, wet coffin of iron.

"We'll take you into the sky," he said in a voice firm and unbending. "But we can't if you keep struggling."

The boy remained motionless. Almost as if he was holding his breath.

Aodhan half expected Illium to question whether they could trust the child's abrupt good behavior, but he said, "I'll carry him." White lines around his mouth, but his hands gentle on the boy's wrists.

That was what the world had never understood: Aodhan might be the artist, but it was warrior-born Illium who had the softer, more vulnerable heart. He'd come down on the side of the victim—always.

It's all right, Aodhan murmured into his friend's mind. *If I can't stand the touch of a broken, wounded child, then I shouldn't be in the position I'm in.*

Illium's lashes flicked up, his gaze searching and protective—but then he stepped back, releasing the child. *I'll fly below you in case he panics at being in the sky and you have to drop him.*

Aodhan had no intention of dropping his passenger, but he knew Illium was right. If the boy began to claw at him . . . Aodhan still wouldn't drop him. Illium had to know that. But Illium was also a rescuer. He couldn't help it, his huge heart his greatest weakness and biggest strength both. But . . . he'd stepped back.

Frowning inwardly, Aodhan returned his attention to the boy. "I'm going to take you in my arms so I can carry you."

No response, but though no one was holding him now, the boy didn't move.

"You start twisting while in the air, we land and walk the rest of the way."

Nothing, the boy a sculpture with hair of moonlight. Deciding there was only one way to find out what would happen, Aodhan bent and scooped the child into his arms, one arm under his knees, the other behind his back. *He's not as light as he looks.* Nothing of a weight to trouble Aodhan, but worth noting. *He's eaten enough not to starve.*

Illium shook his head in a firm negative, refuting Aodhan's implication about the child's presence in the hamlet. Aodhan wished he could be as certain. But he knew how madness slid into your brain in the cold dark. He wasn't sure he'd be sane today if he'd spent even a day longer in that iron coffin.

This boy had grown up inside just such a coffin, for all that his had been a room.

Flaring out his wings, Aodhan looked down at the boy. Those strikingly familiar eyes flicked to him before jerking away. Unable to feel anything but a protective sympathy, Aodhan left his questions aside and took flight into the falling snow.

The boy went rigid in his arms.

Aodhan made sure his grip was secure, then flew on at a far slower pace than that of which he was capable; if this child born with wings had never touched the sky, then this was a wonder for him, and Aodhan would not cut it short.

Wild blue below him, Illium silent about his leisurely pace.

That heart of his. Rescuing kittens, befriending mortals . . . protecting Aodhan.

At times, Aodhan wondered how Illium could survive immortality with such a vulnerable heart. At the same time, he knew that very heart was why Illium would always be the best friend he'd ever have. To the people he loved, Bluebell gave everything. Too much. Until there was nothing left for himself. Honestly, the man needed a keeper, one willing to put Illium first.

A small sharp sound from the boy, but when Aodhan looked down, it was to see no panic on his thin face, only a twisted kind of pain entwined with wonder. Aodhan understood, spoke to assuage his agony.

"Angelic wings can recover even after being fully removed." From all outward appearances, the boy didn't have a congenital issue, as with Jessamy. His wings were simply weak from lack of use, and clipped. Aodhan had seen the scars on the wingtips that indicated a partial amputation, the removal of all hope of flight.

The boy met his gaze, pearl-gray eyes flat and distrustful.

"Illium—the blue-winged angel below—lost his wings in battle not long ago. I have images of him without wings,"

Aodhan would've hated those images, hated the idea of his Bluebell being grounded, had Illium not been posing in a flamboyant cape and matching top hat, a glittering walking stick in hand.

The pictures had made Aodhan grin even when he'd been furious at Illium. In those photos, he'd seen more courage than most would ever understand. Not only had Illium been recovering from grievous wounds at the time, he'd been reeling from the reappearance of his asshole of a father. And still, he'd refused to be anyone but Illium.

Wild, open of heart, and quick of wit.

Snow fell on the boy's face, but he didn't brush off the flakes, his eyes trained on Aodhan. It reminded Aodhan of how young Sameon, one of the little angels at the Refuge, looked at him at times. With the rapt attention of a child being told a tale.

So Aodhan kept on speaking.

"You're hundreds of years younger than Illium. As a result, your recovery will take longer." False hope could be more damaging than harsh truth. At the start of his captivity, Aodhan had clung to the hope that he could build up his strength and escape. Then his captors had brutalized him. Again and again.

It had broken a piece of him in the end.

"You'll also have to build up your strength in the aftermath," he said. "Even Illium had to do that," he pointed out as they overflew the hamlet.

The boy's head twisted without warning, his gaze trained downward. Small, mewling sounds erupted from his throat, one hand trying to reach downward.

A chill breath on Aodhan's neck. *Illium, do you see what he's doing?*

The blue-winged angel looked up, a dusting of snow on his hair and lashes. *Shit. He knows the settlement and he wants what's down there.*

Stomach churning, Aodhan flew on. In his arms, the boy

twisted to stare back at the settlement until the curtain of snow blanked it from view. Small, heartbreaking sounds of loss escaped his mouth—sounds that were eerie and unsettling, given for what he seemed to mourn.

The lights of the stronghold came into focus right as the snow picked up in ferocity; he saw movement in the east wing, efficient silhouettes against the windows. *I've told Li Wei to keep her people in the east wing and make sure the kitten remains with them.*

He landed, keeping his wings outstretched to protect the boy from the heavy precipitation. *Li Wei says Kai was in the kitchen preparing food for us. I've told her she can remain, but that she is not to leave the area until we give her the all-clear. It won't be difficult to keep the child away from her.*

He'd expected a strong reaction from Illium on the subject of Kai's safety, but, shoving his snow-dusted hair back from his face, Illium just nodded. His attention was on the child.

Who screamed and began to twist and claw for freedom the instant Aodhan stepped inside the walls of the stronghold. Crushing him tight to his own body, Aodhan walked quickly into the spacious, high-ceilinged living space that Suyin had used to gather with her people.

He put the panicked boy down by the huge wall of windows that overlooked the front courtyard where they'd landed. "You're not trapped underground." He kept his hands on those bony shoulders. "You can get out at any time." That wasn't quite true, not given what they suspected he'd done, but it was true enough in that this place was no coffin cut off from light.

Illium was already unlatching one of the windows.

The child shot a suspicious look Aodhan's way before darting over to the window and sticking his hand outside. He jerked it back after a few seconds, stared at the snow on his palm. Did the same thing three more times before he exhaled.

With the breath went the primal fear in his expression.

And when Aodhan asked him his name, he answered in a sweet, clear voice. "Zhou Jinhai."

Illium ducked into the kitchen while Aodhan stood beside the boy and spoke in a calm tone that seemed to near-hypnotize Jinhai.

Kai beamed at him from behind the large stone bench on which she was putting together a tray. "I haven't had a chance to make a more substantial meal," she began, but Illium shook his head.

"This is fine for now." His neck prickled at the idea of leaving Aodhan out there alone with the boy. Because, though a child Jinhai might be—and while Illium wanted to find him innocent—he had to accept that there was a high chance of him being a deadly threat.

After picking up the tray, he said, "You can head back to the rest of the staff." It'd be easier if he and Aodhan didn't have to worry about her. "Smoke?"

"I left her with Li Wei." A smile in her eyes, Kai touched the knot of her apron. "I don't mind staying here."

"Thank you, but we really need to focus on the situation." His entire body strained to be back beside Aodhan. "It could be dangerous for you to be nearby—we'll have to divide our attention."

It seemed to take her forever to remove her apron. "Perhaps after we are at the coastal citadel," she said, putting it on the counter, "you will have time to share a mug of mead with me?" There it was, that sweet boldness that reminded him so much of Kaia.

But where such an invitation from his long-dead lover would've caused him to blush and acquiesce, all he felt today was a wave of irritation. He'd given her a clear overview of the security situation, yet she continued to try to flirt. That didn't, however, give him leave to be harsh with her—not when she'd only made the invitation because he'd flirted with her first. Not much. But enough.

He was sorry for that now. He hadn't had any ill-intent and he'd done nothing to be accused of leading her on, for he'd flirted far more with others with no bruised feelings on either side, but Illium didn't like to hurt women even a touch. He could've responded with a playful comment that would've kept her happy until he figured out what he felt for this woman who was an echo of the past . . . but he knew already.

He'd known from the first. Had felt it from the first: a sweet, sharp nostalgia intermingled with affection. No roar of need, of wrenching love. Just a thing old and weathered and of a different time in his life.

Take away his initial shock at her appearance, and that was all that remained.

Frowning inwardly at the quiet knowledge he'd been refusing to face, for to face it was to alter the shape of him, he nonetheless managed to keep his expression warm as he said, "I think we must all lift a glass together. After journeying to the coast together, we will be fast friends."

A fading of her smile, but as with Kaia, bold and determined, she wasn't a woman to give up on what she wanted. "Please do call me if you need any help, Illium—I'll respond at once."

Only after she'd headed safely up the stairs did he move out into the living area. He didn't realize he'd been mentally holding his breath until he saw Aodhan safe and sound.

40

Aodhan had finished lighting the fire already set out on the hearth when Illium reappeared with a tray full of food. His stomach muscles unclenched. That hadn't taken long at all, not considering the fact Illium had been with Kai.

Stopping by where Aodhan stood near the fireplace—while Jinhai was pressed up against the windows—Illium kept his voice low as he said, "He say anything else?"

Aodhan fought the urge to stroke his hand over Illium's wing, the possessive need making his face flush. It was stupid to be irritated about Kai; she wasn't Kaia, who'd treated Illium with such a lack of care. And it wasn't like the young mortal could take Illium from Aodhan. The two of them had been friends too long, the tie between them a thing unbreakable.

"Jinhai," he told his friend, "was the name of his grandfather—Lijuan's father."

Aodhan nodded when Illium raised an eyebrow in a silent question. "It's truth. Suyin mentioned the name once when we were talking about their wider family. The elder Jinhai has been Sleeping an eon."

Nodding, Illium went to put the tray on a table near the windows that Aodhan had noticed already held a fresh pitcher of water and three glasses. Kai's handiwork no doubt. Since she'd had no idea they'd be returning with Jinhai, she must've been expecting an invitation to join them for the meal.

Shrugging off a renewed surge of irritation, Aodhan joined Illium, and they both took a seat. "Eat," he said to Jinhai, and picked up a slice of bread, on which he began to pile on cheese, sliced meat, more.

Jinhai watched warily for a second, then scurried over to join them. His table manners were impeccable. Perhaps not a surprise. Prior to her descent into obsession, Lijuan had been an archangel of great learning and culture, her cruelty informed by intelligence. She'd buried her son in that cavern—but she'd also provided him with clothing, lessons, language.

"Eat slowly," Illium directed when the boy began to shovel food into his mouth. "Otherwise, you'll just throw it all back up."

Jinhai had frozen at Illium's first words, but when that was all he said, the child kept on eating—but at a more reasonable pace.

Aodhan touched his mind to Illium's. *He seems too easily scared to have done what was done to the villagers. At least some of them would've tried to fight back.*

Leaning back in his chair, Illium rubbed at his face. *Sparkle, I want him to be innocent . . . but those people lived in a world where they believed Lijuan a goddess. How do you think they'd have reacted to an apparently scared, starving young angel with broken wings? Especially one who is so clearly the son of their goddess?*

He held up his hand before Aodhan could reply. *Even if the village was set up as Jinhai's kitchen and the home of his guards, I don't think all the residents were aware of his existence. I'd say, at most, they had knowledge of a nearby prison where some neighbors went to work, and that was it—and we know Lijuan inspired devotion. The guards entrusted with the knowledge would've held it close.*

Aodhan's hand clenched on the glass of water he'd just poured, for Illium's thinking aligned with his own. There was no reason for Lijuan to have entrusted an entire village with this secret; the more people who knew, the higher the chance of an accidental leak.

The others would've considered his sudden appearance a boon, a sign of Lijuan's triumphant return. Aodhan glanced once more at the boy. *You think he's capable of being so cunning?*

Illium's face twisted. *I have no fucking idea what the hell is going on.* Rising, he went back into the kitchen, returned with a bottle of mead and two new glasses that he filled, one for him, one for Aodhan.

"Not for you yet," he said to Jinhai. "Mead is a rite of passage after you reach your majority."

The boy said nothing, more interested in his food.

While the honey wine *was* a rite of passage, it did nothing to angelic systems. The taste, however, was a pleasant one familiar from their youth. This dark morn, it threatened to send Aodhan back to a party long ago, when he and Illium had both been lanky young angels finding their feet. It was during that party that he'd had his first sensual experience that had gone beyond kissing; it had been a thing of blushes and delight and exploratory touches of skin on skin in the secret hollow behind a large rock.

Aodhan had recently seen that warrior, for he was now part of one of Caliane's squadrons, and they'd both smiled at the youthful memory that had aged well. The warrior was now much in love with one of Caliane's angelic maidens, and had colored with happiness when he spoke of her.

Aodhan had felt a wave of profound joy for the other man, for he'd helped Aodhan in his darkest hour without ever knowing it. The memory of their long-ago shared joy, and others akin to it—of intimate touch that was welcome, of riotous hugs and embraces from Illium, loving pats on the cheek from Eh-ma, even his parents' absentminded strokes of his hair—he'd repeated them over and over in his mind during his captivity as a reminder that not all touch was unwanted. Not all touch made his skin crawl. Not all touch was a violation.

It hadn't worked to ward off the psychic scars, not for two centuries. But he'd had the memories with him in that time of pain and horror, and he'd had them as a foundation on which to stand when he began to heal at last.

Jinhai, on the other hand . . .

No fond memories of blushing youthful kisses or fumbled explorations for him, no memories of joy at all. Of course, it was all relative.

It might be that Lijuan's visits had been the most joyful thing in his existence.

I hate her more each time I look at him.

Illium's eyes met his. *Yes. I knew she was a monster, but this . . .*

Jinhai kept on eating.

Every so often, however, he'd glance at the window. Three times, he got up, stuck his hand through the one Illium had left cracked open, then returned to the table. By the time he leaned back in his chair, he'd eaten his way through what was in actuality a small amount of food for an angel of his age— immortal childhood growth required fuel, so young angels tended to *eat.*

Still, he appeared satiated. He'd just cracked his mouth in a huge yawn when the watch on Illium's wrist made a noise that had him jerking to attention.

Looking down, Illium tapped a finger on the screen a few times, then took off the device. "Here." He held it out to Jinhai. "You want it?"

The boy hesitated.

Illium grinned—that wicked, playful grin that charmed the world and made Aodhan shake his head in affection. "Let me show you something." He tapped the screen once to bring up an image of blocks. When he tapped it again, the blocks fell apart. "Use your fingers to move them back into place."

From what Aodhan and Illium had discovered in the

cavern, Jinhai'd had no exposure to current technology, but he picked up the game within minutes. Illium continued to give him instructions with the warm patience that made him a favorite of children and small creatures, until even this boy raised in the cold dark offered him a small smile.

Another conquest, Aodhan thought with an inward smile as he leaned back and let his friend take over. His sister had asked him once if he ever got jealous of Illium's way of making friends and charming people wherever he went.

The idea had been such a foreign concept to him that he'd just stared at her. Illium's heart, his unfettered joy in life, his playfulness, all the things that made him so attractive to others, were the same things that had first drawn Aodhan to him. He could still remember Illium coming up to him, asking if he wanted to go play. Aodhan could've never been so brave; he'd been one to stand back, watch the world.

No, he'd never envied Illium's way with people. He adored that part of him as much as he did all the parts most of the world never saw—even when the blue-winged angel pushed him to the edge of endurance.

In front of him, Jinhai fought heavy eyelids.

"You can play after a rest," Aodhan murmured. "If you like, we'll bring in blankets and pillows so you can sleep next to the windows."

A ragged nod was the answer.

Leaving Illium with him, Aodhan went to grab the bedding. He returned to find Jinhai tucked into a large window nook that boasted a cushioned seat. This was an old stronghold—the cold had to be coming through the glass, but the boy had turned that way, curling his body inward. The watch sat on his left wrist, his right hand cupped possessively over it even in sleep.

He didn't stir when Aodhan tucked a pillow under his head and covered him in the blankets. Afterward, he and Illium moved close to the fire, from where the boy had no hope of hearing their conversation. "Can he do anything dangerous with that watch?"

"No," Illium said. "I blocked everything except the games—and the GPS tracker. We don't have to keep him in sight as long as he has that on his wrist. I can find him using my phone."

Clever Bluebell. "He won't be able to get far in this snow, regardless." It was coming down in sheets now. "For better or worse, we're stuck here." He and Illium were powerful enough to fly through the snow, but not with Jinhai *and* the staff.

"Li Wei's people can come into the kitchen if they need to," Illium began, but Aodhan shook his head.

"I spoke to her when I went to get the bedding. Anyone who needed food ate well before our return, and the vampires fed then as well." Li Wei had a timetable and her team knew to follow it. "The ones who had the swing shift are all already asleep, while the rest of them intend to continue their work in the east wing—they won't need breakfast for at least two more hours."

"How about you?" Illium pushed a hand through his hair. "Up for a proper meal? That tray wasn't anywhere near enough for me."

"Yes, and you need a haircut." He tugged on the strands that had already fallen right back over Illium's eye.

A lopsided grin. "Remember that time—"

"—when we were little angels and I gave you a haircut?" He shook his head when Illium grinned. "No. Eh-ma would not forgive such a massacre a second time around."

Wicked laughter in the aged gold. "Come on, scaredy, let's eat." His wing brushed Aodhan's chest as he moved past.

Happy . . . just happy, Aodhan followed him into the kitchen—but made sure to leave the door ajar. He didn't think Jinhai was in any mood to attempt an escape, but he might panic at waking up alone. At least this way, he'd hear the sounds of their voices, be able to find them.

"Yes, let's," he said once he was in the kitchen proper. "I haven't eaten properly for a few days."

Illium had moved enough around the counter by then that Aodhan could see him, so he caught the sudden tightness of his jaw.

He narrowed his eyes. "What?"

"Nothing."

"You look like you're about to bite your tongue in half."

A shrug, the fluid ripple of muscle. "*Someone* keeps biting off my head for daring to care, so zip." He mimed zipping up his mouth—but those golden eyes were doing plenty of talking.

Provoked, Aodhan muttered, "Missing Kai, are you?"

"What?" Illium scowled. "Since she was up when we got home, she's probably asleep now."

Aodhan expected to see yearning on Illium's face at the reminder of the mortal woman. All he saw was irritation. Aimed squarely at Aodhan. "I am not biting off your head," he said as they gathered supplies for the huge sandwiches to which they were both partial.

Illium hummed a happy tune—and ignored him.

"Illium."

His friend opened up a roll of salami that one of the mortals had prepared from hunted meat. "Do you want a piece of this?" He whacked at the salami like it had done him a personal insult.

Temper igniting, Aodhan clamped his hand around Illium's wrist. It flexed under his touch, strong and with the tendons taut. But Illium didn't make any violent gestures. He just said, "I need my hand to chop this."

It was the second time Illium had rejected contact with him and he hated it as much as the first time. Regardless, he forced his fingers to open. "What is wrong with you?" he ground out as he tore a large loaf of sourdough bread in half. "I thought we were—"

"You're standing too close."

Aodhan was not a man inclined to a hot temper. Except with Illium. So fine, Blue wanted to fight? They'd fight until they had this out!

41

"You know what?" he said. "You've had a fucking burr up your butt since you landed in China and I'm over it!"

Illium slammed the knife point down in the wooden chopping block and spun to face Aodhan. "*I've* had a burr up my butt?" His eyes glowed in a way that should've been impossible for anyone who wasn't an archangel.

It terrified Aodhan—not for himself, but for Illium. He was too young, far too young. And it was crystal clear that the Cascade hadn't fully reclaimed the gifts it had tried to force on him. Power lingered in his veins—those veins glowed softly against his skin even now.

But Aodhan was too angry to be distracted by the eerily lovely sight. "You've been snarling at me since the fucking minute you landed."

"I. Have. Not." Illium poked his chest with a pointed finger. "I have been extremely *polite*, you big, sparkling asshole." Then he turned back to the board, pulled out the knife and began to slice the salami with such speed that Aodhan didn't dare interrupt him, lest he injure himself.

He did, however, throw up his hands. "That's your version of picking a fight with me and you know it!" he pointed out. "The last time you were *polite* to me like that was when I was with Ylir."

"That's because Ylir was a prick who treated you like a shiny trophy." Illium's voice caught for a second. "He's the fucking reason we fought and you flew off alone that day. I was off duty for a week, was supposed to go on that courier run with you."

Aodhan blinked, having never thought of it that way. "They would've just waited till the next time I was alone, you idiot! They were stalkers!" Sachieri and Bathar had told him all their plans, all they'd done to prepare to take him. "Don't you tell me you've been carrying guilt over that or I swear I'll kick your blue ass!"

"My ass is not blue. Unlike yours, it doesn't sparkle, either."

"Oh, very mature. I see how you're avoiding the subject." He'd deal with Illium's misplaced guilt before this was done—because it was all part and parcel of the same thing.

Having finished slicing the salami, Illium now began to chop the defenseless meat into tiny, precise squares. "You were all 'Oh, Ylir is so handsome,' 'Oh, Illium, he only calls me cutie because he loves me.'" A roll of the eyes. "You were a fucking blooded warrior and he was calling you *cutie* and patting you on the head!"

"He did not call me cutie!" Aodhan argued.

"Close enough."

It was infuriating but Aodhan couldn't actually argue with that. Because Illium was right. In the language they'd used at the time, it had been a "cute" sounding word. "Stop trying to distract me. We're talking about you, not Ylir."

"*You're* talking about something. I'm just trying to make my goddamn sandwich." He finally stopped chopping to stare down at his mass of pulverized salami. "Shit." Grabbing a pan, he stuck it on the stove. "Guess I'll have mince now."

Fighting the urge to shake him, Aodhan stepped to the

living area door and glanced out. Jinhai was still fast asleep, his breathing so deep and even that it was clear he was in no danger of waking up.

He returned to Illium's side at the counter, picking up an onion from a basket along the way. When he threw it without warning, Illium shot out a hand and caught it, began to peel it with ruthless efficiency. The two of them could both cook—it was part of the training for all young angels, regardless of vocation.

"Still eating onions like they're going extinct, I see," he said when Illium didn't speak.

"Maybe my onion breath will make you keep your distance."

Wanting to scream, Aodhan began to slap together a sandwich. He put on cheese, pickle, whatever else came to hand without really thinking about it.

"Really?" Illium muttered. "You like black olives now? What? Suyin taught you how to appreciate them?"

Aodhan glanced down, saw that he had, indeed, added the hated black olives to his sandwich. Once, he might've stood his ground and forced down the olives just to prove to Illium that he didn't know everything—but he'd grown out of that around the time he got his first wooden sword.

He picked off the seedless olives and put them on Illium's plate.

Rolling his eyes, Illium ate two, then continued to make his monstrosity of a salami-onion-who-knows-what-else mixture—and not talk.

Aodhan had rarely seen his friend in this kind of a mood, but when it happened, it tended to blow over fast. Today, it showed no signs of fading.

This, Aodhan realized too late, was serious. "Are you going to tell me what I did?"

Illium's shoulders knotted at the quiet question. He'd been ready to keep up their fighting as long as it took—it was easier to keep Aodhan at a distance with snark and bite than it was to face how much the other angel had hurt him.

He'd thought he was over it, that—given their renewed comfort with one another—they could just slide back into their previous relationship, but then he'd had to bite his tongue against his natural tendency to look after the people who mattered to him—as Aodhan mattered so deeply to him. And he'd realized that nothing was the same. He and Aodhan, they couldn't just ignore the past year and more.

But the words stuck in his throat, too big to say.

He focused on his culinary creation with an attention that was all but blinding. Like most warriors, he could eat anything. Aodhan would eat even olives if he needed to do so to survive. So he wasn't really thinking about what he was throwing into what he'd decided to call a stew.

Sounded better than "screw-it-all-salami."

An echo of Ellie's laughter in his mind, how she would've grinned and told him he should stick to that name for his mess of a creation. But the thought was a fleeting distraction, his skin burning from the force of Aodhan's attention. "Stop staring at me."

"I can't even look at you now?" Aodhan was the one with a knife this time, and he whacked a giant hunk off the sourdough he'd broken in half. "What's next, you're going to banish me to my room? Won't work. I banished myself for two hundred years and I'm not going back there."

Illium's hand squeezed the handle of the pan before he turned to pin Aodhan with a disbelieving gaze. "You're making bad jokes about something you refused to talk about for fucking centuries? What's changed? Let me guess. You and Suyin opened up to each other, had long heart-to-hearts."

"If we did, what business of yours would it be?"

Illium threw something else into his angry stew. Chili peppers? Cinnamon? Who the hell knew? Who the hell cared? "None," he said, even as his breathing accelerated. "It's none of my business at all. I've only been your friend for five hundred fucking years."

"Enough!" A tone in Aodhan's voice that Illium had heard very, *very* rarely over their many years of friendship.

Then he turned off the stove with a decisive hand, and shifted so that they stood face-to-face, toe-to-toe. With Aodhan's slight height advantage, they weren't exactly eye to eye, and the fact he had to tip his head back a fraction to meet the blue-green translucence of Aodhan's gaze infuriated Illium even more.

"What is *wrong* with you?" Aodhan bit out, all bright light ablaze with emotion. "Why are you so angry? You've been angry since the moment you landed, and we both know it, so don't you try to deny it."

Illium wasn't about to beg for attention, not from anyone—and especially not from Aodhan, at whose side he'd stood through thick and thin, pain and hope. But neither was he about to allow his friend to pin the current fucked-up state of their relationship on him.

"You're interested in how I'm doing all of a sudden? Funny, when you were fine ignoring me for an entire year. Guess you forgot how to write letters or make phone calls." He slapped his forehead. "Oh, my bad, you didn't forget. I just didn't make your list." Then, despite his urge to touch Aodhan, even if it was to shove him away, he stepped back. "I'm giving it to you—the distance you made it clear you wanted. Now get the hell out of my face so I can finish making my food."

Excuses flittered through Aodhan's mind, some of them even believable, but he brushed them all aside, his skin hot. He *had* frozen Illium out over the past months. It had been a self-protective act driven by angry desperation—and it had been a cowardly thing that shamed him.

"You don't let go, Blue," he found himself admitting, anguish in his voice. "You hold on so tight that I couldn't breathe."

Illium's face went pale, the spark fading from his eyes as

he dropped the red pepper he'd been holding onto the chopping board. "You really do see me as a cage."

The whispered words hit Aodhan like a blow to the solar plexus. "No! *No!*" He went to grab Illium's shoulders, but the other man stumbled back, his legendary grace nowhere in evidence and his hand clutching at the counter to his left to maintain balance.

"Shit." Aodhan spun to slam his hands down on the counter. "You kept *looking after me.*" He glanced at Illium to see incomprehension on his face. "I needed looking after for a long time, I'll accept that."

He hated what he'd allowed himself to become in those years after his capture, *hated* it, and he'd finally taken responsibility for his actions. Only, Blue refused to see that. "But I don't need that kind of care anymore," he bit out. "I'm a warrior angel you trust to watch your back in any battle, but in anything else? You second-guess me, try to double-check my instincts, attempt to wrap me up in cotton wool."

"Looking after you is a crime now?" Illium snapped, his hand fisted on the counter, and his wings bunched in.

It devastated Aodhan to hurt Illium, but they had to lance this boil, clear the slow-acting poison of it. "Remember that fight we had—I had information about the Luminata through my contacts, and you came down on me like a ton of bricks."

Aodhan could still remember the rage that had scalded him in the aftermath. "As if I was still that broken angel in the infirmary, unable to defend myself, my mind so wounded that I was nothing but prey."

Illium swallowed, his gaze bruised—but the spark, it had reignited. "Do you know how hard it was for me to watch you fight your way back to yourself?" Raw emotion in every word. "Now you're pissed at me for being protective?"

"Yes." Aodhan wasn't going to back off, not on this point. "If you want us to stay friends, you can't pull the protective shit, Blue. I don't have the capacity to deal with it anymore." It was as if he'd woken out of a long sleep and any hint of being coddled or protected enraged him. "It reminds me of who I was for a long time—and I fucking hate that pathetic creature!"

Eyes afire, Illium stepped closer. "Don't you *dare* talk about yourself that way!" He scowled, no longer in any way distant now that he was defending Aodhan. "You survived an evil that would've killed other angels!"

Aodhan had been told that over and over, and it made no difference. "I let those bastards scar me to the point that I put *myself* in a cage." He slammed a fist against his chest, his anger a hot, hard thing that cut. "But I've broken free at last—and I won't let anyone else put me back in a box. Any fucking kind of a box."

Illium folded his arms, his biceps flexing. "Caring for you enough to look out for you isn't trying to control you," he argued, red slashes of color on his cheekbones. "It's what normal people do for those they love."

"Oh?" Aodhan rose to his full height, faced his friend. "When was the last time you allowed me to do anything protective for you?"

"When my asshole father decided to reappear like a bad smell," Illium shot back. "Or was that another sparkling angel who dropped out of the sky onto my mother's rooftop?"

"Listen to yourself. You had that on the tip of your tongue because it's one of the very few times in two hundred years where I haven't been taking but giving."

Illium's eyebrows lowered. "You're not a taker, Aodhan. If there's one thing I know, it's that. You give away your art. You give away your time. You moved to the cauldron of death because Suyin needed a second!"

"Cauldron of death?"

A one-shoulder shrug. "It was all that came to me. But my point stands. You don't take, Aodhan. You give."

"Except when it comes to you," Aodhan whispered, suddenly exhausted. Bracing both hands on the counter, he shook his head. "We've fallen into a pattern where you protect and shield me from the world, Blue, and I won't have it."

This time when he raised his hand and touched the side of

Illium's face, his friend didn't push him away. "We were never unbalanced before I broke. That's why we worked. Each as strong as the other."

Illium's throat moved. "Adi, I can't help looking after my people." A frustrated plea. "That's who I am."

"Is it? Or is it someone you've had to become?" Lady Sharine was now awake, but she'd been asleep for a long, long time, Illium her caretaker as much as her son. Then had come Aodhan.

Two of the most important pillars of Illium's life had shattered, and he'd used his wide shoulders to prop them up. "It's time for me and Eh-ma to stand on our own two feet." He gripped Illium tighter. "It's time for us to be your support rather than the other way around."

"I never minded," Illium said, raising his hand to grip Aodhan's wrist with a strong hand callused from relentless sword work. "Not for a single instant. Not when it came to you, and not when it came to Ma."

"I know." That just made their crime all the worse. They'd corrupted Illium's generous nature, exacerbating his tendency to give until he had nothing left for himself.

That it had been without intent didn't alter the damage done.

"I *know*," he repeated. "But my need for that kind of protection is in the past now. The man I am today? What I need is for you to treat me as an equal, as you did before Sachieri and Bathar."

Illium sucked in a breath. "You really are ready to talk about that." He made a face. "I guess I should stop sniping at Suyin and thank her."

Illium's protectiveness toward his people had always been laced with a big dose of possessiveness. If he had a flaw, it was that. And in the grand scheme of things, with his giving heart to balance it out, it was nothing.

"I haven't said a word to Suyin about this." Aodhan squeezed the side of the other man's face. "If I was ever going to talk to anyone, it was always going to be you. *Always*."

The simple, honest words lay between them, a peace offering.

Releasing his wrist, Illium turned back to his aborted meal. "Want a bowl of angry stew? We can sit by the fire and eat and you can talk if you want."

Aodhan fought his urge to bristle, because there Illium went, taking care of him again . . . but they did have to talk about this. It was time.

Our memories make us.
Even the darkest of them all.

—*Archangel Raphael*

42

The fire was still going, the large room warm, but Aodhan stoked it up further after glancing at their sleeping guest—and prisoner. The boy was huddled into himself. Possibly because of cold, but more likely as a result of a life lived in the dark.

"He's sleeping peacefully despite that tight fetal position," Illium said in a quiet tone after he put their food on a low table Aodhan had carried over to place in front of a large sofa that faced the hearth.

It had been a popular seat while Suyin's people were in residence—but only among the mortals and vampires. The winged members of the household tended to default to the armchairs. No official stance, just a thing of comfort—it was difficult to create sofas with backs and cushions that allowed egress for wings as well as personal space.

To share a sofa often meant an inevitable brush of wings against another.

That might've been a point of difficulty for him and Illium when Illium first arrived, but they were past that now . . . though nothing was back to normal. A tension hovered between them, a knowledge of drastic change.

So be it.

He'd been stuck in amber far too long. He needed to grow, to break out of that rigid shell. That it'd leave behind shattered debris was manifest—and a fact he hadn't considered enough.

Not once, however, had he thought of Illium as a piece of that debris. No matter how angry he'd been, how angry he still became at times, Illium was as much a part of his life as the sky and the air. A necessity.

He couldn't imagine—didn't want to imagine a life without his Blue.

"Here." Illium thrust a bowl of stew into his hand. "I tasted a spoonful. It's weirdly delicious."

Taking it, Aodhan sat. Illium followed, half his wing lying atop Aodhan's. With every other person in this world, Aodhan was always aware of any such contact. Even with those whose touch he welcomed, some small part of his brain was always conscious of the physical contact.

The sole exception was Illium.

Any contact between them felt natural, just the way it should be. Today, however, he found himself conscious of the warmth and weight and strength of Illium's wings. Another time, he'd have thought nothing of reaching out and examining a feather, checking a tendon. But . . . things had changed.

Aodhan had changed them.

Sitting back, he forced himself to eat a bite of the salami concoction. "This is the strangest stew I've ever eaten, but it's good."

"Told you." Illium propped his feet up on an ottoman he'd dragged over, then leaned forward and grabbed a hunk of the bread that Aodhan had chopped. Chopped, not sliced. The weird shapes went well with the angry stew.

They ate in silence for a while, until Aodhan found himself speaking. Jinhai was too far away to hear them, even had he been feigning sleep. Which he wasn't. That kind of almost-not-breathing only occurred when an angel was in a deep resting state so profound it was close to the healing rest of *anshara*.

"I think," he said, "what scarred me most of all was the mundanity of Sachieri and Bathar."

Putting down his empty bowl, Illium picked up half of the enormous olive-free sandwich that Aodhan had prepared. And he listened.

"They were so ordinary," Aodhan continued, his food forgotten. "It wasn't like with Lijuan—and seeing her megalomania in full bloom really brought that into focus for me. She was evil on a grand scale. A being of power and age who either chose to use that power in a terrible way—or who lost herself over the course of her long lifetime."

Illium snorted. "You're being too kind." A glance at the window nook. "She was evil. She chose evil. Over and over again, she chose evil."

Aodhan couldn't do anything but agree. "She was also what we think monsters should be—a storm of malevolence. Not an angel you'd walk past and not notice except as a fleeting passerby. Not dangerous. Not a threat."

When Illium nudged at his bowl to remind him to eat, Aodhan snapped, "Leave me be." He knew he was being irrational, but at this point in time, even the smallest hint from Illium that he needed care of any kind was sandpaper on his skin.

Illium's chest expanded as he took a deep breath, but rather than arguing, he returned to demolishing his half of the sandwich.

Aodhan put down his bowl. He had too much inside him, needed to release it. "But Sachieri and Bathar, I never really noticed them. I knew of them in a vague way because they were a limited part of Elijah's wider court, but otherwise, they were just ordinary angels going about their business." He looked at Illium. "Does that make me sound arrogant?"

"No," Illium said at once, his eyes staring off into the distance. "In simple terms, they weren't a part of your life or your duties—you had no reason to pay them any special attention. You know of Priya Anjalika, don't you? She's shy and small and hides away in her office, but you know of her because she's part of your world.

"But if I asked a senior squadron commander in Titus's court about her, he'd just look at me blankly. She might be an important component of the Tower's internal machinery, but she's not a threat he has to monitor—and is otherwise not in the orbit of his attention."

"You put it so clearly." Cutting through the fog. "Priya Anjalika, however, is critical to the Tower." A specialist in accounts, she could do sums in her head faster than anyone else Aodhan knew. "Sachieri and Bathar were only tied to Elijah in the most nominal way, and otherwise just lived their lives."

Aodhan thought back to all he'd learned of his captors in the aftermath. "Sachieri had lands that mortals and vampires farmed for her, and Bathar managed a small number of properties he'd acquired over the years. Pooled together, their income allowed them to live a life comfortable and settled."

"Normal," Illium murmured. "Ordinary angels living an ordinary life."

"Not people who rode into battle, or people who picked fights or started controversies. They might've been the neighbors of my parents or a strolling couple I ran across in an art gallery—immortals who found happiness in a calm walk through eternity."

He realized he was leaning forward, his hands fisted on his thighs. "That's why I felt no sense of threat when Sachieri waved me down from the sky. It was gray that day, but she was wearing a gown of vivid yellow—impossible to miss."

He'd seen her before he realized she was in distress, and for a heartbeat, his mind had noticed only the beauty of the composition, that splash of shining yellow against the craggy rocks and sky-piercing forest.

"The way she was collapsed on the ground under a huge tree with broken branches," he told Illium, "I thought she'd tangled her wings on a sharp branch that she hadn't noticed and fallen, needed help . . ."

Lifting his hand, he pressed it over his heart, rubbed. "The crossbow bolt struck my throat before I knew what was happening. And her face . . . right in front of me as I staggered and bled, this greedy, triumphant look to her as she punched a bolt into my heart." A memory of blinding shock, his brain struggling to comprehend what was happening. "I should've moved, acted faster, but—"

"Screw that, Adi." Having put aside his sandwich, Illium leaned forward in an echo of Aodhan's pose—so he could turn and glare at Aodhan. "They might not have been angels of power, but Sachieri was four *thousand* years your senior, Bathar not much younger.

"You were only three hundred, with nothing of their life experience—and none at all with evil that wears a friendly face. Hell, even Raphael would go down if you took out his heart. Maybe only for a second, but that blow is a massive shock to our systems."

Aodhan looked down at the ground. "I know you're right, but for so long, I kept running those moments in my head, kept telling myself that there was a way I could've escaped— even though I knew full well I was close to collapse the instant they destroyed my heart." Sachieri had chosen the heaviest possible bolt, fired it with a precision she'd honed over constant practice—all for that one brutal instant.

"After she hit my heart," he continued because now that he'd started, he'd tell Illium all of it, "he shot me in each wing. Then he sliced off half of one wing." Aodhan couldn't remember the pain of that, his mind already shutting down as his young body struggled to heal catastrophic damage.

"Fuckers." Illium hissed out the word, his eyes wet. "*Fuckers.* I wish we could make them rise from the dead so we could torture them over and over again."

Jerking up his head, Aodhan gripped the back of Illium's neck, squeezed. "*No.*" He held the angry, devastated gold of his friend's gaze. "I won't have it, Blue. I won't have their evil reaching out from beyond death to take hold of you. Don't you let them do that."

Illium's jaw worked. "I can't not hate them."

"Fine. But don't you allow their poison to seep into your blood." He squeezed the strong column of Illium's neck once more, Illium's skin hot and smooth under his touch. "They were punished. They're dead, and worse, forgotten by the vast majority of our kind. If you give them residence in your head, then you keep them alive."

Illium stared at the fire . . . but gave a jagged nod.

No doubt, it'd come up again in the future—if and when it did, Aodhan would deal with it. He *could* deal with it because he'd long moved past hate, banishing his captors to the oblivion they deserved. But he knew that had their roles been reversed, had his laughing, playful Illium been the one taken and tortured, he would've hated, hated hard and for a long, long time.

"Their very normalcy," he said, picking up the thread of the story, "it broke my trust in the world."

Illium's wings began to glow, his body rigid, but he didn't interrupt.

Aodhan ran his knuckles down his friend's spine regardless, pulling him back from the edge of the abyss on which he walked. "I didn't trust my instincts after returning to the Refuge. How could I? When these two people who seemed so normal had done that to me? When the ordinary, everyday people who were their staff had helped them? How could I trust anyone?"

Illium's body remained a thing of granite, but he reached out to place one hand over Aodhan's knee. As if anchoring him to the here and now so that he wouldn't fall into the past. Or perhaps anchoring himself from falling into a rage. They sat that way, one hand on the other, as Aodhan kept on speaking.

"You know what they did to me." Sachieri and Bathar had created panels in the box that they could unlock and lift at will, so that they could reach in and touch him . . . possess him. "I couldn't escape them, they made sure of it." Whether that meant starving him, or wounding him over and over again.

"But the worst, the absolute worst of it all was how Sachieri would sit with me and tell me how very beautiful I was, how much she loved me, and how she knew I'd love her back if she just gave me a little more time."

He shook his head. "She was as sane as you or me—yet she seemed to believe every word she spoke. Bathar was sane, too. But he enjoyed coming up with new and cruel ways to hurt me. It made me wonder if I could ever trust the faces people wear, if I could ever believe what came out of their mouths."

Wings stirring, he thrust both his hands through his hair. "Then what happened in the Medica . . ."

The memory sat between them, a living, breathing malevolence.

Keir's assistant at the time of Aodhan's rescue had been an angel named Remus. A healer held in high esteem and considered honorable. As such, all those who'd watched over Aodhan's badly wounded body had taken Remus at his word when he'd told them that Aodhan was becoming stressed having them around all the time, that he needed space alone to heal.

Remus had made even Illium leave.

And then he'd whispered in Aodhan's ear that Aodhan was a "broken doll" and that broken dolls needed masters. Lost in nightmares, Aodhan had nonetheless seen the man for the monster he was, and blanked him. Then Illium had caught Remus in the act—the end result of that had been a beating so bad that it had almost separated Remus's head from his spine.

He would've died then and there if Aodhan hadn't managed to call Illium back from the edge. His splintered bones and crushed organs, however, hadn't been the end of Remus's punishment. The instant he healed enough to walk, he was banished from the Refuge. The angel was a pariah among their kind, shunned and alone for all eternity.

But none of that erased what Remus had done, what he'd *been*.

"Remus was meant to be a healer. Keir, wise and perceptive, trusted him to look after me. And he did that? Try to break me? To make me into his puppet?"

Exhaling hard, he rose, his wing sliding out from under

Illium's. The sudden break in contact, the loss of the heavy warmth, it made his stomach clench, but he couldn't sit still. Crossing to the mantel, he pressed his hands against the old and polished wood, staring down into the dance of the flames below. "It screwed me up for a long time."

"Was that why you didn't want me to touch you?" Illium asked, his voice gentle. "It's okay if that's how it was, Adi. I was never mad at you about that. I just wanted you to heal, any way it took."

Aodhan swiveled, saw that Illium's expression held no hurt, just worry . . . and love. A love that had stood beside Aodhan through time, through pain, through anger. "No," he said very precisely. "You are one of the few people about whom I've never had a question in my mind." No matter what else got screwed up between them, this, Aodhan would not do—ruin the trust that had bonded them since childhood.

So he told the truth, even though it scraped off his skin, left him raw and exposed. "I didn't want you to touch me because I felt dirty and wrong and broken."

Illium gripped at his own hair, his jaw clenched. "How could you—" A hiss of breath. "I want to shake you sometimes." Releasing his abused hair, he took two deep breaths, then leaned back into the sofa. "Look at me, being all calm and civilized even though I'd rather wash your mouth out with soap."

Aodhan felt his lips twitch. Such an unexpected moment of light in this walk into evil. So very Illium. "Your control is astonishing," he said—and, if Illium wanted to shake him, he wanted to hold Illium right that moment.

The blue-winged angel had made this so much better, so much easier. "I know it was a stupid thing to think," he muttered. "But I wasn't exactly in a healthy mental space. Talking with the healers, that helped. And having Eh-ma around, ready to hold me at any time, that helped even more."

Illium's expression softened. "You permitted her touch because you knew she wouldn't understand why you were flinching from her."

"I think we both underestimated her, Blue. But yes, back then, that's why I let her close even though I felt like I was contaminating her." He'd had to fight every second not to pull away. "Then slowly, it became okay. She was Eh-ma and she was fractured, too, and it was all right."

The heat from the fire glowed against his wings. "She was the reason I started to accept that while I wasn't the same man I was before it all happened, being different wasn't such a bad thing.

"The art I made after I could create again, it was different, too, and Eh-ma taught me that there was nothing wrong with that. 'We grow, Aodhan' she said to me. 'Our scars change our brushstrokes.'"

"She's extraordinary, isn't she?" Illium's smile turned a little crooked. "Sometimes, I think that I must be biased, because I'm her son, but then I hear about another thing she's done, and my pride expands all over again.

"Titus calls her his small but fierce sun, and she is that, don't you think?" The light from the fire picked up the silver filaments in his feathers, this angel strong and courageous and as fierce a light in this world as his mother. "Even when she was at her most lost, she glowed with life and warmth."

"Yes." A simple answer, because it was all true. "But Eh-ma wasn't the only reason I started to come back to myself." He took a step toward Illium. "The—"

A shrill sound from the window nook.

43

Jinhai had jerked awake and was staring out into a world gray with dawnlight under a rain of snow, both his hands pressed to the glass. They began to move toward him as one, and were by his side by the time he began scrabbling at the latch Aodhan had closed to keep out the cold.

Aodhan didn't stop him, just said, "What is it?"

His voice made the boy jolt, his eyes rounding as he stared at Aodhan. As if he'd just realized he wasn't alone. Chest heaving, he turned, looked at Illium, then back at Aodhan. Then he did the oddest thing. He reached out a single trembling hand and touched Aodhan's arm before jerking back his hand as fast.

"We're real," Aodhan said. "You didn't dream us."

Jinhai went as if to speak, but then wrenched his face to the glass again, making small, mewling sounds in his throat as he pressed his hands to the clear pane, his body straining.

"What's out there?" Illium asked. "Is it danger?"

A quick shake of the head.

"Do you want to be outside?"

Another shake of the head, those eyes so like his mother's—but with a heartrending innocence to them—looking imploringly at Illium.

"Talk to us," Illium said with the same patient gentleness as earlier. "We've helped till now. We'll continue to help you."

Skittering eyes, jagged breath.

A trapped animal sound.

Neither one of them pushed, for that would only engender fear.

Then, a single word potent with teary need: "*Quon.*"

A name. A person.

Aodhan looked out into the steadily falling snow, saw only a sheet of white. "Is Quon out there?"

Jinhai nodded.

Two chairs, Illium said, his cheekbones blades against his skin. *A very large bed.*

"Does he need help?" Aodhan searched the landscape, but knew the boy could be hiding behind a tree, in the shadow of one of Zhangjiajie's pillars. "I'll go out and bring him—"

A sudden darting movement, Jinhai's hand locking around Aodhan's forearm. "He hurts you." The melodic clarity of his voice suddenly a rasp of sound. "He wears your skin."

Fuck.

Aodhan echoed Illium's mental reaction, though he managed to keep it from escaping his mouth. "Quon did that to the people in the hamlet?" When the boy only stared at him, he said, "Took off their skins?"

A spasmodic nod. "Take the skin. Wear the skin. Be the person." It was a singsong sound. Almost as if Jinhai was repeating something he'd heard.

"Who said that?" Aodhan murmured, while Illium remained in the background, his eyes on the snow outside. "Quon?"

"Mother said. Wear many skins. Many faces."

Ice crawled through Aodhan's veins. "Your mother? His mother?"

"Our mother."

Do you think she realized they didn't understand she was speaking metaphorically? Revulsion in Illium's voice, directed at the Archangel of Death. *Surely even Lijuan wouldn't turn her own children into monsters?*

Blue, she buried them underground. They were always going to be monsters. Aodhan met his friend's eyes for a moment, wished he could grab hold of him in a hug, protect him from his own soft heart.

Even as the thought passed through his head, Illium said, "You stay with Jinhai." He shook his head when Aodhan would've argued. *He's bonded to you, will panic if you try to leave.*

Aodhan looked down at the way the child clung to him. Illium might as well not have been present for all the attention Jinhai gave him—though he still wore Illium's watch. As if he'd forgotten Illium now he had no use for him. That, too, was disturbing. But one horror at a time.

"Be careful."

A speaking look from the man Aodhan had banned from looking after him, but Illium didn't point out the hypocrisy of his statement. Instead, a small flash of a smile flicked over his lips as his voice entered Aodhan's head: *If a crazy child can bring me down and skin me, he deserves to wear my stupid dead pelt.*

Scowling at the other man was a waste of time—Illium was already heading to the door. He reappeared outside the window soon afterward, a dazzling brilliance of blue in the white.

Aodhan's heart stopped.

Sometimes, he forgot the sheer depth of Illium's masculine beauty, and then it'd strike him hard without warning, especially when light sparkled in Illium's eyes and a playful smile flirted with his lips. But it faded too soon into solemn vigilance as he said, *Ask Jinhai how he knows his brother is out here.*

When Aodhan did, Jinhai said, "I know. He knows. Two skins. One son."

After repeating that to Illium, Aodhan said, *I don't know what Lijuan thought she was doing, but it appears she achieved some type of bond between them.*

Or—Illium frowned as the snow settled on his hair, his shoulders, his wings—*they might be twins.*

Twins were rare in angelkind, but when it did happen, those births came with a high chance of some kind of a mental connection. Parents of angelic twins knew to watch for that during early childhood. Without intervention, the bonded ones could often begin to act like one being, the stronger personality overwhelming the weaker.

"Has Quon always been in your life?" Aodhan asked the slender boy who stared out the window. "And you in his?"

Jinhai touched his own face with fluttering fingertips. "Two skins. One face. One son."

Twins, he confirmed to Illium. "Can you point toward your brother's exact location?"

Jinhai did so without argument and Aodhan passed on the direction to Illium. His friend took off in a flurry of swirling snow in front of a rapt Jinhai, soon disappearing into the leaden sky. Aodhan's heart thundered, every part of him straining to follow Illium into the fall of white.

He hated that Illium was out there alone in this cold and unfriendly place filled with hidden dangers, wished he could protect Illium as Illium had so long protected him. Would Illium even allow such protectiveness? No, was Aodhan's instinctive reaction, but then he paused. Had anyone ever asked Illium? After all, Aodhan's Blue had simply shouldered responsibility after responsibility.

The only person on whom Illium openly relied was Raphael, and that was a relationship that had been born during his childhood. While he took emotional comfort from Elena, he didn't expect her to protect him—he saw it as *his* duty to watch over her. As he'd watched over Eh-ma. As he'd

watched over Aodhan. As he'd watched over Kaia until the
day she was placed on her funeral pyre.

Illium blinked the driving snow from his eyes, then winced
at the shards of ice the sky decided to throw down like
deadly confetti. It wouldn't do him any damage, but fuck it
was cold. *I hate the cold,* he muttered to Aodhan, the mental
contact a thing of ease, the groove long worn in their minds.
  No you don't. You just hate it when it's work not play.
  Illium's responding grin faded as fast as it had come. So
without effort they fell back into their old ways, into paths
trodden over hundreds of years. But that was the problem,
wasn't it? Old ways. Old patterns.
  Flying as low as he could without risking a crash into the
trees, he scanned the ground without surcease, but saw no
signs of life. The snow had erased all footprints, all evidence
of life of any kind. But he didn't stop looking. Illium knew
one set of bonded angelic twins. The two always knew each
other's location, even when divided by an entire state. If Jinhai said his twin was out here, he was out here.
  Thinking he'd seen a flash of movement, he landed in
warrior silence, and allowed the snow to obscure his wings.
Then he listened. Only to hear the soft, hushed silence that
snow alone could nurture.
  Shaking off the white, he rose once more into the sky to
continue his search—though he had to pause every so often
to slide more snow off his wings. Such pauses weren't a usual
part of his snow flying, but he was moving at slow speed
today and the snow was coming down like water.
  Aodhan, I can't see any sign of a second child. He wiped
a hand over his eyes, felt ice on the tips of his lashes. *If Quon
is out here, he's better at hide-and-seek than Naasir.* And no
one was better at hide-and-seek than the fellow member of
the Seven who'd once played with their childhood selves.
  Cubs, he'd called them. But of all those who'd known

them as children, it was Naasir who'd most quickly adapted to dealing with them as adult warriors.

"Cubs grow," he'd said with a shrug when Illium asked him once. "Life moves. Only the old and the stupid don't move with it. The old have earned their rest, and the stupid will be eaten by predators."

Sometimes, Illium thought Naasir was the wisest person he knew.

You're sure? Open disbelief in Aodhan's voice. *Even Lijuan couldn't have trained her child to be such a stealthy hunter. His brain, for one, isn't fully developed.* True enough. As with mortal teenagers, angelic youths had a way to go before total physical maturity.

I'll take another look now the light's a bit better, Illium said, because he wouldn't risk abandoning a child out in the cold and wet. *And I'll fly back, check near the cavern, too.*

When he did, however, all he found was another whole lot of nothing.

A thought pricked the back of his mind, a memory of sadness and love forming out of air and ice.

Landing in the courtyard of the stronghold with that haunting memory a ghost that walked beside him, Illium made a note to stop in Africa on his way home, whenever that might be. He wanted to see his mother, wanted to let her spoil him and cherish him and look after him.

Yes, he'd missed the mother he'd had in early childhood, and it felt good to be with her without worrying over her, but mostly, he wanted to do it for her. Now that she'd woken from her long sleep, she carried within her a terrible guilt for the mother she'd been to him while inside the kaleidoscope.

She tried to hide it, was good enough at it that he'd only caught a glimpse when she'd thought he wasn't watching. It broke his heart to know that she blamed herself for a thing that had never been her fault. She could no more have stopped her mind from shattering than he could stop a quake from ravaging the earth. Not after the life she'd lived, the cracks in her psyche.

She'd told him of all of those cracks during his most recent visit. "At last," she'd said, "the cracks have callused over, become scars. And I'm always conscious of not allowing further cracks to take root without my knowledge.

"Some would say this is the business of adults, not a child," she'd added, "but you've earned the right. You should know why your mother left you for all those years."

"You didn't leave me," he'd protested.

"Don't protect me from owning up to my mistakes," she'd chastised him—then kissed him on the cheek. "Let me own up to the hurt I caused my sweet boy."

A squeeze of his hand to stop him from speaking. "I tell you my past not as an excuse, but so that you are aware of the rich tapestry of history, and how it can alter a person—and so that you can be on guard in your own life against the wounds that fester deep below the surface.

"I didn't know I had such wounds, you see, and so I wasn't prepared for how I might be affected—how I might be damaged—by other blows of a similar nature."

"You couldn't have predicted that Aegaeon would turn out to be a giant flaming asshole," he'd muttered.

She hadn't told him not to talk about his father that way; they both knew the description was only the truth. Rather, she'd taken his hand and said, "But don't you see, Illium? I *should* have seen the cracks in his facade, shouldn't have permitted him to treat me—and you—the way he did."

"Until he left, he was a fine father." A grudging admission he'd made only so she didn't take on more unnecessary blame. "He was with me as much as an archangel could be. So wipe that idea from your mind."

She'd tapped him gently—so, so gently—on the back of his head. "Let your mother speak."

He'd grinned and hugged her instead. The champagne of her laughter had covered them in sparkling joy. "Scamp."

Afterward, she'd said, "Let us not argue. We'll leave you out of it. But the way Aegaeon treated me . . . I will not talk to you of my relationship with him. No child should hear such things."

"Ma, I know he had a harem—"

"*Illium.*"

He'd shut up. As a child, he'd known he was in big, fat trouble when she brought out that particular tone. Turned out it worked just as well now that he was an adult. "Sorry."

"So you should be. Let your mother have a few illusions."

"I've erased the memory from my mind." He'd mimed washing his brain.

Her renewed laughter had been a familiar thing and yet not. It had been such a long time since she'd laughed so much and with such brilliant clarity to her that his breath caught on every single occasion.

"My inner fragility—those cracks I couldn't see," she'd said after the laughter, "they made me vulnerable to Aegaeon's brand of charm. I felt . . . important, felt seen. Me, Sharine, not the revered Hummingbird. And because he was an archangel, I had no fear that my past losses would repeat themselves."

Slender fingers brushing back his hair with maternal tenderness. "Do you see, Illium? I made a choice out of a deep-rooted fear that I'd never faced. I hid from my pain, and so a woman willing to accept crumbs from an archangel's table is what I became. Don't do what I did. Don't hide. Don't pretend. Confront what hurts you, know the shape and form of it so you can conquer it."

Her words rang in his head as he entered the stronghold. Once under shelter, he took a few seconds to shake off the clinging snow, then strode into the warmth of the living area with the awareness of a dread truth heavy on his shoulders.

44

Jinhai wasn't holding on to Aodhan, his eyes no longer trained on the snowy landscape. He sat on the sofa in front of the fire, intent on a string game that Aodhan must have taught him.

The two of them had played the same game as children, weaving shapes in the string with their movements. Aodhan had always made the most creative patterns, but Illium had been faster. Balance, he thought. Yin and yang. No strong one and weak one. No protector and protected.

Aodhan's eyes went straight to Illium when he walked in the door. "Anything?"

Shaking his head, Illium grabbed a chair and carried it to in front of the fire. He sat so he faced Jinhai, but not so close that he was intruding into the boy's space—more as if he was simply drying his wings. Angel feathers had a natural oil that couldn't be felt to the touch, but that helped them repel water. It wasn't foolproof, however.

That time Illium had crashed into the Hudson, Raphael had told him his wings had become waterlogged. Mostly due to injuries that had disrupted the normal rhythms of his body. Today, it wasn't about that. The heat just felt good against his chilled body. His position also made him less threatening.

"Here." Aodhan, who'd disappeared into the kitchen, returned to put a cup of hot mead in his hands. "I threw it on the stove to warm after you left."

The first sip was nectar in his blood. "Thanks." He sighed. "It's good." After taking a few more sips, he leaned forward, the drink held loosely between his hands—and reached for Aodhan's mind. *Adi, I need to ask Jinhai a few questions. I have a theory. Could be ass-backward wrong, but I won't know until I ask.*

Aodhan moved to sit on the arm of the sofa on Jinhai's far side, in a pose that appeared more protective than guard-like. *You think he's behind the carnage at the hamlet.* His jaw was a tense line.

Illium looked at his friend, met the clear blue-green so hauntingly beautiful. *Yes.*

A quiet exhale from Aodhan, his features tight. *Ask. If he ignores you, I'll nudge him along.*

But when Illium shifted his attention to Jinhai and said, "Will you tell me about Quon?" the boy smiled.

"Quon protects me." Putting aside the string, Jinhai hugged his legs to his chest with arms too skinny to fight off even a moderately strong adult—mortal or immortal. "Quon plays with me."

"You like Quon?"

An enthusiastic nod. "He's strong. Not like me. Quon can talk to Mother." His face fell. "I just hide. I get scared and I hide, but he's never scared."

"He sounds like a good brother," Illium said, while Aodhan sat motionless.

"Yes." Jinhai rocked back and forth. "But Quon does bad things sometimes." This last was a whisper. "Quon gets angry, and does bad, *bad* things."

"Like steal other people's skins?" Illium kept his voice even, not accusatory.

A jerking nod, Jinhai's eyes going to the windows. "Quon wanted to have a family." A soft confession. "So he wore the son's skin. But the mother didn't love him. She cried. It made him angry."

Dear Ancestors, Illium. Horror in every syllable of Aodhan's mental voice. *He's so small. How could he have done all that?*

I think he's older than we assumed—and he's the son of an old archangel. Given how much he resembled Lijuan, Jinhai would've likely always been a slight man, his bones delicate, but his life had further stunted his growth. There was a good likelihood the physical damage could be reversed—the boy had immortal cells after all, and immortal cells could heal almost any damage that wasn't congenital.

The same couldn't be said for the mental harm done to him.

Instead of asking straight-on about the horrors he and Aodhan had unearthed, he said, "Did Quon not like the animals?"

"A dog tried to bite him. After that, he didn't like them." Jinhai's eyes got wet. "I told him I still liked the dogs and the other animals, and I wanted to keep them, but he was so mad."

That explained what had happened to the animals—but not how. Not when it came to the animals and not when it came to the mortals and vampires. "How did Quon clean up after himself? It must've taken a lot of work."

Slow blinks of the boy's eyes, followed by a sly smile. "Quon made *them* do it," he whispered. "The ones who called him Son of the Goddess. Quon hates mess. He made them dig a big hole in the forest, then after, he made them cover it up like it was, with leaves and stones and dirt, so no one could see. Quon is smart."

Illium's skin prickled. "How did they know him? Because of how he looks?"

A tilt of Jinhai's head. "They always knew him," he said. "In the dark, they knew him."

The guards, Aodhan said in Illium's mind. *He manipulated them into becoming his murderous army.*

Illium could see Aodhan's pain in the unyielding line of his spine, the way his gaze lingered on Jinhai. Others might condemn the boy, but Aodhan understood him in the way of another being who'd been to the black heart of the abyss.

His own chest tight, Illium said, "Didn't Quon's . . . acolytes have family in the hamlet? Didn't they hesitate?"

"No. The Son of the Goddess told them the others were monsters only pretending to be their family."

There had to be more to it than that, a subtle long-term manipulation—and perhaps even dangerous mental abilities developed young by a child whose physical growth had been so badly stunted. All that immortal energy would've redirected itself to the one part that *could* grow: Jinhai's mind. "Did the worshippers set Quon free?"

Jinhai stared down for a while, then unfolded his legs to the floor and sat up straight. The eyes that met Illium's now were harder, crueler, the smile on his lips a thing of slicing evil. "I had to get into their skins first."

He even sounded different, older, more composed. "They were used to following Mother's orders, but I heard them whispering that she was gone, that they didn't know what to do. So quiet they whispered, but I can walk in silence—and I walked to the chains often to listen."

Leaning forward in an echo of Illium's position, he said, "So they just kept doing what they'd always done. Bringing me food from the village. That's why Mother put that village there. For me." Pride was a blaze that lit up the gray of his eyes and made his skin glow with a subtle power that should've been impossible.

Yes, this child was very, very dangerous.

"Did the others who lived in the village know about you? That you were Lijuan's son?" Illium asked.

"Of course not. They were nothing." He waved off all those lives in the same careless manner another man might wave off the extermination of a nest of insects. "My servants knew never to tell or their Goddess would punish them."

"Were they all vampires?"

Another sly smile. "My blood, they love. So delicious. An addiction."

The words raised every tiny hair on Illium's body. "You convinced them you needed to be released."

"I whispered to them from the chains, said things like Mother used to say. I put worms in their heads until they were mine." His head jerked toward Aodhan, though Aodhan had done nothing to attract his attention. "The sunbright one," he whispered. "That's what Mother called you. She wanted your wings." Hard, envious eyes drilling into Illium now. "And yours. Pretty wings."

Looking sideways, he fingered his own limp and faded feathers. "Ugly." A spitted-out word.

"They'll heal." Aodhan's voice was grit. "You are an immortal."

"I am a god," the boy said in the way of someone saying their hair was black or their eyes were brown. As if, to him, it was simple fact. "I am Mother's son."

"Where are your worshippers?"

A shrug. "I wanted to see what wearing their skins felt like."

"Didn't they fight?"

The boy frowned. "I was their god. They cut each other's heads off for me. The last one knelt down so I could behead him." He flexed his hands. "It took a long time. I'm weak."

No one, no matter how loyal, would kneel without protest for such torture if they weren't being controlled in some way.

Worms in their heads.

The boy's features altered in front of Illium even as the eerie statement reverberated in his mind. "Quon shouldn't have done that," Jinhai whispered. "We were all alone after that." Rubbing at his belly. "After a while, I couldn't find anything to eat. I went back to my hole, but there was no food there, either, so I went back out."

"Why didn't you come toward the other angels in the area?" Illium knew the boy had to have spotted angels flying this way and that from the stronghold.

"Mother said," he whispered. "Mother said I wasn't to be seen. I was her secret. Her special secret." A bright and horribly innocent smile. "I was to be her new skin, her new life."

She was mad, so mad, Aodhan said. *Why did we not see it until of late?*

Because she was also very old and very clever. Her insanity had also been the kind of affliction that could look like nothing more than megalomania, or a hunger for power. Both of which were acceptable in the angelic world. "What will you do now?" he asked the son she'd doomed to the same madness. "And what will Quon do?"

A lost look. "Quon says he will be a god like Mother. He says I can stay with him. But he will be the god."

Illium nodded, as if everything about their conversation was rational. "Will you stay here with us for the time being?"

"Yes." Jinhai's expression brightened. "Mother said you were strong. The sunbright angel and the bluebell angel. She would have you in her court. Quon says you can serve him now." He looked out at the snow. "And it's cold outside. It's warm here. Quon likes it here, too. Quon says we can stay."

"I have to tell Suyin first," Aodhan said to Illium when the two of them moved into the hallway to discuss what to do next.

Illium scowled. "I'm not about to keep this from Raphael."

"I wouldn't ask you to—but beyond it being my duty as her second, it's a thing of respect to go to her first. This is her territory, and sadly, this is her family."

Illium folded his arms, but he didn't have any good arguments to the contrary. It wasn't as if Lijuan's son posed any direct threat to New York. He was, however, a very real threat to China. "You have reception?"

Taking out his phone, Aodhan glanced at it. "Yes."

While he remained in the hallway to make the call, Illium returned to the warmth of the room that held a boy whose mind had split in two. He'd heard of this type of mental wound, but had believed it to be a far less defined division—a blurring of personalities or a veil falling over the person's mind, as had happened with his mother.

But this was nothing akin to that.

To all intents and purposes, Jinhai and Quon were two different people.

Having spotted an old game set on a bookshelf in the room, he grabbed it, set up the board on the low table in front of the fire. "A game?"

Jinhai jumped at the invitation.

He knew the game very well. It was one taught to most angelic children, to help them with their mathematical prowess. Partway through, he said, "I won't wear your skin," and his voice had shifted again, as if his mind couldn't settle. "I don't want to be all alone again."

A child is not to be blamed for the actions of evil.

—*Archangel Raphael*

45

To say that Raphael hadn't anticipated the reason behind Suyin's call was a vast understatement.

"I wanted to tell you this myself, Raphael," she said, her voice quiet. "You have been a good friend to me, and it was two of your Seven who unearthed this latest horror."

Raphael understood exactly why Illium hadn't come to him with the knowledge. This went beyond politics and into the complicated and emotional realm of family. "There's no doubt the child is Lijuan's?" He couldn't wrap his mind around the idea that Lijuan, a being of death and rot and evil, had borne a child.

"Illium and Aodhan have agreed to bring Jinhai to me—they are fashioning a carrier as we speak, with what I'm told is the child's enthusiastic agreement. So I have not yet seen him with my own eyes, but the images Aodhan sent . . ."

A shuddering breath. "He is hers. I've authorized Aodhan to send you the images, too, so you will see. Illium has informed me that there are scientific tests that can be done to confirm Jinhai's bloodline, and we will do those, but I do not need them to know."

"There were periods when Lijuan disappeared from public view," Raphael murmured, "but none of us saw anything unusual in that. Even Michaela did that a few times." And the former Archangel of Budapest had loved attention and adored being the muse of artists as well as the fantasy of millions, mortal and immortal.

"My aunt's people were also so loyal to her that they would help her hide many things."

"But to hide an angelic child? To allow that child to grow up alone in the dark?" Were Lijuan not already dead, Raphael would've killed her then and there. "That isn't loyalty, Suyin. It's the same kind of blind faith that led to so many of her people supporting her goal to shroud the world in death."

"I won't argue with you there," Suyin said. "But I ask your advice—should I share this with the rest of the Cadre?"

Raphael paused, gave the question serious thought. By every measure, this was a private family matter. And judgmental eyes were already looking Suyin's way. On the flipside, it appeared the boy could be a treacherous threat. "Can you control him on your own?"

"I can cage him." Bitter words. "But a jailer is not who I want to be. And when I think of what was done to him . . . Where is the moral line, Raphael? I want him in the care of healers of the mind, not locked up like an animal."

"I agree with you." Despite the terrible darkness of the child's crimes, Raphael struggled against the idea of simply imprisoning or executing a being who'd never been given a chance to become anything better.

Jinhai had to be given a choice—and a foundation on which to make that choice. "I think," he said at last, "so long as you take the necessary measures to keep him from harming others, this isn't Cadre business."

Truth was, some on the Cadre would kill the boy rather than allow any piece of Lijuan to exist. But the child should not be judged by the crimes of his mother. "I can assist you. My mother will also help." Raphael knew Caliane well enough to be certain of that. "Three archangels being aware of the problem is enough for now."

"He will need to be caged, even as we seek to help him," Suyin said, the bitterness back in her tone. "Lijuan has won there. Made me like her."

"No, Suyin. You won't consign him to the cold dark. You'll contain him in the light. And once he has the power of flight, you'll ensure he has the opportunity to take to the sky."

"I thought to put him in an old stronghold half a day's direct flight from my new citadel, with a dedicated security and healing team," Suyin said. "No vampires or mortals, only angels old enough to be immune to his strange abilities. I can fly to him often, speak to him."

"Keir is currently in my city," Raphael told her. "A short trip to check on a few of the war-injured who aren't yet back to full health. Do you want me to alert him of this, and ask him to make plans to join you?" he said in an effort to take a little of the load off her shoulders. "You know he can be trusted." The senior healer had worked with Suyin after her escape from Lijuan.

"Yes, I trust Keir." Exhaustion in her voice as she said, "Do you think there is hope? Or am I just delaying the inevitable? Will I end up having to execute Jinhai when he transforms into a maddened adult with ever more deadly abilities?"

Raphael looked out over the lights of his city, thought of all he'd learned in his millennia and a half of life. "There are some that say a child damaged young will remain forever damaged."

"I've heard the same."

"But I've witnessed at least one child beat the odds and become far more than could be expected of them, did you only know the circumstances of their early childhood."

Raphael's spymaster had survived a childhood marred by his father's obsessive jealousy—a jealousy that had ended in the viscous scarlet of his mother's lifeblood, and the ashes of his father's body. The murder-suicide on a lonely atoll had left behind a scared and grief-stricken child, the silence around him profound.

Jason had been thought mute when he first appeared in the Refuge.

But though the spymaster had plenty of scars, he was no monster and never would be. At times, Raphael thought that Jason's deepest secret was that he felt too much, too strongly. That was why he strove to keep a certain distance between himself and the world.

Then there was Naasir, intelligent and unique and a favorite of all. He, too, had been born in a place cold and without love, a place teeming with the ghosts of the innocents who'd gone before him. Yet his heart was a thing magnificent, as wild and as ferociously protective of his people as the tiger that was his other half.

"And," he added, "I've seen an archangel so lost in madness that she turned two thriving cities into silent graveyards." In eliminating the adult populations of those cities, Raphael's mother had also created thousands of orphans with broken hearts, many of whom had curled up and died of that heartbreak.

Raphael had helped dig their small graves, his tears lodged in his throat and his scream a keen in his head.

"I call that same archangel a friend now," Suyin whispered, "and she is one of the calmest heads on the Cadre."

"Exactly so." Caliane made no effort to hide from or obscure her past. It was a silent shadow she carried with her always. All those deaths, all those souls, they haunted his mother, and in so doing, they made her a better ruler and a better archangel—while creating in her a weakness that could be exploited by the unscrupulous.

Better that than the bringer of death she'd once become.

"We are not mortals," he said to Suyin. "Our lives are

endless in comparison to theirs—as a result, our minds and hearts have a far longer period over which to heal. I think, if this child has spent decades in the dark, we should give them that same time in the light, to find a better path."

"You speak what is in my heart, Raphael." Suyin's quiet voice held untold agony. "I will hope for him—and I will ensure that those who died at his hands have a respectful burial according to their rites. I will not simply ignore their lives as Lijuan might've done."

A solemn pause before she said, "Jinhai didn't—doesn't—truly grasp what he did. He knows people are dead, but he seems to have no comprehension of such being a bad thing. And to orchestrate *that* while yet a boy? Not only murder, but the rest."

"Yes." Raphael, too, worried about what lived in the boy. "I won't stand in your way if you decide he can't be permitted to live—but, Suyin, I think I know you well enough to predict that such a decision will haunt you."

"No, I will not let Lijuan make me an accomplice to the murder of a child." This time, it was rage that vibrated through Suyin's voice. "Jinhai never had a chance, did he? It's as if he grew up surrounded by toxic sludge. The cancers were inevitable."

After Suyin hung up to deal with the situation, he turned to his hunter, who'd arrived while he was speaking to the other archangel, but had stayed quiet. Damp tendrils of hair curled at her temples, the near white of it dark with sweat, and her body clad in black hunting leathers bristling with weapons.

Her wings were a magnificence of midnight and dawn.

A vampire had gone bloodborn a couple of hours to the south, and she'd volunteered to handle it. "Got to keep my hand in," she'd said. "Being a hunter is part of who I am."

He'd caught a slight panic in her gaze, tied to her awareness of just how much her life had changed since they'd fallen together. In her lived the knowledge that one day in the future, she might no longer have the right to call herself a hunter. Raphael didn't believe that to be a true threat—she was hunter-born, the hunt in her blood. She could no more stop being a hunter than he could stop being an archangel.

She would, however, one day lose the friends with whom she'd grown into her hunter self. But that day existed in a far distant future. Her compatriots were currently in the prime of their lives. Her partner today had been the irreverent Demarco, a mortal who reminded Raphael of Illium.

He didn't know Demarco well, but he would remember him long after he'd passed beyond the veil immortals so rarely crossed.

"Elena-mine. A good hunt?"

"Yeah, we got the vamp." Arms folded as she leaned against one side of the doorway, she shook her head. "Older one. Stupid to allow his control to fray after all this time—and for what? A bad breakup that left him enraged to the point he surrendered to bloodlust."

Unfolding her arms, she straightened up. "I was just going to wave at you to let you know I was home, then head up for a bath, but then I heard you mention Her Evilness. What's happened?"

When he told her—for she was welcome to all he knew, his consort in the truest sense—she hissed out a breath. "I thought I understood evil, but this . . ." Striding over, she cupped the side of his face. "You okay, Archangel?"

No one else would've thought to ask that question. Elena alone understood how the specter of madness haunted Raphael. Both of his parents had gone mad. One had died. One had survived. Each had caused carnage.

"Yes." He wrapped her up in his arms and in his wings, needing her close.

"Raphael, I'm sweaty and—"

"*Hbeebti.*"

She locked her arms around his torso, the lithe muscle of her warm and possessive. "Not that I'm not happy to see you," she said softly against his neck, "but that's a knife hilt that's digging into you."

He laughed, the sensation unexpected after the ugliness of what he'd just discussed with Suyin. Then, surrounded by the fierce *life* of his Elena, he told her the full extent of what Aodhan and Illium had discovered.

"Fuck." A shake of her head against him, tendrils of her hair clinging to the white of his shirt. It had grown out in the time since she'd woken, the tiny feathers at the ends now all gone, and the length enough for her to braid it back out of the way as she'd done today.

Every so often, however, he'd catch a glimpse of light arcing through her wings. She'd told him she didn't feel anything, and as far as they'd been able to determine, her power levels remained appropriate to her age as an immortal—though the Cascade *had* left her one lingering gift: she healed faster now, the archangelic cells in her body having accelerated her immortality.

"It disturbs me that I interacted with Lijuan as an elder archangel during the time she was torturing her child," he admitted. "Because that was what it was: torture."

"You won't get any disagreement from me."

"But I never saw any signs of such depravity. I saw that she was old and wise and not necessarily 'nice'—but so few of the old ones are. It makes me question my ability to judge my fellow members of the Cadre."

Elena pushed back so she could look up at him. "No one saw it," she pointed out. "Not a single person outside of her inner circle. I know angels well enough to predict that almost none would've countenanced the mistreatment of a child—especially not back then, before she turned so many of her people into obedient followers."

She put a hand on his chest, over his heart. "The news would've spread if Lijuan had brought in anyone but her most fervent acolytes. Trust me, Archangel, she put a firewall of unquestioning devotion around that information—and she was still stable enough to appear normal."

Raphael went through a list in his mind, of Lijuan's most trusted courtiers and generals. "I can't believe this of General Xi. He saw her as his goddess, but he was a good man in many ways—especially back during the time of Jinhai's birth."

"Mortals have countenanced a hell of a lot of cruelty in the name of religion," Elena pointed out. "And Lijuan had Xi since he was real young. I'd like to think he didn't know, that she used others who were less intelligent, less likely to question her, but unless Suyin's people dig up records that make it clear, we're never going to know for sure."

"No. The boy's words certainly can't be trusted, not given his state of mind." Raphael pressed his lips to the top of Elena's hair. "I think I will join you in that bath, Elena-mine. I feel the need to wash off this darkness."

She stroked a hand down his back, her knuckles brushing the underside of his right wing. "Aodhan and Illium?"

"I haven't spoken to them, but I know Illium will be all right. It's Aodhan about whom I worry." He'd never told Elena what had happened to the angel made of light, and she'd never asked, for that was a piece of private history for Aodhan to share.

But she understood enough to wrap her arms around him again and say, "Illium's there. You know those two will be fine as long as they're together."

46

Jinhai was silent on the flight to join Suyin, though it was a silence awash in wonder. The snow had stopped falling, the landscape a pristine carpet of white under cool winter sunlight that turned Aodhan into a star on one side of the sling that held the boy, while Illium took the other.

Jinhai was interested in everything, looking around with wide eyes.

Illium saw in his curiosity a glimpse of who this young angel might've become had he not been molded into a monster. For Lijuan had never been less than intelligent—and the same intelligence burned in the eyes of her son.

Driven by the situation, they'd accelerated the closing up of the stronghold. Now, only a day after they'd found Jinhai, Li Wei and her team traveled in three all-terrain vehicles on the ground below and just far enough behind them that Illium and Aodhan could check for threats on the road.

A grumbling Smoke traveled with them.

Li Wei had chafed at the rush that meant things weren't up to her standards, but she was also a senior member of staff for a reason. She'd prioritized the list of tasks, mobilized her people, used Illium while Aodhan kept watch on Jinhai, and got the job done so they could leave this morning at first light. It had to be this way—Suyin was the only one who could deal with the boy, both because she was an archangel, and because she was his kin.

He and Aodhan landed often, but each time, they did so at a distance from Li Wei's team, while still keeping them in sight. The sightline to ensure the team was never out of Illium's or Aodhan's protective watch, the distance a precaution in case Jinhai's mental powers were more virulent than they'd initially judged. He'd had a long time to work on his guards, so it was probable he needed continuous access to manipulate—but there was no point in taking chances.

As for the regular landings, it was to give the boy a chance to stretch his legs, as being carried in a sling for a long period could be difficult on the body. Jinhai appeared to appreciate the breaks and used them to explore what there was nearby, but he never made any move to escape, too excited for further flight.

"I know he orchestrated a massacre," Illium said to Aodhan during one stop, while the boy examined a frozen bloom on the edge of the clearing, "but right now, all I see is a child."

Aodhan, seated right beside him on a large rock from which they'd cleared the snow, opened his wings in a slide over Illium's, closed them back in. "Mentally speaking," he said, never taking his eyes off Jinhai, "he's younger than his chronological age."

Illium agreed. "My gut says he's around eighty, but he acts more like a child of fifty." In mortal terms, it'd be the difference between a ten- or eleven-year-old and a sixteen- or seventeen-year-old.

An enormous gap in maturity and experience.

Illium had been offered a gorge aerie at Jinhai's age and had already begun to run drills with what eventually became his squadron. He hadn't accepted the offer, aware his mother wasn't yet at a point where she could let him go, but that the offer had been made had been a source of enormous pride for him.

"Did she keep him immature on purpose, you think?" he asked Aodhan. His friend had always had a better insight into why people did the things they did. It was what made him such an extraordinary artist. He saw inside people, to their dreams and hopes and secrets.

"I don't have enough information to say for certain." Aodhan pushed back his sleeves, his skin warm against Illium's when he put his arm back down. "But it could just be a consequence of his life. A flower won't grow if deprived of light. How could he grow? He was in a place designed to make him small, make him *less*."

In the distance, Jinhai went to pick the frozen bloom, hesitated, left it where it was. Again, a sense of loss stabbed at Illium. He'd never forget what they'd discovered in the hamlet—hell, the images would haunt his nightmares—but he found himself unable to simply condemn this boy. It would be like condemning a dog that had been trained to bite.

Jinhai's most authoritative source of information about the world had been an insane and cruel archangel. The others around him were his jailors. Where was he supposed to learn empathy when Illium very much doubted anyone had ever been kind to him.

"I wonder," he said, "who I would've been had it been my mother who went into Sleep and my father who raised me?" Looking out into the snow-draped dark green of the trees, he shook his head. "I wouldn't be this Illium, that I know."

Aegaeon was brash and selfish, a man capable of an intense and calculated cruelty, all of which he concealed behind a mask of bluff charm. Illium's mother might've had a fractured mind during much of his childhood, but she was innately good and kind, and oh, how she loved.

Never, in all his life, had Illium questioned his mother's love for him.

Aodhan's hand closing around his nape, his skin a little

rough in the same way as Illium's. Every so often, especially with repetitive injuries such as the small stresses caused by regular weapons-work, immortal cells decided to callus rather than heal damage over and over.

Aodhan ran the pad of his thumb over the pulse in Illium's neck. "Don't let that fucker get into your head," he ordered in a voice that vibrated in Illium's bones. "You know that would make him happy."

Illium scowled. "I'm having a crisis of personality and you tell me to knock it off? Sensitive." Also exactly what he'd needed to hear. He'd rather gnaw off his own foot than do anything that might give Aegaeon even a tiny smidgen of joy.

Right then, Jinhai returned to the frozen bloom, ripped it off, then stomped on it.

They flew on.

Regardless of their regular breaks, since they were traveling with a small party and following a trail already cleared of major hazards, they made much better time than the initial caravan and caught up with Suyin within a matter of twenty-four hours.

She'd flown back toward them, not wanting to expose the rest of the survivors to Jinhai or Jinhai to them. With her had come General Arzaleya, a compact and deadly woman with wings of a red so dark it held undertones of black, hair the shade of burnt oak, and skin like Dmitri's—it held its light brown color no matter the season. She also had Dmitri's air of competence, her strikingly pale eyes watchful.

"I'd have thought she'd leave the general with the caravan," Illium had murmured to Aodhan when he first spotted Arzaleya's wings. "She's the third in rank, right?"

Aodhan had looked thoughtful. "Suyin has a decision to make, and, by my calculation, the caravan is now at the safest part of their trek. Vetra is also there. And one—or two—of us three will join her soon, so there is little to no risk."

Illium hadn't had the chance to dig further on that before the group landed. Also with Suyin and Arzaleya was a small squadron of senior angels who were to guard Jinhai until Suyin assigned him a final team.

Aodhan had already warned her to rotate that team out with multiple others to ensure Jinhai couldn't work his tactics of manipulation on them—his abilities might not be strong enough to affect angels, but he was still a master at subtle psychological ploys.

Suyin had brought along senior healer, Fana as well. Not a specialist in ailments of the mind, but of a skill and kindness that would make her a help to Jinhai until the arrival of the specialist healers. Aodhan knew Keir himself was on the way—Jinhai could have no better help.

Jinhai's face lit up with piercing joy the instant Suyin landed in front of them. "Ma!" he cried. "Ma!" The happiness and hope and childish innocence in his voice was heart-wrenching.

He was almost to Suyin when he slowed down, a questioning lilt in his voice as he said, "Ma?"

"I am not Lijuan, child," Suyin murmured. "But I am kin. I am your cousin and your archangel."

Jinhai seemed momentarily nonplussed by that. A second later, he exploded, launching himself at Suyin with hands fashioned into claws. "I am her only skin! I am her! I am her skin!"

Though everyone reacted to protect Suyin, she was an archangel, had no need of their assistance. She controlled the boy without doing him harm, her arms locked around him as she took them to the snowy ground. When he stopped screaming and struggling at last, she held him tight as he sobbed for his mother.

To harm a child is an act of
dishonor beyond forgiveness.

—*Angelic Law*

47

Later, after Jinhai had worn himself out and fallen into an exhausted sleep, Suyin told Aodhan and Illium to join the caravan. "I will go with Jinhai to his new home. For better or worse, he sees the familiar in me, and I think it's best he begin to learn to look at me with trust. As such, I need you to protect the caravan."

Aodhan struggled against an immediate disagreement. He knew he couldn't allow himself to become too attached to the child; Jinhai might speak to the part of him that knew what it was to be trapped and tortured, but the boy's path had to diverge from his if he was to heal.

Though . . . "In the future, I would like to see him at times if he will receive me as a visitor. Would that be acceptable to you?"

Suyin's smile was soft. "You will always be welcome in my territory—and Jinhai could do no better than to have you as a man from whom he can learn." She turned to Illium. "I thank you, too, for watching over this broken child rather than executing him at first sight."

"It wasn't my right or my decision." Illium flowed into a graceful bow, going down on one knee while flaring his wings out behind him. A powerful, dangerous butterfly in the snow.

Aodhan had seen him do the same thing in a mocking way, but today, it was very serious, a show of respect for this archangel who had in her as much empathy as power.

Suyin's face softened further. *I see again why he is so dear to you, Aodhan.*

Aloud, she said, "You are a light in this dark world, Illium." She held out her hand, and Illium took it as he rose. "I'm glad to know you, glad to learn from you."

When Illium tilted his head in a wordless question, she said, "You are a power. I see it. We all do. Arza tells me that the Cadre has watched you since long before the Cascade, for you were a power even as a boy.

"And yet you hold on to your sense of self with a ferocity that defies even the Ancient who is your father. You do not buckle under the weight of eternity." She released his hand, but held his gaze. "You show me a different path—and it is a path I will endeavor to follow."

A flush of color on Illium's cheeks. "You honor me, Archangel Suyin."

"Just Suyin to you, Bluebell. You saved my life in battle and it is an act of courage I will never forget." With that, she glanced over to where Jinhai slept in the sling. "I will go now, so I can return soon to my people. It won't be an easy transition for the poor child, but nothing is easy in this land right now. But he will have light, and when he has healed, he will have the sky."

Aodhan looked up as she rose into the air, a slim and lovely angel with more steel in her than the world saw. He wasn't sure Suyin herself knew it, not fully. She, too, after all, had spent time as a prisoner and it had marked her.

"I like her." Illium sounded reluctant. "Not because of the compliment." He blushed again, kicking at the snow. "I've always liked her, I suppose. But seeing her here, in her archangel skin, the weight of all that's happened on her shoulders . . . I see why you respect her so much."

Aodhan's lips curved as he took in his friend's face. It continued to hold a touch of suspicion engendered by his possessive heart, but intermingled with that was admiration.

"There, Blue," he murmured. "That wasn't so hard, was it?"

A scowl was his only reply before Illium took off, dusting Aodhan in a tempest of snow.

Laughing so hard that it caused Li Wei to look over at him with a startled grin on her face, he shook his head to dislodge the white, opened out his wings, and took off into the sky after his Blue.

They reached the caravan before darkfall, their presence more than welcome.

"Shall we stop for the night?" Vetra asked, and it was clear she was more than ready to hand the responsibility of being in charge to Aodhan. "We have another hour of light, but it'll be pushing it."

"I agree," Aodhan said. "Slow and steady is the pace we want to maintain."

This entire group had a long journey to make. Not because of distance—that could be covered by a well-maintained vehicle within two days, allowing for rest breaks for the driver. No, the trouble lay in the obstacles in their path—the dead patches, the eruptions of black fog, unexpected slips across the roads caused by the heavy snowfall.

Sunrise, and the vehicles crawled on. The winged cohort paced the ground cohort, on constant alert. Illium was the one who spotted the fog eruption some distance up ahead, in the dead center of their projected path.

Aodhan made the call to halt the caravan while he and the rest of the team found a workaround—a detour along their main alternate route at this point would mean going backward by several painstaking hours. Illium did multiple high-speed flights to confirm their less-preferred alternate route was clear.

"Damn he's fast." Anaya, a senior angelic commander,

whistled when Illium took off into the winter-blue sky for the second time. "Also, hot. Do you know if he's single?"

Aodhan stiffened. "You'll have to ask him." He was irritated by the question, though why he didn't know—it wasn't exactly a surprise. Illium had always had plenty of admirers, mortal and immortal. Kai, for one, was still making eyes at him, though Illium had been too busy to respond.

"Maybe I will." A dazzling smile from the smart, funny woman who was just Illium's type. "Who knows? Could be he's feeling lonely out here far from his people."

He's not far from his people, Aodhan thought mutinously as she walked away, *I'm* here. Though he tried to put the small byplay out of his mind, he kept returning to gnaw on it. He wanted to slap himself for it, but he couldn't stop and he didn't understand why.

No romantic relationship, not even Illium's love for Kaia, had ever impacted his friendship with Aodhan, so it wasn't as if Aodhan was afraid of that. Or maybe he was. After all, they'd been on rocky ground this past year—and a lot of it was Aodhan's fault. He knew it, admitted it.

He had no right to be in any way irritated by any romantic entanglement in which Illium chose to indulge.

That thought was firmly at the forefront of his mind when Illium returned from his latest sortie. "All clear," his friend told him, before bending over with his hands on his thighs, his chest heaving and sweat dripping down his temples.

"You flew at maximum capacity." Elsewise, Illium could leave everyone in his dust without effort.

"Yeah." It came out a puff of air. "Figured the faster you had the info, the less chance of other fog hellholes opening up before the caravan gets past." All of that spoken in short, staccato bursts.

Aodhan found himself touching the back of his hand to Illium's cheek. "Thank you."

A quick grin that melted the tension in Aodhan's spine. What was he worried about? Him and Blue? Fighting or annoying one another or eating angry stew together, the two of them were stuck like glue.

But there was one thing he had to say, one apology he had to make. "Keir told me something when I first began to speak to him about Sachieri and Bathar." He'd already mentioned his talks with the healer to Illium.

"Yeah?" Illium's breathing was yet unsteady, but he'd straightened up, his hands braced against his hips.

"He warned me that I might one day strike out at the ones I love the most." He held the aged gold of eyes that, to him, meant home, meant safety. "He said that it would be an unconscious thing, but that I'd choose them as targets because I knew they were safe, that they wouldn't forswear me even when I was an ass."

"Keir doesn't use words like ass," Illium said, but there was a slight tremor in his voice that had nothing to do with his breathlessness.

Aodhan ran the back of his hand over Illium's cheek once more, ignored the small attempt at levity. "I forgot what he told me even as I struck out at the person who means more to me than anyone else." Illium was the sun in his system, the person without whom nothing else functioned quite right. "I took advantage of your loyalty and generosity, and I'm sorry for that."

"Shut up." Illium swallowed hard. "I'm glad you felt safe enough with me to be utterly insufferable."

"I'm still sorry." He waited until Illium met his gaze. "Not for what I want or how I've changed, but for how I've hurt you by my actions—and by my silence." He hadn't used it as a weapon, but that didn't alter that it had drawn blood. "I will never again do that." A promise that was a vow. "I will never again lock you out."

Blinking hard, Illium glanced away.

Aodhan moved close enough to take Illium's chin in his hand, tug gently until his best friend in the world would look at him again. The gold shone with a sheen of wet, the same emotion rocks in Aodhan's throat. "Always, Blue," he said, his voice husky. "Me and you? We're always."

Their breaths mingled, the sounds of the world fading away, until it was just Aodhan and Illium, Adi and Blue, Sparkle and Bluebell. Then Illium gave a lopsided smile and their entire world righted itself.

Nothing more needed to be said. Not here.

Leaving Illium to recover, Aodhan told the rest of the team to prepare to shift toward the secondary alternate route. It only took them an hour to move out—quick when you considered the number of people and vehicles involved. Aodhan didn't see Illium after that except at a distance, his friend doing his job as an advance scout, sleek and fast.

As for Anaya, she was busy with the rear guard.

A position to which Aodhan had shifted her prior to this flight. Nothing to do with Illium being out front. It just made logical sense.

Illium wasn't scheduled to stand night guard when they made camp, as Aodhan needed him fresh for his scouting duties the minute day broke. It was just as well, because he was wiped. The unpredictable eruptions meant constant high-speed flights to find a clear route, and then relentless worry as people passed beneath.

In a smart move, Suyin and General Arzaleya had split the caravan into multiple small "pods" far enough apart from each other that one eruption wouldn't take out a large chunk of the population. It slowed them down, but the tradeoff was worth it in terms of safety.

At one point, they'd ended up with the caravan split in two when an eruption occurred in between, and had to work out a route to bring them back together. So far they hadn't lost a single pod, but everyone's nerves were at a fraying point. It didn't help that, given the persistent disruptions, they'd only made it halfway to their projected goal for today.

The only reason they could rest easy tonight was because

Illium had located a patch of rocky ground on which to make camp. Not the most comfortable, but the one type of material—aside from bodies of water—that the fog didn't seem to like. It was too bad there wasn't enough of such ground to take them safely to the coast.

With Suyin and the general both gone, Aodhan had to be front and center, and would only catch a short rest break at some point during the night. He was plenty strong enough to handle it, but that didn't stop Illium from worrying about him.

Not that he'd say that aloud. All those scouting runs alone? They'd given him time to think about everything Aodhan had said to him—especially when it came to that first big fight in Elena and Raphael's Enclave home. Hard as it was for him to admit, he *had* jumped down Aodhan's throat that night.

He'd never have reacted the same way had it been any other member of the Seven. The fear and rage he'd felt when Aodhan was taken, the agony of the aftermath, none of it gave him the right to treat Aodhan as . . . less.

His gorge roiled.

He'd never, not once, thought of Aodhan that way, but you'd never know it from his overprotective hovering. No wonder his best friend had been so angry with him. Aodhan had apologized for using Illium as a target for his anger, but Illium had apologies to make, too, and he would as soon as Aodhan had a free moment.

To distract himself for the time being—and because he was sweaty and filthy after the long day—he made his way a short distance from the camp and to a small but deep lake that hadn't frozen over, most likely due to underground geothermal vents. While those vents had kept the water liquid, they hadn't appreciably warmed it up.

Still, it had been cleared as safe, and angels were built for the cold. Everyone else was making do with wipes, or by warming up enough water for a rubdown in the privacy of their snow-resistant shelters.

The angels who'd decided to take advantage of the lake

did so fully clothed. This wasn't the time or the place to be caught with your pants down. Illium did take off his boots and stash them in a tree, but—if need be—he could fly and fight bootless.

That done, he shot up high into the sky before arrowing down to the lake. He didn't splash as he went in, his body an aerodynamic blade that sliced deep, deep into the dark depths. The icy chill was welcome, its quiet embrace equally so.

He was feeling as good as his troubling thoughts would let him when he broke the surface and sleeked back his wet hair. Another angel swam lazily over from a short distance away. Anaya, that was her name. Her golden hair had gone dark in the water, her curvy body hidden beneath, and her face awash with admiration.

"Nice dive," she murmured, a look in her eye that he could read all too well.

"Thanks." He'd intended to do another dive, maybe swim, but now said, "I'll see you tomorrow. I'm under strict orders to eat and sleep."

No insult in her expression at his rejection of her silent offer. "To be honest, I should do the same. But if you want to play when we're not so stressed . . ."

Illium's usual response to such invitations was a grin and a nod. He never made promises he didn't intend to keep, but he also hated to hurt others when they'd made themselves vulnerable to him in such a way.

Today, however, he said, "Lovely as you are, Anaya, I find I'm no longer in the market for casual romps." A truth; he hadn't been compelled to share his sheets with anyone for some time. It just . . . didn't feel right.

Anaya sighed. "Pretty *and* faithful." Her smile said he was forgiven for not accepting her offer. "I hope your lover appreciates you."

Parting from her on a friendly wave without correcting her misapprehension, he swam to shore to shake out his wings. Once out, he didn't linger. He didn't want to linger.

Not here.

After he'd retrieved and put on his boots, he flew back through a clear sky, his wet clothing ice in the winter cold. He still wasn't sorry about the dip. He'd needed it. Quick change into his alternate set of clothing and he'd be fine.

He caught the lights of the camp well before he reached it. More, he caught the sparkle of Aodhan. His best friend sat alone beside a firepit, his seat what looked to be a fallen log, and his brow furrowed as he stared at his phone. Lips curving, Illium arrowed away from the firepit to land near the tent that held the supplies of angels who hadn't yet put up a shelter for the night.

It took him only a couple of minutes to change—into jeans and a sweater of fine black wool designed to fit around his wings thanks to four sleek black zips. He had another set of leathers, but what the hell, the softer fabrics felt good on his skin right now—and the sweater was one of his favorites.

Dressed, he deposited his wet gear with the laundry team; they'd ensure it dried as they traveled—the trucks had been fitted with rooftop racks for just this purpose. Then he hit the small tent that held the food supplies for this quarter of the caravan. The vampire on duty handed him two warm buns filled with spiced meat.

"Seriously?" Illium said, his mouth already watering. "We're cooking on the road?"

"You don't know my great-great-great-great-great-grandchild," the grumpy old vampire muttered, his mustache so big and fluffy that it was its own continent. "She's not about to have a cold dinner when she can whip this up. Just be grateful I saved a few for the latecomers."

"I'll kiss her when I see her next."

"She'll paddle your behind for daring."

Laughing, Illium accepted the buns, several protein bars, and two bottles of water, then somehow managed to carry it all to Aodhan.

Who was now full-on scowling at his phone.

48

"What?" Illium said. "An astronomical rise in the price of ultramarine blue?" He knew full well that was one of the hues Aodhan and his mother used when painting his wings. He even knew the two still, at times, made it the old way—from crushed lapis lazuli.

"Ha-ha." Despite his morose tone, Aodhan took the food Illium held out, placing it on an upturned crate in front of him that had clearly been put there for just that purpose. "No, it's a notice from the team Lady Caliane sent over to meet us on the coast—they're gathering building supplies for the new citadel and associated city. Small hitch."

Sliding away his phone as Illium managed to fit himself on the log, too, their wings overlapping, he shook his head. "You don't want to know more, trust me. It's admin." He picked up the bun, took a bite—and groaned in pleasure.

Illium's blood warmed.

"Do you think Dmitri does admin?" Aodhan said after he'd swallowed that first bite. "I never thought of that part of being a second before I came here."

Illium shrugged. "I think Dmitri has a finger in every possible pie when it comes to the Tower—but he's been second for a long time. Our Dark Overlord's got minions." He demolished another quarter of his own bun. "You know that vampire, Greta? She hates people and mostly doesn't talk to anyone, but she's Dmitri's right hand when it comes to admin stuff."

"Her?" Aodhan stared at him. "You're sure? She only grunts when I say hello."

"I've seen her smile. Once." Illium had been so shocked his mouth had legitimately fallen open. "I think she's just ancient and can't be bothered, but she enjoys the work, so she stays on."

"How do you know about her?" Aodhan drank half a bottle of water.

"Because I talk to everyone." In stark contrast to Greta, Illium liked people. "One time, I brought her a bottle of that fancy blood from Ellie's café empire." He would always find it hysterical that Ellie, one of the hunter-born, was the CEO of a thriving blood-café business. "She stared at it like it was a dead frog—looking over those half-glasses she wears."

"Why does she wear those?" Aodhan muttered after swallowing the last bite of his bun. "Vampirism would've fixed any vision problems long ago."

"Because she's Greta." Illium finished off his bun, drank some water. "Anyway, couple months after the dead-frog stare, my Tower apartment's air-conditioning gets upgraded. No one else's. Just mine. Moral of the story is: be nice to the admins."

Aodhan chuckled, his shoulders brushing Illium's as they sat side by side. "You're all wet." Reaching out, he ruffled Illium's hair.

It should've felt friendly, joking, but their eyes met, and it was . . .

Aodhan dropped his hand, and they both stared into the fire, but they didn't move apart. And when Illium picked up a protein bar and offered it to Aodhan, the other man took it, and they talked about different things. About the journey to come, about what might be happening with Jinhai, about Suyin.

To occupy his hands and calm the odd sensations in his body, he played unthinkingly with the small metal disk that he carried always. When he yawned a few minutes later, his eyes beginning to close, Aodhan said, "Sleep, Blue."

He then walked over to grab a bedroll, spread it out by the fire. "Should be warm enough for you—no snow predicted tonight."

Illium knew he was right, but he fought the grit in his eyes to get to his feet. Shoving the disk that had once been a pendant into his pocket, he said, "Hey, Adi?"

Bedroll set up, Aodhan rose with the blanket in his arms. "No, I'm not going to tell you a bedtime story."

Illium grinned—because this Aodhan? The funny one with a quiet wit? It was a private aspect of his best friend that he shared with a rare few. And it was a part of him that had been silent for a long and painful eon. "I wanted to say I'm sorry, too."

It wasn't hard to do that, to admit his mistake, when he knew his words—his understanding—would matter a great deal to Aodhan. "I did react badly that night in the Enclave." He brushed his fingers over the heavy warmth of the other man's wing. "I couldn't see it then, but I do now, and I'm sorry."

Aodhan looked at him for a long moment. Then, sliding his free hand around to the back of Illium's neck, he tugged Illium close for a hug that melted Illium from tip to toe, no more chill in him. He slid his arms around Aodhan's muscled body, allowed Aodhan to envelop him in his wings.

It felt right. All the way down to his very core.

"Apology accepted." Soft words against his ear, a warm breath, as Aodhan ran one hand down his back.

Illium should've done the same . . . but he turned his face toward Aodhan's neck, his lips a mere breath away from the stardust of Aodhan's skin. Aodhan didn't flinch, and affection, warmth, love, it morphed quietly into a thing that stirred butterflies in Illium's abdomen and had Aodhan going motionless.

They broke apart, their breathing not quite even.

Aodhan swallowed. "You need sleep." It came out rough.

"Yeah." But he wasn't about to leave this unfinished. If this past year had taught him anything, it was that he had to listen—and he had to speak. "Sh—" He cleared his throat. "Should I apologize again?" He was the one who'd altered the tenor of their embrace by turning his face into Aodhan's neck in a way that wasn't a thing of best friends.

A sudden panic had him rubbing his hands on his thighs. "We can make a deal to forget it." It had nothing to do with the fact they were both male—angels were not like the majority of mortals. Their kind lived far too long to see sexuality as an inflexible construct. Angels knew that growth was infinite.

It might hold linear for some, split off into different dimensions for others.

No, his panic had to do with the fact his friendship with Aodhan was vital to an eternity lived in joy. "If you want, I can bleach my brain, no problem."

Aodhan was starfire in the light from the flames, his smile a startled sunrise. "No," he said. "Don't apologize and don't forget." Then he cupped the back of Illium's neck again in a way that was so familiar and so welcome, and pressed his cheek to Illium's . . . before bending his head and pressing a kiss to the curve of Illium's neck.

A shiver rocked Illium's body, his hands clutching at Aodhan's hips. Everything inside him felt curled up tight, on the verge of flying apart.

Rubbing his cheek against Illium's, Aodhan squeezed his nape. "You're so tired, Blue." Then he stepped back, brushing his knuckles over the line of Illium's jaw. "Rest. We'll figure this out later."

And because he *was* tired, and he knew these minutes seated with him might be the only rest Aodhan got that night,

Illium lay down on the bedroll with his back to the fire and
his wings wrapped around himself. The blanket Aodhan
opened out over him was a bonus. He'd slept in far worse
places, so it didn't take him long to fall into a deep sleep,
despite the nerves twisting him up.

Sparkles of light fluttered over his irises, followed him
into the welcome dark. He was on the precipice of dreams
when he thought he heard Aodhan murmur, "Does she walk
in your dreams, Blue? Is she our phantom third?"

49

There wasn't much time to talk in the grueling days that followed, but Aodhan was always aware of Illium—and he worried constantly about him. "Don't go so far out of range," he snapped one day. "We can't help you if you've flown so far ahead that none of the other scouts can keep you in sight."

"What's crawled up your butt?" Illium muttered, shoving back his hair.

"I'm serious, Illium." He wanted to shake the other man. "Stay within range of the others." As protective as Illium was of others, he had the tendency to take risks when it came to his own safety.

A quick—irritated—salute before Illium took off, but when night fell and they made camp, it was beside Aodhan that he landed. And when Aodhan finally had to sleep, it was Illium who watched over him. When Aodhan snapped at Illium for shoving food into his hand, Illium snapped back, pointing out that Aodhan couldn't do his job if he was "falling flat on his face."

Tired and worried about the increasing eruptions of black

fog in their way, along with several toxic patches that had formed in the short time since Vetra overflew the route, Aodhan muttered something under his breath about "Bluebells with a savior complex."

Illium's eyes narrowed, but rather than snapping back, he said, "You're exhausted." He pointed to the bedrolls he'd already spread out under the thick branches of a tree that had sheltered the ground from a build-up of snow. That this tree and its brethren had taken root in the stony ground they'd chosen for their campsite was a testament to the power of nature.

"Sleep, or you'll be useless," Illium added. "Then I'll have to take over, and the next thing you know, we'll all be wearing glittering capes and dancing to Elvis songs." A sigh. "Man, I really wish he'd been compatible for vampirism."

Aodhan was still irritated, but now he was irritated at how well Illium was handling his haywire emotions. "Stop managing me."

Literally throwing up his hands, Illium said, "Fine. I'm going over there." He pointed to the far side of the site. "Nowhere near your sparklehole vicinity."

But as Illium went to walk away, Aodhan found himself saying, "Don't go." He slumped down with his back to the tree and closed his eyes right afterward, so he wouldn't have to meet Illium's gaze—he knew he was behaving atrociously.

A sigh, then the rustle of a familiar pair of wings nearby, Illium's shoulder brushing his as he sat on the bedroll beside his. Maybe others couldn't tell wing sounds apart, but Aodhan had long ago learned to pinpoint several of the most important people in his life. Illium was at the top of the list.

"I'm doing it again," Aodhan said, angry with himself. "Using you as a target."

"No, you're not. You always get short-tempered when you're critically low on sleep. You mutter and you stomp and you're kind of adorable—and weird as it is, I'm glad to see that part of you return."

Aodhan scowled without opening his eyes, his mind rolling back to a past where . . . yes, Illium was right. He'd been this way before the torture and the trauma; this wasn't a result of Sachieri and Bathar's evil. This was him and his "one bad trait" according to his own mother.

"He's the sweetest boy, but he needs his sleep," he'd overheard her saying to a friend while he was sulking in the corner one day. "It's the only time he ever acts up—when he's missed the hours he needs."

"Sleep, you grump." Illium's voice wasn't hard or angry.

It was worried.

Aodhan could feel his shoulders bunching up again, his muscles tensing. He knew he was being unreasonable—especially since he'd been ragging on Illium to be careful. But the things inside Aodhan that had broken a long time ago, though they'd finally begun to heal, the scars were hard and rigid and without flexibility.

"I don't know how to bend on this," he said, his voice sleep-blurred. "I can't . . ."

"It's okay, Adi. I can bend until you're ready."

"What if . . . the scars are so unyielding."

"It takes a long time for them to soften?" Illium chuckled. "I waited two hundred years for your first waking. What's another couple of centuries?"

The last thing Aodhan felt before sleep sucked him under were Illium's fingers stroking through his hair, a tender caress that was wanted, was beloved.

Suyin returned when they were an estimated three days of ground-travel out from the location of the new stronghold. That estimate was predicated on a number of eruptions, the detour required by a new toxic patch that Illium had scouted up ahead, and the heavy snow buildup on the road.

Remove all that and they could've reached the citadel within the day.

"He's as well as can be expected," she told them when they asked about Jinhai. "At present, he's basking at being inside a large stronghold where he has the freedom to move as he wishes. I also told him that he can think about how he wants to decorate his room and—once we are settled in the new citadel—I will get him the paints, wallpapers, and carpets."

It was an architect's thought, that last, and Aodhan was thankful for it. It'd mean a great deal to the youth to have ownership of his private surroundings, to actually be able to influence how he lived. It might even redirect a little of his manipulative tendencies in a healthy direction.

"He's also cooperating with Keir's attempts at counseling," Suyin added.

"The healer got here fast."

Suyin nodded at Illium's interjection. "He flew on one of the mortal machines all the way to Caliane's territory, then she had a combat squadron escort him across to the stronghold."

"Does Keir have any thoughts on Jinhai's future mind health?" Aodhan knew the boy's journey would be a long one, yet still he hoped for an answer that would spare Lijuan's son centuries of mental anguish.

But Suyin shook her head. "Not yet. He says he must assess first—at present, he says a lot of Jinhai's cooperation is an act, a scheme to show himself as he believes Keir wants to see him. Keir is not discouraged, for he says it is the merest beginning." She spoke those words as if they were a talisman.

"His wings?" The question came from Illium.

"Keir and Fana recommended a medical amputation, to which he agreed." Lines around Suyin's mouth. "Arza helped him make that decision by locating images of you after you lost your wings, Illium."

Illium nodded, his hands braced on his hips and his hair damp at the temples from his most recent scouting run. "Smart."

"Jinhai stared at the images for hours. He's seen your wings with his own eyes, so he believed me when I told him they would grow back—and grow back stronger. And . . . they were useless appendages to him. He wasn't emotionally attached and actually seemed excited to lose them."

A strand of white hair that had escaped her braid danced across the thin and unsmiling lines of her face. "Keir and Fana agree that we'll have to maintain a careful watch to ensure he doesn't attempt to destroy his wings when they begin to grow. Given his age, it'll take considerable time for him to achieve full growth, then flight strength—until then, they'll once more be dead weight to him."

Aodhan couldn't imagine any winged being feeling relief at such a loss, but then no other winged being had lived Jinhai's life.

"I'll be returning to see him on a regular basis," Suyin added, "but first, let's get my people home." Dark eyes met Aodhan's. "I would speak alone to you, my second."

Illium stepped back. "I'll grab Vetra and Xan, and we'll catch the general up on our current situation."

Once they were alone, Suyin asked Aodhan to walk with her along the river, on the rocky shore of which the caravan had stopped for a break. "Arza has accepted my offer that she stand at my side as my second."

Aodhan waited to be stabbed by a sense of loss, of jealousy, of the panic of having made the wrong call—but inside him bloomed only a warm surge of happiness. For both of them. She needed a permanent second and he wanted to go home. To New York. To the city where a certain blue-winged angel might drop by at any moment. "She's who I hoped you'd choose."

"You did well to conceal your partiality." A faint smile. "I'm glad I took her with me to settle Jinhai. It allowed us time alone, and I saw how she is in difficult situations." Stopping, she turned toward him and held out a hand, palm up.

When Aodhan enclosed it in his own, she said, "You are extraordinary, Aodhan, and I will never forget you and all you did to help me take these first steps into my reign. I hope you will not be a stranger to my lands."

"I promise you I will honor our bond in the eons to come, sire." With that, Aodhan went down on one knee, his wings spread in a bow of respect to his archangel.

When he rose, he was no longer her second—though she asked him to maintain the appearance of it until they reached the location of the new citadel. "We need to minimize disruption on this last leg of the journey. Arza is in agreement. My people love you, too."

Aodhan agreed, and they separated to take care of their own tasks.

His first one was to find Arzaleya. She was seated on a rock cleaning her sword but stood at once when she spotted Aodhan. "Aodhan, I hope this won't impact our friendship?" Pale eyes searched his face. "Suyin was adamant you didn't wish for the position."

"I'm not the right second for her, Arza," Aodhan confirmed. "I'm one of Raphael's Seven and I have no wish to change that."

Her smile held unhidden relief, her body relaxing from its at-attention stance. "I'll be contacting you often for advice," she said with a wry look. "I've long been a general, but being second, that is another thing altogether."

"Contact me as often as you need," Aodhan said. "If I have one piece of advice, it is that you must walk into the future. Don't fight progress. Nudge Suyin if you have to, but if China is to heal, it can't stay stuck in the past."

Arzaleya's expression turned solemn. "Yes, we think the same there." She held out her arm.

Aodhan had never before touched her, but today, he grasped the other angel's forearm in the way of warriors. It was the beginning of his good-bye to China, but there was still much to do until his departure, and he got on with it.

"Why are you planning on leaving right after we reach the coast?" Illium demanded when he shared his plans that night, while they stood in the privacy afforded by the dark— and by the wall of trees behind which they'd stopped to speak. "Suyin will need help with building, everything else."

"Because you can't have two seconds." Neither Suyin nor Arzaleya had made any demand of him, but that was because they trusted in his heart and in his intellect. "Right now, I'm the one everyone turns to instinctively. Only once I'm not here will Arza have a chance to grow into her position."

Illium gave a grudging nod. "Yeah, I can see that. What about me? Raphael sent me to assist Suyin."

Aodhan gripped the arch of Illium's left wing, ran his hand down the curve in a touch of stunning intimacy between angels. Illium flushed, ducked his head a little, and when he looked up, his eyes were wild gold. "*Aodhan*."

"I don't want to be apart from you." Aodhan's journey was far from over, but one thing he knew: he wanted to do it with Illium by his side. "But we can't be selfish. China has borne so much, needs help. I believe Suyin will want you to stay behind, help with the build."

Jaw tense, Illium nonetheless nodded. Because he was a warrior. Because he had honor. Because he was Aodhan's Blue, the most unselfish angel Aodhan had ever known.

"What am I going to do with you?" Aodhan murmured, overwhelmed by tenderness. "You and that heart of yours really need a damn keeper."

A playful smile that did nothing to hide the depth of Illium's emotions. "Do I hear you volunteering?"

Aodhan thought of the metal disk in Illium's pocket, of the way Kai watched him, of the centuries Illium had carried that particular torch. Then he thought: *Fuck it, Kaia and her damn doe-eyed descendant can fuck right off.* What he felt for Illium? It was a thing of eternity and forever, and he wasn't about to step back and be self-sacrificing.

If Kai wanted him, she'd have to fight Aodhan.

Shifting until their boots touched and their body heat warmed the winter air, he cupped the side of Illium's face and said, "No, I'm not volunteering," in a voice gritty with need and hard with confidence. "The position is already mine."

Then he kissed Illium.

Kissed him hard and deep, his hand fisted in the silken blue-tipped black of his hair and his wings wrapped around him. Kissed him until Illium groaned and grabbed fistfuls of the back of his shirt.

Pushing his back up against a tree, Aodhan braced one arm over Illium's head while spreading his wings to block out the night, and he kept on kissing him. It should've been awkward, new, but it wasn't. It was the most perfect kiss in all his existence. Because it was Illium.

His body was all sleek muscle and strength, his lips softer than Aodhan could've guessed, the taste of him as familiar as his laughter. Aodhan swore he could taste Illium's joy in his kiss and it filled him up and made him voracious at the same time. He gave back as much as he took, wanting Illium to remember this, remember them.

Breathless in the aftermath, both their chests heaving, he pressed his forehead to Illium's and said, "I'm never letting you go."

All my loves leave me in the winter snow.

—*Illium*

50

When, all too soon, the time came for Aodhan to fly home, it was Illium who walked him to the beach area from which he intended to take flight. It was Illium who hugged him tight and whispered, "I'll fucking miss you," in his ear.

Face pressed to the side of his, Aodhan wrapped Illium up in his wings, suddenly terrified of leaving him in this land yet full of deadly mysteries. "You'll be careful? Promise me. No racing off to explore interesting things. Who's going to spoil your temperamental cat if you're gone?"

Illium's breath on the skin of his neck as he huffed. "I'm not an idiot." It was a mutter, but he continued to hold on. "Am I allowed to ask you to be careful on the trip home? I'm not being overprotective," he added quickly. "You're exhausted, Adi. We just arrived here yesterday, and you shouldn't really be going on such a long flight—"

"I'm heading to Amanat," Aodhan interrupted, having intended to share that with Illium before being distracted by his worry. "Suyin spoke to Lady Caliane just before, arranged it." His former archangel had hugged him, too, tears in her eyes. "I'll stay there some days."

"Oh. Good." Illium's arms turned bruisingly tight before he pulled away.

Aodhan had to force himself to let go. Of all the people in his eternity, it was Illium whose touch reached into the deepest, darkest places in his soul, bringing with it light and hope and all the vivid brightness that made him a favorite of so many.

But it was Aodhan he called his best friend.

And Aodhan whose hair he gripped as he pressed a hard kiss to Aodhan's lips. It was over too fast, Illium stepping back with the jerky movements of a man who didn't trust himself close. They'd barely touched the edge of this new horizon between them, and already, it was a thing of potent power.

Wings backlit by the rising sun, Illium swallowed. "I'll see you in New York."

A lump in his throat, Aodhan nodded. "New York." It came out a rasp, his emotions choking him.

That playful smile a little shaky at the edges, Illium said, "Don't get blinded by the big city excitement and forget me."

Aodhan couldn't speak, his throat all but closed up. *Never,* he managed to say mind-to-mind. Then he spread his wings and took flight, but he looked back again and again . . . and the dot of blue on the sands, it never moved.

Illium, watching him fly away.

The image haunted him during his sojourn in Amanat. It wasn't that he and Illium had never been apart before this past year. They were warriors and members of the Seven. Both of them had also worked as couriers in their youth. It wasn't in their nature to cling to one another.

No, it was something about that particular good-bye that troubled him, but he didn't understand what until the day Lady Caliane found him walking in the forest outside Amanat, the chattering monkeys of the local troop following along in the trees, and the wild horses shadowy ghosts in the mist.

Having not expected the archangel, Aodhan said, "Lady Caliane. Is something amiss?"

"No, young Aodhan." She folded back her wings, in her warrior avatar today—faded leathers of gray-blue, her hair braided, and a sword riding her hip. "I was flying for the joy of it, and caught a glimpse of your light." The searing blue of her eyes held his. "Would you mind the company on this walk?"

Aodhan was solitary by nature, had been that way even before his abduction, and he and Lady Caliane weren't in any way friends. She was an Ancient, while he was a whisper off half a millennium in age. But he was comfortable with her— for she was both the mother of his sire and the best friend of Lady Sharine.

"I don't mind," he said. "But I'm afraid I may not be the best company."

"Things weigh on you," Caliane said as they began to walk in the cool quiet of the forest. "I have seen you walking in silence often, in Amanat and outside."

Aodhan went to give her a generic, polite reply but the memory of his earlier thoughts made him stop, think. *Best friend to Lady Sharine.* Two very different women, but there had to be a core of similarity hidden beneath that had made their friendship endure.

After all, look only at the surface and Aodhan and Illium were polar opposites. No visible sign of the value they both placed on things like honor and fidelity. No indication of the drive inside each of them, their ambitions for the future running on parallel tracks. And no sign at all of the love that meant one would die for the other without hesitation.

Perhaps, with Eh-ma so far from him, he could ask Lady Caliane for guidance. "May I ask you a personal thing?"

"Yes, child." A smile that turned her from beautiful to astonishingly lovely. "You remind me of my son when he was young. Oh, your coloring is different and so are your personalities, but my Raphael can be as solemn, as thoughtful. Tell me what troubles you."

"You know I left Illium in China. The final image I have of him—on the beach watching me go—I dream of it, think on it night and day, and I don't understand my obsession." It was hard for him to talk of such private things to anyone, far less an Ancient who was mostly a stranger to him, but he forced himself to keep going.

"Our duties mean we've often been apart. Why then, does that one image haunt me?" He wasn't sure he'd ever said so many words to Caliane and was half-convinced she'd tell him she had no time for such foolish concerns of the young.

"Ah." Caliane's exhalation of air was somehow portentous. "Sharine's son is a beautiful being, and I say this not about his outer shell, but his heart. I have seen this, though I wasn't there when Illium was born, nor when Aegaeon deserted them in the most cruel way possible." Her voice was a sharp knife, bloodying Aegaeon.

"I was also not there when Sharine's mind fractured, or when Illium was separated from his mortal love. And, child, I was not there when you were stolen away, or when you retreated from the world."

Aodhan didn't ask how Caliane knew of his history. Archangels had their ways. He didn't care, either, because her words had made him freeze under the snow-draped trees, his mind awash in the images she'd put together piece by relentless piece.

Aegaeon's desertion.

Kaia's forgetting of their love.

Lady Sharine's broken mind.

The long winter of Aodhan's withdrawal.

But for Raphael, *all* of the most important people in Illium's life had left him in one way or the other.

Aegaeon by choice. Lady Sharine without, but the effect had been the same.

Kaia hadn't made a choice, either—but Aodhan couldn't be merciful toward her because she *had* made the choice to speak the secrets that led to the erasure of her memories and the breaking of Illium's heart.

Illium was surely not the first angel to have whispered angelic secrets to a mortal lover. Love made people do many things transgressive and not at all sensible. Angelkind didn't care if one mortal knew their secrets—so long as that mortal kept their own counsel. No one would've known Illium had told if Kaia had held his whispers close. But she hadn't loved Illium enough to keep her silence.

As for Aodhan, he'd been abducted against his will, but the withdrawal, that had been a choice. Not at the start, when he'd been so horrifically emotionally wounded, but later. Later, he'd chosen to stay separate, keep everyone at a distance.

Even his beloved Illium.

Father. Mother. Lover. Best friend.

Illium had spent a lifetime watching people leave him.

Then Aodhan had done it again a year ago. Joining Suyin's court had just been an escalation of the leaving that had already been taking place, beginning that night in the Enclave.

Breath jagged, he bent over, hands on his thighs. "I didn't—" He couldn't speak, his chest was compressed with such vicious force. He'd thought often of how Illium watched over people, how he'd been forced into the role of a caretaker, but never had he seen the other side of the coin.

Abandonment.

No wonder his Blue held on too tight at times.

No wonder he had difficulty letting go.

And no wonder he was afraid Aodhan would forget him.

All those messages he'd sent Aodhan, all the care packages, all the things Aodhan had seen as overprotective hovering, they'd been Illium's way of reminding Aodhan of his existence. As if Aodhan would *ever* forget him.

Caliane didn't attempt to touch him as she said, "We often don't see the hurt we put on those we love most. And he is so bright, Sharine's son, so full of life and laughter. He hides his bruises well, I think, your Bluebell, using that joyous self as an impenetrable shield."

Heat burned Aodhan's eyes, seared his throat. "How could I not see?"

"Oh, child. You're young." Husky laughter. "You think you've had so much time to heal from your wounds, but in immortal terms, you've had but a heartbeat. I Slept more than a thousand years to get over my madness, and I yet bear wounds that are open and raw."

"I'm meant to be his best friend and I was so stuck in my own head that I didn't see." Aodhan wasn't going to give himself a pass over this. "He's the most important person in my universe." A simple, profound truth.

Caliane's wings were pure white in his peripheral vision as she spread them slightly, then pulled them back in. "You both have healing to do, growing to do. But you have one advantage over me and Sharine."

Aodhan rose to his full height, feeling oddly old and heavy. Beaten. With the knowledge of all that Illium had borne and kept on smiling. It had taken Aodhan's most recent abandonment for him to flinch and try to retreat. And even then, he'd forgiven with a wild grace that humbled Aodhan. "Advantage?"

Caliane's eyes—those extraordinary eyes she'd passed on to the archangel who was Aodhan's sire—were ablaze with light, fierce with emotion. "You are in the same time and place, able to hold on to each other, uplift each other. Do not squander that prize, young Aodhan."

Aodhan felt an almost uncontrollable urge to take flight, return to China. But to do that would be to go against the unspoken wishes of an archangel. "I need to go back, need to find a way." He'd ask Suyin; she wouldn't deny him, even if it threw a wrench in the smooth transition of seconds.

"Oh, you young ones. Always moving before you think." A faint affectionate smile. "This is a new realization for you, a new understanding. Let it settle. Think on what it means— and ask yourself if you can be the friend he needs."

Aodhan flinched as if struck.

But Caliane was shaking her head. "I say this not as an indictment, but as advice. In all the times you've come to Amanat, including all the short runs you did to deal with important tasks for Suyin, I see a growing fierceness of independence in you—you don't even like it when my maidens dare bring you trays of food."

Heat burned his cheeks. "I'm sorry. I didn't mean to be rude."

"You never were," Caliane said. "That doesn't mean my maidens are not clever and able to work such things out on their own. They had no idea what to do about a visiting angel who wanted no assistance whatsoever, approached me for advice for they know you are dear to my own son. I told them to let you be and treat you as a resident rather than a guest, that you'd find your own way to food and supplies."

Aodhan hadn't even noticed the subtle change in how the people of Amanat treated him. "Thank you, Lady Caliane."

"You have stood beside my son with fidelity and courage. That matters a great deal to a mother." She began to walk again, and because he was lost, he fell in with her. A wild horse materialized out of the mist at that very instant, and she stroked its dark flank as they walked.

"My friend Sharine is also generous of heart." An incredible depth of warmth in Caliane's tone. "She gives without fear, without compunction. I think her son has inherited this tendency. Can you accept him giving to you? Or will you break his heart by insisting he not care for you in the way that is his?"

Aodhan thought of the care packages that had made him feel suffocated and trapped, suddenly wanted to gather each and every one close to him, hold on like a miser. But—"Care is one thing, but he can be protective beyond reason, and I *can't* be protected anymore." It would tear open barely healed things inside him.

"Is there no middle ground?" Caliane asked, then held up a hand. "Do not answer me now. This is what I mean when I say you should fly home and think." Power pulsed off her now, a vastness of age and strength, but that wasn't what held him in place. No, it was the wisdom in eyes that had seen more yesterdays than he could imagine.

"Look into your future, young Aodhan, and ask yourself if you want to hold on—or set him free. Because if he is like Sharine, then he won't let go even if you hurt him—not unless you do an act of cruelty akin to Aegaeon's. My friend's heart is too generous and it's a beautiful flaw that she's bestowed onto her son."

"Eh-ma has changed," he pointed out.

"Yes." Caliane's smile held pure delight. "She is glorious, is she not? It gives me much pleasure to watch her confound Titus and even more pleasure to see her bloom ever brighter. But I think her boy walks a different path."

Her smile faded, and she patted a good-bye to the horse, who ambled off to rejoin his brethren. "I would be sad to see his joy diminished—but at times, a short, sharp pain is better than drawn-out suffering." She looked up at the canopy, a woman astonishing in her beauty, her eons of life a pressure against his skin, and her insight an echo in his head.

When she spread her wings, he said nothing, just watched her rise into the air . . . and he thought of Illium, and of the brutal collision of their competing needs. Could Aodhan let him go? Did he *want* to let him go?

"*No.*" A single hard word. Because Illium *was* the most important person in Aodhan's universe, a man without whom Aodhan's future would be a desolate wasteland. Even at his angriest and most distant, he'd never imagined eternity without Illium.

But his wasn't the only heart on the line. For that was the other question Lady Caliane had asked of him: Did Aodhan need to let Illium go for Illium's sake?

He shuddered, his wings drooping to scrape the damp, snow-dusted forest floor.

Who'd look out for Illium if Aodhan wasn't there? Who'd hold him when no one else even knew he was hurting? Who'd cherish him for both his gifts and his flaws?

No, Aodhan had to figure a way forward into a future where neither one of them ended up fractured and lost.

Time passes like an inexorable river,
bringing change with it.

—*Archangel Suyin*

51

Illium ran into Kai on his way back from the beach, where he and Smoke had gone for an early morning amble to shake themselves awake. Caught up in the endless work of building a new citadel—and using the work to stop missing Aodhan so much—he hadn't had a chance to speak to her except for the odd fleeting greeting.

The morning light was a glow behind her, and she had a brightness to her step, her smile pure happiness. His heart hurt, she reminded him so much of Kaia, young and awash in a vivid delight in life.

"Illium," she said, a small basket held to her side. "You've been to the water?"

Illium inclined his head, and as he did so, he caught the haunted, besotted look shot Kai's way by a young man unloading equipment to the right. "An admirer?" he asked gently.

Her eyes sparkled. "He has asked me to be his wife. We've known each other many years." Affection, perhaps even love in her tone . . . and yet Illium knew that he could have her if he pushed the merest fraction.

It had nothing to do with ego. It was the fact he was an angel. There were very few mortal women who'd turn down an angel. He could have her, and perhaps, if she proved compatible with the toxin that turned mortals into vampires, she could be forever by his side. If not, he could still cherish her for all her mortal years, their lives entwined and memories of shared joy her legacy.

But when Kai smiled and walked off to join her admirer, Illium didn't stop her. The mortal male's relief was a dazzling gratefulness, his love for Kai a shining glow, and Illium could've told himself that he'd chosen the noble path—but it was far more complicated than that.

Bending down, he petted Smoke, then the two of them headed off to breakfast.

He was still chewing over his reaction to Kai's new love when he got stuck into the work—while Smoke, healthy and sleek, prowled away to do things feline and secret. She was a smart kitten, didn't bother with the building site. Quite unlike a couple of the other pets, who'd had to be corralled in a safe zone after they kept on getting underfoot.

As one of the most powerful people in the area and one who'd helped rebuild Raphael's Tower, Illium was in constant demand. Not only for physical labor, but to consult on structural issues—he was no architect or engineer, but he did have information on new building materials and methods that Suyin appreciated as she slowly rebuilt her own knowledge.

He was also good at sweet-talking outside suppliers over the phone, and using salvaged computer systems to track down useful items that might be stored in warehouses within a doable flight distance. The most useful computer was a laptop Aodhan had picked up from the main office in Lijuan's central stronghold. It contained within it access passwords to Lijuan's entire administrative network.

"Good to see he listened when I told him to recover computers from major strongholds," he'd said to Yindi when he unearthed that laptop inside a truck that held only salvaged items of tech—all labeled in Aodhan's distinctive flowing hand with the date of recovery, plus the location.

"He insisted," Yindi had answered, her dark blue feathers all but black in the shadowy light of the day. "Even when I argued against it because of the weight of the items." Rolling her eyes, she said, "I feel the biggest idiot now."

Illium had laughed at Yindi's self-effacing tone, but inside, he'd felt a quiet delight that had nothing to do with her. It was good to know that even when infuriated with Illium, Aodhan had kept his advice in mind . . . kept Illium in mind.

As a result of all the calls on his attention, he ended up too occupied to worry at the unfinished business with Kai . . . but at night, when they stopped work for reasons of safety, he sat by a fire with a dozing Smoke snuggled at his side, and brought out the small disk he'd carried with him for an eon.

It was a pendant that Kaia had given him—a charm for protection—but it had now lost all detail. He'd run his fingers over it too many times, rubbed it too much. It gleamed a dull brown in the firelight as he stared at it and waited for the bite of pain. All he heard was the echo of Kaia's laughter . . . and it made him want to smile.

She'd been so beautiful and bright, his Kaia. Also, selfish and thoughtless. He could admit that now, with the clarity wrought by time and maturity. He could see how young she'd been. How young he'd been. He could look beyond the rose-colored lenses they'd both worn.

It made him think of words his mortal friend, Catalina, had once spoken to him, while reminiscing of her love for her beloved Lorenzo, who'd beaten her beyond the veil.

"My granddaughter, Adriana?" she'd said as she pulled out a sheet of cookies in the small kitchen of her little Harlem bakery redolent with the smells of vanilla and butter and melted sugar. "The girl sighs over a boy. He brings her roses, and writes her poems, and all is perfect."

Laughter, as warm and full-bodied as when Illium had

first met her and Lorenzo. "So sweet, sí? How it should be for young ones." A light slap of his hand when he tried to steal a cookie. "But you know what real love is, Illium?"

She'd plated four of the cookies, then slid the saucer across to him. "Real love isn't so shiny and pretty as they show in the cinema. It has . . . dents in it, real love. Bandages here and there—maybe even a patched-up crack or two."

"You're not selling it to me, Catalina," Illium had joked.

She'd flapped a tea towel at him. "To know a person's bad habits along with their good ones? To see them at their worst and at their best? To fight and play with them through all the seasons of this life? And to still wake up every morning happy to see their face? This is love."

Sorrow in her face then, her gaze going inward. "Oh, how Lorenzo drove me mad at times. My hair, it would be on fire from it. But I would give up all the years of my life that remain if I could see him just one more time, hear his voice say mi corazón as he holds me close."

Illium and Kaia, their love had been like Adriana's with her boyfriend. Sweet, joyful, puppy love. A thing of flowers and rainbows, no clouds on the horizon until the end. When he'd lost his feathers for her.

"It wasn't about being grounded," he said to a dozing Smoke, the admission an eon in the making. "If I'd been so stupid out of love, if I'd had a good reason for my mistake— then I could almost forgive myself for the pain I caused Raphael for forcing him to do that to me."

He'd never forget the look on Raphael's face the day he'd had to take Illium's feathers. The archangel had held Illium after, every muscle in his body rigid. Illium had cried, not from the pain, but from the shame of having so badly wounded the man he most respected in the entire world.

I'm sorry, Rafa. A broken statement, the long-forgotten name permitted a child, coming to the fore. *I'm so sorry.*

Raphael had pressed a kiss to his temple and just kept on holding him tight, telling him without words that even though he'd fucked up monumentally, Raphael wouldn't forsake him. "I was so ashamed, Smoke." Until it was in his every breath.

When Smoke pricked up her ears, he scratched her between those ears. "But I was just a kid, wasn't I? Hell, I was barely older than Izzy." His eyes widened. Dear Ancestors, Izzy was *green*. If he made the same mistake tomorrow, would Illium forgive him?

"In a heartbeat." His throat tightened. Because it had never been about Raphael, for the archangel had never held Illium's mistake against him. He was also open in his pride of the man Illium had become.

No, the forgiveness had to be Illium's own.

Smoke meowed and butted her furry head against a hand that had gone still. Laughing, he scratched her a little more. "Yeah, I think that lovestruck kid can let go of the shame. He's more than made up for it in the life he's lived since then." He stroked Smoke over her back, and thought again of his lack of a passionate response to Kai.

As part of that, he probed at the bruise of Kaia's loss, a thing he hadn't done for some time . . . and found that it was no longer tender.

When had that happened?

Staring into the flames, he realized he couldn't pinpoint the instant. He just knew that the pendant had become less about Kaia and more about habit at some unknown point in time. In recent years, his main focus had been on his work as one of the Seven . . . and on watching Aodhan return to himself.

The memory of Aodhan's startled smile after Illium altered the tenor of their relationship, it made his gut tighten and his heart squeeze. He touched mental fingers to the image of his Adi's smile, and thought of the kiss that had melted him to the bone. Part of him was furious that he hadn't taken it further, cemented their new relationship.

But of course, it wasn't about the physical. Not between them. Not when it came to the heart of it. Their bond was a thing intimate and layered, the pleasure to be found in tangling limbs and wings just one aspect of the whole. Even as he flushed at the idea of touching Aodhan in such a way, being touched by him, his hunger a painful ache, he tried not to worry about the distance between them.

Tried not to listen to the gnawing whisper at the back of his brain that said now that Aodhan was far from him, he might look back and decide their renewed friendship and nascent brush with intimacy had been a thing of circumstance, that he didn't actually want to reconcile after all, much less go further.

"Stop being a drama queen, Bluebell." His mutter made Smoke complain, and he petted her back into a doze in an effort to calm himself, her fur soft under his touch, and her body delicate despite her newfound health.

It didn't work, a quiet panic taking root at the back of his brain.

Swallowing hard, he slipped Kaia's pendant back into a pocket.

It was as if Kai was everywhere he turned in the days that followed—or perhaps that was simply his mind zeroing in on her as he came to terms with the cataclysmic change in his perception of himself. No longer the mourning lover was he, but rather a man who saw that first love as exactly that: a soft, lovely thing to be cherished as a memory of youth.

The man he was today? That man understood Catalina's comment about dents and bruises. That man was marked by a love far more profound, a love that had built over centuries of loyalty and friendship, sorrow and laughter, anger and devotion, a love that defined him—and it was a thing quite apart from Kaia, bold and impatient and dazzling to his young heart, or her pretty, sweet descendant.

"You'll break more than one heart when you go," Arzaleya said to him one day, as the two of them stood with drinks in hand at the end of a long and exhausting day—

while an inquisitive Smoke poked around nearby. "I'm hearing that you've turned down all offers."

"Who even has the energy for that after the days we're putting in?" Illium kept his tone light, in no mood to share his constant state of stress where Aodhan was concerned. It didn't matter that his best friend had stayed in frequent touch, Illium couldn't shut up that stupid panicked voice in the back of his brain.

He didn't even understand what was driving the asshole thing.

Arzaleya's low and earthy laughter broke into his cycling thoughts. "Isn't that the truth? I, for one, have no desire to tangle wings with anyone." Rubbing the back of her neck, she said, "I respected Aodhan always, but I'm now in awe of him."

She resettled her wings, the fading sunset picking out the ruby and scarlet tones of the filaments that made up her feathers. "To step into the role he did, at the time he did, with China in the state it was . . ." She blew out a breath. "I don't know how he did it. It's just dawning on me, the task I've taken on—and that's after Aodhan did all the groundwork."

This was a conversation for which Illium had plenty of time.

They spoke about the jobs on Arzaleya's plate, and of the future of the territory, were joined at some point by Yindi, Xan, and others. Illium stayed for a while, enjoying the company. But tiredness got to him at last. "It's bed for me. Good night." He hadn't slept the previous night, having taken a security shift.

The others shouted out good night, and he headed off after picking up Smoke's sleeping body. When he heard whispered giggling halfway through his journey, he glanced to the right just in time to see Kai running off with her hand in that of the mortal who loved her.

Again, he waited for the blow of pain. Again, it didn't come.

All he felt was a warm affection for the descendant of the woman he'd loved as a young man just finding his wings. There was no envy or jealousy in him, nothing but the heart's ache that comes with memories of times long past.

Looking up at the diamond-studded sky, he took a deep breath. No more clinging to the past because he was panicked about the future. No using a faded ghost as a talisman against the unknown to come. To make his love for Kaia into nothing but a habit of comfort, that would devalue them both.

Going to the tent he'd put up when the snow began to build on the ground, he placed Smoke on his bedroll, where she'd be comforted by his scent. Then, though he was exhausted, he flew far enough out to sea that the waters were deep and the waves wouldn't wash anything back to shore.

The pendant was flat and small and thin on his palm when he pulled it out of his pocket. Hovering above the night-touched ocean, he lifted it to his mouth, pressed a gentle kiss on it. "Good-bye, Kaia. It was my joy to have known and loved you."

Despite everything, he would never be sorry for having loved her, for she was part of the tapestry of his life, one thread weaving into the next. He wouldn't be who he was today without her, and her memory would stay with him into eternity, a treasured part of his history.

But their time had passed lifetimes ago.

Heart at peace, he opened his hand and allowed the charm to float gently into the arms of the endless ocean.

52

Though he'd come to peace with his memory of Kaia, Illium remained edgy about Aodhan in the days that followed. He hated that they were so far apart when they'd just found their way back to each other. He'd had a nightmare the previous night that Aodhan would use the time apart to convince himself that he had to break the bonds of their relationship to find freedom.

What the fuck was wrong with him?

Aggravated with his own misbehaving subconscious, he slammed a beam into place, went to pick up one more. Suyin had asked him to track down some supplies, but he needed the physical outlet right now; he'd do the computer work once he'd burned off the tumult in his body and mind.

When Arzaleya waved him down from the sky, he thought about pretending he hadn't seen her, but it wasn't the general's fault he was feeling pissy. He landed. "Yeah?" He shoved back the snow-damp strands of his hair at the same time, remembering how Aodhan had told him he needed a haircut.

"Package for you." The other angel handed it over. "I saw

it coming in and knew you wouldn't be back to your tent till nightfall. Figured you might want to see it earlier. You should probably take a break anyway."

Arzaleya raised an eyebrow. "You're wearing out the crew with how fast you're moving, and how much material you can shift on your own. Give them a breather or I'll be dealing with a revolt."

Illium scowled, but he didn't argue. Fact was, he liked getting packages, and he was curious about who'd sent this and what was inside. If he had to guess the identity of the sender, he'd say Ellie or his mother. "I might grab something to eat."

It wasn't until after he'd wolfed down a filled roll, drunk half a bottle of fresh juice, and petted an insistent Smoke that he sat down on his favorite stone above the beach and looked at the package. It had come by angelic courier and was stamped with the seal of the Tower . . . but in the field for the sender's identity was a name most unexpected: *Aodhan*.

He ran his fingers over the fluid black strokes, his cheeks suddenly hot. His fingers turned clumsy as he tried to tear open the box, until he finally made himself stop and take several deep breaths. Then he retrieved a pocketknife from his pants. The blade sharp as a razor, it took but a stroke to cut open the seal.

Inside was a small blue bag as familiar to Illium as his own sword. From Catalina's bakery, it proved to hold her famous angel-wing alfajores, the filling in between coconut-infused dulce de leche. She'd come up with the initial recipe for the dulce de leche, while Lorenzo had struck on the idea of making the cookies in the shape of angel wings.

No one made cookies like Catalina. And she usually only made these in the holidays, which meant Aodhan must have placed a special order. Toes curling, Illium bit into one as he checked the other items.

A jar of his favorite peanut butter—a spread that Aodhan abhorred—a new book from a mortal author that Illium loved, a small bag of gourmet cat treats, a sealed pack of caramel-nut popcorn from Illium's favorite snack store . . . and a handcrafted belt buckle that had been polished to a high, silvery shine. It was simple but for the feathers engraved on it and the stylized *I* hidden in among the feathers.

Putting aside the bag of cookies, he took off his belt. "You won't like those," he warned Smoke when she went to poke her nose into the bag. "Here, this is for you." He took out one of the cat treats Aodhan had sent, and placed it in front of her.

Pouncing on it with glee, she ran off down the sand to enjoy it in some secret spot. He didn't worry; she always found him when the day came to an end. Smoke taken care of, he replaced his belt buckle, and put the belt back on. It felt different. Heavier in a way that had nothing to do with actual weight.

No, it was as if it was full to the brim with all the emotions thick in his blood.

He swallowed, ate another cookie, and didn't look for a letter or a note. Despite his beautiful penmanship, Aodhan wasn't much for writing—even the messages he sent were short and to the point. No, Illium's Adi spoke with his art, with his hands, with his talent. And with a belt buckle that he'd fashioned personally for Illium.

Closing up the box with care, he flew it to the tent.

He took the cookies with him when he returned to work, sharing them with the crew—who were happy to see him now that they'd caught up. No point hoarding the alfajores when they'd go stale now that he'd broken the seal. And he had what mattered most—confirmation that Aodhan hadn't forgotten him. Stupid, how the fear haunted him . . . or maybe it wasn't.

His mother had forgotten him.

It was a thing about which he tried not to think, tried not to look full in the face. Not even Aodhan knew about it. He hadn't told. Ever. And he'd never *ever* bring it up with his mother. It would destroy her. But during the worst years, when she'd wandered the far depths of the kaleidoscope,

there had been three terrible times when she'd forgotten Illium.

Only three times.

Seconds-long pauses where she'd looked at him without
recognition.

Then the wrench at the unraveled threads of her memory
as she fought to remember.

A forgetting and a remembering that had happened so fast
he could've lied to himself, told himself he'd imagined it.
Except he hadn't. He knew how his mother looked at him,
how her eyes warmed with love and with joy no matter if she
was aggravated or annoyed by him . . . but those three times,
she'd glanced at him with nothing more than polite inquiry
in her gaze.

Three points of horror in his life, as he wondered if this
was it, the final loss, his mother gone forever.

He brushed his hand over the belt buckle, a talisman
against the dark. And unlike the pendant he'd carried for so
long, this one wasn't a memory of sorrow, but a gift of hope.

Grinning, he got back to work.

Thanks for the belt buckle. It's perfect.

The new citadel is going up piece by piece and I have to
say, it's shaping up to be the kind of building that will make a
mark. It's not the Tower and it's not Caliane's Amanat. It's
very much Suyin's Citadel.

Send more cookies next time. They were a hit.

Smoke approves of your offering. You may present her
with more.

No extra weirdness to report.

Aodhan's lips kicked up as he finished reading the message on his phone. He might be new to being the one who
did the looking after, but it appeared that he was getting
it right.

And because he remembered how his silence had hurt
Illium, he made an effort to send back a message. He wasn't

as good at this type of thing as Illium, but that had never mattered between them.

I'll order two dozen cookies next time. And I won't forget Smoke.

Send me a few images of the citadel in progress when you have time—it's strange not to help build it after being so involved in the planning process.

It's good to be home in New York.

He almost ended it there, but then made himself add the rest. Both because it was true—and because Illium deserved to know: It's not the same without you.

Illium, open of heart and far too quick to forgive, replied with: Miss you too. Might even watch a horror movie in your honor. But I draw the line at blood and gore.

Aodhan stared down at his phone. "What will I do with you, Blue? You let the people you love take total advantage of you." His fingers closing over the phone, he looked to the horizon, searching for wings of blue that were on the other side of the world.

You and that heart of yours really need a damn keeper.

Do I hear you volunteering?

No, I'm not volunteering. The position is already mine.

Aodhan intended to hold on to that position with teeth and claws. He'd never thought of himself as a possessive angel, but when it came to Illium . . .

Eyes narrowed as he stared out at the New York skyline from the Enclave land that had once held Elena and Raphael's home, he checked the time, then called Illium. He picked up after a couple of rings. "Sparkle," he said, the shouts of the rest of the crew background music, and his smile in his voice. "Can't talk long. Crew needs me to bring through another beam."

"I just need you to answer one question."

"Yeah?"

"Is Kai still flirting with you?" He carried on before Illium could answer. "Because if she is, I'm flying back there even if it causes a diplomatic incident—and I'm going to make damn sure she understands that you belong to me."

A taut pause, Illium's voice a little rough as he said, "Do I?"

"Yes." No games now, no crossed signals or things unsaid. "And I belong to you." It was still hard for him to say that, to give control over himself to another person . . . but this wasn't just another person.

This was Illium. His Blue.

"I said good-bye to Kaia." Illium's voice was husky now. "Over the ocean. Her charm sleeps in the deep now."

Aodhan sucked in a quiet breath, for this, he had never expected. "Are you sure, Illium?" He might not have liked Kaia, but he'd always understood that she was one of the defining features of Illium's youth. That was why he'd never made any comment about Illium's attachment to the charm, no demand that he give it up.

"Beyond any doubt. It got to be habit and comfort more than anything else—just a physical anchor when I needed it." The way he said that, it made Aodhan realize he'd really thought his decision through. "As of today, I've swapped that anchor for another—I've touched my fancy new belt buckle so many times that it's all smudged. Guess I better stock up on polish."

Aodhan's lips twitched. "I'll make you something smaller to play with." The other angel had always had a way of fiddling with things—whatever was around, whether that was a throwing knife, a pebble, a paintbrush in Aodhan's studio, anything with which he could occupy his hands.

It was only after Kaia that he'd become obsessed with that charm.

"And no," Illium said, "Kai is engaged to be married to a mortal who worships the ground on which she steps." No anguish in his voice, nothing but a kind of affectionate happiness.

Aodhan truly exhaled for the first time since his return to

New York. "I want you home—I'll look for you until the day you land." Then he admitted another thing. "I've just stocked up on ultramarine blue, silver, and multiple other oil paints. I'm going to paint you diving from your aerie in the gorge, that day in the storm, when you almost got struck by lightning."

Delighted laughter down the line. "I've never seen you so furious. I swear you had sparks shooting off you."

"I'll probably be furious all over again while I paint. I can't believe you decided to dance with lightning." Aodhan had lost half his immortal years that day, he was sure of it. "Come home soon, or I'll end up with so many paintings of you they'll call it my Bluebell era."

More laughter that faded off into something softer, more intimate. "How long do you think your Bluebell era will last?"

"All the eons of our existence."

Six months later

Six months later

Lightning cracked the sky as it had that day when Illium danced with death, rain thundering to the earth, but Aodhan took off from the Tower roof with no hesitation. According to all his calculations, and—given Illium's last check-in—the other man had to be about four hours out from the city.

Aodhan wasn't about to wait any longer.

Illium's spoiled and adored Smoke was already at the Tower, having come home in a cargo plane a week prior—in the care of the pilots, both of whom had pets of their own and could be trusted with the precious cargo.

She'd waited by the window since her arrival, and he knew she watched for Illium.

Just like Aodhan.

Rain stabbed at his cheeks, dripped from his hair, slid off his wings in tiny jewels, but he flew on. The wind wasn't strong enough to be a real problem, but the sky hung heavy overhead—and lightning set the horizon to glittering white fire. Aodhan's heart pounded; Illium was coming from that direction.